SAXON: *The Emperor's Elephant*

TIM SEVERIN, explorer, filmmaker, and lecturer, has retraced the storied journeys of Saint Brendan the Navigator, Sindbad the Sailor, Jason and the Argonauts, Ulysses, Genghis Khan and Robinson Crusoe. His books about these expeditions are classics of exploration and travel.

He made his historical fiction debut with the hugely successful Viking series, followed by the Pirate series. *Saxon: The Book of Dreams* was the first in the new Saxon series, and this, *Saxon: The Emperor's Elephant*, is the second.

Visit Tim's website to find out more
about his books and expeditions:
www.timseverin.net

Follow Tim on Facebook:
Facebook.com/TimSeverinAuthor

TIM SEVERIN

SAXON

VOLUME TWO

The Emperor's Elephant

PAN BOOKS

First published 2013 by Macmillan

This edition published 2014 by Pan Books
an imprint of Pan Macmillan, a division of Macmillan Publishers Limited
Pan Macmillan, 20 New Wharf Road, London N1 9RR
Basingstoke and Oxford
Associated companies throughout the world
www.panmacmillan.com

ISBN 978-1-4472-1215-7

1 3 5 7 9 8 6 4 2

A CIP catalogue record for this book is available from the British Library.

Map artwork by Stephen Raw
Typeset by SetSystems Ltd, Cambridge CB22 3GN
Printed and bound by CPI Group (UK) Ltd, Croydon, CR0 4YY

Visit www.panmacmillan.com to read more about all our books
and to buy them. You will also find features, author interviews and
news of any author events, and you can sign up for e-newsletters
so that you're always first to hear about our new releases.

The Emperor's Elephant

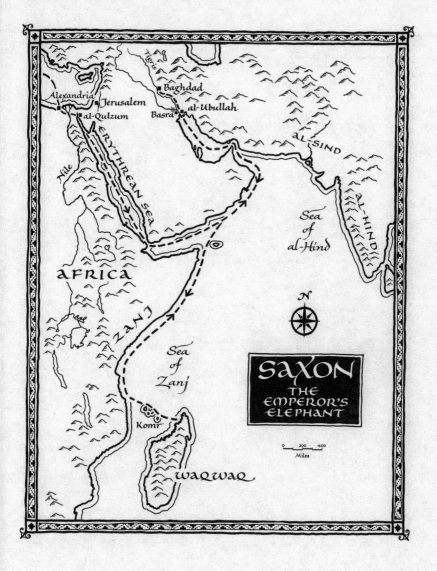

Alexandria
Jerusalem
al-Qulzum
Baghdad
Tigris
Basra
al-Ubullah
al-SIND
Nile
ERYTHREAN SEA
AFRICA
ZANJ
Sea of al-Hind
al-HIND
N
Sea of Zanj
Komr
SAXON
THE EMPEROR'S ELEPHANT
0   200   400
Miles
WAQWAQ

Prologue

They think it is a fragment from a shattered human skull. Bone white, it has the same dished shape, and is thin enough to be from a dead child. The clerks in the royal chancery glance at it with distaste as they pass my desk, giving me a wide berth. Possibly they imagine it is a gruesome memento from King Carolus's disastrous campaign against the Saracens in Hispania fifteen years ago. They know that I took part in that failed invasion and that, though wounded, I survived the bloody ambush of his army's rearguard during the retreat through the mountains. If the clerks presume that my swordsmanship saved me, they are wrong. The real reason was my friendship with the Saracens after I had lived among them and gained their trust, even though I was a spy.

Doubtless they also puzzle why the king himself still consults me from time to time, bypassing the royal council. They would be surprised to know that their most Christian and devout lord, Carolus, believes that dreams are a guide to the future. He asks my advice because I am someone who has been known to interpret the meaning of dreams and is himself a dreamer. Yet I am increasingly reluctant to provide the king with clear answers. Experience has taught me that dreams are rarely false but they often mislead. When their truth is finally revealed, the shock is all the greater. In the year before the Hispania campaign I dreamed of a giant Carolus on his warhorse and he was crying tears of blood. I had no idea then that it signified he would lose a third of his army and his favourite nephew and my patron, Count Hroudland, in that wretched ambush. And even if I had foreseen what was to happen, I could not have changed the outcome.

So when a dream provides me with a glimpse of the future, the prudent course is to hold my tongue.

Recalling the past requires similar caution. The story I will set down touches on a royal secret being kept from Carolus, here in Aachen. Should he learn what I am concealing from him, I would be disgraced. So I intend the tale as a purely private record of a journey to distant, little-known lands. That is why I have placed the little bone-white chip with its ragged edges in plain view on my desk. People steer clear of bits of skulls – though that is not what it is – and this will keep my written pages from prying eyes.

Chapter One

THE NORTHLANDS

*

I LAY FACE DOWN on the soggy ground, trying to ignore the throb of pain in my left shoulder. The wound left by a Vascon spear point had healed cleanly, leaving a puckered scar, but the change of season still brought on a deep-seated ache. The dampness seeping through my clothes from the leaf mould beneath me was making matters worse. The only sounds were random splashes and drips as the oak forest around me shed a recent rain shower. Though it was mid-morning, the underfloor of the woodland remained gloomy and dank. The spring foliage of the giant trees blocked much of the daylight and the air was heavy with the loamy smell of decaying vegetation. Directly in front of where I lay, a glade some thirty paces across was open to the sky. Whenever a cloud moved away from the face of the sun the fresh raindrops glistened on blades of new grass and gave the clearing a clean, inviting look.

It was a deception. The centre of the glade was hollowed out. The pit was ten paces long, five wide and sheer sided. Dug to more than the height of a tall man, the empty space had been criss-crossed with a web of light withies to support a false covering of woven hurdles. The workmen had then spread a thin layer of turf sods that mimicked solid ground. In the very centre of the trap they had placed a pile of leafy branches cut from a bush believed to be the beast's favourite food. The bait to the pitfall.

Very slowly, I raised my head and looked to my left. An arm's length away Vulfard, the king's chief verderer, was nestled. His leather leggings and jerkin, moss coloured and streaked with mud, blended perfectly with the shallow trench he had scooped out for himself. Even his weather-beaten complexion, darkened by a lifetime in the open air, matched the colour of last year's leaf fall. His grizzled hair was cut very short, and his forest-green cap with its single eagle feather was placed beside him. He sensed my movement and turned to face me. Light brown eyes flecked with yellow reminded me of the gaze of a canny dog fox and his flinty expression told me that I was to remain absolutely still for as long as he decided was necessary. Otherwise we would waste the two weeks we had spent preparing for the beast: scouting the best spot for the trap, the breakneck dig and the tedious labour of carrying away the spoil, and a final meticulous sweeping up to make sure that no trace of man remained. The labourers had finished their task just before sunset and had withdrawn from this remote corner of the forest. After they had left, Vulfard had gauged the likely direction of next morning's breeze. Then he had placed his watchers. There were just three of us. Vulfard and I were hidden upwind. His son Walo was stationed a stone's throw to our right where he could look down the track along which we expected the beast to approach. Walo's task was to scare away any large animal that might blunder into the pitfall. We did not want a stag or boar crashing through the flimsy covering. Our sole prey was the beast itself.

I relaxed and laid my head down into the crook of my arm, then closed my eyes. We had lain in wait for sixteen long, tedious and uncomfortable hours and nothing had happened. I was beginning to doubt that the beast existed at all. No one had actually seen the living creature. We were relying on reports of massive tracks left in soft mud; hoof prints larger than those of any known animal. Foresters had noted the stubs of branches ripped off seven and eight feet above ground, the splintered ends left pale and mangled. The best evidence of the beast's existence was its dung. Great piles of it contained undigested twigs and leaves that allowed Vulfard to guess the creature's diet and then devise a plan to catch it alive. The sceptics had laughed and said we were wasting our time. The unknown beast was nothing but a very large wisent, that breed of shaggy-headed, brutish wild cattle that roamed the forest. Wisents were rare but there were still enough of them in the forest for the king, who loved his hunting, to have killed one or two of them each season. It always put him into a great good humour.

Vulfard had disagreed with the doubters. He quoted a retired forester, dead these five years past, who had assured him that the gigantic beast and a few others of its kind had retreated into the furthest depths of the great forest and still lived.

A twig cracked loudly. The sound came from the far side of the glade. Startled, I raised my head, then remembered my instructions and froze in place. A hind was approaching. She was stepping delicately down the trail straight towards the pitfall. The swell of her belly showed that she would soon give birth to her fawn. She reached the edge of the glade and paused cautiously. At that moment there was a movement from my right. Walo, clad in forest colours like his father, had risen silently to his feet. Without a sound, he waved his arms. For a moment the hind failed to notice him. Then, with a sudden start she recognized danger and spun around and bounded away, disappearing back down the path she had come. Walo cast one quick glance towards his father, seeking his approval, then sank down again out of sight.

I breathed a sigh of relief. I had been troubled by the heartless way the labourers had teased Walo. He was an easy target. His arms and legs were too short for his body, and the slack mouth and the half-closed eyelids in a moon face made it look as if he was about to drop off to sleep at any moment. Nor did it help that his speech was slow and often slurred, and what he said was sometimes what you might expect from an eight-year-old boy, not an adult. His appearance made it difficult to tell Walo's age, but I guessed him to be in his mid-twenties. Vulfard was fiercely protective of his son. He had rounded angrily on the man who grumbled that Walo was too simple-minded to be made a lookout. The royal verderer had snarled that he would withhold the man's wages on account of his insolence. Then he had sent the fellow packing. I feared that if Walo botched this task, the men's taunts would make his life even more difficult.

I must have fallen into a doze soon afterwards, for the next thing I knew I was jerked awake by a deep wheezing grunt. The sound was so hoarse and powerful that it seemed to reverberate right inside my own chest. I had never heard a sound like it, but the message was unmistakable. It was a challenge.

I could not stop myself. I twisted round and looked behind me. The sight was something from a nightmare.

An enormous animal stood among the tree trunks, some thirty paces behind us. How such a bulky and massive creature had managed to come so close and in such silence was shocking. Even Vulfard, the most alert of huntsmen, had been taken off-guard.

The beast had ambushed us. At the shoulder it stood taller than the very largest stallion. The body bulged with muscle and was covered with a coarse blackish-brown pelt. The creature was a grotesque version of farm oxen that I had known as a child. They had been domestic animals, plodding, slow and placid. The creature that now stood close behind us was larger, stronger, hostile, and infinitely more dangerous. I stared with horrified fascination at its horns. They projected from its brow in a long forward curve, half the length of my arm, then swept upwards to end in a deadly sharp-pointed hook. They were designed to pierce, gore, and then fling aside a victim. They were weapons for killing.

Unbidden, the name of the beast surfaced in my mind. Vulfard's informant had called it 'aurochs'. In Frankish this meant 'ancient ox', an apt name for a throwback that belonged to a distant age when all manner of gross creatures walked the forest. I had failed to foresee that beasts that deserved this name might still claim mastery over their ancestral domain.

The huge beast gave a second resounding grunt. Louder, more aggressive than before, the challenge was even more obvious. The animal resented our presence. We were trespassers, and the carefully sited trap had gone disastrously wrong. We had planned for the aurochs to approach from the far side of the glade and we had placed ourselves downwind. But the beast had come from behind us, sensed our presence, and come to investigate. Now we were the ones who were trapped.

The beast tossed its head angrily. A great gob of drooling spittle flew through the air.

My guts turned to water. I was so frightened that I doubted I could even get to my feet. For a stupid moment I thought that if I stayed absolutely motionless the creature would ignore me.

Then the aurochs swung its head from side to side, displaying the terrible horns in a further warning, and I saw the creature's eyes. They had a mad, glaring look, a white rim around the darker, gleaming centre. There was no chance that the creature would leave us alone.

It was so close that I could see the slick wetness inside the flaring nostrils of its broad black muzzle. The aurochs snorted angrily yet again, then gave another threatening side-to-side shake of the horns. The creature stamped down, pawing at the ground. The hoof dragged a deep furrow in the soft earth, and the monster lowered its head. It was about to charge.

At that instant, Vulfard saved my life. He was either very brave or very foolish. 'Lie still, Sigwulf!' he rasped, then he sprang to his feet, snatching up his cap. Spinning round to face the aurochs, he waved his cap in the animal's face and taunted it with a shout. Then he turned on his heel and ran directly towards the pitfall.

It was impossible that such a huge animal could move so fast. One moment the aurochs was standing still. The next, it had gathered its huge haunches and sprung forward, head down, the great legs moving in a blur. The ground shook under me with the sudden thud of its hooves, followed by a waft of musty air as the animal raced past where I lay paralysed with fear. In a heartbeat it was closing the gap as Vulfard sprinted to escape the deadly horns.

He ran out into the glade. Now he was on open ground and totally exposed. Yet he kept his nerve. With perhaps three paces to the lip of the pitfall he glanced over his shoulder and, at the very last second, swerved to one side. The aurochs charged on past him, unable to halt its headlong rush.

As the huge beast stepped on the false ground the covering of hurdles collapsed immediately. With a great flurry of broken sticks and earth sods the huge creature tumbled into the pit, bellowing with rage.

Perhaps Vulfard had mistaken the precise location of the hidden pit. Or misjudged the length and reach of the long horns. The verderer was unbalanced and teetering on the very edge of the pit when the aurochs dropped forward. With amazing agility for such a bulky creature, the aurochs twisted sideways in mid-air. The tip of the right horn snagged the verderer's jerkin, just below the armpit. One moment Vulfard was on the edge of the pit; the next he was dragged down with the enraged beast.

Aghast, I lurched awkwardly to my feet and ran forward, my legs already wobbly with fear. Reaching the edge of the pit I looked down. Nothing could save Vulfard. He had landed alongside the animal and managed to push himself upright in the gap between the side of the pit and the aurochs' hindquarters. For a brief moment he was clear of its horns. But the enraged monster squirmed round and I watched as it drove a horn straight into Vulfard's chest. The horn spiked Vulfard like a pig on a roasting spit, passing right through him. With a savage twist of its head the aurochs tossed Vulfard high into the air. The verderer spun, then fell back. The aurochs caught him on both horns, then tossed him again. I prayed that death would come to Vulfard quickly, so badly broken was his body. It flopped limply as the aurochs flung its victim upwards again and again. After several lunging, maddened attacks the brute allowed the wreckage of what had once been a man to drop into the churned mud of the pitfall's floor. To my horror the aurochs then backed away into the small space available, lowered its head and deliberately spiked the corpse again. Lifting Vulfard on its head like some grisly trophy, the aurochs shook its head from side to side as a terrier might shake a rat in its jaws. A terrier would have growled its anger; the aurochs bellowed and bellowed hate and frustration.

Only when Vulfard's mangled corpse was a bloody pulp did the aurochs finally drop its victim into the slime and mud. Little by little, the frenzied bellowing died away, and from where I stood above, I could see its flanks heaving in and out. Then the beast raised its huge head to me, its mad, white-rimmed eyes glaring malevolently.

In the terrible, empty interval that followed I became aware of Walo standing on the opposite side of the pit. He too had been looking down at the gruesome death of his father. Tears were streaming down his face, and he was shaking violently. For a desperate moment I thought that Walo would hurl himself down into the pit to try to retrieve his father's body or avenge his killer. Instead, as the aurochs ceased its bellowing, Walo threw back his head and, between great sobs of anguish, let out an awful, long-drawn-out howl.

Chapter Two

MY SUMMONS TO the royal chancery had arrived three weeks earlier. The compline bell in the dome of Aachen's basilica was tolling when a nervous-looking young clerk with rabbit teeth knocked on my door. He stared at the ground and mumbled his words because I had not had time to slip on the eye patch I usually wore in public. The Franks and my own Saxon people believe that someone who has eyes of different colours bears the mark of a person touched by the evil one. One of my eyes is blue, the other a greenish hazel. This oddity saved my life as a teenager when my bitter nemesis, King Offa of Wessex, invaded and seized my family's insignificant little kingdom. Offa slaughtered my father and brothers but, fearful that ill luck would follow my murder, he spared my life, choosing instead to exile me to the court of the king of the Franks and the most powerful sovereign in Europe whose rule now extends from the Atlantic coast to the dark forests beyond the Rhine. That exile had a cruel streak. Offa anticipated that I would suffer all the disadvantages and sorrows of a *winelas guma*, a 'friendless man', a prey to all who would harm or exploit him. Against all odds I had prospered. My service in Hispania had been rewarded with an annual stipend and the gift of a small house on the edge of the royal precinct.

The young messenger on my doorstep also made it clear that he preferred not to come into the house. I guessed it had something to do with the fact that I shared my home with a foreigner of sinister appearance. Osric's dark Saracen skin, sardonic manner, and the twisted leg must have made him an alarming figure to the desk-bound gossips in the government bureaucracy. Osric had once been a slave, charged by my father with my upbringing. Now he was my trusted companion and friend.

I stepped back inside the house, put on my eye patch, and collected a heavy ankle-length cloak. At that late hour the braziers in the chancery offices would have been allowed to burn out, and the place was notoriously draughty. Then I followed the messenger along the footpaths that criss-crossed Aachen's royal precinct. We had to go carefully in the fading light as the place was still a construction site. Piles of sand, brick or cut stone were dumped here and there, apparently at random. Temporary workshops and storehouses sprang up overnight, forcing one to make a detour. A familiar track was suddenly blocked by recent scaffolding, or fenced off by a barrier to stop one falling into a trench being dug for the foundations of a new building. For as long as I had known Carolus, the king had been pressing forward with his grand design to make himself a new capital in the north, the equal of Rome, and he was sparing no expense. His treasury, the tribunal building, and the garrison block were complete. But the towering council hall, large enough to seat an audience of four hundred, was still a shell, while his most ambitious structure, the royal chapel, was not yet ready for its ceremonial consecration. It had acquired bells and marble columns and a pair of great, ornate bronze doors that had been locally commissioned and made a fortune for the foundry owner. But an army of workmen still had months of labour before they finished cementing into place the brightly coloured mosaics that would dazzle the congregation.

We met no one on our way to the chancery except for a few late-comers hurrying towards the basilica. From inside came the words of a psalm energetically sung by a large choir, and I caught a faint whiff of the burning incense. I hastened my pace a little and tried to stay in the shadows, not wanting to draw attention to my absence from the service. With each year Carolus was becoming more and more devout and he expected his entourage to be the same. Those like myself who had little or no religion risked his displeasure if they failed at least to make an outward show of faith.

At the entrance to the chancery my guide plucked up the courage to tell me that he was eager to attend the last of the service, and – as I had anticipated – it was Alcuin of York who wished to see me. I assured him that I knew where to find Alcuin's office. With a grateful bob of his head, the young man hurried off, leaving me to find my own way.

I had first met Alcuin of York thirteen years earlier, on the day I had trudged into Aachen as a footsore and callow youth accompanied by a limping slave. Alcuin was scholar, churchman and tutor to Carolus's own family. Royal confidant and mentor, he was the man the king consulted on delicate matters of state. Indeed, I had known Alcuin long enough to know that he would still be on his knees in the front rank of the congregation, and there was no point in hanging about in a chilly corridor. So, briskly, I made my way to his office and, wishing that King Offa could witness my self-assurance, I did not bother to knock but pushed open the door and boldly walked in.

It was more a monk's cell than a bureaucrat's work place. A simple wooden cross hung on one whitewashed wall. Directly opposite was a large plain desk with an uncomfortable-looking wooden stool placed so that anyone looking up from his work would directly face the crucifix. Apart from the shelves that lined the remaining walls, the room was bare of furniture. Three candles of expensive beeswax had been arranged on the desk in an iron sconce. In a sign of economy, just one candle was lit to illuminate the sheet of vellum, pen and ink bottle left there. Alcuin had evidently been working late and had only left the room to attend compline. He would be back shortly.

I closed the door behind me and restrained an impulse to read what it was that Alcuin had been writing. Instead, I sauntered over to the shelves and picked up an item that had caught my eye. It was totally out of place in such austere surroundings. It was a tremendous drinking horn, almost a yard long. I recognized the shape from drinking vessels of similar style used at palace banquets. But they were half the size of the one I held in my hands and were made of glass or cow horn. I brought it closer to the candle flame, trying to identify the material. The dark surface had been polished to a high shine, and there was a broad silver band around the open end. I peered inside. It would hold an impressive quantity of liquid, and when I sniffed, I distinctly picked up the smell of ale. At that moment I heard the scuff of footsteps on the flagstones outside. Hurriedly I replaced the great horn on the shelf and turned, just as Alcuin came in.

It was typical of Alcuin that he did not seem to notice the cold of the evening. He was wearing only a plain dark brown gown and had sandals on his bare feet. Gaunt and of a little more than ordinary height, he would have been approaching his fiftieth year. His hair had thinned and receded, accentuating the severely intellectual look of a high forehead and the narrow, clever face. Pale skin and faint freckles told of his northern origins, and grey eyes retained the sharply penetrating gaze that I remembered from previous interviews. I thought he looked tired and over-worked.

'Sigwulf. Thank you for coming so promptly,' he began, apparently unconcerned to find me loitering in his office. He did not suggest that I remove my cloak so I anticipated that the interview would be brief.

'You've heard about the gifts from Caliph Haroun, I presume,' he said. He had a distinctive way of speaking. Each word was carefully selected and precisely delivered as if he was delivering a lecture. I listened closely. Alcuin had a well-earned reputation as someone who came straight to the point and I was intrigued to know why I had been called to his office at this late hour.

'I'm told that the knight keeps good time,' I replied. The caliph's most talked-about gift was a mechanical clock. On each hour, the tiny figure of a knight in armour emerged from a miniature pavilion and dropped a metal ball that chimed against a metal dish. No one had ever seen such a marvel of ingenuity.

'Let us hope the knight does not rust. We have no craftsmen capable of repairing him,' Alcuin observed drily.

There was nothing unusual about Carolus receiving gifts from foreign rulers. The palace kept inventories of the various items and their value – jewels, coin, inlaid armour, furs, carved ivory, rolls of expensive cloth and so forth. A few pieces were selected for display but most were consigned to the royal treasury, a windowless building with walls three feet thick that had been built against the side of the as-yet-unfinished council chamber.

'What do you know about this caliph?' Alcuin asked me.

'Only common knowledge,' I replied cautiously. 'His capital is a city called Baghdad. It's very far away, beyond Jerusalem and the Holy Land. He lives there in great splendour and is hugely wealthy. The quality of his gifts is proof of that.'

Alcuin gave me a patient look as if to rebuke me for my

ignorance. 'Haroun al Rashid is one of the three most powerful rulers on this earth.' He spoke as if to a promising but lazy student. 'The other two being the emperor in Constantinople and, of course, our own Carolus. The most significant of Haroun's many titles and honorifics is Commander of the Faithful. He regards himself as supreme overlord of all Saracens.'

'Surely the emir of Cordoba contests that claim,' I murmured. I had received my shoulder wound during the failed expedition by Carolus's army into Hispania in support of a rebellion against the emir. I recalled that the rebels, Saracens themselves, had appealed for help from distant Baghdad as well as from Carolus.

'You are correct. The emir of Cordoba refuses to acknowledge the caliph's authority. I won't trouble you with the details, but Haroun's forebears killed every member of the emir's family they could hunt down after seizing the caliphate. The sole survivor fled to Hispania where he established his own independent dominion. The two dynasties hate one another.'

I glimpsed the direction Alcuin's comments were leading. 'So Haroun sends valuable gifts to Carolus as a gesture of appreciation and friendship.'

Alcuin rewarded me with a slight smile. 'Sigwulf, I'm glad that you are still reasonably quick on the uptake.'

'My friend Osric tells me that the Saracens have a saying: "My enemy's enemy is my friend."'

A worm of doubt was stirring in my mind. Did my summons from Alcuin have something to do with Osric?

Alcuin's next statement made matters no clearer. 'Custom and diplomacy dictate that Carolus responds to Haroun's generosity by sending valuable gifts of equal rarity back to him. The king has consulted me for my recommendations.'

'Not an easy task,' I said blandly.

Alcuin gave me a sharp look. Perhaps he thought I was teasing him. 'This will be more than a matter of sending the caliph a parcel of sword blades,' he snapped.

Frankish sword smiths were renowned for the quality of their weapons and a consignment of sword blades was a standard item among the gifts that Carolus despatched to fellow rulers.

Alcuin quickly regained his usual even tone. 'The caliph must have known about Carolus's menagerie because Haroun's gifts included an elephant.'

I gaped. The collection of animals in Carolus's menagerie included wolves, bears, leopards, peacocks, lynx and even a panther sent by the basileus, the emperor in Constantinople. The thought that they might have been joined by a living elephant was tantalizing. I thought how dearly I would love to see an elephant.

Alcuin was enjoying my evident amazement. 'Regrettably the creature did not survive the journey here,' he added.

My imagination soared. I had heard about elephants. Everyone had. They featured in many tales about the fabled east, and my boyhood teacher, a defrocked priest, had described how the ancient Romans trained them as instruments of warfare. But no elephant, as far as I was aware, had set foot in Europe for centuries. They were wondrous beasts.

'The death of this particular animal is most unfortunate,' Alcuin went on. 'The elephant had been specially selected. Its skin was very pale, almost white – a very great compliment from the caliph to Carolus. Apparently, white is the royal colour in Baghdad. Anyone who enters the inner city must be dressed in white.

'What did the elephant die of?' I asked.

'You will have to ask the man who was in charge of its transport from Baghdad. He is full of apologies.'

If I had been more alert, Alcuin's words would have prepared me for what was to follow. But I was still too intrigued by the idea of an elephant arriving in Aachen to notice what he had implied.

Alcuin had not finished. 'I'll introduce him to you at another time. You'll like him. He's most civilized and obliging. He's a Radhanite by the name of Abram.'

'A Radhanite?' I repeated. I had no idea what Alcuin meant.

'The Radhanites are Israelites by faith.' Here I detected a brief glint of disapproval, 'They spend most of their lives on the road, moving from one market to another, trading, trading, always trading. They've spun themselves a web of contacts and associates that reaches from Hispania to India.'

Reluctantly I abandoned my daydream of seeing an elephant, and tried to concentrate on what Alcuin was saying. 'If a city or town prospers by trade, you can safely say that it has its share of Rhadanites, if only a family or two. In Carolus's domain we are aware that they favour the trade artery of the Rhone and several families are settled in the riverside towns. But you never know where or when you've come across one. They merge into the background. It is said that they recognize one another by secret signs.'

He paused. 'Our king has decided that he will match Caliph Haroun's generosity by sending to Baghdad a selection of creatures as unique and special as a nearly white elephant.' Up until now, Alcuin had amazed and intrigued me. Now he stunned me. 'Sigwulf, the king has specifically directed that you be placed in charge of their transport to Baghdad.'

His statement was so unexpected that it was some moments before I found my voice. 'What sort of animals will I be transporting?' I croaked.

Alcuin treated me to a sardonic smile. 'That I will leave to

Carolus himself to inform you of. He will have finished chapel by now and have arrived back in the royal apartments. He is expecting to see you . . . without delay.'

The interview was over. Dazed, I fumbled my way towards the door and found myself back in the corridor. It was only as I closed the door behind me that I realized that when I had asked which animals I was to take to Baghdad, Alcuin's eyes had flicked towards the enormous, silver-mounted drinking horn.

*

The night sky had clouded over and the covered arcade that linked the chancery building with the royal living apartments was in near-total darkness. The middle section of the arcade was unfinished and littered with paving slabs, yet I found my way without stumbling or tripping. I had taken that same route many times, usually well after sunset, though the excursions had been much less frequent in recent months. They had occurred on the nights when I was summoned by Bertha, one of Carolus's large brood of daughters. She had swooped on me soon after my arrival as a young man in Aachen, judging me to be naïve, and – as I came to understand – exotically attractive with my strange eye colours and foreign background. The passage of time had cooled her ardour and I had slipped far down the list of those whom she took to her bed. Yet she still liked to tweak the string occasionally and would reel me in when she sought variety among her lovers. I knew very well that the relationship was increasingly unstable and very dangerous. If her father learned of the extent of his daughter's wanton activities, he might decide to put a stop to them by making an example of someone he considered to have been particularly presumptuous and brazen with a royal princess. As an interloper within the Frankish court, I was the obvious candidate for exemplary punishment. I dreaded what penalty might be exacted – execution or castration were both possibilities – and I had already resolved to extricate myself from the relationship with Bertha. But I was wary. To deny her might make her vindictive, and, to be truthful to myself, I still found Bertha most alluring. She took great care with her appearance, staining her lips with berry juice and applying a delicate coat of powder to cover the first blemishes in her once flawless complexion. Doubtless she tinted the long flaxen braids that her attendants spent hours brushing and arranging. But her body needed no such artifice. As she matured, Bertha's statuesque figure had become ever more voluptuous and desirable.

The king's living quarters took up the entire first floor of a substantial building in the north-east corner of the royal precinct. At the foot of the broad sweep of stairs I ignored the smirk on the face of one of the guards, recognizing him as one of the men who took bribes to look the other way when I was visiting Bertha. His colleagues searched me for hidden weapons and passed me on to an under-steward who was already hovering and waiting to take my cloak. Carolus's household staff were well used to dealing with late callers to see their master. It was the king's habit to take a long nap in the afternoon and then work far into the night. If Carolus was restless, he was known to slip out of his official apartments in the small hours of the morning and wander about the royal precinct, unescorted, checking on what was going on. On one heart-stopping occasion I had almost bumped into him as I was on my way to a tryst with Bertha, and I was still not sure if he had seen me hastily dart away.

After a short delay the under-steward led me up the stairs and to a set of double doors. He knocked discreetly before easing them open just wide enough to let me slip inside.

I had to squint. In contrast to Alcuin's dimly lit office, Carolus's private audience chamber was ablaze with light. Clusters of tall, fat candles burned everywhere. They were suspended in holders from the ceiling beams, fixed on great iron floor stands, held in wall brackets. Many were fitted with polished steel mirrors. The effect was to heat the room, make it as bright as day and flood one's senses with the sweet scent of beeswax. The spacious room itself gave an impression of comfortable opulence. The windows were filled with panes of glass to keep out the weather. Linen panels painted with colourful pictures of hunting scenes decorated the walls. A day couch covered with cushions and a rich carpet was where Carolus could take his afternoon nap. Another expensive-looking rug served as a cloth on a broad table, and beneath its edge was a glimpse of table legs intricately carved into animal shapes. Half a dozen folding chairs were made of some dark, exotic wood, and – inevitably – there was a crucifix. In Alcuin's study the cross had been plain and unadorned, hung against a white wall. Here the cross was four times the size, standing on a base of pale green marble and placed where it was immediately visible to a visitor. Its arms were studded with patterns of semi-precious coloured stones that glowed in the candlelight.

Carolus loomed beside the table, his presence dominating the room. I had forgotten what a big man he was. He was taller than me by at least a head, powerfully built with heavy bones, wide shoulders, large feet and hands. His luxuriant hair had gone grey but was carefully trimmed and oiled, and he wore the long drooping moustaches so fashionable among the Franks. As usual, he dressed modestly for someone of his exalted rank though the materials were of the very best quality. The wool of his deep-blue hose and tunic was as fine as silk, and the soft leather of his shoes and garters had been dyed pale blue, then over-stamped with leaf designs in silver. He wore very little jewellery – a heavy gold ring inset with a large red stone on his right hand, and a torc of twisted gold around his thick neck. Despite the warmth in the room he was wearing a waistcoat of short fur that I guessed was otter skin. It was left open at the front because Carolus, King of the Franks and Patrician of the Romans, had grown a noticeable paunch.

I bowed.

'Sigwulf, I have a mission for you,' said the king briskly. Like Alcuin, he too preferred to come directly to the point. In contrast to his advisor's clear, quiet tones the king spoke in a surprisingly high, thin voice. It was unexpected coming from such a bulky frame.

I stood meekly, unable to tear my gaze away from the object that Carolus was holding. It was another of those huge silver-mounted drinking horns, the twin of the one I had just seen in Alcuin's study. In the king's massive grasp it seemed not quite as out of proportion.

'This is from my grandfather's time,' said the king, observing my gaze and turning the great drinking horn this way and that.

I remained silent and waited.

'Alcuin mentioned the elephant that the caliph had chosen for me?' the king asked.

'I am very sorry to hear that the creature did not survive the journey, Your Majesty,' I murmured politely.

'No matter. I will send in return a creature that is equally spectacular.' Carolus hefted the horn as if he was proud of it. 'Nothing the size of an elephant, of course. But two of these will be the equal!'

Carolus was boyish in his enthusiasm. I had no idea what he was talking about.

'My verderer, Vulfard, tells me that it's possible,' he said.

He must have noted the puzzled look on my face or remembered that I was an outsider who had not grown up among the Franks. 'Sigwulf, this is the horn of the largest, most dangerous animal in my kingdom. The man who hunts the aurochs requires skill and courage. If he succeeds, the horn is a mark of his bravery, a supreme trophy.'

The king's large grey eyes scanned my face, his expression momentarily serious. 'Sigwulf, you will take a pair of live aurochs to Baghdad for me, a bull and cow. They will be my elephants. Breeding stock for Haroun's menagerie. That Saracen friend of yours will be a help.'

Carolus had an astonishing memory. It was one reason why his grip on more than half of Europe was so effective. He remembered small details and combined them with a shrewd judgement of people. Osric had played a vital part with me during the Hispania campaign.

Abruptly Carolus broke into a high-pitched laugh, almost a giggle. 'I'm beginning to sound like the quarrelling hunters of the fable,' he said, smiling at me to share his joke.

This time I knew what he was talking about. The tale was of two hunters, preparing to hunt a bear, arguing so bitterly over who should get the bear's pelt that they fell out before they got started and never managed to kill their prey.

'First we must catch our aurochs,' he said. 'I've given Vulfard all the men he needs. You are to join him and learn how the animal lives in the wild, what it eats, how it behaves, and so on. You must get to know how to look after the beast so that it survives the journey, unlike that unfortunate elephant.'

The king walked across to the table and set down the aurochs' horn. I thought my interview was at an end and prepared to take my leave. But then he said over his shoulder,

'Sigwulf, take off your eye patch. You need both eyes for what I'm going to show you.'

Obediently I took off the eye patch. Carolus had known about my different-colour eyes since my first arrival at his court.

When he turned to face me, he held an object I had not expected: a book.

Carolus could neither write nor read. Bertha had told me so. She had revealed that her father kept a stylus and wax tablet by his pillow so that he could practise his letters in secret but was making little progress. He knew how to write his name, of course. He had developed an impressive royal signature full of flourishes and cross-strokes. He scratched it on official documents prepared by his secretaries, and although he might puzzle out a handful of words, reading an entire book was well beyond the limits of his capability.

Carolus's initial boyishness had been replaced by something almost conspiratorial, as if he was about to share a secret with me.

'Besides learning how to look after an aurochs, you will procure some other animals as my gifts for the caliph Haroun,' he said.

'At Your Majesty's command,' I answered. There was no mistaking his tone of voice; this was an order and I had no choice in the matter. He had no need to remind me that I was an exile from my homeland and depended on Carolus for my entire existence. I was completely at the king's disposal.

'Alcuin told you that the elephant that died was near-white? And that white is the royal colour in Baghdad?'

'He did, Your Majesty.'

The king opened the book. 'Besides a pair of live aurochs, I have decided to present the caliph with a selection of different and interesting animals, all of them white.'

There was a note of self-congratulation in his voice. I sensed that what he was about to say had not been discussed with Alcuin beforehand. It made me all the more attentive and a little uneasy.

The king was turning the pages of the book, searching for something. From where I stood I could tell that the pages were covered with coloured pictures though, as they were upside down, it was difficult to work out exactly what they were.

'The caliph has his own menagerie at his Baghdad palace.' Carolus had a slight frown on his face and was talking to himself as much as he was addressing me. 'Alcuin informs me that his animal collection is a wonder of the world. There are strange beasts from countries as far away as India and beyond.'

He was finding it difficult to locate the right page. He reached the end of the book and began to search through it from the beginning again.

'I must send animals that he does not already have. Animals that will amaze him, and flatter him because they, too, are white. Ah! Here is one!'

He turned the book around and held it out to show me.

The book was a bestiary, a volume where the artist had drawn pictures of strange and remarkable animals. The illustration that the king had selected was of an ice bear.

'Imagine the effect when Haroun sees a bear that is white, and so big and powerful!' said Carolus triumphantly. 'He will understand that in the north we have creatures every bit as remarkable as his tigers and lions.'

I swallowed hard, my mouth had gone dry. 'Your Majesty, if I understand correctly, your wish is that I take an ice bear to Baghdad, as well as two aurochs?' A worrying image had surfaced in my head. An animal accustomed to ice and snow

25

would die from heat on the way to Haroun's capital. An ice bear would never survive the trip.

'Not a single ice bear, Sigwulf. A pair of them,' muttered the king. He was already leafing through the pages of the bestiary again. He quickly found what he wanted, and again held up the page for me to see.

'And at least two of these. More, if you can get them.'

This time it was a drawing of a bird of prey. The artist had accurately sketched the elegant pointed wings, the neat head and fiercely hooked beak. He had tinted a bright yellow eye and the grey talons, but left the sleek body uncoloured so that the bird was off-white on the page except for a very light sprinkling of dark speckles.

Now I was on firmer ground. There were several such birds already in the royal mews. The Franks knew them as gyrfalcons or vulture falcons, and prized them so highly that their use as hunting birds was restricted to the king himself and his most senior lords. I felt a mild sense of relief, imagining that gyrfalcons were unlikely to suffer from the heat in the same way as an ice bear. Only one thing made me hesitate. The plumage of the gyrfalcons I had seen on their perch blocks in the royal mews ranged in colour from silver-brown to a bird that was nearly black. I had never seen one that was as white as the illustration on the page, and I wondered where I could find white gyrfalcons.

The king provided the answer. He loved his hawking and was very knowledgeable about his birds of prey.

'Sigwulf, my mews master will give you the names of the traders who deal in vulture falcons. You'll buy only pure-white birds from them. You'll have ample funds.'

'Where will I find these traders?' I ventured to ask.

'Far in the north.' Carolus's reply had the vagueness of a

monarch who expected his orders to be carried out. 'Whether gyrfalcons or ice bears, it's all the same. The further north you go, the whiter are the creatures. They match the ice and snow.'

But the king had not finished. He was already leafing through the bestiary once more, and this time he found what he wanted near the opening page.

'And while you are getting the ice bears and falcons, I want you to track down this creature for me.' He held up the page.

It was a woodland scene. A beautiful maiden was seated beneath a tree laden with ripe fruit. The artist had shown her wearing a long, soft flowing gown and her hair hung loose around her shoulders. She looked exceptionally demure. There was an impression of grassy sward and bright flowers around her bare feet. In the background were low bushes. At the far left of the picture appeared the edge of a forest, and among the tree trunks lurked two men dressed as huntsmen. One was holding a spear, the other a rope noose. They were obviously hiding in ambush and about to pounce. Their intended prey was not the vulnerable-looking young woman, but a graceful four-legged animal that at first glance was either a young stag or a fine pure-bred horse. It was shown in the very centre of the composition, part kneeling and part lying on the grass and had laid its head trustingly in the young woman's lap. This placed her in some danger because from the centre of the animal's brow protruded a wicked looking spike, a single long horn with a distinctive spiral.

The animal was white.

A large blunt finger tapped the page. 'Find me a unicorn.'

The king was so certain of what he wanted that I knew it would be wise to conceal my astonishment. Of course I had heard about the unicorn, just as I had heard about elephants. But I had never heard of anyone who had actually seen a living unicorn any more than someone who had seen a real elephant. Dimly I recalled my teacher telling me of a wild beast with a single horn that the Romans put on display in their circus games. As I looked at the vicious spike on the forehead of the creature in the picture it occurred to me that the same Romans also should have trained such an animal for war. It would have been at least as deadly as an elephant.

'As Your Majesty commands,' I said with a confidence I did not feel.

Immediately he detected the uncertainty of my response. 'Is there a problem?'

I took a deep breath. 'Your Majesty has mentioned that white animals are commonly found in the lands of ice and snow. Their colour matches their surroundings. But it seems to me from this picture that the unicorn lives in places where the climate is quite warm, a place of forests and flowers and fruit-bearing trees.'

Carolus took another look at the picture of the unicorn, and for a moment I thought he was about to change his instructions. But obtaining a unicorn was too close to his heart for him to abandon the idea entirely. 'I admit that a unicorn will be difficult to obtain. By all accounts it is a notoriously shy and timid beast. So just one example of the animal will be sufficient. I don't expect you to bring back two of them.'

I dared one last attempt to get him to re-consider. 'Your Majesty, would not a professional huntsman have a better chance of capturing a unicorn? Someone like Vulfard?'

I had gone too far. The king brought down his heavy eyebrows in a scowl.

'After Vulfard has secured the aurochs,' I amended hastily.

The king regarded me for a long moment, and, despite the warmth of the room, I felt a sudden cold chill in the air. 'I think you, Sigwulf, would be more suited than Vulfard for this enterprise. The unicorn has a weakness: it cannot control its animal passion. If it sees a young maiden, it will emerge from hiding and lay its head adoringly on the maiden's lap. Then it can be taken.'

The goosebumps rose on my skin. I wondered how much Carolus knew about my affair with his daughter. This interview was getting more difficult by the minute, and it was time to leave the room. I bowed again and began to sidle towards the door. He stopped me with a single barbed phrase, 'Sigwulf, there's one more thing to discuss . . .'

I braced myself. This surely had something to do with Bertha.

'Have you had any more dreams that I should know about?' he asked.

I swallowed with relief. Carolus knew my dreams. They were strange and vivid and, if interpreted correctly, foretold the future. But interpretation was very difficult, often contradictory, and to help me I had used the Oneirokritikon, an ancient book on how to interpret dreams, written by a Greek named Artimedorus. The copy that had come into my possession was in Arabic and Osric had translated it for me. But less than twenty pages of our translation survived – the rest had been lost during the war in Hispania – and we kept them hidden beneath a floorboard in the house.

'I've had very few dreams in recent times. Nothing of note,' I answered truthfully.

He nodded, seemingly satisfied. 'Well, if there is something I should know about, please tell Alcuin. He will keep me informed.'

I left the audience chamber feeling distinctly queasy. I had always thought of Carolus as a benign and understanding overlord. Now I was not so sure. This time he had been self-absorbed and imperious, even threatening. Perhaps that was the inevitable result of more than twenty years on the throne, ruling such a vast kingdom. Day after day he was dealing with a multitude of problems and had to manage a circle of courtiers with their competing rivalries and jealousies. I was glad to be out of his sight.

I collected my cloak from the under-steward and, deep in thought, descended the stairs. The wind had got up and was driving a chill, slanting rain between the pillars of the arcade at ground level. The corrupt guardsman gave me a sly wink as I walked past him, and his gesture confirmed my worries: I had allowed myself to drift dangerously close to the intrigues and conspiracies of court. I should be thankful that the king had jolted me out of my seductively comfortable life. In Aachen I was achieving nothing of note, and the mission he had given me was my chance to put my abilities to the test, engage myself in something worthwhile, and indulge my curiosity for seeing new countries and my love of travel. Not least, it was the ideal excuse to put a safe distance between Bertha and myself.

Stepping out from the shelter of the building, I turned and looked into the wind. The night sky was velvety black. Tilting back my head I let the cold raindrops splatter on my face and trickle down my neck. It was time I woke up.

Chapter Three

NOW THAT THE AUROCHS was their captive, they starved the beast of food and water. Only after three days, when the animal was close to collapse, did the foresters drop a loop of rope around the deadly horns and tangle its legs with heavy cords. Then, very cautiously, they began to dig away one wall of the pit, bevelling the earth into a ramp. Nevertheless, the aurochs still had the strength to try to gore its enemies as they prodded the creature up the slope and into a heavily barred cage on wheels. No one was willing to go down into the pit and delve into the slimy mud to retrieve what was left of Vulfard. His battered corpse stayed submerged in the muck and excrement as the trap was filled in; there was no Christian burial.

All that time Walo refused to leave the scene. He slept in the same little trench where Vulfard had hidden beside me in the ambush, and begged scraps of food from the foresters. Despite their charity they treated him with caution. At times he ducked and cringed away if anyone came near him, or, without warning, he made sudden aggressive movements as if to strike them. He was increasingly haggard, his face and clothes filthy. I feared that his mind was close to total collapse. When everyone was ready to depart, I coaxed him into coming with me as we trailed along behind the aurochs' cage, its solid wooden wheels creaking with the strain as it was manhandled over tree roots and ruts until we were on the better surface of the road that brought us to Aachen. There I managed to trace his family, only to learn that his mother had died when he was still an infant. Vulfard had raised him up on his own, almost entirely in the forest, and now no one wanted to take on the responsibility of looking after him. When we finally returned to Aachen with the aurochs, Walo finished up at my own home, sleeping in an outhouse by his own choice, as he felt more at ease there than in the main building.

'We could take Walo north with us,' I suggested to Osric. We were seated on a bench in front of the house, soaking up the sunshine of a spring morning and discussing the journey to collect the white animals. The sounds of sawyers shaping beams and trusses for yet another royal building carried clearly from the nearest construction site.

'He could turn out to be a liability,' Osric grunted. Grateful for the warmth, Osric was massaging his crooked leg. In his belted woollen tunic and sturdy leather boots he dressed like a Frankish tradesman, though his black eyes and swarthy skin hinted at his Saracen origin, as did his habit of wearing a cloth wrapped around his grey felt skull cap.

'His father saved my life,' I said. 'And Walo's showing signs of recovery. He's speaking an occasional sentence. If we leave him behind, he'll just slip back into a wordless daze. There's no one here to look after him.'

I tried to sound casual and reasonable but my friend knew me only too well.

'I get the impression that you've another reason why you want Walo to accompany us?' he said pointedly.

Osric was the only person with whom I regularly discussed my prophetic dreams.

'It was the night after my interview with Carolus,' I admitted. 'I dreamed I was trudging through a pine forest and heard a strange buzzing sound – very loud. Two wolves were running towards me between the trees. The buzzing noise came from a great mass of bees clinging to their fur. The insects covered the wolves so thickly that they seemed to have grown a second skin that hummed and rippled. The wolves paid no attention to the bees but I was terrified. Out of nowhere, Walo appeared . . .' I paused, remembering the bizarre scene.

'Go on,' prompted Osric.

'Walo was acting like a madman. He went straight up to the wolves and stroked their heads, and they sat down obediently, their tongues lolling out. Walo sat himself on the ground between them and many of the bees swarmed across and onto Walo until he, too, seemed to be wearing a coat of bees. Then I woke up.'

Osric was quiet for a long moment. 'What does the Oneirokritikon have to say?'

I hesitated before replying. Both of us knew that the dream book could be as dangerously ambiguous as any charlatan fortuneteller.

'Artimedorus writes that seeing a madman in a dream is a good omen. He points out that madmen are not hindered in anything they have set their hearts on. So to dream of someone who is insane means that a business venture will succeed.'

'An unlikely argument,' Osric observed sardonically.

'Enough to persuade me that taking Walo along with us would be more than repaying his father's sacrifice. Walo could prove a lucky mascot.'

'You'll be exposing him to situations for which he is completely unprepared, perhaps to a new danger.'

Puzzled, I looked at my friend. 'What do you have in mind?'

'The last I heard, King Offa still rules Mercia as ruthlessly as before. He has his informants at Carolus's court. He's still your enemy, and he might well still be thinking that he was foolish for not killing you when he wiped out the rest of your family. Now he has his chance to finish the job.'

'But we're not going anywhere near Mercia.'

Osric's face clouded momentarily. 'Offa will have heard about the caliph's splendid gifts to Carolus and the preparations to send a mission to Baghdad in return. His agents may even have reported that you have been put in charge of the mission. Mercia and Frankia are on good terms.'

It was true. Relations between the two kings, Carolus and Offa, had become increasingly cordial of late. They were exchanging letters regularly and recently there had been a formal trade agreement between their kingdoms. All of a sudden I felt foolish. If Offa knew how high I had risen in Carolus's favour he might now see me, the legitimate heir to the plundered throne, as a threat. Offa was brutal and ruthless. Regretting that he had let me live, he might try and undo his mistake.

'I doubt that the spies will think it's worth reporting that I'm being sent to gather together the white animals,' I replied.

'Offa hasn't tried to harm you while you are at Carolus's court. That would be an insult to the Franks. But once you're away from Frankish territory on this animal-collecting trip, you'll be vulnerable . . .' Osric let his voice trail off.

'Then we'll make sure he doesn't know exactly where or when we are going,' I said firmly. Osric's caution was oppressive.

He treated me to a sceptical glance. 'Offa's no fool. He'll work that out for himself.'

His remark hit home. Carolus's mews master had already

told me that the source for white gyrfalcons was the market in Kaupang, on the furthest border of the kingdom of the Danes.

My friend grimaced as he tried to stretch his crooked leg. 'Just how far north is this Kaupang?'

'A month's travel. The market is temporary, just a few weeks every summer. Traders come to it from all over the Northlands.'

'And just as I was hoping to enjoy a few weeks of summer warmth,' Osric grumbled.

'Everything is being arranged by the chancery and we should be back before the summer's over,' I assured him. 'There'll be an armed escort from here to Dorestad on the Rhine, a ship from there direct to Kaupang where we purchase the white bears and falcons, then back home.'

Osric shook his head in disbelief. 'And a moment ago you said that we would conceal the timing of our journey. Not with an escort of Frankish troopers clattering along with us, we won't.'

'Then I'll have the size of escort reduced to the bare minimum. Just enough to make sure we arrive in Dorestad without being robbed. We'll be carrying a small fortune in silver coin. Carolus is providing a massive budget.'

'Sufficient to buy a unicorn?' My friend was gently mocking.

'We'll do our best to find one, and if we fail, the king will have to accept our excuses.'

Osric sighed. 'That part of our mission is probably a fool's errand. But I can see that you've already made up your mind about Walo coming with us.'

I got to my feet. 'I must go and check how soon the chancery can have our escort and money ready for us.' As I made my way across the royal precinct, I wondered if I should have been more honest with Osric. The Oneirokritikon had offered an alternative explanation for my dream. According to Artimedorus, a dream of bees was only a good omen for farmers. For everyone else, to dream about bees was highly dangerous. Their humming signified confusion, and their stings were symbols for wounds and hurt. If the bees settled on the dreamer's head, it foretold his death.

*

We rode out from Aachen on the first day of June when the faint glow of dawn was barely visible in the sky. I hoped our small party would be unremarkable among the early travellers already taking the rutted highway leading out of town. Osric and I wore the sober, practical clothes that marked us as smalltime merchants. Walo was dressed as our servant. I had removed my eye patch to make myself less noticeable and would replace it only when it was full daylight. Our escort of two burly troopers had been persuaded to leave behind the helmets and armoured coats that identified them as members of the royal guard. Each man led two pack ponies, his sword hidden among their straw-lined panniers stuffed with the bottles of Rhenish wine that purported to be our trade goods. Our real wealth was in the leather saddlebags slung from the saddle of my horse and Osric's: shiny new silver deniers from the king's mint at Aachen. Each coin was the size of my fingernail and the moneyers had stamped them with Carolus's monogram on one side, and the Christian cross on the other. There were three thousand of them, a dazzling prize for any lucky thief.

As the morning wore on, I was alarmed to see Walo attracting attention. He stared rudely at the people coming towards us along the road, gazing at them with open curiosity. Some scowled at him in return. Others met his stare and, noting his moon face, looked away and hurried their steps. Ignoring their reaction, he swivelled right round in the saddle to turn and watch their backs long after they had passed.

'Walo sticks in people's memories,' Osric muttered as he rode up alongside me. 'Let's hope that Offa's spies don't hear that you are travelling with Vulfard's son. We'll be easy to track.'

'There's not much I can do about it,' I admitted.

'Does Walo know where we are going and why?'

'I got him in one of his better moments, and told him that the king was sending us to obtain white bears, hawks and a unicorn. But I didn't say where we were going.'

'What was his reaction?'

'He accepted everything I said as perfectly normal. He only asked if a unicorn sheds its horn every year.'

'Why on earth would he want to know that?'

'He told me in all seriousness that if the unicorn loses its horn each year, then it is a sort of deer. If not, then it is more like a wisent.'

Osric raised an eyebrow. 'For all his strangeness, he knows a lot about the animals. Let's hope he doesn't blurt out the reason for our journey to some stranger along our route.'

'He shies away from strangers. Maybe he doesn't trust them,' I reassured Osric. 'But I'll keep a close watch on him.'

We left the town and emerged into gently rolling country-side. The rich soil was intensively cultivated, and here Walo gawked at the prosperous brick-built farms with their tiled stables and cattle byres, the barns, pigeon lofts and orchards. I guessed that his previous life under his father's care had been almost entirely spent in the great tracts of untamed forest that the king reserved for hunting. Edging my horse closer to Walo I took it on myself to try to explain what was happening on the land. Here a flock of sheep was penned next to an open-sided shed. Two men were shearing while their comrades were carrying away the fleeces to drop them into rinsing baths. A little further on I described why an ox team was ploughing the ground so late in the season. It was the new agricultural system recommended by the king's advisors. The field had been left fallow for the previous year. When we came to a watermill, the turning paddles astonished him and I doubted he understood my long-winded description of their function. But I needed to hold his attention while, off to one side, Osric discreetly bartered with the miller for a bag of oats for our horses.

By noon, the day had turned very warm and it was time to break our journey. Passing a large, ramshackle farm, I spotted a water trough in one corner of the farmyard. I turned aside and led our little pack train into the yard to ask permission to water our animals. Two ill-tempered guard dogs promptly burst from their kennel, barking and snarling. They were large, vicious curs. We pulled up immediately, unable to dismount. Our horses skittered nervously, edging sideways and back. The dogs circled, hackles raised, occasionally rushing in to snap at their heels. One dog, the largest and boldest, leapt up in an attempt to sink its teeth into a guardsman's leg. He kicked out at the brute with an oath and I feared that he would reach for his hidden sword. After a little while, when no one appeared from the farmhouse to call off the beasts, I pulled my horse's head around and prepared to lead our party away.

At that moment, Walo, who had not spoken all morning, suddenly broke his silence. I did not make out the exact words but he called out some sort of command. At the same time he threw a leg across his saddle and slid down from his horse, leaving the reins dangling. He then strode straight towards the angry dogs. I was sure they would rush him and attack, but he called out again and they backed away. He kept walking forward, both hands held out palms down, and his voice dropped to a more normal tone. As he spoke, the frenzied barking subsided to low, frustrated growls. Walo moved even closer, and the dogs' hackles sank down. Finally, when Walo was standing right over them, he gestured at them to return to where they had come from. Silently the brutes trotted off to the side of the farmyard, heads low and their tails drooping.

Without a backward glance, Walo returned to his horse and gathered up the loose reins.

'Not as addled as he appears,' the trooper who had nearly been bitten observed grudgingly. The dogs had settled themselves down at the far side of the yard. Their ears were pricked and they were watching Walo's every movement, ignoring the rest of us.

A farm servant eventually emerged to give us permission to water our horses and, with my eye patch back in place, I negotiated the purchase of a couple of loaves and a large chunk of cheese for ourselves. We removed our horses' packs and saddles, found ourselves a shady spot beside a barn, and began to eat our midday meal.

'What's the plan when we reach Dorestad?' Osric asked me. The bread was stale and he dipped his crust into a cup of water to soften it.

I spat out a morsel of grit. The mix of rye and barley flour had been poorly sieved. 'In Dorestad we locate a shipowner called Redwald. He makes the voyage to Kaupang every year.'

'What about our escort?' Osric flicked a glance towards the two troopers who were throwing crumbs to the farm doves that had fluttered down to peck at the leftovers.

'They'll help us load the wine aboard, then return to Aachen with the horses.'

'Leaving us to the tender mercies of this Redwald.'

'The mews master assures me that Redwald can be trusted,' I replied. Osric had good reason to be suspicious. The ship captain who had carried Osric and me into our exile had tried to rob us and sell us into slavery.

'And what if this Redwald learns just how much coin we are carrying? Never underestimate the power of silver and gold to make a man change his loyalty—'

A peculiar sound made me stop and look up. At first I thought it was the cooing of one of the doves that were strutting around our feet. Then I realized that someone was blowing on a musical instrument. It was Walo. He had wandered off by himself and was leaning up against the wall of the barn in the sunshine, his eyes closed. He held a simple deerhorn pipe to his lips and was gently playing the same few notes, over and over again.

*

After five uneventful days on the road we arrived at Dorestad. It was one of those clear windless June mornings when a handful of small, puffy clouds hang almost motionless in a sky of cornflower blue. The port was an untidy sprawl of warehouses, sheds and taverns that spread along the bank of the Rhine for more than a mile. Dozens of staithes and jetties projected out into the dark waters of the broad river like the teeth of a gigantic comb. They had been built on wooden posts hammered into the soft stinking ooze of the foreshore. Moored against them were watercraft of every description ranging from rafts and river wherries to substantial seagoing cogs. Not wanting to attract attention, I was reluctant to ask for Redwald by name so we picked our way along the riverbank between heaps of discarded rubbish, broken barrels, handcarts and wheelbarrows while I tried to identify those vessels that looked large enough to make the voyage to Kaupang. We had gone nearly the full length of the waterfront when a gangling, ruddy-faced man with a bulbous nose and unkempt, thinning grey hair stepped out from behind a pile of lumber and caught my horse by the bridle.

'Another two tides and you'd have been too late,' he said.

I looked down at him in surprise. I judged him to be a dock worker. He was wearing a labourer's grubby canvas smock and heavy wooden clogs.

'Too late for what?'

'A passage to Scringes Heal.'

'I have no idea what you're talking about,' I said curtly. He showed no sign of letting go the bridle so I was forced to add, 'Can you tell me where I can find shipmaster Redwald?'

'You're speaking to him,' the man replied. 'You must be Sigwulf. I had word that you'll be needing passage. Scringes Heal is what the northmen call Kaupang.'

Behind me Osric gave an unhappy cough. Clearly we had failed in our attempt to keep our mission secret.

The shipmaster glanced towards my companions, a wary and disapproving expression on his face. 'I wasn't told that there were so many in your party.'

'Only three of us are for the voyage,' I said.

Redwald put up a hand to rearrange a stray wisp of long hair across a bald patch on his scalp. 'No point in discussing our business in public. Your companions can wait here while we settle terms.'

'Osric is my business partner. He needs to hear what you propose,' I answered frostily.

Redwald swung round and gave Osric a cursory inspection. 'Very well. Come with me.' He let go of the bridle and stamped off along the nearest jetty, his clogs echoing on the planks.

Osric and I handed the reins of our horses to Walo, and followed. At the far end of the jetty was moored a solid-looking cargo ship. Big and beamy, with a thick single mast, it looked like the sort of vessel to trust. I was not so sure about its uncouth master.

Redwald jumped aboard then waited while Osric, hampered by his stiff leg, clambered over the ship's rail and onto the deck. I followed them to where a length of sailcloth had been rigged to provide a patch of shade. Redwald growled an order and a sailor came scrambling up a ladder from below deck. He brought three stools and, as soon as he had set them down, Redwald sent him scurrying off to the local tavern to bring back a jug of ale and three tankards.

With the sailor out of earshot, Redwald waved us to our seats and got down to business. His tone was far from friendly.

'Why did the mews master send *you?*' he demanded. 'There's a rumour going around that you're going to Scringes Heal to buy falcons. Until now I've bought them as his agent.'

I didn't enquire as to the source of the rumour but it was further proof that my attempt to keep our mission secret had failed. 'This is a special requirement,' I told the shipmaster. 'Carolus requires only birds that are white.'

Redwald snorted. 'I can recognize a white bird when I see one.'

I guessed that the shipmaster was irritated because he turned a profit on his transactions as agent for the mews master, inflating the price he had paid for the birds in Kaupang.

'I'll be paying a bonus if we return from Kaupang with all our purchases alive and in good condition,' I said.

His eyes narrowed. 'What purchases are you talking about? I've never lost a gyrfalcon yet.'

'The king also wants a pair of ice bears brought back from Kaupang.'

Redwald threw back his head and guffawed, showing several gaps among his yellowing teeth. 'Difficult to find. And shitting all over my deck if you obtain them. I'll charge you extra for that.'

The sailor returned with the ale and mugs and poured out our drinks. Redwald had been speaking to me in Frankish, but now he switched to his local dialect as he muttered to the sailor that his two visitors were a couple of troublesome dolts. His dialect was almost identical to the Anglo-Saxon I had spoken as a boy so I understood every word.

Keeping my temper in check, I said in my mother tongue, 'Transporting ice bears should present no problems if they are caged securely.'

Redwald's head jerked round. 'So you speak Frisian.'

'Not Frisian . . . my own Saxon tongue,' I told him.

'I should have known,' he growled. I wondered what he meant by this remark, but already he had changed the subject. 'What have you got in those panniers on your horses?' he demanded bluntly.

'Good-quality Rhenish wine. Once we reach Kaupang, I intend to do a little trading on my own account.' I had hoped to make myself sound suitably devious, to encourage him to think that I, too, was unprincipled enough to make a profit on the side.

Instead he scowled. 'You leave your wine right here on the dockside. Half my own cargo is wine. I don't need competition.'

I saw my opening. 'I've a better idea that will suit both of us. I'm willing to add my wine to your own stock so that you can sell it for me on commission.'

He swirled the contents of the wooden tankard in his hands while he thought it over. 'Here's what I can do,' he said finally, 'I'll bring you and your companions to Scringes Heal and back again, but I'll take no responsibility for the health of the animals. That's your lookout. In return, I take a thirty per cent cut from the sale of your goods.' Abruptly he thrust out his tankard towards me. 'Is it agreed?'

I touched my tankard against his. 'Agreed.'

A draught of juniper-flavoured ale sealed our bargain. I watched Redwald over the rim of the mug and wondered why he had not asked how I was going to pay for the gyrfalcons and the ice bears. He must have known that they would be very costly.

*

Some hours later, I was standing beside the shipmaster on the cog's deck and feeling apprehensive. Redwald had ordered his sailors to cast off from the jetty the moment we had brought aboard our wine and I had dismissed the escort troopers. Dorestad was already several miles behind us, and the last trace of daylight was bleeding from the sky. I could scarcely make out any difference between the black surface of the Rhine and the distant line of the riverbank. The cog was floating downstream, carried along by the current, her great rectangular sail barely filling with the breeze. There was no moon, and soon there would only be starlight to see by. As far as I could tell, we were rushing into blackness and out of control.

'How do you know which way to steer?' I asked, trying to keep the anxiety out of my voice. Osric and Walo were below deck, keeping watch over the silver coin in our saddlebags, for we had agreed that someone should be awake at all times.

'I use my ears,' Redwald grunted.

I could hear only the creak of ship's timber and the soft slapping of water running down the sides of the ship. From somewhere in the distance came the harsh croak of a heron. A moment later a slowly flapping shadow passed across the sky as the bird flew over us.

Redwald's explanation was a joke, I thought. 'And what if there is night fog?'

He belched softly, exuding a stale whiff of ale. 'Don't worry, Sigwulf. I've navigated this river all my life. I know its twists and turns and moods. I'll bring us safely to the open sea.'

He spoke a quiet order to the steersman, and I sensed the slight tremor under my feet as the blade of the side rudder turned. It was too dark to tell whether the cog had altered course.

Redwald had spoken Frisian to both the helmsman and to me. Out on the river he seemed more relaxed, less gruff. It was the right moment to sound him out.

'How many times have you made the trip to Kaupang?' I asked.

He considered for a moment. 'Fifteen, maybe sixteen times.'

'Never any trouble?'

'Pirates once or twice, but we drove them off or managed to out-run them.'

'What about bad weather?'

'With decent ballast my ship can handle heavy weather.' He sounded very confident but the fact that he immediately spat over the side — a gesture every countryman knows is intended to appease the weather — reduced his credibility.

'Ballast?' I asked. I had no idea what he was talking about.

He was standing close enough for me to see the affectionate way he laid a hand on the wooden rail. 'It's what you stow low down in a ship to make sure she doesn't fall over in a gale. I've a couple of tons of quern stones stowed beneath all that wine.'

He belched again. 'God only knows why in the Northlands they can't make decent querns for themselves, but their wives prefer the stones we bring from the Eifel. That's the way of the world: stones for hard-working women to grind their flour while their menfolk guzzle wine.'

I peered forward into the darkness. Occasionally a pale shape appeared and swooped past the bow before vanishing into the gloom – seagulls. I recalled how excited Walo had been when he saw his first gull flying upriver from the sea. Living in the forests, he had never seen a gull before. He had asked me if these were the white birds we were bringing back for the king. Redwald had laughed aloud.

The shipmaster's voice broke into my thoughts. 'I suppose that Saracen companion of yours has his own contacts at Kaupang.'

The shipmaster was observant and shrewd. He had identified Osric as being a Saracen, or perhaps someone had already told him.

'Osric knows no one at Kaupang, as far as I know. He's never been there,' I replied sharply. I wondered why Redwald was fishing for information.

'Then he'll have a chance to meet some of his own people. Saracen traders get to almost as many faraway places as us Frisians. A few show up in Kaupang each year. Buying slaves and furs mostly, and they pay in coin –' his significant pause alerted me – 'so it will be handy to have someone who can check for counterfeits.'

'I'm sure Osric will help in whatever way he can,' I said neutrally.

'Northmen aren't happy with coins –' again, the slight pause – 'they think that a clever moneyer can adulterate the metal in a way that can't be detected. They prefer to put their trust in lumps of chopped-up silver jewellery.'

'What about gold?'

'Don't see that very often. Maybe the occasional Byzantine solidus. Goldwork tends to be set with precious stones and spared the hatchet.'

'You seem to be as expert in gold and silver as in guiding a ship through the dark,' I said, intending to flatter him. His reply surprised me.

'There's a tidy profit from acting as a money changer.'

It was my turn to change the subject. 'You said in Dorestad that you should have known that I can speak Saxon.'

Redwald chuckled. 'The name Sigwulf is rare among the Franks. Much more popular among Northmen and Saxons. So what brought you to the court of King Carolus?'

He put the question lightly but I detected again that he was showing more than casual curiosity.

'It was not my choice. Offa of Mercia despatched me there, to get me out of the way.' It was an honest answer and designed to evoke a response. It succeeded.

Redwald sucked in his breath. 'Offa's a right mean bastard. I trade regularly in his ports and I wouldn't want it widely known that I've taken a passenger he doesn't like. Could damage my business.'

'Then make sure I don't come to the attention of anyone in Kaupang who might report to Offa that I arrived there with you,' I said quickly. It was a flimsy safeguard for my future, but better than nothing.

'That I will do,' Redwald assured me bluntly.

There was little more to be said so I turned and groped my way across the deck, stepping carefully to avoid loose ropes and other dimly seen obstacles. As I reached the ladder down into the hold where Osric and Walo had prepared sleeping places for us among the bales and boxes of the cargo, Redwald's voice came out of the darkness behind me.

'Get a good night's rest, Sigwulf, however hard your pillow.'

I paused with my foot on the top rung. My pillow was to be a saddlebag containing the king's silver.

*

We emerged from the Rhine mouth the following afternoon, though it was impossible to say at what point we had left the river and reached the sea itself. The colour of the water remained the same murky greenish-brown, and the flat, dull Frisian shoreline lacked any headlands to mark our departure. As soon as the vessel began to rise and fall on the gentle swell, poor Walo turned pale and began to moan softly. He gripped the ship's rail with such desperation that his knuckles showed white. Redwald gruffly advised him to take deep breaths of fresh air and look at the horizon to steady himself. Walo closed his eyes even more tightly, whimpering with distress. Before long he was seated on deck, head down between his knees and retching miserably. Osric remained below, guarding our saddle-bags, and I took the precaution of eavesdropping on the cog's six-man crew in case they were planning any mischief. They talked among themselves in Frisian and their only topic of conversation was the weather. I gathered that they were expecting an easy passage to Kaupang as the wind at this season was usually from the south-west and favourable. Reassured, I ducked beneath the edge of the large rectangular sail that smelled of fish oil and tar and made my way forward to the bow where I could be alone.

A thin veil of light cloud covered the sky, and the sensation of facing out across an empty sea towards a hazy and indistinct horizon played tricks on my mind. It seemed that I was adrift in a great, limitless void. There was only the undulating sea swell ahead, the steady rhythm of the vessel's movement beneath me, and an infinite, trackless space across which I was scarcely moving. I felt isolated and detached, free of my day-to-day existence and from whatever lay ahead on my new endeavour. Next winter I would be twenty-nine years old. No longer was I the naïve and inexperienced youth who had arrived at Carolus's court. I had matured and grown more worldly wise from all that had happened to me, and it would be normal to have put down roots. Yet I continued to feel like a stranger among the Franks in spite of Carolus's generosity and favour. I was still unsettled and restless, and always hovering in the background were my strange dreams and visions. They came without warning and though I had learned to be very wary how I interpreted them as omens of the future, they still disturbed me.

I looked back to where Redwald stood stolidly at the helm. Every so often he glanced up at the sail or looked out across the waves, his gaze watchful and calculating. He knew his ship intimately, how she handled in a seaway, how she responded to every shift of the wind, how best she carried her cargo. To that knowledge he added his vast experience of the sea to hold the cog steady on her course. Here, I thought to myself, was an example that I should follow. I knew myself far better now than ever before, and the time had come for me to have more confidence in who I was. I should be more purposeful, more open.

I reached up behind my head and unfastened the lace that held my eye patch in place. With a flick of my wrist I tossed it overboard.

*

Absorbed in my thoughts, I stayed on the foredeck until a noticeable chill in the evening air eventually obliged me to seek a less exposed spot towards the stern. I rejoined Redwald to find that the shipmaster had covered his thinning hair with a shapeless woollen hat almost as grubby as his worker's smock. He immediately noticed my missing eye patch.

'The crew will have to think up a different nickname for you,' he said with an amused smile.

'Why's that?' I asked. I had expected him to react with dismay when he saw that my eyes were different colours. Mariners were supposed to be superstitious.

'They've dubbed you "Odinn".'

My own father had been a follower of the Old Ways so I was familiar with the story. The god Odinn sacrificed one eye for a drink at the well of knowledge and wore an eye patch afterwards.

'What are they calling Osric and Walo?' I enquired.

'"Weyland" and "the troll",' he replied.

It was a cruel jibe: Weyland was the crippled smith to the old gods.

'I hadn't realized that Frisians follow those quaint beliefs,' I retorted sourly. Neither my father's paganism nor the devout Christianity of men like Alcuin appealed to me. As far as I was concerned, trying to make sense of my own strange dreams and visions was enough.

'Just sailors' humour. But you'll want to be careful in Kaupang about mocking the old gods.'

I sensed there was something more to his warning. 'You seem to be worried about what will happen when we get there.'

Before answering he reached up under his hat to scratch his scalp. 'Kaupang is the outer fringe of the civilized world. There's no law there, and none wanted. People resent outside interference, particularly when it comes to religion.'

'So they suspect that anyone sent by Carolus is either a spy or a missionary.'

'Let's just say that Carolus is not popular.'

'Then how do you manage buying gyrfalcons there for the king?'

'I work through a middleman. It was several years before I had his confidence.'

I spotted the trap Redwald was setting. He was determined to have his usual commission on purchasing gyrfalcons for Carolus's mews master. I decided it was easier to fall in with his plan.

'Then I'll depend on you to buy the birds after I've selected them. You can do the bargaining and I'll provide you with the money.'

He gave a satisfied grunt and tilted back his head, checking the sky. Streaks of high cloud were beginning to form, their pink undersides catching the last rays of the sun, now below the horizon.

'We could be in for a bit more wind later tomorrow,' he observed.

'Does that mean we'll have to seek shelter?'

He shook his head. 'Safer to stay away from a lee shore. Besides, the wind will push us along nicely and keep us clear of any pirates who might be watching from the coast.'

I looked back in the direction we had already come. There was nothing to be seen except a darkening expanse of the grey sea flecked here and there with a breaking wave. Suddenly the cog felt small and very isolated and vulnerable, and that made me ask, 'Redwald, what gods do you pray to in a storm?'

He chuckled. 'Every god that I can think of. But that doesn't stop me from doing everything possible to keep my ship afloat.'

Chapter Four

THE WIND, THOUGH BLUSTERY, stayed fair for the next three days while Redwald steered his chosen course without any sight of land. In response to my questions he told me that he took the direction of the waves as his guide, together with the angle of the sun and stars whenever the clouds allowed. But it was a mystery to me how he managed to calculate so accurately the distance we had covered. Late one morning, he gestured over the bow and announced casually that we would be at Kaupang next daybreak. I looked in that direction but saw nothing. Another couple of hours passed before I made out a narrow dark smudge just discernible against the hazy line where a grey overcast sky met a sullen-looking sea. It was our landfall. Judging by the crew's lack of any reaction, they thought this feat of navigation was unremarkable. They made minor adjustments to the set of the sail, and then went back to the everyday routine of repairing worn tackle and hauling up buckets of water from the bilge and tipping the contents overboard.

Slowly the cog wallowed towards the coast. It was a raw land, rugged and desolate. Thick, gloomy forest covered dark hills that rose gradually towards a range of mountains whose bald peaks were purple-grey in the far distance. As we drew closer, it was possible to make out the jumbled boulders of a rock-bound shore without any sign of human activity. The wind had already eased to a soft breeze and in the late afternoon it died away completely. The cog was left becalmed, the big sail sagging. We were perhaps a long bow shot from the shoreline, and I supposed the vessel had come to a complete halt. But watching more closely I realized that the cog was caught in some sort of current. She was being carried sideways towards a spit of land where the swell heaved and broke on a hidden reef, each surge and retreat sucking back the foam in whorls and patterns. Unnerved, I turned to look at Redwald, for it seemed to me that the cog must drift helplessly onto the rocks.

'Is it far to Kaupang?' I asked, trying to hide my alarm.

'Just around that point,' he answered calmly.

He seemed utterly unconcerned by our situation and I wondered if he had noticed a gathering grey murkiness out to sea. To add to our troubles, a fog bank was beginning to form.

An hour dragged by and there was nothing to do except observe the shoreline slowly edging past. Behind us the fog bank grew thicker, swallowing up the sun as it sank towards the horizon. Now the mist was oozing towards us. The first wisps arrived, cool and moist, caressing our faces. In a very short time it had wrapped itself around us and we could see no more than a yard or two in any direction. It was like being immersed in a bowl of thin milk. From where I stood beside the helm I could see no further than the mainmast. The bow was totally invisible. When I licked my lips, I tasted fresh dew. The fog was settling. I shivered.

'Have you been in anything like this before?' I muttered to Osric standing at my shoulder. Walo had gone below deck, taking his turn to guard our saddlebags.

'Never,' he replied. Long ago he had been shipwrecked on a voyage from Hispania to Britain aboard a ship trading for tin. It was as an injured castaway that he had been sold into slavery.

'Why doesn't the captain drop anchor?' I wondered.

I did not know that sound carries well in a fog. 'Because the water's too deep,' came Redwald's voice somewhere in the mist.

I watched the droplets of water gather on the dark tan of the sail, then trickle down, joining into delicate rivulets before dripping to the deck. Somewhere in the distance was a faint sound, a low, muted rumble repeated every few seconds. It was the murmur of the swell nuzzling the unseen rocks.

The cog drifted onward.

Perhaps half an hour later Redwald abruptly growled, 'Sweeps!'

There were indistinct movements in the mist. Blurred figures moved here and there on the deck, followed by several thumps and dragging sounds. The crew were preparing the long oars that had been lashed to the ship's rail during the voyage.

There were more noises and some clattering as the sweeps were thrust out over the side, splashes as their blades hit the water.

'If you want to make yourselves useful, lend a hand,' came Redwald's gruff voice again.

I fumbled my way to where I could just make out a crewman standing ready to pull on a sweep. He moved aside enough to let me join him. I gripped the soaking-wet wood of the handle.

'Pull away!' Redwald ordered. After a few moments I picked up the rhythm, a slow steady dip and pull. Osric must also have found his place at another oar handle, and not long afterwards I became aware of a figure ducking past me. I recognized the shambling walk, and knew it was Walo. He must have sensed that something was wrong and clambered up from the hold. I decided there was no point in worrying that our silver was unguarded. It was more important that every man aboard helped keep the cog off the rocks.

I began to count the strokes and had nearly reached five hundred when, abruptly, Redwald called on us to stop rowing. Gratefully I stood straighter, my arm muscles aching. I turned to my neighbour and was about to speak when he raised a finger to his lips and gestured at me to stay silent. He cocked his head on one side and I understood that he was listening intently. I tried to pick out the sounds, and heard the noise of small waves breaking. The sound came from directly ahead. We were off the reef, but very close.

'Row on!' came Redwald's command.

We returned to our labour and this time I had counted another four hundred strokes before we were told to stop. Once again we listened. Now the swash and rumble of the breaking waves came from a different direction and seemed to be more distant.

'Row on!'

We must have rowed for perhaps three hours, stopping and listening at regular intervals. The fog and the gathering darkness soon made it impossible to see the surface of the water and the blade of the sweep. We trusted entirely to Redwald's commands. Eventually, during one of the listening pauses, I heard him tell one of his men to take the helm. Then I heard the shipmaster's clogs thump along the deck as he moved forward.

'Row on!' This time Redwald's command came from the bows. Then, every twenty or so strokes, I heard a splash very close by.

'What's the captain doing?' I whispered to my oar comrade.

'Soundings,' he hissed back irritably, as if I was an imbecile to have asked.

The explanation meant nothing to me so I kept on heaving on the handle of the sweep until finally Redwald's voice came floating back. We were to stop rowing and the crew were to go forward and drop anchor.

Gladly I helped pull aboard the heavy sweep and laid it on deck. From the bow I heard a heavier splash which must have been our anchor hitting the water, then the thrum of rope, and more activity as the crew made fast.

Redwald's gangling shape loomed through the fog, an arm's length away.

'All set for the night,' he announced. 'You and your friends can get below and rest.'

'When will we finally reach Kaupang?' I asked him.

'We're there,' he said flatly.

'How can that be?' I blurted in surprise, unable to keep the disbelief out of my voice.

There was a throaty chuckle. 'What did I tell you when we left Dorestad?' he demanded.

I thought back to our departure as we sailed down the Rhine's current in the fading light of evening.

'You said something about listening,' I replied.

'Exactly,' the shipmaster said. He brushed past me without another word.

I held my breath and listened intently. The ship was lying quietly to her anchor. There was no longer the creak of ropes and timber, not even the sound of water moving past her hull.

In a moment of absolute silence and through the pitch darkness, I heard the bark of a dog.

*

I awoke with a stiff neck and aching shoulders after an exhausted sleep. At first I blamed my hard pillow, the saddlebag packed with silver, but the moment I stretched and felt the soreness in my muscles, I recalled the hours spent hauling on a sweep. I could hear the muffled sounds of distant activity and sunlight was pouring into the hold through the open hatchway. I rose gingerly and made my way to the foot of the ladder to the deck. Fresh blisters on my palms made me wince as I hauled myself up the rungs and emerged into a fine, bright morning. There was not a breath of wind. The fog had gone completely.

Turning to look over the bow, I blinked in surprise.

We were anchored within a stone's throw of a landing beach. In dense fog Redwald had managed to guide the cog into a broad, sheltered inlet. It was little wonder that his crew had such confidence in their captain.

A couple of dozen boats lay drawn up in an uneven line on the shingle. They ranged from two-man skiffs to middling-sized cargo vessels. Their crews must have been ashore, for these boats were empty and unattended. Three much larger ships were berthed alongside a rough stone jetty and here the day's work was already well underway. Men were hoisting cargo from the holds, carrying sacks and packages ashore, rolling barrels down gangplanks. At the root of the jetty stood a stocky, shaggy pony. It was harnessed to a wooden sledge already heaped with boxes, and the animal's master was tying down the ropes that held the load in place. As I watched, a mongrel wandered up, circled the pony cautiously, and made as if to cock its leg. Someone must have thrown a stone, for suddenly the mongrel yelped and ran, tail between its legs. I wondered if it was the same dog that had barked the previous evening.

'Kaupang must be just over there,' said Osric. My friend was already on deck, leaning on the ship's rail. He pointed inland to where a rough track led past a couple of weather-beaten shacks and over a small ridge. 'Seems as though our captain's expected.'

A small open boat was coming to us, rowed by two men

while a third stood in the stern. He cupped his hands around his mouth and called out. 'Redwald! The knorr leaves for Dunwich at noon. You can have her space alongside as soon as she's gone.'

Redwald shouted back, 'I've got passengers you can take ashore for me right away!'

I was surprised that Redwald was being so obliging. 'There's no hurry. Osric and I can wait till later,' I said to him.

'I want you off my ship,' he grunted. He jerked a thumb towards the jetty. 'See that big vessel? That's the knorr. Her captain will want to come aboard and have a chat before he sets sail.' When I made no move to step away from the ship's rail, Redwald shot me a meaningful look from his pale blue eyes and added, 'Dunwich is a port on the English coast. Part of King Offa's domain. Gossip spreads fast.'

There was a slight bump as the rowing boat came alongside.

'But Walo stays aboard,' I said.

Redwald scowled. 'Then tell him to keep out of sight.'

I was about to climb down into the waiting skiff when the shipmaster laid a hand on my shoulder. He slipped his sailor's knife and its sheath from his belt and held it out to me. 'Here, take this, and don't loiter in Kaupang after dark. Come back to the ship before dusk. The knorr will be gone by then.'

I took his knife without a word and lowered myself into the skiff. Osric followed, and as we were rowed ashore I looked back at the cog, wondering what to make of Redwald. He had ordered me off his ship because he wanted to avoid trouble with King Offa. Yet he seemed genuinely concerned for my safety ashore. He also knew that we were carrying a fortune in silver. I fretted that Walo was not the right person to have left on guard. At the landing place a man was melting tar in a cauldron over a driftwood fire. The unmistakable smell of hot pitch hung in the still air and a flock of seagulls squabbled at the water's edge, tearing at a shapeless piece of carrion with their orange and yellow beaks.

'Redwald is worried that King Offa will get to know that I'm in Kaupang,' I said to Osric as we walked up the beach and out of earshot of the skiff's crew.

'Then we must take care not to draw attention to ourselves,' he answered. 'If Kaupang's a seasonal market, there'll be plenty of strangers who arrive here just for a short visit. We should be able to blend in.'

We stood aside to allow the pony and loaded sledge to go past at a lunging trot, the driver slapping the reins and shouting encouragement. Then we followed them along the track as it led up the slope of the beach to where it skirted the grove of alder trees and then crested the low ridge. On the far side, we found an untidy straggle of humble single-storey dwellings, their walls and roofs made of weathered grey planks. Among them were several much larger buildings shaped like huge upturned boats and roofed with turf. It took a moment to realize that this was Kaupang and our footpath, where it broadened, was Kaupang's one and only street, unpaved and chaotic.

'So this is the great market place of the north!' observed Osric dubiously.

Scores of makeshift sales booths were little more than crude hutches. Rocks and turf sods had been piled up to make their walls, and sheets of canvas rigged to keep out the rain. Other shops were open-sided sheds. Much of what was for sale was merely heaped up on the ground, jumbled together, and left for prospective buyers to browse. Despite the chaos and clutter, the place was swarming with customers.

We strolled forward, picking our way around untidy displays or squeezing between rickety stalls set up at random.

'I don't see many takers for Redwald's shipment of household querns,' I murmured. There were some women in the crowd, but not many. They wore loose linen dresses reaching to their ankles and most of them had tied up their hair in scarves. That was a shame because, from what I glimpsed, they had fine, lustrous hair and wore it long. By far the majority of Kaupang's customers were men. In general, they were burly, heavily bearded and exuded a certain swaggering arrogance. One passerby stared into my face, and then gave me an odd look – he must have seen my different-coloured eyes – and I was glad that Redwald's dagger was very obvious in my belt. A drunk came swaying out of a ramshackle building that did duty for a tavern. He pitched forward on his face in the dirt in front of us. Like everyone else, we skirted around him and carried on walking.

In the area where foodstuffs were for sale, the most common offering was fish: split, dried and hung up like laundry, dangling in long strings that gave off a pungent smell. I could see little sign of the sort of farm produce normally found in a country market. There were no vegetables or fruit or fresh meat, just a few eggs and some soft white cheese in tubs being sold by one of the very few women stall holders.

'I wouldn't risk my teeth on that lot,' Osric commented, nodding towards a handful of knobbly oatmeal loaves displayed in a wheelbarrow.

We drifted on to where farm implements were for sale. Here the traders had laid out axes, saws, cauldrons, hammers, chisels, lengths of chain and barrels of massive iron nails. It was also possible to purchase rough slabs of raw iron, ready to be heated and moulded into tools. I thought sourly of Osric's nickname of

Weyland, and that made me look more closely at some of the men in the crowd. A big ox of a man standing near me was examining an axe. His shirt front was open. Hanging from a leather thong around his neck was a T-shaped amulet. I recognized Thor's hammer.

'Let's see if we can track down a seller of hunting birds,' I suggested.

'Maybe over there.' Osric pointed towards one of the larger open-sided sheds. Some sort of unidentifiable animal skin had been nailed to a cross-beam high enough to be seen above the heads of the crowd.

We pushed our way through the press of people and found ourselves in front of a display of anchors, rolls of sailcloth, fishing line and hooks, balls of twine, ropes and nets. The air reeked of pine tar. The proprietor was a scrawny, pockmarked fellow who was trying to sell a coil of rope to a customer. The local language was close enough to Saxon for me to understand most of his sales talk. The rope was dark, greasy and – if the man was to be believed – cut from the thick leathery skin of a large animal he called a hross-hvalr, and far superior to rope made from strands of flax. His client, a thick-necked man with half an ear missing, was fingering the rope doubtfully and saying that he preferred thin strips of good-quality stallion hide so that he could plait his own rope. 'One horse's skin is as good as another. You will save yourself the labour of all that plaiting,' wheedled the shopkeeper.

His client was not persuaded and dropped the heavy rope's end with a disdainful grunt, then wandered off. I waited until he was out of earshot, then asked the shopkeeper. 'Excuse me, I heard you speaking of a "hross-hvalr" just now. Is that some sort of horse?'

The man looked me up and down. He must have seen by

my clothes that I was not a seafarer and therefore an unlikely customer. He was about to turn away when perhaps he noticed the colour of my eyes because he hesitated. His expression, which had been dismissive, changed to one that was more wary.

'Why would you want to know?' he asked.

'Just curiosity. I'm a stranger to these parts and "hross" sounds much like horse.'

'You're right in that,' the man agreed.

'I'm told that many of the animals native to this region are white. I'm wondering if this type of horse is also white.'

'I've never seen a live hross-hvalr,' said the merchant. 'I get offered lengths of rope made up from their skin. It's always the same colour as that one there.' He nodded towards the coil of rope on the ground. It was a dull, grey-black.

A thought occurred to me. 'So you don't make the rope yourself?'

'No, it comes ready made. The hross-hvalr lives far in the north where the winter nights are so long that there's plenty of dark time for a man to fill in the hours sitting by his hearth, slicing up skin into rope.'

'Perhaps I should ask someone from that area,' I suggested.

The man paused before replying, cautious about giving information to a stranger.

'If you can help me find what I'm looking for,' I coaxed, 'I would gladly pay a small reward.'

He cocked his head on one side and looked at me sharply. 'What exactly is it that you are seeking?'

I hesitated, aware of my own doubts. 'I'm looking for an unusual sort of horse, a white one. It's called a unicorn.'

There was a startled pause, and then he threw back his head and hooted with laughter. 'A unicorn! I don't believe it!'

I stood there, feeling foolish and trying not to show it.

He laughed so hard, he almost choked. 'In these parts you'll find Sleipnir before you come across any unicorn. A hross-hvalr is a horse whale,' he gasped finally.

I waited until he had regained his breath and, curbing my irritation, asked him again who had supplied him with horse whale rope.

'His name is Ohthere,' he told me. 'He owns a large farm on the coast and so far north that it takes him almost a month to get here, sailing every day and anchoring each night. He shows up in Kaupang every year, probably the only time he meets anyone outside his own family.'

'Where can I find this Ohthere?'

The shopkeeper was still chuckling. 'At the end of the street, on the outskirts of town. He always sets up a big tent there, on the right.'

'Thank you,' I said, stepping back. 'You've been most helpful.'

'And tell him that Oleif sent you!' he called after me as I trudged on, Osric limping beside me.

'What did he mean about finding Sleipnir before we came across a unicorn?' Osric asked.

'It was his way of saying that there's no such creature as a unicorn. Sleipnir is the horse Odinn rides. According to the old beliefs, Sleipnir travels on eight legs.'

We were passing one of the large boat-shaped houses with a turf roof. Three men stood in the open doorway, deep in conversation. Judging by the tints of grey in their neatly trimmed beards, two of them were in their mid-forties. Their companion was younger, perhaps in his twenties. All three were dressed in the same unobtrusive style – loose trousers of dark wool, a long shirt belted at the waist and soft knee-length boots. Two of them were bare headed; the third wore a round felt cap with an unusual trim of alternating patches of glossy dark and light fur.

Osric nudged me with his elbow. 'Over there,' he murmured, flicking a glance towards the strangers.

At first sight there was nothing noteworthy about them apart from the fact that their skins were a darker shade than most visitors to the market and they appeared to be more neatly groomed.

'Look at their belts,' Osric prompted under his breath.

I took a second glance. Their broad leather belts were stitched with complicated interlocking red and green patterns in loops and whorls. The buckles were ornate and of massive silver.

'Slave dealers,' muttered Osric. There was sadness in his voice and I remembered that once he too had been traded as a slave.

I felt the pressure on my arm as he steered me so we passed close enough to the three slave-dealers to overhear their conversation.

The three men ignored us as we sauntered past and when we were at a safe distance I asked, 'What were they talking about?'

'I picked up a few words. Enough to guess that they come from Khazaria, well beyond Constantinople.'

'Redwald mentioned that Saracen traders come to Kaupang to buy slaves. I'm surprised that the emperor in Constantinople allows Saracens to cross his lands to get here. They could be spies,' I added.

Osric grimaced. 'Trade leaks through frontiers. Slaves bought in Kaupang can finish up serving in the palace at Constantinople.'

Presently we found ourselves in the rougher end of Kaupang's market. Rubbish littered the ground and the buildings were even more seedy. Stray dogs, scabby and malnourished, nosed for scraps at the side of the roadway. A group of what looked like vagrants were squatting or lying in the shade of one of the flimsy sheds. There were tear streaks on the grimy faces of some of the women and girls, the men looked sullen and bored. They wore no chains but I knew at once that they were for sale. They could have been taken prisoner in local battles, kidnapped by slave catchers, or sold into slavery to pay debts. I tried not to think of my own people made captive when King Offa conquered us. Most would have been allowed to stay on and work the land, paying their taxes to their new lord, but others would have been sold. It was my good fortune to have been sent into exile.

At the far end of the roadway, at the point it turned back into a footpath, we finally found where hunting birds were sold. A dozen or so birds were fastened by cords around their legs to a line of wooden blocks on the ground. They watched our approach with their fierce, bright eyes. The ground around their perches was soiled with their droppings. Fresh bloodstains and shreds of mouse carcasses on the blocks showed that they had been fed recently. The smaller merlins and sparrowhawks were easy to identify, and Carolus's mews master had taken me on a tour of the royal mews so I was able to distinguish the big gyrfalcons from their cousins the peregrines. Disappointingly, of three gyrfalcons only one was white. The plumage of the others was patterned in dark brown and black. They were not what I was seeking.

A whip-thin lad, scarcely ten years old, had been left in charge. Mindful that I had agreed with Redwald that he would be negotiating with the bird sellers, I contented myself with asking the boy if he knew where I might find a man called Ohthere. My question was drowned out by a sudden furious outburst of barking. A pack of mangy dogs rushed past, nearly knocking the lad off his feet. Their jostling and yapping disturbed the hunting birds. They fidgeted on their perches, fluffing up their feathers.

'Where can I find Ohthere?' I repeated. The lad had knelt down on the ground to calm the white gyrfalcon, gently stroking its plumage. When he looked up at me, I thought that he did not understand my Saxon. The dogs had bunched in front of a stout wooden pen a little further down the road and were snapping and snarling hysterically at its bars.

'Ohthere?' I asked again.

The lad continued to stroke the gyrfalcon. He raised his free hand and pointed. A heavily built man, roaring and cursing, had emerged from a leather tent close beside the wooden pen. He strode angrily towards the frenzied pack, and began laying about him with a stout stick.

Osric and I waited until the stranger had succeeded in beating back the dogs before we approached him.

'Would you be Ohthere?' I enquired politely. 'Oleif said I might find him here.'

The man turned to face me, stick in hand. He was someone with whom I would avoid a quarrel. Watchful grey eyes were set in a craggy face under bushy eyebrows. He had a dense, black beard and although he was of no more than ordinary height, his barrel chest strained the fabric of his jerkin. Muscular forearms and thick, blunt fingers grasping the stick made it clear that he was not to be trifled with.

'I'm Ohthere.' His tone of voice, assured and forceful, matched his appearance.

'I'm hoping you can tell me about the horse whale, the hross-hvalr. Oleif said they are found in the region where you have your farm.'

Ohthere studied me. I was sure he had seen the colours of my eyes, but he showed no reaction. 'That's right. Horse whales haul out on the beaches near me.'

'Haul out?'

'They clamber out of the sea and lie on the land, sunning themselves. That's where they breed and raise their pups. What did you expect?'

'I had hoped that they were a sort of horse, and maybe some of them have white skins.' This time I did not want to make an idiot of myself by mentioning unicorns.

Thankfully Ohthere did not laugh. 'They're sea animals, big and bloated. Odinn only knows how they came to be called horses. They're more like whales. That part of their name is accurate.'

'And none of them are white?'

'Not that I've seen. The only white thing about them is their teeth. Great long fangs. They fetch a good price for carving into ornaments and jewellery.'

Now I knew what animal he was talking about. At Carolus's court I had seen chess pieces, sword handles and pendants that were said to have been carved from the massive teeth of a sea beast. An image flashed into my mind from the Book of Beasts that Carolus had showed me. As he flicked through the pages, I had caught a quick glimpse of a drawing of a great ungainly animal lying on a rocky shore. It had a bulging body, a tail like a fish, a mournful-looking face, and drooping whiskers. It was not a unicorn, and not what the king had wanted.

Ohthere must have read the disappointment on my face. 'I've heard rumours of a small whale that is as white as snow. But it's only a rumour.'

'Thank you for your help. I'm sorry to have disturbed you. Those dogs must be a nuisance,' I said. Several of the curs had sneaked around behind us while we were talking, and were again at the bars of the pen, snarling and growling.

'If they get too close, they'll be sorry,' said Ohthere. 'Here, let me show you what I've got inside.' He led me over to the wooden enclosure.

It was more of a large strong cage than a pen. The sides were made of stout timber posts and a number of heavy slats had been laid across to form a roof.

I peered inside.

All that was visible were two grubby yellow shapes on the ground. At first I mistook them for a pair of large and dirty sheep, sound asleep. Then one of the shapes moved slightly and I saw a snout with a black tip and two bright black spots. They were eyes.

'Yearling ice bears,' Ohthere announced beside me. Without warning he lashed out with his stick and caught one of the dogs across the rump. It ran off with a howl.

'They don't look that dangerous,' I said, still gazing at the bears. They were both slumped on the ground. The two black eyes had closed.

'That's because they're half-starved.'

'How did you get them?' I asked. I was utterly disappointed. I had expected to see a wonderful white creature like the one drawn in the bestiary. Instead, these two creatures looked sick and feeble, and their dirty fur was the colour of urine. They also smelled of piss. I wondered what impression such dejected and mangy animals would make on the caliph of Baghdad in return for his gift of a white elephant to Carolus.

'The Finna traded them to me,' Ohthere replied. 'They had killed the mother bear. They let me have her skin as well. I've already sold it.'

'Who are the Finna?' I was already wondering if I should travel onwards and contact these people in my quest.

'They roam the mountains and wastelands near my farm. A native people and always on the move. They come to me, asking to trade metal in exchange for feathers, horse whale teeth and skin rope. You never know when they will turn up or what they will bring for barter. This year they produced two bears.'

Ohthere stared in at the two animals. 'It's been impossible to get them to eat properly. They'll eat a couple of mouthfuls and leave the rest. I've tried seal blubber, mutton fat, chicken, milk. I'd say they're pining for their mother.'

One of the young ice bears had risen to its feet. It was somewhat bigger than I had imagined, the size of a large mastiff. It padded slowly towards the far side of the pen. The gait was strange, sinuous and soft.

'How big will they grow?' I enquired.

'If they live, they'll be as big as their mother, and her pelt was two fathoms from nose to tail.'

'They don't look very dangerous.' A dog had poked its muzzle between the wooden bars and was barking shrilly at the moving bear. Scarcely were the words out of my mouth than the bear made a sudden pounce, lashing out with its paw. The movement was almost too quick to see. The claws raked the face of the cur. The dog screamed and fled, blood spraying from the wound.

'You see my problem,' said Ohthere. 'You don't want to get too close when you're trying to coax them into feeding.'

'I thought ice bears are white?'

'In winter the fur is the same colour as the snow and ice. If they were healthy they would not look so shabby.'

'Are they for sale?' I asked, turning to look at him.

'Why else would I have brought them to Scringes Heal?' he

said ruefully. 'I was hoping that they would regain their appetites, but it seems I was wrong.'

'I'll make you an offer,' I said.

Ohthere looked at me in surprise. 'What would you want with them?'

'I'm collecting white animals for King Carolus.'

A smile split the heavy black beard. 'I can see you are no trader. You would not have been so honest about the identity of your client.'

He frowned at the cage. 'Come back tomorrow at about this same time. By then I'll have had time to think about a price. Mind you, I don't suppose that these two bears will survive much longer. You could finish up delivering only their skins to Carolus.'

As Osric and I walked back towards our ship, I brooded on the discouraging start to our visit to Kaupang. We had found only one white gyrfalcon for sale, and though we were lucky to have come across a pair of ice bears, the two animals were so sickly that it was virtually certain they would die long before they could be brought all the way to far Baghdad. As for a unicorn, the mere mention of such a creature made people burst into mocking laughter.

Chapter Five

WHEN WE GOT BACK to the harbour, Redwald's cog was already tied against the jetty. A gang of local men was helping his crew unload the cargo. There was no sign of the knorr so she must have sailed for Dunwich. Redwald himself was at the foot of the gangplank, deep in conversation with a tall, bony man whose face seemed vaguely familiar.

'Find any of the animals you were looking for, Sigwulf?' the shipmaster asked me cheerfully. Clearly he was in a good humour.

'A single white gyrfalcon, and two young ice bears.'

'Gorm tells me he's hopeful of having a second white gyrfalcon for sale, but someone will have to go and collect it from the trapper.'

The tall man was a dealer in hunting birds, and now I saw his resemblance to the skinny lad who had tended the agitated gyrfalcon. They were probably father and son.

'Unfortunately, the two ice bears aren't at all healthy. Their owner fears that they will soon die,' I said.

'That'll be Ohthere,' said the bird dealer.

'He's a farmer who got the bears as cubs from some people he called the Finna,' I explained.

Redwald laughed. 'Some farmer! Ohthere's farm is as far north as anyone has dared to settle, and he explored and cleared the land himself. He's as hard as nails.'

Clearly he already knew Ohthere well, and I made a mental note to be vigilant in my dealings with regular visitors to Kaupang market. They seemed to form a close-knit circle and were likely to serve their own interests when it came to setting prices and negotiating deals.

'I've offered to buy the bears and he's thinking about the price. I'm going back to see him tomorrow,' I told the shipmaster.

Redwald watched as a porter balanced his way down the unsteady gangplank with several bottles of my Rhenish wine cradled in his arms. 'Then I'll come with you. I've got my own business in town that needs attention,' he said.

'There's something else I need to discuss with you before then,' I told him, with a sideways glance at Osric.

Redwald was quick on the uptake. He turned to the bird dealer. 'I'll see you tomorrow, Gorm, at your place.'

As Gorm walked off along the jetty, Osric and I followed the shipmaster up the gangplank. When we were out of earshot of the crew, I asked Redwald to be more discreet in his market dealings. 'I would prefer that as few people as possible know why I've come to Kaupang,' I told him.

He shrugged dismissively, then shocked me by saying, 'It's about time we discussed just how you're going to pay for the goods.'

'What do you mean?' I demanded sharply.

'Come with me and I'll show you,' he grunted.

He escorted us down the ladder into the hold, almost empty now except for a few remaining sacks and packing cases. Walo was seated on a sack, guarding our precious saddlebags with the silver coin.

'I presume those bags contain your funds,' Redwald announced bluntly.

There was no point in denying it. I nodded.

'Mind if I take a look?'

'As you wish,' I said, though I felt a stab of suspicion.

I asked Walo to bring one of the bags across and he handed it to Redwald.

The shipmaster hefted one of them approvingly. 'Carolus's denarii?' he asked me, raising an eyebrow.

'Fresh from the Aachen mint.'

Redwald unlaced the saddlebag's flap and picked out one of the silver coins. He held it up to the light falling in through the open hatch. 'The Aachen stamp has been changed,' he announced. 'The cross in the centre is different, more ornate than before. Mind if I use this coin as a sample?'

'A sample for what?' I asked, my suspicions now thoroughly aroused.

'I'll show you.'

Keeping the coin, he handed the saddlebag back to Walo and then made his way into the gloomy shadows beneath the overhang of the deck. Rolls of spare sailcloth lay on a shelf built into the stern. Pushing them aside, he reached his arm into the space, felt around for a moment, tugged, and there was a soft thump as something shifted. It was too dark to see what he was doing, but when he turned to face us he was holding a bundle wrapped in oilcloth.

'Tools of my other trade,' he announced cryptically. From the package he extracted a set of small weighing scales, their weights, a soft leather pouch fastened with a drawstring, a tiny flask and a fist-sized object wrapped in a cloth bandage. Unwinding the bandage, he produced a flat stone, smooth and black, and laid it on top of a packing case. He unstoppered the tiny flask, dripped a small amount of oil on the surface of the stone, then wiped it. With quick, firm strokes he rubbed

Carolus's coin up and down on the stone, leaving a thin silver streak.

Next, he tipped out the contents of his leather pouch. A jumble of odd-shaped items rattled out on the surface of the packing case. Some were chunky, others flat or slightly dished, many had jagged edges or were thin strips folded over, twisted, and then hammered flat. They were all a dull grey.

'The sea air takes the shine off them,' said Redwald, picking out a flat piece about two inches across, one edge smoothly curved. It took me a moment to recognize a scrap of tarnished silver, probably chopped from a silver platter.

Redwald rubbed it against the stone, leaving a second silvery streak, parallel to the first.

'See any difference?' he asked Osric who had been watching him closely.

Osric shook his head.

'It takes experience,' Redwald told him. 'The mark from the coin shows good silver, more than nine parts silver to one of copper. I happen to know that the platter fragment is silver mixed with copper, three parts to one.'

He swept up the pile of broken silver pieces and dropped them into the pouch. 'As I told you, Sigwulf, the Northmen don't trust coins. If Ohthere sells you those bears, he'll want most of his payment in broken silver. And he'll probably expect a couple of pieces of worked jewellery, something bright and gaudy, that he can trade to the Finna in future.'

He began to wind the bandage back around the black stone. 'It's going to be a tedious job demonstrating to him that every one of your coins is genuine. I'm not looking forward to it.' He grimaced. 'But first we have to agree a price for those bears.'

*

Next morning, I set out with Redwald and Walo for our meeting with Ohthere. Osric had volunteered to stay onboard the ship and watch over our silver hoard. He claimed that his crooked leg was hurting after the previous day's walk. But the truth was that he and I were both feeling guilty that Walo had not yet had a chance to get off the ship and see Kaupang for himself.

Once again Kaupang's street was thronged with customers, and as we made our way through the press of people Redwald drew my attention to two brawny individuals loitering outside one of the small wooden houses.

'Hired guards. Every year that same house is rented by a dealer in precious gems and metals.'

At that moment the crowd ahead of us hurriedly parted to allow a group of half a dozen men to stride through. They were armed with swords and daggers and their leader was a big, red-faced fellow with a truculent expression. Walo had fallen behind to examine some wooden trinkets on a stall and was in their path. Redwald hastily turned back, grabbed him and pulled him aside. After the group had disappeared into one of the taverns, Redwald explained quietly that the man at the head of the group was a minor jarl, a local lord. His companions were his retainers and it was wise to steer clear of such people as they took offence easily.

A few steps further on, Walo again needed to be rescued. He had halted in front of a display of skins and furs, and the stallholder snapped at him to stop fingering the merchandise. Redwald quickly intervened. 'That's a sealskin, Walo,' he explained.

'It is like a big otter,' said Walo, stroking the glossy pelt.

'He can handle it all he wants, once he's paid for it,'

grumbled the vendor, an old man with a long, lugubrious face and a heavy scarf wound around his neck despite the warm day.

'Where did those white skins come from?' I asked him. In a pile of smaller furs were several pelts that were a soft, lustrous white.

'Winter fox and hare,' said the old man.

My hopes rose. 'Can I obtain these animals alive?'

'They're no good to you, Sigwulf,' Redwald intervened. 'By the time you get the creatures to the caliph they'll have turned back to their normal brown. The animals are white in winter only.'

'How about this, then? Fit for a jarl's cloak,' coaxed the old man. Struggling with the weight of it, he unrolled a massive white bearskin. The head and paws were still attached. I had witnessed the injuries inflicted on a dog by the hooked black claws of a yearling bear. Now the huge teeth set in the gaping jaw of an adult made me shudder. There was no need to confirm with the old man that he had purchased the bearskin from Ohthere.

We found Ohthere himself on the edge of town, as before, staring moodily in through the wooden bars of the stout cage. The two yearling ice bears were slumped on the bare earth, eyes closed. They lay so still that it was difficult to tell whether they were even breathing. Just inside the cage's heavy door was placed a wooden water trough. Beside it were two trenchers heaped with what looked like strips of yellowy-white pig fat with thick black rind.

'They're still refusing to eat,' said Ohthere, his frustration evident. He had his wooden stick with him and put the tip between the bars of the cage and pushed one of the trenchers closer to the nose of an ice bear.

Both animals ignored him.

'What are you trying to feed them?' asked Redwald.

'Whale blubber, from my own larder.'

'You must be getting desperate,' teased the shipmaster. It was obvious that the two men were on friendly terms.

The shipmaster turned to me. 'Ohthere has a weakness for whale blubber and hoards the stuff like a child. Don't know why. It tastes vile.'

Ohthere snorted. 'Not everyone thinks so. Wait here a minute.' He strode off in the direction of his leather tent.

Redwald peered in at the two ice bears. 'Are you sure about buying them, Sigwulf? They look as though they're not long for this world.'

'I'll have to take that chance. They're the only ones available, and maybe we can find a way of making them eat.'

Redwald shrugged resignedly. 'Leave the negotiations to me. At least I should be able to get them cheaply because they're half-starved.'

'I've already told Ohthere that they are for King Carolus,' I confessed. 'I'm afraid that will have put up the price considerably.'

Ohthere emerged from his tent holding a slab of something in his hand. We walked across to meet him as he held it up for our inspection. One side had a thick skin, dark and slightly wrinkled. The rest of it was pale yellowish-white, two inches thick, and resembled solid jelly.

'Best whale blubber, air dried,' he announced. 'Here, try a bite.'

He took a sailor's knife from his belt, cut off a small cube, and offered it to me.

I popped the piece of whale blubber into my mouth and

chewed cautiously, not knowing what to expect. The taste was surprisingly pleasant. As I bit down, I felt the oil squeeze out and run down my throat. It was vaguely soothing and reminded me faintly of hazelnuts.

At that moment Ohthere gave an annoyed grunt. He was gazing over my shoulder. 'What's that idiot doing!' he growled.

Alarmed, I swung round on my heel.

It was Walo. We had left him standing beside the bear cage and had failed to keep an eye on him. He had unfastened the heavy door to the cage, opened it, and was crawling inside on his hands and knees.

'He'll get himself killed,' I blurted, and started forward. But Ohthere's grip on my wrist stopped me. 'Don't rush and don't shout. It'll only upset them. We need to get close enough to speak to your man quietly and tell him to back out.'

He glanced at Redwald. 'The fewer the better. Best you stay here.'

Slowly and deliberately Ohthere and I began to walk towards the cage. Walo was fully inside now, crouched on all fours, facing towards the two ice bears. To my dismay I saw that both animals had raised their heads and were staring at him. The gap between them and Walo was no more than four or five feet.

'I suspected he wasn't quite right in the head,' Ohthere muttered.

Walo had turned his back on the bears and was pulling the door shut behind him. I was appalled to see him then put an arm out through the bars and push in place the peg that served as a catch. He was now locked in with them.

'At least they can't escape, whatever happens,' Ohthere said quietly.

Just then there was a low growl close to my right knee. My heart flew into my mouth. One of the scavenger curs had come between us, hackles raised, and with a continuous, rumbling deep in its throat was keeping pace with us.

Ohthere's hand shot down. He grabbed the dog by the neck, squeezed fiercely, and the growl suddenly choked off. We halted while Ohthere bent down, placed his other hand around the dog's throat, tightened his grip and held it until the dog's frantic thrashing stopped. Calmly he laid its corpse on the ground.

Meanwhile Walo had made himself comfortable. He was sitting inside the cage with his back against the bars, facing the ice bears. They were still lying on the ground, but were fully alert, heads up, their black eyes fixed on the intruder.

I was about to creep forward but Ohthere warned quietly, 'Better keep our distance.'

Walo had pulled something from his pocket, and was holding it to his lips. A moment later I heard the same four notes he had played in the farmyard back in Frankia, softly repeated.

First one bear, then the other, rose slowly to its feet. But they did not approach him.

Unperturbed, Walo kept playing. I was aware that beside me Ohthere had turned and gestured urgently at Redwald to stay back.

After a little while Walo put the whistle back in his pocket. Then he began to crawl on all fours towards the two bears, sliding the trenchers across the ground in front of him.

When he was very close, well within reach of the slashing claws, he halted. He crouched even lower, his face almost on the earth, and stretching out his arms, pushed the two trenchers sideways, away from one another.

'He's making sure the bears don't quarrel over their food,' said Ohthere, barely whispering.

Walo straightened up, sat back on his heels and waited. For several moments nothing happened. Then both ice bears padded forward a step or two, lowered their muzzles and sniffed the offering. Another pause, and finally both bears began to feed on the blubber.

I breathed a sigh of relief, expecting Walo to leave the cage. Instead, to my astonishment, he crawled even further forward until he was right between the animals, then he turned and sat cross-legged. Out came his deerhorn pipe and he started playing his simple melody again. On either side of him, the two young bears gulped down their food.

Redwald tentatively came forward to join us and I overheard Ohthere make a comment to Redwald. He spoke in hushed tones, and it took me a moment to understand him. The word he used for a bear was one that I had not heard since I was a lad. My own Saxon people consider the bear to be a creature with mystical powers, so they often refer to it with respect and indirectly, not as a bear, but as a beowulf. Now Redwald had used the same word, saying that if he had not seen it with his own eyes, he would never have believed that anyone could tame the beowulf. The hairs on the back of my neck rose in prickles: beowulf means 'bee wolf'.

In front of me was my dream in Aachen – Walo seated between wolves and covered with swarming bees. According to Artimedorus, if bees appeared in a dream with a farmer, they foretold the successful outcome of an endeavour. For all others, it was an omen of death.

From a safe distance we watched until the bears had eaten their fill. Only after they had curled up and fallen into a contented sleep did Walo cease playing his pipe. Then he unfastened the cage door and crawled out to rejoin us. He seemed completely unconcerned, as if nothing unusual had happened.

'I'd like to hire him to look after the bears. What's his name?' Ohthere said to me.

'Walo. His father was King Carolus's chief verderer.'

Redwald gave me a warning look, making it clear that I was to hold my tongue. Addressing Ohthere, he said, 'Walo is not for hire. Sigwulf has already offered to buy your two bears. But they will surely die if Walo does not feed them. In which case, the best price you will get for them is the value of their pelts.'

I kept my expression neutral. By now I knew Redwald well enough to recognize when the Frisian was about to drive a bargain.

'Ohthere, I suggest we make a deal,' Redwald continued. 'Walo stays on with you, looking after the bears until it's time for me to take my ship back to Dorestad. In return you will receive a payment midway between the bears' value alive and the price you would get for their skins.'

Ohthere considered for a long moment. 'On one condition – if the bears die before it is time for shipment, then it is Walo's fault, and I still get my money.'

'Agreed!' said Redwald. Turning to me, he said briskly, 'This is a good moment to sort out with Gorm how we obtain the additional white gyrfalcon he says he can supply.'

Leaving Osric to explain to Walo his new duties, Redwald and I went across the road to where Gorm and his son were watching over the line of birds of prey standing on their blocks.

'I have a reliable supplier who specializes in gyrfalcons,' Gorm told us. 'He usually brings at least one white gyrfalcon

for the Kaupang market, but this year he is delayed. I don't
know the reason, and I can't spare someone to go to find out, or
bring back the birds he has caught.'

'What about sending your son?' suggested Redwald.

The bird dealer stooped and picked up the half-eaten body
of a mouse where it had fallen on the ground beside a perch
block. He held it out towards one of the merlins. The fierce
beak snapped the bloody morsel from his fingers. 'Rolf's too
young. The trapper won't trust valuable birds to a boy.'

'How far away does this trapper live?' I asked.

Gorm scratched his chin. 'His name's Ingvar and he's
probably still in the high country where he does his trapping.
That's a three-day ride from here.'

Gorm's skinny son was shifting anxiously from foot to foot.
I caught his eye, and saw how eager he was to prove himself.

'If this Ingvar really does have a white gyrfalcon, I'm willing
to accompany your son and fetch it,' I said.

I must have sounded too keen because Redwald immediately
put in, 'You'll have to lower the bird's price if Sigwulf goes to
such trouble.'

Fortunately, Gorm accepted Redwald's argument and after
only a small amount of haggling it was agreed that Gorm's son
and I would ride to seek out the elusive trapper and bring back
any birds he had caught. Osric had come across to join me and,
stepping aside for a moment to confer, we quickly came to the
conclusion that it was best if he stayed aboard ship to safeguard
our silver hoard while I was away. In the meantime Ohthere
could take in Walo so the lad could tend the ice bears. That
would leave Redwald free to get on with his business in the
market.

'The sooner we start out, the better,' I called out, turning
back to Gorm, and almost immediately regretted my enthusiasm

when young Rolf went off at a run, and within minutes re-appeared dragging our mounts by their rope bridles. They were two of the small shaggy breed that we had seen pulling a sledge up from the landing beach. There were no stirrups and once seated in the plain leather saddle, my dangling feet nearly touched the ground. I wondered if the diminutive animals were capable of carrying us far inland.

*

I had misjudged them. They set off at a scampering gait – half trot, half run – that was ideally suited to the difficult terrain. Rolf led the way confidently and I had only to let my little mount follow him at the same jolting pace as it dodged and weaved around the bushes and boulders along a trail no wider than a footpath. Our route was directly away from the sea and our progress was impressive, though at times I felt my spine was being rattled out of shape. For the first few miles the land was level, a mixture of sour bogland with stands of willow and alder, and tussocky rough pasture. We saw scarcely a dozen houses – basic cabins with log walls, a turf roof, a shed or two, and a small fenced enclosure for sheep or scrawny cattle. We spent our first night at the furthest of them where the land-holder's wife recognized Rolf. She gave us a place to sleep in the hay shed, and provided a meal of hard cheese, bread and milk, together with a satchel of the same provisions for our onward journey. Her husband was away at Kaupang market, she said.

The next morning the track veered more to the north-west and began to climb, gradually at first, then more and more steeply, winding its way up the ragged flank of a mountain range. Our ponies scrambled up the slopes with the agility of goats, their unshod hooves finding footing on the loose surface of stones and gravel. We left behind the bright sunshine of the coast and before long the grey of an overcast sky matched the sombre colours of the landscape. We were climbing into a wide, bleak landscape of rock and scree where stunted plants clung to tiny patches of thin soil. Ahead of us always loomed the mountains, the very highest peaks streaked with the last traces of the winter snow. Occasionally we crossed rivulets where ribbons of clear water trickled between the rounded stones, and we stopped and allowed our ponies to drink. I saw little wildlife apart from flocks of small, darting birds and several ravens, hovering like black rags in the breeze. Once, less than fifty paces away, I glimpsed a fox slinking away behind a boulder. Rolf spoke hardly at all, either from shyness or because he found my Saxon difficult to understand, even though it was close enough to his own tongue for us to agree on practical details. He never hesitated in our direction and appeared to know his way even when the last vestiges of a track petered out and we were riding across a rock-strewn wilderness.

We passed the second night of our ride in a lonely hut built entirely of stones ingeniously laid one upon the other in a single spiral course so that it made a cone shape and did not need a roof. The hut, if I understood Rolf correctly, belonged to the bird trapper we were seeking. It was empty except for some mouldering deerskins in one corner, a wooden stool with a broken leg, and the charred remains of a fire beneath the blackened smoke hole. Rolf had brought two small bags of oats for our horses and, once they had fed, staked them out on a rope long enough to let them pick and nibble at the mosses and tiny plants that grew among the rocks. Our own supper was the last of the cheese and bread.

The following morning was distinctly chilly and I was glad to get a fire going, using dried wood that I found stacked behind the hut. I was painfully saddle sore, the inside of my knees bruised and my buttocks tender. So I was glad when Rolf announced, 'Today, Ingvar.'

We rode on, the landscape growing ever more barren until, shortly after midday, we were entering a high valley sheltered on both sides by mountain ridges. Another stone hut similar to the first one stood close beside a small stream, and this time it was in use. Two small horses, penned into a small enclosure, whinnied a greeting as we approached and I saw clothes draped to dry over a low rock wall. But there was no sign of Ingvar himself.

A hanging length of sacking closed the entry to the hut, and after we had tethered our ponies I followed Rolf inside, bending double under the single large flat lintel stone. There were no windows, and barely enough light to see by. The place smelled of wood smoke and soot. It was clean and sparsely furnished – a single stool, a couple of sheepskins pushed against one wall to serve as a bed, some bags hung on pegs, and a large black iron pot on a tripod. The pot contained three inches of cold, congealed stew. A length of fishing net lay on the bare earth floor just inside the doorway. The mesh was small, only suitable for catching sprats. I was puzzled why anyone would need fishing net in the mountains. The little streams we had passed were too shallow and stony to net for fish and we were very far from the sea.

'Where do you think Ingvar's got to?' I asked the boy.

He rolled his eyes expressively and shrugged.

'Maybe we should go looking for him,' I suggested.

He shook his head. 'We wait.'

I left the hut to look around for clues as to what might have happened to the mysterious bird catcher. Not far away was another shelter scarcely larger than a pigsty, with side walls of rock and a flimsy roof made by scraps of worn canvas thrown over some branches.

I crouched down and peered into the small entrance. There was a rustling of feathers. I thrust my head further inside and when my eyes had got used to the near-darkness I saw a pole rigged across the width of the shack. Attached to the pole by a leather strap around its foot was a huge bird: dark, hunched and motionless. It was a mountain eagle, far larger than a gyrfalcon. I was both impressed and disappointed. An eagle was not what I had come to find, but to have captured such a magnificent bird of prey was an achievement. I heard rustling again. It came from the ground on my right, from what looked like a chicken coop made of wooden slats. Unable to restrain my curiosity I reached in and dragged the coop out into the light where I could see it better. Inside were a score of very ordinary pigeons. I sat back on my heels, baffled. It made no sense that someone should take the trouble to go deep into the mountains to trap pigeons that could be caught much more easily near any farm.

Rolf was calling to me, and I returned to find that he had taken down one of the hanging bags and found stale bread and tear-shaped chunks of smoked meat, dark with a reddish purple tinge. We were very hungry so while the ponies drank at the little stream, we sat down on nearby rocks and began to eat. The meat, though a little tough, was delicious. It was with the third or fourth bite that I realized that the chunks, the size of a plum, were the smoked breasts of a small bird. Rolf did not know the bird's name, only that it lived beside the sea. Like the fishing net, it was another Ingvar mystery.

The man himself appeared some hours later as the sun was dropping behind the mountains. Rolf spotted him first, a distant figure making his way down the slope of the mountain ridge, a small sack in his hand. As Ingvar reached the level ground and came walking towards us, I was overwhelmed by the eerie sensation that I was about to encounter someone I had met before. It was akin to the moment when I understood my dream of Walo and two wolves. But this time I was seeing a double: Vulfard, Walo's father, had returned from the bottom of the aurochs' pitfall, alive and unharmed. He and the bird trapper were uncannily similar in height and build and manner. Both were tough and wiry and had the same quick, light step, holding them very straight. Ingvar's complexion was perhaps a little darker, but he had the same alert, foxy expression that I had seen on Vulfard's face. I found myself looking for a cap with a feather, just like Vulfard's, but Ingvar was bareheaded. Only when Ingvar was right in front of me did I see that where Vulfard's eyes had been light brown flecked with yellow, Ingvar's were a dark brown and they slanted above much higher cheekbones in the same narrow face. Something that Redwald had said to me earlier as we walked through the crowds in Kaupang's market place told me that these facial features were signs that one of Ingvar's parents was a native Finna.

'You are welcome,' he said in a clear, sharp voice. I was relieved to hear that his speech was easy to understand.

'Gorm suggested that we come to find you. He missed you at Kaupang's market,' I said.

'I'll come to Kaupang as soon as I'm ready,' the trapper answered.

'Do you know when that will be?'

'Maybe this week,' he answered. The sack he was still holding moved slightly. Something alive was inside. 'After I have washed, we will eat, then talk.' Without another word he turned and walked away towards the shed where I had seen the captive eagle.

A little while later as the light was fading, Ingvar brought out the iron pot and the tripod from his hut, lit a fire, and reheated the stew. He added onions from a bag, some herbs, and a dozen more of dried breasts of the unidentified little bird.

'Rolf tells me that this is from a sea bird,' I commented. The hot meat was even more succulent than it had been when cold.

'I don't know its name in your language. We call it a lundi. In flight it flutters its wings like a bat and, in summer, the beak is striped like a rainbow.'

He sounded like Ohthere with his liking for whale blubber, and I tried to recall if this bizarre-sounding bird had been pictured in Carolus's bestiary. But I could not remember seeing it there.

Ingvar leaned forward and stirred the stew with a stick. 'In the nesting season I travel to the coast and net the birds in the cliffs. Their flesh keeps well, is nourishing and light to carry, and is ideal for when I am in the mountains.'

'Is that why you have a fishing net?' I asked.

'That net is for a different purpose.'

'Gorm told me that you can supply him with white gyrfalcons.'

The trapper studied my face, his expression serious. 'Is that why you have taken the trouble to find me in the mountains?'

'I came to this country, hoping to buy white gyrfalcons.'

'Then tomorrow, if the spirits favour us, you may have your wish.'

My tiredness vanished. 'Tomorrow you will catch a white gyrfalcon?'

'If the spirits wish,' he repeated.

'May I come with you to see how it is done?'

There was a long pause as he considered my request. 'You are the first person who has taken the trouble to come to find me in the mountains. If you give me your word that you will be quiet and calm and not disturb our quarry, you may come with me.'

It was very like what Vulfard would have said.

Then the trapper took me aback by adding, 'And it will do no harm that you are a seidrmann.'

'What do you mean – a "seidrmann"?' I asked.

'Your eyes are of different colours. That is the mark of a man who is at ease with the Otherworld.'

*

Ingvar and I set out next morning while it was still dark, leaving Rolf to look after the horses. The trapper had insisted on an early start, saying that we must be in position by the time the gyrfalcons began to hunt. He was carrying the same small sack he had brought down from the mountain the previous day, and once again its contents moved and shifted with a life of its own. The climb up the ridge was a stiff one and I was embarrassed that Ingvar had to stop from time to time so that I could catch up with him. The result was that it was already full daylight by the time we reached a natural ledge some fifteen paces broad on the shoulder of the mountain. It was, according to Ingvar, the ideal site to trap a gyrfalcon. I was gasping for breath and my legs were shaking with fatigue as I stood there gratefully sucking in deep breaths of the clean fresh air, and gazing out to the blue-grey haze on the distant horizon. It was going to be a warm, windless day. Below me rank after rank of hills and ridges fell away to where, beyond view, lay Kaupang and the market. Without knowing quite why, I felt confident that we would add to the number of white animals for the distant caliph in Baghdad.

I turned to speak to Ingvar. He was gone. I was alone on

the ledge. For an instant I was close to panic, remembering childhood tales of men who could dissolve themselves into thin air. Then I saw his sack. It lay on the ground at the foot of the rock face, still bulging and moving.

I waited for a few moments and – as unexpectedly as he had vanished – Ingvar reappeared, ducking out from a narrow cleft in the mountainside, its entrance hidden in such deep shadow that it was invisible from where I stood. He carried a couple of long, thin whippy lathes, a coil of stout cord, a ball of light twine and – I was interested to see – a length of the fine-mesh fish net.

He gestured at me to hurry in helping him clear away the pebbles and dust from the level patch where I was standing. When that was done, he hammered two wooden pegs into cracks in the rocky ground, about six feet apart. Lashing the two lathes end to end to make what looked like a long fishing rod, he threaded the rod along one edge of the net. Next he bent the rod into an arc and attached the ends to the two ground pegs. Finally, he fastened down the trailing edge of the net with heavy stones. Belatedly I understood what he was creating. It was a bow net. The wooden hoop would lie flat on the ground until he tugged on the cord and it would swing up and over, dragging up the net and trapping anything beneath it.

In the area where the net would fall, Ingvar now placed two stones, one fist-sized, the other somewhat larger and heavier. He untied the neck to his sack, reached in and pulled out a live pigeon. It flapped and struggled as he tied it by the leg to the larger stone. Weighed down, the protesting bird made short fluttering hops but could not escape. I realized that the pigeon was to be our bait, in the same way that Vulfard had placed fresh leaves in the centre of the pitfall for the aurochs. But

Ingvar had a surprise for me. He reached again into the sack, groped around and pulled out a second bird, not a pigeon but a smaller bird, the size of a thrush, pearly grey with a black stripe on its head. This he also placed in the centre of the trap, attached to the smaller stone.

'Why do you need two birds in the trap?' I whispered.

'The gyrfalcon strikes so fast that he can snatch away his prey before the trap is sprung. The smaller bird will provide a warning that a falcon is in the area.'

'A lookout?'

He nodded. 'The smaller bird is very watchful, not like the foolish pigeon. We call it the "shrieker". When it sees a hunting falcon in the sky, it screams and flutters, jumps up and down, trying to escape. Then I know to be ready.'

'Won't the falcon strike at the little "shrieker", as you call it?'

He gave me a patient look. 'If there was a nice plump pigeon nearby, what would you do?'

He scattered a handful of oats on the ground in front of the two birds and beckoned me to follow him to the hidden cleft. As he retreated into the shelter he laid out two cords: a strong one fastened to the hoop to pull it shut, and the other, no more than a thin line, to the free leg of the pigeon.

The cleft was just wide enough for us to sit side by side, hidden from view but looking out over the captive birds. I remembered Vulfard and my vigil in the forest, waiting for the aurochs. Instead of a forest glade rimmed by oak trees, I was watching over a flat, dusty ledge on which two staked birds pecked at grain.

Ingvar did not take his eyes off the tethered birds. He wound a couple of turns of the stronger cord around his right fist, and held the lighter line with the fingers of his left hand.

He reminded me of a fisherman getting ready to strike the hook into the jaws of a pike.

'For these last two months I have ben watching a gyrfalcon nest nearby,' he said in a low voice. 'The birds use the same nest year after year. It's a family that often produces white birds. This year the chicks hatched much later than usual. That is why I delayed going to Kaupang market. I had to wait until they were old enough to look after themselves.'

'So that there's another generation for the future?'

'Exactly. If I caught a parent too soon, the young would die and I would destroy my livelihood.'

'What if an eagle swoops down on the bait, not a gyrfalcon?' I asked.

'Then the spirits are against me. A gyrfalcon, if it is white, gets a much better price than an eagle, nearly three times more.'

'Why would anyone pay more for a falcon when an eagle is so much larger and more impressive?'

'Have you seen how a gyrfalcon hunts?'

I shook my head.

'There is no finer sight in the entire world. It patrols the land, flying low, until it frightens up its prey. Then it takes up the chase. The gyrfalcon is faster than any other bird. It can twist and turn, strike from above or below, and knock its victim from the sky. By contrast the eagle is a farmyard fowl.'

The floor of our hiding place was bare rock, hard and uneven. My backside, already sore from riding, had gone numb. I feared that I would soon get cramp. I longed to get up and stretch.

All of a sudden the little grey bird in front of us crouched down, pressing itself against the ground. Then it began to hop and flutter, screeching in panic. The pigeon continued to peck greedily at the grain.

I held my breath in anticipation. Between the agitated cries of the small bird, there came a shrill bird call, *kree, kree, kree*, distinct in the still mountain air. Ingvar tensed. 'A gyrfalcon is circling above. Keep very still!' he hissed.

With his left hand Ingvar tweaked the thinner of the two lines.

In response the pigeon jumped a few inches off the ground and flapped indignantly. Ingvar waited a couple of heartbeats and tweaked again. Once more the pigeon fluttered, drawing attention to itself.

There was a brief pause, no more than the time it took me to release a slow breath, and then with a sudden rush of wind a white shape hurtled from the sky like a thunderbolt. A burst of pigeon feathers flew up. I heard a distinct thump as the falcon struck its victim, the talons driving into the pigeon's back. Then the predator – it was a white gyrfalcon – was crouching over its victim, shoulders hunched, the hooked beak stabbing down into the pigeon's neck with an assassin's thrust. The pigeon's head flew off. It was all over in the blink of an eye, and in that instant Ingvar tugged firmly on the stouter cord, the hoop of the spring trap swung over, and the gyrfalcon was in the net.

Ingvar gave a whoop of satisfaction and sprang to his feet. 'We must secure the falcon before it hurts itself,' he said. The captive was thrashing and tumbling inside the net, frenziedly struggling to escape.

I tried to rise but had lost all feeling in my legs. I threw out a hand to help myself and, in my clumsiness, grabbed Ingvar by the back of his jerkin. My tug threw him off balance just as he was about to leave our hiding place and he fell across me. He swore at me, fearing to lose his prize. In that same moment, there was a second rush of wind and, from nowhere, another bird of prey came flashing down, striking deep into the swirling turmoil of the net. It was a second gyrfalcon, as white as the first.

The second bird's headlong attack was its undoing. Its talons struck through the net into the pigeon's carcass, closed, then caught in the mesh. The second gyrfalcon also became a tangle of fury, jerking and twisting to get free.

Ingvar had regained his balance. He burst out of our hiding place, slipping off his jerkin. Racing up to the second falcon, he threw the garment over it, trapping it in its folds.

'Quick! There's a spare net in the cave,' he called to me.

I ran back, found the net, brought it to him and together we managed to wrap the furious gyrfalcon in its mesh.

Ingvar worked with calm efficiency, not losing a moment. Deftly he disentangled the second falcon's claws from the mesh of the spring trap and handed me the bird, still wrapped. The dark brown eyes circled with bright yellow skin glared at me in fury as I clutched the struggling creature to my chest, determined not to let it escape. Meanwhile, Ingvar had pulled a length of cloth from his pocket. Gently he eased back the hoop of the trap. Slipping an arm under it, he dropped the cloth over the bird, smothered its thrashing wings, then enveloped its head. As soon as the bird's head was covered, it became less agitated.

Ingvar gathered up the falcon and rose to his feet. 'Bring your bird, we must seal them quickly.'

We hurried back to the cave where Ingvar produced a fine needle and thread, and with infinite care – though it made my stomach clench – ran stitches through the eyelids of the first falcon, then drew them together.

'It doesn't hurt them,' he said, seeing my squeamishness. 'And once the eyes are sealed, they are less likely to hurt themselves.'

It was true. Both birds stopped their frantic attempts to get free as soon as their lids were sealed, and we were able to set them down, to stand quietly on the floor of the cave.

Finally, Ingvar relaxed. 'That's the first time it has happened to me in twenty years of trapping,' he confessed.

'Two birds at a single time?'

'The second falcon must have decided it could snatch away the dead pigeon.'

'Are they the same birds you hoped to trap?' I asked.

'One of them is. It's the male from the nesting pair I've been watching.'

'And the other?'

'Had it been the female, I would have released it so that it could feed the chicks.'

'So you don't recognize it?'

'Never seen it before. It's a different female. She must have been on passage, and just happened upon us. That's what is so difficult to explain . . .' The words died on his lips as he stared into my eyes, his expression wondering. 'Unless the spirits had been asked to help.'

I knew what he was thinking: I had used seidrmann's powers to summon the second bird from afar.

The look on Ingvar's face was unsettling. I had an uneasy feeling that my journey to Kaupang was slipping out of my control.

*

At Ingvar's hut that evening the trapper wrung the necks of all but three of his remaining stock of pigeons. The survivors would later be fed to our captive birds. He let the little 'shrieker' go free.

'It served me well,' said Ingvar as we watched the bird fly away, flitting over the boulder-strewn landscape. 'I can trap another one next year.'

Rolf was given the task of plucking the dead pigeons for our supper, and we sat beside the cooking fire, adding dry sticks from the woodpile to produce a good roasting blaze.

'Tomorrow we set out for Kaupang. You and I each carry a gyrfalcon, and Rolf carries the eagle,' Ingvar said.

He selected a crooked branch, cut off a short section with his hunting knife, and began to scrape off the bark. 'Rolf will need a travel perch for the eagle. That's a heavy animal. If he places one end of this on his saddle tree, it will take the eagle's weight.'

I watched the shavings curl up from the knife blade as the stubby perch took shape, and it occurred to me that Ingvar, a hunter living in the wilds, might know something about the mysterious unicorn. I was still smarting at the memory of being laughed at, so I raised the subject cautiously. 'I read in a book that no bird can match the eagle for its courage.'

'What book is that?'

'It's called a bestiary, a book about notable animals and their behaviour.'

In Carolus's bestiary an eagle had been drawn on the page opposite the picture of the gyrfalcon, and I had read what was written underneath.

'It claims that parent eagles train their fledglings to endure pain by holding them up and making them stare directly into the glare of the sun,' I continued.

Ingvar held up the half-finished travel perch to check its shape. 'Can't say that I've ever seen eagles doing that. But if a cuckoo can get other birds to raise its young, why shouldn't eagles have their own special way as parents?'

'There was also a picture of a wild animal like a horse but with a horn. It's white and very shy, yet it can be tamed. Have you ever seen or heard of such an animal?'

He paused, knife in hand, and regarded me thoughtfully. 'Are you sure it's a horse, not a deer?'

It was an echo of what Walo had asked when we set out from Aachen. He had said that if a unicorn shed its horn every year, then it was a sort of deer.

'I don't know,' I said hesitantly. 'The book doesn't say.'

'My mother's people know of a wild deer that could be the animal you speak of. If you are gentle with it, the animal can be tamed.'

His mother's people, I presumed, were the wild Finna. 'And is this a white deer?'

'Some are.'

'Can you draw me a picture?'

Using a twig Ingvar scratched an outline of the animal in the dust. The body, legs and head could well have been a unicorn. But when he came to sketch a full set of branching horns, it was clear that this was not the creature of the book.

He saw the disappointment on my face. 'It's not the animal you are seeking?'

'No. The animal I'm looking for has a single horn, a spike that springs directly from the forehead. You cannot mistake it. The horn is made in a spiral like the strands of a rope.'

Ingvar's face was alert with sudden interest. 'There is such an animal. Some years ago I came across a broken piece of its horn.'

My heart gave a lurch. 'Where was this?'

'I had gone to the coast to catch those birds whose flesh you so enjoy. A broken piece of its horn was lying on the beach, just a small fragment. Maybe the creature had been fighting with a rival and damaged the spike.'

'Do you still have it?'

He flipped his knife in the air, caught it by the blade, and held it out to me.

'Take a look,' he said.

The handle was dark wood, much polished with use. Where it tapered towards the hilt was a creamy yellow band, the width of my little finger. I looked at it more closely. It had been inset into the wood, and was a section of pale horn or some sort of ivory. Without question, the surface bore the distinctive spiralling twist of the unicorn's horn.

*

The moment I got back to Kaupang, I placed the gyrfalcons in Gorm's care and hurried off to check on Walo and the two ice bears. Ohthere was standing in front of their cage, chewing on what I supposed was his favourite whale blubber.

'If they get any bigger I'll have to build them a larger, much stronger enclosure,' he said as I joined him.

In the week I had been away, the two ice bears had thrived more than I would have imagined possible. They had grown several inches in height and length, put on weight, and their fur was losing its ugly yellow tinge.

'So Walo's doing a good job,' I said.

Ohthere nodded. 'Twice a day he crawls in there, plays that wretched pipe, gives them food and water, brushes their coats, scratches them behind the ears. I won't be surprised to see him rolling around and wrestling with them one day.'

'So he's tamed the bears.'

'Not at all! If anyone else goes near them, they start that

snaky movement, side to side with their heads. A warning that they're about to lash out. They won't let anyone near them except Walo.'

'Where is he now?'

'With Osric. The two of them are helping Redwald. That crafty rogue drove a shrewd bargain over the price of my bears.'

As I walked away, heading into the town, he called out, 'And tell Redwald that I want to talk with him about who's going to pay for their food. They're consuming eight chickens every day, and all the lard I can get my hands on.'

I identified Redwald's place of work by a pile of quern stones. They were heaped outside one of the small, wooden houses just beyond the slave market. Inside I found Redwald standing in the light from the window, moodily rubbing a piece of broken silver jewellery against his touchstone. He looked round as I entered and treated me to a smile of genuine welcome.

'Back already, Sigwulf! How did you get on?'

'Two more white gyrfalcons, one male, one female. And an eagle, but that's of little interest.'

He reached up and brushed back the strand of hair, which, as usual, had slid away from his bald patch. 'Carolus's mews master will find a place for that eagle.'

'And pay you handsomely?' I suggested.

'Of course. I'm a Frisian. I never miss a chance to turn a profit.'

'Yet you don't seem to have sold many of the quern stones.'

He waved dismissively. 'They have their uses. Everyone knows that Redwald brings a cargo of wine to Kaupang each year as well as quern stones. So when they see the display, they know there's a decent drink nearby. It avoids open competition with the other taverns.'

'Is Walo with Osric on your ship?'

'You'll find both of them next door. I've rented half that building.'

It was one of the long boat-shaped structures with a turf roof and, when I entered, I found that wooden partitions divided the interior into a line of rooms, each with its own door, all firmly closed. The first one I looked into contained an array of barrels and crates. I recognized the wine that had been Redwald's cargo. The next was a drinking den, with several rough-looking customers seated on benches with their cups and tankards. They gave me a less-than-welcoming reception as I peered in. I closed the door hastily and went to investigate the next room that proved to be much smaller, with a single table and a couple of stools. Walo and Osric were bent over the table, sorting through a pile of fresh plant leaves.

'Walo, I've seen the ice bears. You're doing a splendid job,' I congratulated him.

Walo bobbed his head and grinned happily.

'How did you get on with the trapper?' Osric asked.

I told him about the two white gyrfalcons and described the sliver of unicorn's horn that decorated Ingvar's knife.

'I've got something to show you,' said Osric. He glanced at Walo. 'Can you find somewhere to put these leaves so they dry in the sun?'

'What are those?' I asked my friend as Walo carefully gathered up the leaves.

'Black horehound is your Saxon name for the plant. Chewing the leaves staves off sea sickness.'

I waited until Walo had left the room and was about to ask Osric why he had left our silver unguarded, when my friend forestalled me.

'Hear me out, Sigwulf,' he said flatly. 'The silver's in safe keeping . . . what's left of it. The only times I've been off the ship were when I knew Redwald was safely in town, and it's just as well that I came ashore.'

He held my gaze, his dark eyes troubled. 'I had a chance to talk with one of those Khazar slave traders while you've been away.'

'Is there something wrong?'

'There could be.' Osric lowered his voice. 'The Byzantines won't be pleased when they learn about our mission to Baghdad. The Khazar confirmed that the basileus in Constantinople is at war with the caliph. It's an all-out conflict, Christian against Saracen.'

I recalled that the caliph styled himself Commander of the Faithful. 'Do you think they will try to disrupt our mission?'

'The basileus would prefer Carolus to despatch troops to help him fight his battles, not send exotic animals as presents to the foe.'

'Maybe Constantinople won't find out what we are about,' I said.

My friend shook his head. 'Not a chance. The Greeks place their spies everywhere. No one pays more for gathering intelligence on their neighbours. I wouldn't be surprised if they allowed the Khazars to travel to Kaupang on condition that they brought back information for them.'

'But the slave traders don't know why we've come to Kaupang.'

'I'm afraid they do. I as good as told them.'

I was shocked. Osric and I had agreed to keep our mission a secret. We would explain our presence in Kaupang only to those who, like Ohthere and Gorm, could supply white animals. By being discreet, we should avoid coming to the attention of King Offa who was sure to have his informers at the market.

I opened my mouth to ask Osric why he had been so reckless, when he held up a hand and cut me short. 'I think you will agree it was worthwhile.'

My friend reached under the table and brought out a long, thin package wrapped in heavy purple velvet cloth and secured with a cord of crimson silk. 'I mentioned to the Saracen that I had originally studied to be a doctor. He said he had acquired an item likely to be of great interest to a medical man.'

'Sounds as though he was trying to sell you something.'

'He was, and I was sufficiently intrigued to ask him to show me what he was talking about.'

I waited for Osric to continue. His slim brown fingers were untying the knots in the silk cord. Slipping off the binding, he set the package on the table and gently unrolled the square of velvet to display what it contained.

A complete unicorn horn.

I felt something tighten in my chest, and for several moments was lost for words. The horn was exactly as depicted on the brow of the unicorn in Carolus's bestiary. Two inches thick at the base, it was the length of my outstretched arm and tapered to a fine point, the twisting spiral impossible to mistake.

My hand shook as I reached forward and picked it up. It was a little lighter than I would have expected, and the same faded yellowish-creamy colour as on the haft of Ingvar's knife.

'Where did the slaver get it?' I asked, my voice husky with shock. The material felt more like ivory than horn.

'He wouldn't tell me directly, only that it was in trade. I suspect that he was lying. Slavers will raid remote villages to grab their victims, and they take the chance to pillage the settlements. I think this is plunder.'

I ran my fingers along the length of the horn, feeling the

twist of the spiral glide beneath my touch. 'Why would it be of value to a doctor?'

'Items of great rarity are often considered to have medical value. For example, pearls are ground to powder and taken with a herbal infusion as a treatment for convulsions.'

'Did the Khazar know that it is a unicorn's horn?'

'He wasn't sure what it was. Only that it was something very unusual.'

I passed the horn back to my friend. 'What did you tell him it was worth?'

'I tried to avoid giving a value, but then he said he was thinking of offering it to one of Kaupang's dealers in precious stones and jewellery.'

'So you bought it.'

My friend treated me to one of his thin-lipped smiles. 'It was expensive – twelve hundred silver denarii.'

'The cost is not important,' I assured him. 'It would have been a disaster if we had lost the horn. Besides, by the time Redwald has finished haggling with Ohthere and Gorm over the price of the bears and the falcons, he'll have saved us at least that much.'

'The Khazar insisted on being paid at once,' Osric explained. 'I had to use our coins from the Aachen mint. That's how the slaver worked out that we must be agents for Carolus himself. He as much as told me so.'

He began to roll the horn back inside the velvet cover. 'The Khazars know we've purchased white bears, and are buying up any white gyrfalcons that are for sale. They'll be wondering what Carolus wants these animals for. If they also know that white is the imperial colour in Baghdad, they'll be stupid not to have made the connection between Carolus and the caliph.'

I was so elated at having proof of the unicorn's existence

that only now I thought to ask Osric what he had meant when he said the unused portion of our silver hoard was in safe keeping.

'I handed the last few coin bags over to Redwald,' he answered calmly. 'He's put them in that secret cubby hole aboard his ship.'

I stared at him. 'Was that wise?'

Osric was unperturbed. 'Ohthere was pressing to be paid for the ice bears, and by the time he had a down payment and the Khazar got his coin, less than a third remains.'

A faint shadow of doubt clouded my satisfaction. I wondered if we were putting too much trust in the shipmaster. Even a third of Carolus's original funds was a temptation for someone sufficiently unscrupulous.

*

Freed of the necessity to mount guard over our silver hoard, Osric and I redoubled our efforts to obtain clues as to where the unicorn itself might be found. We could not interrogate the Khazars because they packed up and left Kaupang abruptly, less than a day after selling the unicorn horn to Osric. So instead we split up and worked the market, asking traders and their customers, sailors down by the landing place; anyone who looked as though they might provide us with information. We were met with blank looks, humorous and sometimes ribald inventions and – as often as not – outright laughter. If we had picked up the slightest hint about where the unicorn lived we would have travelled there immediately, but with each passing day there were fewer people to answer our questions. Midsummer's day was the highpoint of Kaupang's annual market and soon afterwards a number of traders began shutting up shop and heading home. The fine weather also left us. Mornings that dawned full of bright sunny promise turned into afternoons when masses of close-packed clouds sailed overhead and a chill west wind rattled the canvas covers on the remaining stalls. The gusts brought sudden, heavy showers. When it rained, Walo usually stayed with his ice bears, and Osric and I would take shelter in the building where Redwald had rented rooms.

It was on such an afternoon that I decided not to wait to be drenched by a downpour from a bank of smoke-coloured clouds moving in rapidly from the sea. Already there were rumbles of distant thunder, and a curtain of heavy rain trailed below the storm's underbelly. Hurrying my steps, I reached the building ahead of Osric. The drinking den was crowded and several of the clients smelled of wet manure, so I made my way to the smaller room where Osric and Walo had checked their horehound leaves. I stood by the small window, looking out and waiting for my friend. The light dimmed as the storm swept in, and the rain began to come down in a solid cascade, splashing up from great puddles in the rough ground behind the building. I jumped as a flash of lightning lit the sky at no great distance, rapidly followed by an enormous crash of thunder. I came to the conclusion that Osric had got out of the downpour elsewhere so was surprised to hear the door of the little room open behind me. I turned to greet him, but the two men who entered were strangers.

'Shouldn't last long,' I commented cheerfully. I tried to recall where I had seen them before. They were both thickset, rather jowly men dressed in plain, unremarkable clothes. The shoulders of their jackets were only speckled with raindrops so they must have ducked in to shelter just before the cloudburst. The taller one had a heavy, rather stupid-looking face that emphasized his hulking menace. His colleague was even less attractive, with a bull neck and deep-set black eyes that looked as if they had been poked in his pudding-like head with the point of a charred stick.

Neither man responded directly to my greeting. They edged further into the little room, then the taller one closed the door behind him, leaned against it, and folded his arms.

'Odd-eyes aren't welcome in this town,' said Pudding Head nastily. Another crash of thunder drowned the rest of his words.

'What do you mean by that?' I asked. It was a feeble response as I tried to work out why the men wanted to pick a quarrel.

Pudding Head moved closer. 'A seidrmann brings bad luck.'

'I may have odd eyes, as you call them, but I'm no seidrmann.'

He laughed coarsely. 'Then why do you keep company with a cripple who looks as if he came from Niflheim and a moon-struck idiot servant?'

Niflheim was the home of the dead. Osric's dark skin must have seemed outlandish to these yokels.

'I'm not a magician,' I repeated, a tight knot of fear gathering in my stomach. Belatedly I recognized the two men. They were the same pair of guards that I had seen from time to time outside the jewellery shop. The jeweller himself had closed up and departed from Kaupang a week earlier so I wondered who now employed them or whether the two men were acting on their own. I could only suppose that they were planning to rob me. I looked for a means of escape. The window behind me was too small, and the ruffian at the door was too burly.

The heart of the thunderstorm was now right over Kaupang. Outside, the torrential rain fell in a steady roar. Peal after peal of thunder shook the building. The air suddenly felt chilly, though that was not what made me shiver. Pudding Face pulled out a knife. The two men were not here to frighten me or even to beat me up. They intended to kill me.

I had long since returned to Redwald the sailor's knife he had loaned me, and now my only weapon was the knife I used for cutting up food, a blade just four inches long. I pulled it from my belt as I backed away towards the window and saw the look of disdain in the hard, black eyes of my attacker.

I had fought in pitched battles, on foot and on horseback, and with sword and shield. But being trapped in a small room by a pair of cut-throat killers was outside my experience.

Pudding Head was circling to my left, my exposed side, his knife held low in front of him. He jabbed it towards me menacingly. I jumped back out of range, then realized that he was intent on driving me round the little room in a circle, until my back was to his colleague Stupid Face. There I would be clasped in those thick arms and held while his companion put the blade into a fatal spot.

I backed away further, felt the edge of a stool against my knee, and – not taking my eyes off the knife man – picked it up to use as a shield. Pudding Head took a half-pace forward, his expression cold and calculating.

I bellowed for help, shouting at the top of my lungs. With sudden desperation I knew there was little hope of being heard over the crash of thunder and the drumming of the rain and, even if I was, my cries might well be mistaken for a noisy brawl in the nearby drinking den.

Nevertheless, I kept yelling and yelling, thrusting the stool at Pudding Head's head making him step back.

He waited his moment, then suddenly reached out with his free hand and grabbed the stool, and used it to propel himself forward. I tried to dodge his knife, but he was too quick. I felt a sharp burning sensation as the blade cut me, on my right side, sliding off a rib.

I yelped from fear and pain. He had not let go of the stool, and for a moment we wrestled together, each trying to tug the stool from the other. My initial surge of energy was ebbing rapidly. I would either drop the stool or be forced backward within range of Stupid Face guarding the door.

I shouted again for help, and the cry had scarcely left my throat when there was a great splintering and smashing of wood. The man with his back against the door was propelled head first into the room as someone shoulder-charged the door from the passageway outside, carrying away its hinges.

Ohthere. He burst in, carrying the same heavy stick that he had used to fend off the dogs from the bear cage. He wielded it as a cudgel. Before Stupid Face could recover his balance, Ohthere drove the blunt end of the stick hard into his stomach. The man doubled up with a grunt. Ohthere then stepped across to where I was fending off Pudding Head and brought his stick down with a resounding crack on the hand that held the knife. I made the mistake of letting go the stool, and Pudding Face had the wit to swing it at Ohthere, who failed to duck in time. The edge of the stool caught him on the side of his head and he staggered back. Taking advantage of the moment, both attackers turned and bolted for the door.

I was too exhausted to do more than take jagged gasps of breath and press my hand against my wounded side, feeling blood.

'How badly are you hurt?' asked Ohthere.

'Nothing fatal,' I managed to answer. Then, dizzy and in shock, I staggered to the stool that lay on the floor, righted it, and sat down. 'Who were they? They were trying to kill me . . .'

Ohthere was rubbing the side of his head. 'I've no idea. But they'll have made themselves scarce by now.'

'Should we report the incident?'

'There's no one to report to. The only law in Kaupang is the one you take into your own hands. If you can track them down, you could take revenge. But if they are the jarl's men, it's a waste of time. They'll have his protection.'

I noticed that Ohthere's clothes were soaking wet. 'It was lucky you came by, despite the rain. Otherwise I'd have been done for.'

He gave a dismissive shrug. 'A little damp won't stop me from calling on Redwald to arrange the final payment for the bears. I heard shouts and recognized your voice.'

'I got a good look at the two men. Perhaps Redwald knows where to track them down,' I said.

I got up from the stool and hobbled out of the building, leaning on Ohthere's arm. The rainstorm had eased as rapidly as it had started. The last few raindrops were flicking down, and the ground outside was muddy slop. Just before we reached the door to Redwald's office, I turned to Ohthere. 'Could you find Osric for me? He's good at dealing with wounds.'

'Of course. I left him at my place, with Walo.'

While Ohthere squelched off, I paused for a moment to gather my thoughts: Northmen rarely killed those whom they believed to have magical powers. They feared retribution from the Otherworld. If there was a different motive for the attack, someone must have known that I was by myself, sheltering from the rainstorm. Immediately Redwald sprang to mind. The shipmaster, I recalled, had identified to me the same two brutes when they were on guard outside the jeweller's shop. Redwald's office was just a few steps away. He could have spoken with the two would-be assassins in the adjacent drinking den to tell them that the moment was right. Redwald already had his hands on what remained of our silver hoard aboard his ship. If he killed me, all that would remain would be to dispose of Osric, perhaps on the voyage back to Dorestad. With us out of the way Redwald could also claim his commission from Carolus's mews master for bringing back the gyrfalcons, and probably get a reward for obtaining the ice bears as well.

I limped into the shipmaster's office, alert to his reaction when he saw that I was alive.

Redwald was seated alone at his changing table, leaning forward and concentrating, and he ignored my arrival. He was placing matching weights into the two pans of his moneyer's weighing scales to check the balance. When he looked up and saw blood on my shirt, he made a sucking sound through his teeth.

'What happened to you?' he asked as I sank down on a bench facing him.

I told him of the unprovoked assault and described the two men. 'I think they were previously guards for the dealer in precious stones, the man who had his premises a little way along the street.'

I watched him closely for signs of guilt but he only tugged at an earlobe as he considered his reply. 'You could well be right.'

'Do you know anything about the dealer?'

He sat back with a sour smile. 'I make it a policy to stay clear of him. His line is in gems and fine ornaments. If he thought I was infringing on his trade by doing more than changing money and handling broken silver, he would try to put me out of business.'

'Would he set his men on me because I'm with you?'

He shook his head. 'Only a madman would carry a commercial rivalry that far.'

'Surely you don't believe they tried to kill me because they thought I practise black magic!'

'No, though it's common knowledge that Ingvar caught two

gyrfalcons in the same trap when you were with him. Everyone says that's not natural.' He paused and gave me a look of shrewd calculation. 'What about King Offa? You told me that he had a grudge against you.'

'How would he have found out that I'm in Kaupang?' I said.

'Of course he has his agents here, though I wouldn't know who they are, or want to,' Redwald answered. 'I don't pry into King Offa's affairs. My trade with Mercia is too valuable . . .' His voice tailed away, and a heavy silence hung in the air between us. 'There's a coincidence, though. If your identification is correct, one of the attackers came to see me last week. He wanted money changed.'

Redwald reached inside his tunic and pulled out a small soft leather pouch. 'Northmen trust gold coins even less than silver ones. They get rid of them as quickly as possible.'

He untied the little pouch and shook the contents on the table, a mix of half a dozen gold coins of varying thickness, shape and size.

He picked up one of the coins and handed it to me. 'Take a look.'

The coin was the size of my thumbnail. It was recently minted so the markings were clear. I recognized the wavy lines of Saracen writing.

'That was one of the coins that your mysterious attacker – if we have the right man – wanted me to change into silver,' Redwald said.

I turned the coin slowly in my fingers. 'Advance payment for a murder?'

'Possibly. Equally, it might have been his gambling winnings or part of his legitimate wages from the jeweller, though the latter would have been very generous.'

Unwisely I took a deep breath and winced as I felt the stab of pain from my wound. 'I'll get Osric to translate the writing after he's bandaged the gash in my side. If we know where the coin comes from, that might tell us who was behind the attack.'

'You don't have to ask Osric. Turn the coin over and read what it says,' said Redwald.

I did so. Among the Saracen symbols was an inscription in Roman letters: 'Offa Rex'.

'This is Offa's coinage?' I said, puzzled. 'Why the Saracen writing?'

Redwald leaned back on his chair and I recognized the look that he had on his face when he was about to impart one of the secrets of his trade. 'A couple of years ago, Offa decided to issue a coin in gold, not his usual silver. He wanted to expand Mercia's trade with Hispania. Having a coin that the Saracen recognized would make payments easier. So his mint master took his mould from a genuine Saracen coin, a gold dinar, and changed a single detail – inserting Offa's name.'

'So those cut-throats were Offa's hirelings.' The thought that Offa had not forgotten my existence and was prepared to have me killed made my stomach twist.

'Not so fast,' warned Redwald. He slid a second gold coin across the table towards me. 'This was another coin your knife-wielding friend wanted me to change for silver.'

This coin bore a cross on one side, and two stylized heads on the other. Both wore crowns, one with long pendants hanging almost to the shoulders. I looked up at Redwald questioningly. 'Where does this one come from?'

'Constantinople. That's a Byzantine solidus.' Redwald raised an eyebrow. 'The figure on the left is the young Basileus Constantine.'

'And the one with the dangling decorations?'

'His mother, Irene. She acts as regent. Can you think of any reason why someone in Constantinople wants you done away with?' He gave a bleak smile. 'Just in case they try again, I think we should bring forward the date of our departure from Kaupang. I seem to remember that I gave my word to deliver you and your friends safely back to Dorestad ... and that's when I'll be paid my bonus.'

At that moment Osric limped into the room. He made me stand up and peel off my tunic so that he could examine the wound. As he cleaned the gash with a rag soaked in rainwater, I reflected to myself that either Redwald was innocent of my attempted murder or he was a most ingenious liar. He had provided me with two suspects. The first was King Offa whose agents had hired the killers to rid their master of a long-standing nuisance. The second was the basileus in Constantinople. As Osric had pointed out, the Emperor of the Greeks had reason to wreck Carolus's mission to the caliph.

I racked my brains trying to understand how the Greeks could have known why Carolus had sent me to Kaupang. The Khazars could not yet have carried back their report to Constantinople. Then I recalled Osric's other warning: the Greeks have their spies everywhere. Their sources at Carolus's court could have alerted the basileus even before Osric and I left Aachen.

*

Redwald lost no time in preparing for us to leave Kaupang. He sold off the rest of his wine cheaply and arranged for the remaining quern stones to be left with a local factor. On the morning before the cog was due to set sail, I went with Walo to fetch the three white gyrfalcons and the eagle. They had been left in the care of Gorm, and the bird dealer's son had already picked the stitches from the eyelids of the more recently captured birds so that they could see, and had been gentling them so that they were easy to handle.

Gorm himself helped us carry the birds down to the cog where she lay against the jetty. Climbing down into the ship's hold, we found two of Redwald's sailors slinging a long wooden bar by ropes from the deck beams. It was a travelling perch.

While Gorm and I looked on, Walo wrapped sacking around the wooden bar so that the falcons' talons could get a firm grip.

'Here, you can't do that!' shouted one of the sailors. Walo had picked up a length of light rope, and was hacking it into short lengths with the knife he used for cutting up the ice bears' food.

'Let him be,' said Gorm sharply. 'He knows what he's doing.'

Walo had begun rigging the lengths of cord so that they dangled beside the perch.

'What are those for?' I asked the bird dealer.

'So the birds can reach out and get a grip on the cords with their beaks when the ship rolls,' Gorm explained. He turned to Walo. 'How about you staying on in Kaupang? I could use a really good assistant.'

To my alarm Walo's moon face went pale, and his half-closed eyes began to glisten with tears. He shook his head violently and looked at me pleadingly. He was frightened of being abandoned.

'That's all right, Walo,' I reassured him. 'I need you to look after the ice bears. You can remain with Osric and me.'

Walo mumbled something, and I had to ask him to repeat what he had said. 'The bears have no names,' he muttered.

Gorm hastened to make up for his blunder. 'Sigwulf, I think that Walo believes that you were going to leave the ice bears behind because you hadn't given them any names.'

My mind went blank and I looked at the bird dealer. 'What do you suggest?'

He chuckled. 'My son has been calling them Modi and Madi these past few days. Maybe that fits.'

'Why's that?' I had never heard either name.

'They're gods, sons of Thor. Modi means "angry", Madi means "strong".'

I looked across at Walo. 'Will those names suit?' I asked.

He brightened and gave me a shy nod.

'Then it's time we got Modi and Madi down to the ship,' I told him.

He reached inside his shirt and pulled out his deerhorn pipe that hung on a leather thong around his neck. 'They will follow me here,' he said.

I was lost for words. The two animals were no longer the feeble, sickly creatures that had arrived in Kaupang. They were larger and heavier, active and quick, and they enjoyed mock fighting. Rearing up on their hind legs, they battled and growled, seizing their opponent's neck or limb in their formidable jaws and twisting and tugging. It required little imagination to picture the danger if they ever got loose.

Gorm came to my rescue. 'I've got a better idea, Walo. We'll bring them to the ship on a sledge.'

And that was how it was accomplished. Redwald's sailors built a double-size sledge on top of which they constructed a sturdy cage. It had to be large enough to contain both bears at the same time because Walo assured us that the animals would become distressed and unpredictable if separated. He himself sat inside the cage with the bears while they were moved in case they needed calming. After much coaxing we harnessed four terrified horses to the sledge. Then all of us – Gorm and his son, Redwald, Osric, Ingvar the bird catcher, Osric and myself – hauled on drag ropes and we set out for the dock. Our progress along Kaupang's rutted and pot-holed street, even with the bears securely caged, caused uproar. Merchants shuttered their shops while we passed, stallholders evacuated their stands, and only the most curious of their customers remained to gawk at us. Every step of the way we were accompanied by a horde of wildly excited dogs, snapping, snarling and barking.

We reached the jetty where Redwald's crew waited until the top of the tide, then slid the entire contraption across and onto the cog's deck where it was fastened down with strong ropes. While this was being done, I was concluding a last-minute purchase with Ingvar's help. Among the pack of curs attracted by the commotion of our departure were several dogs with short fox-like faces beneath high-set triangular ears. Of medium size, they were stocky and active and had curly tails. They gave an impression of sharp intelligence and it occurred to me that if their thick coats of short dense fur were washed and cleaned, they would be off-white. Like everything else in Kaupang, they were for sale.

Thus we loaded five dirty and quarrelsome dogs as extra cargo. The rest of the pack lined the beach in a noisy frenzy as the gap widened between ship and shore, and we left Kaupang to the same sound as our arrival – the barking of dogs.

Chapter Six

FRANKIA

*

FREQUENT SWIGS OF black horehound leaves steeped in hot water helped Walo find his sea legs on the southward voyage. Thanks to him, all our animals were in good health when our ship turned into the estuary of the great river we had left three months before. From there, Redwald worked the tides, anchoring during the ebb and riding the flood to bring us upriver by easy stages to Dorestad. In the last week of July, the cog tied up to a staithe in her homeport and I found a royal courier waiting for me as we docked. His instructions were to escort me to Aachen with all speed. Any white animals we had collected were to be trans-shipped and to proceed upriver by barge on the first stage of their journey to distant Baghdad. It seemed that the mission to the caliph was to go ahead.

Leaving Osric and Walo in charge of the animals, I said a hurried farewell to Redwald, interrupting him as he stood at the foot of the mast, supervising his crew unlace the great sail from its spar, ready to carry it ashore. I had already offered to deliver the captive eagle to the palace mews master on his behalf. But he had declined gruffly, saying that I was not a

Frisian so he could not trust me to drive a hard enough bargain over the price.

'I owe you an apology,' I said.

He tilted his head to one side and gave me a knowing look. 'You had your doubts about me, didn't you?' he said.

I felt my face go red. 'That's right. But you've done as you promised, and brought us back safe. I want to thank you.'

He clapped me on the shoulder. 'That was just good business. I seem to remember that I was promised a bonus if you and all the animals got here in good condition. I'll settle up with Osric and he can pay me from the rest of your silver hoard.'

He reached into an inner pocket, produced a small coin, and held it out to me.

'You'd forgotten about your share from the sale of the Rhenish wine,' he said.

The coin was the dinar with Arab script and Offa's name, the same gold coin that my attacker had asked Redwald to change for silver.

'That's too much,' I said. 'Besides, I bought the wine with funds from the royal treasury. You should credit them with any profit.'

'I'll haggle with the treasury in my own time.' He pressed the coin into my hand.

I had no wish to be rude so I slipped the dinar into my money belt. 'I'll spend it in Baghdad when my mission is over,' I told him.

'That coin will be a useful reminder,' he said.

'A reminder of what?'

He made a wry face. 'That money has a very long reach.'

*

Aachen had altered while I had been away. Summer was the building season, and the royal precinct resounded to the constant tapping of hammers as teams of tilers crawled over the vast roof of the future banqueting hall. The web of scaffolding had been dismantled from the façade of the basilica and re-erected around the treasury. The arcade leading to Carolus's private quarters was no longer an untidy muddle of bricks and paving slabs. Several houses on the fringes of the precinct had been torn down to make extra space for the royal building programme, and there was a new stable block I could not remember seeing previously. There was no time to take in any further details because my escort whisked me straight to the royal apartments and handed me over to the major domo, a plump, watchful man whose sharp eyes immediately took in the suspicious-looking package in my hand. It was early afternoon, a time when I knew the king liked to take a nap. Yet the major domo waved aside the guard who wished to check whether what I was holding was some sort of weapon and immediately brought me up the familiar broad staircase leading to the royal apartments. Without knocking, he eased open the door to the king's private audience room and slipped inside.

A few minutes later he reappeared and held the door ajar. 'The king will see you now.'

It was the same audience chamber as before, though in daylight it seemed even more spacious and airy than when candle-lit. Carolus was alone in the room. His slightly dishevelled appearance suggested that he had only just got up, and the silk cover of the couch he used as a day bed was rumpled. He yawned and stretched before addressing me, looking down from his great height.

'I'm told that you've brought back two ice bears,' he said.

I was reminded that the king's long and successful reign

depended partly on his excellent intelligence system that brought news from all parts of the kingdom.

'Two ice bears, three gyrfalcons, five dogs, Your Majesty – and all of them white,' I replied.

'Dogs?' Carolus grunted irritably. It seemed that being disturbed during his afternoon nap left him out of sorts. 'I didn't ask for dogs.'

'They were available so I purchased them with surplus funds. I apologize if this went beyond my instructions,' I said apologetically.

'Any good for the chase?' the king demanded.

He was passionate about his hunting, and I suspected that he was thinking of putting the dogs into the royal kennels.

'I've been told that these dogs make excellent guard dogs and can pull sledges. But I heard nothing about hunting,' I answered tactfully.

'Not a lot of sledges in Baghdad,' grumbled the king, 'but I suppose we should add them to the list.' Carolus's gaze sharpened. 'What about the unicorn? Did you bring one back?'

I took a deep breath. 'No, Your Majesty. There is no unicorn.'

His eyebrows came together in a scowl. 'My Book of Beasts states otherwise. Last month I was unwise enough to mention my hopes for a unicorn to my councillors, and one of them failed to hide his smirk. I dislike being thought a fool.'

Carolus's ill-humour was making me nervous. 'I meant only that there is no unicorn among the animals we brought back. The animal itself does exist of course.'

The shrewd grey eyes regarded me suspiciously. 'Go on, but don't try to hoodwink me.'

'Your Majesty will recall you showed me the horn of an aurochs as proof that such an animal is real?'

'Go on.'

'Here is the proof that the unicorn exists.' I held up the velvet-wrapped package. 'I obtained this in the Northlands though no one could tell me where to find the living creature.'

'Show me,' ordered the king.

With a showman's flourish I whisked off the purple velvet cover and offered the unicorn's horn to the king. He took it from me and stood for a long moment, grasping the horn in his large, strong hand, turning it this way and that.

'Remarkable,' he said finally. A delighted smile replaced the scowl.

He whirled about, giving me a fright, and using the unicorn horn as a pointer, rested the tip on a deep-red gem set in the crosspiece of the great jewelled cross that dominated one side of the room.

'Know what this is, Sigwulf?' he demanded.

'No, Your Majesty.'

'A precious carbuncle. It represents the blood of Christ.'

He lowered the unicorn horn and turned to face me. 'And where has God hidden the precious carbuncle to demonstrate its great worth?' he demanded.

I shifted my feet uncomfortably. 'I do not know, Your Majesty.'

'In the skull of the asp or within the head of a dragon. That is where you find the carbuncle.' He looked triumphant. 'There are those who question that fact, just as they question the existence of the unicorn, but no more!'

He twirled the unicorn's horn. 'Sigwulf, you are to press ahead with the embassy to the caliph. You must cross the Alps before the snow closes the passes on your way south.'

'And the aurochs?' I ventured to ask. I noticed that he used the word embassy rather than mission. It seemed that my task had acquired extra status.

'I'm still sending the aurochs as my giant beast, though it can't match his elephant in size. You'll be taking just a single one. My verderers could not trace another.'

He hefted the horn again. 'But this I will keep with me. I will enjoy seeing the expression on the face of my doubting councillor.'

It was strange to see the king as elated as a child with a new toy. 'Sigwulf, you've done well. I shall not forget the service you have rendered.'

I took it as a dismissal, bowed, and backed away towards the door.

'Go and see Alcuin,' were the royal parting words. 'He will arrange all that is needed and can provide the necessary letters of introduction. And you'll find he has an additional gift for you to hand over to the caliph.'

*

Amid all the bustle and clatter of the building works it was reassuring to find that Alcuin was just as I remembered him – tall and spare, dressed in the same dark gown and sandals, a calm, watchful expression on his intelligent face, and his same habit of coming straight to the point.

'How did you get on?' he asked as he opened the door to his cell-like office and saw me on the threshold. 'Do come in.'

This time there was no aurochs horn on display, and he waited for me to finish recounting the outcome of the visit to Kaupang before he sat down again behind his desk. 'A fair result,' he said.

There was no other seat in the room, so I remained on my

feet feeling like an errant schoolboy facing his master. 'I wish we had been able to bring back a unicorn. That was what the king wanted most of all.'

'Really.' He put just enough scepticism into that single word to make it clear that he thought this had been an impossible quest.

'I managed to bring back an example of the creature's horn. I've given it to the king,' I told him.

'I look forward to inspecting it,' he murmured politely. However, the scepticism did not leave his eyes. Both of us knew that charlatans sold fakes to gullible clients.

'The king mentioned that there's an additional gift that I am to carry to Baghdad,' I said brightly, hoping to change the subject to something more positive.

'I'll come to that in a moment. First, you need to be aware of a recent political development.' He put his elbows on the desk and steepled his fingers as he studied me carefully.

'You are aware of the route the embassy will follow?' he asked.

'Upriver by barge, then across the Alps to Rome, from there by sea to the Holy Land and then . . .' I fell silent. My grasp of the geography of the eastern lands was hazy.

'. . . Or possibly up the river Nile,' he continued for me, 'then by caravan across the desert, and finally by ship to Baghdad. A very long journey, with many risks: blizzards and avalanches in the mountains; sand storms in the desert; gales at sea. Fortunately, as I mentioned before, you will have a very competent guide who has made the journey in the reverse direction, bringing that unlucky elephant. I've arranged for him to come here so I can introduce you.'

Alcuin lowered his hands to lie flat on the surface of the

table. Their backs were faintly mottled with light freckles, and there was a smudge of ink on his right index finger.

'What I have to say is best explained before he gets here. It concerns other than the physical dangers.' His tone remained restrained and calm, but his expression was very serious. 'Recently there have been overtures from Constantinople, proposing a marriage union between the royal houses of Frankia and Byzantium. There was even a hint of a wedding between Carolus and the regent empress Irene.'

It occurred to me to say that Carolus was already married, and for the third time. He also had a string of mistresses. But of course that was no obstacle to a political union.

Alcuin held my gaze. 'The proposal was declined as diplomatically as possible. Nevertheless, the Byzantines are sure to have seen it as a snub.'

More of a slap in the face, I thought, from someone who was in the process of sending rare gifts to the caliph instead.

'Sigwulf, you will be travelling through regions where the Greeks, the Byzantines, are very influential. They would dearly like your embassy to fail. You will need to be on your guard, even in Rome itself.'

The image of the gold solidus gleaming on Redwald's desk in Kaupang sprang into my mind. 'Perhaps Carolus can ask the pope to offer the embassy additional protection?' I ventured.

'Pope Adrian is a staunch friend. I'm sure he will do everything he can to assist a ruler whose allegiance to Holy Church is without question.'

Alcuin paused, perhaps he was aware how bland his last statement had been. His next words brought a dash of icy realism.

'Pope Adrian is nearly ninety years of age so there is always the question of who will succeed him. There are factions and counterfactions in the Eternal City and they will take advantage of any opportunity to further their own candidate, including serving Byzantine interests.'

Alcuin's eyes were red-rimmed from lack of sleep. I wondered how many hours each day he was obliged to spend giving government advice. 'Fortunately, I have a good friend in Rome whose advice will guide you through those murky undercurrents. I have personally written a letter of introduction for you,' he said.

'The additional gift for the caliph . . . ?' I reminded him.

Alcuin's careworn expression was replaced with something more cheerful. 'Yes, and it's something you will appreciate.'

He stood up and went to the shelves that lined the wall on his right. They held his writing materials. He took down what I had assumed was a thin stack of fresh vellum but now I saw was a newly sewn book that had been lying with its spine against the wall.

'The king's own idea. I've seldom seen him so excited about a project,' said Alcuin, placing the book in my hands. 'I had to assign four of my best copyists to get it ready in time.'

I looked down at the volume. It was expensively bound in what I guessed was fine goatskin. The cover was stamped and dyed with interlaced patterns in green, blue and red, and the detailing was outlined in gold leaf.

'A hurried job but the best we could do,' Alcuin explained. 'Carolus is concerned that not all the animals he is sending the caliph will survive the journey. If that happens, you are to use this book to show the caliph what creatures had been selected for him, apologize for their loss, and enquire if there are any replacements that the caliph might prefer.' Alcuin allowed himself a tight smile. 'You will also take the opportunity to point to the animals that Carolus himself would like to receive for his own zoo.'

Carefully I lifted the cover of the volume. The fresh stitching made the binding stiff, and the leather still had the chalky smell of the alum tanning.

It was another bestiary. The first page had an illustration of a lion with a heavy, curly mane, roaring over a small, sleepy-looking cub. Underneath was a paragraph summarizing the creature's habits and nature.

A lion always sleeps with its eyes open and evades the hunter by using its tail to sweep away the tracks left by its paws in the sand or dust. The mother lion gives birth to five cubs the first year, four cubs the second year, and so forth. The cubs are born dead. They come to life when the mother breathes in their faces, and the father roars over them.

Below were several lines in Saracen script. I presumed they were the Arab translation.

Alcuin's voice brought me out of the book. 'Sigwulf, think of it as a catalogue, as a list of possible gifts that might be exchanged between a king and a caliph.' He was smiling at me, half in amusement, half in warning. 'Carolus wonders, for example, if by any chance the caliph can send him a griffin. You'll find it on the third page.'

I turned to the correct illustration. It showed a bizarre, fierce-looking creature that had the body and tail of a lion but the head and wings of an eagle. The griffin, according to the description written underneath, was an enemy of horses and large enough to fly away carrying a live ox.

I looked up at Alcuin. 'It seems a lot more extraordinary than a unicorn,' I commented.

'That is not your concern, Sigwulf. What matters is that the king believes the creature may exist.'

'Do you think that there's really such an animal as a griffin?' I asked him.

Alcuin permitted himself a delicate shrug. 'If there is, and you find one, then you will have added to our knowledge of the creatures God placed on this earth. Another wonder of God's creation.'

I thought his reply was tactful but still sceptical.

'Is this an exact copy of the bestiary that Carolus showed me?' I was itching to look through the bestiary at my leisure and to discover what other bizarre and strange animals were thought to exist.

'The copyists had permission to add creatures shown in other books in the palace library.'

I closed the book gently and carefully so as not to distort the fresh stitching. 'In Kaupang a hunter told me about a wondrous bird that has a beak striped with all the colours of the rainbow. That would make a very striking gift between monarchs.'

'I'm sure the caliph already has more than enough parrots in his zoo,' said Alcuin drily.

'Not a parrot. A sea bird that eats fish and lives in cliffs. It flutters its wings so fast that, in flight, it flies like a bee. My informant couldn't tell me its Frankish name.'

'And it tastes delicious,' interrupted Alcuin.

'That's right! Dark flesh, with a flavour like pigeon.'

Alcuin broke into a sudden, boyish grin. It was something I had never seen before. 'In my youth I spent three years at a monastery on a remote island off the coast of north Britain. In spring time we caught and ate those birds by the dozen, their eggs too. But I don't think you'll find them illustrated in that book. They're called puffins.'

I must have looked crestfallen because he added, not unkindly, 'And that gaudy beak is only colourful in summer. The rest of the year it looks very ordinary.'

I thought back to the white furs I had seen in Kaupang's market, winter furs from creatures that wore much more drab colours for the rest of the year. It occurred to me that animals, like humans, could deceptively change to suit the occasion.

Alcuin was still chuckling when there was a discreet knock on his door. He gestured at me to open it. A chancery clerk was standing on the threshold, soberly dressed in a brown tunic, grey leggings and lightweight summer shoes. Then I noticed that his clothes were of very expensive fabric and beautifully cut. He was in his late thirties, of about my own height, slim and fit-looking. From a cap of short black curls to the beardless, fine-boned face with its pointed chin, everything about him was neat and self-contained.

'Come in, Abram,' said Alcuin from behind me. 'I want you to meet Sigwulf. The two of you will be in one another's company for many weeks. I'm sure you will get along well.'

The newcomer's brown eyes rested for the barest fraction of a moment on the book in my hand, before he gave me a pleasant open smile, showing small, even teeth, and said, 'I understand you have just returned from a most successful venture to the Northlands, a region I would dearly love to visit. Perhaps you will be able to tell me all about it.'

Maybe it was because he reminded me of Osric, my closest friend, that I took an instant liking to Abram. They both had the same quietly intelligent look, the same dark skin and fine features and self-assured poise, though of course Abram was many years younger and did not have Osric's lop-sided stance with his damaged neck and badly set leg.

'It'll be the other way round, Sigwulf,' observed Alcuin as the visitor joined us. 'I doubt anyone has travelled to more countries than Abram has. He's more likely to be telling you about foreign countries. How many languages do you speak, Abram?'

The newcomer spread his hands in a depreciating gesture. 'Just a few.' His Frankish was perfect, without the trace of an accent.

'Just a few with absolute fluency, you mean,' chided Alcuin. He turned to me. 'Abram speaks a dozen languages well, and I suspect he has a working knowledge of the same number again. He's being modest.'

Abram deflected the compliment with a slight shrug. 'I hope to be more successful as a dragoman for Sigwulf than I was in delivering a live elephant to King Carolus.'

'A dragoman? That's a word I've not heard before,' I said.

He turned to me and there was a twinkle in his eye as he made a small circling motion with his right hand, touching first his chest and then his brow. 'In Rome you may call me your "dragumannus", in Arab lands your "tarjuman", and if we reach the realm of the Khazars, a "tercuman".'

He had succeeded in making me laugh. 'Plain Frankish will do for now.'

'Then I am your dragoman. I'm sure you noticed the similarity between the different words. They all have the same meaning: someone who acts as guide and interpreter.'

Abram's mention of the elephant prompted me to ask Alcuin about the condition of the aurochs that had cost Vulfard his life.

'It left Aachen the same day that we received word that you

had got back. The plan is to assemble all your animals at Dorestad and to take them by water as far as possible. It makes their transport easier.'

The bell for tierce tolled faintly, the sound muffled by the substantial brick walls of the chancery. 'Time for chapel,' said Alcuin. He handed me a single sheet of vellum, rolled and sealed, which had been lying among the documents on his desk. 'Here's the letter for my friend in Rome. His name is Paul. He works for Pope Adrian as his Nomenculator.'

'Nomenculator?' I asked.

'The official who deals with requests for favours from the pope.' Alcuin got to his feet. 'Let's hope that you don't have to call upon his professional intervention.'

He accompanied Abram and myself out into the corridor. 'Sigwulf, the chancery is finalizing your travel documents. Carolus has designated you as his special envoy. He is determined that your embassy is a success.'

There was an awkward pause as Alcuin hesitated. The sound of the church bell came from our right, from the basilica. To the left lay the offices of the chancery. I realized that Alcuin was giving me a chance to accompany him to the church service. When I made no move, he pulled the door closed behind us, turned on his heel abruptly and strode off, sandals clacking on the stone flags. I had a shrewd idea he was disappointed: he would have preferred an ardent Christian to be taking Carolus's gifts to the caliph. But Abram was an Israelite and Osric's origins were in Hispania. If the white animals did reach Baghdad, they would be brought before the caliph by a Jew, a Saracen and someone who was not even a churchgoer.

Chapter Seven

I SPENT MOST OF the next day alternately arguing and pleading with the treasury's senior bookkeeper. A stickler for detail, he demanded full and proper accounts for the funds I had taken to Kaupang. When I was unable to provide them, he showed his displeasure by restricting the amount of silver allowed for the new mission. He provided instead a document authorizing me to requisition supplies from royal stores along the road. I considered going directly to Carolus to put a stop to this bureaucratic nonsense but was wary of being seen again in the royal apartments. There was too much risk of encountering Princess Bertha, and early the following morning I slipped out from Aachen feeling relieved that I had avoided her. I was on my way to rejoin Osric and the others. As arranged, Abram was waiting for me an hour's brisk ride along the now-familiar road. With him were three mounted servants in charge of half a dozen packhorses. The men had the vigilant yet patient manner of seasoned travellers and I guessed they were Abram's regular attendants.

'I hope we don't run out of money,' I confided to Abram after explaining my tussles with the skinflint in the treasury.

'I can arrange cash for us along the way,' he answered.

'As far as Baghdad?'

He gave an easy smile. 'As far as necessary.'

The sun was burning off the dawn mist and the day promised to be blisteringly hot. The horse provided to me by the royal stables had already worked up a sweat and we paused for a few minutes to allow the animal to cool down. The dragoman took the opportunity to introduce his attendants to me. One of them was a cook, good at producing a decent campfire meal, and another was handy with making running repairs to the tents and other equipment strapped to the horses. There was no need to ask about the third man. He had a serviceable-looking sword dangling from his saddle and was evidently a bodyguard. Never before had I felt so well prepared when starting on a journey.

'Does your cook prepare special meals for you?' I asked as we moved off at a gentle amble. It was a leading question for I was curious to know more about my travelling companion. I presumed his attendants were his co-religionists but he had made no mention of the fact.

'I try to follow the dietary laws of my faith,' Abram replied. 'Fortunately, Radhanites are allowed broad dispensation due to our wandering way of life.'

He turned in the saddle to check on our little pack train, and I stole a sideways glance at my companion. He rode well, his handsome face alert as he watched the passing traffic.

'Alcuin told me about the constant wayfaring, but that's almost all he knew about your people.'

The dragoman showed no sign of resentment of my probing. 'We originated in Mesopotamia many centuries ago, according to one theory. Others say that we came out of Persia.'

'What do you believe?'

'Under the present circumstances I prefer Persia. In that country's language "rah" means a path and "dan" is one who knows. So a Radhanite is "one who knows the way".'

'Then Persian is one of those dozen languages that Alcuin said you speak.'

He acknowledged the compliment with a graceful shrug. 'Once you've acquired six or seven languages, the rest come easily.'

'I've yet to reach that stage.'

'So Frankish is not your mother tongue?' He regarded me with polite interest.

I shook my head. 'No, I grew up speaking Saxon. I learned Latin as a child, Frankish and Arabic later.'

'Then, like me, you are a wanderer.'

'Not by choice,' I admitted, and found myself confiding to him how Offa had forced me into exile.

He heard me out, his expression turning to one of sympathy. When I finished I realized that instead of learning more about Abram, it was the reverse.

'Is there anything about our mission that worries you?' I asked him, hoping to divert the conversation back to what I had intended.

'Getting the animals across the Alps before the first snowfall of winter,' he said, guiding his horse around a deep rut in the road surface.

'The ice bears would enjoy seeing some snow,' I said cheerfully. I was relaxed and carefree, happy at the thought that I had a dragoman to recommend how far to travel each day, where to spend the night and find our food.

'You might consider taking a different route, avoiding the mountains entirely.' He made the suggestion diffidently.

'The royal chancery decided we go by river barge along the Rhine as far as possible. At some stage we'll shift the animals onto carts and haul them over the mountain passes.'

Abram sighed. 'The Arabs have a saying: "Only a madman or a Christian sails against the wind." It seems that a Christian also chooses to travel against the current.'

'Is there an alternative?'

'You could use the river Rhone instead . . . and have the current help you.'

I wondered if this was an excuse for Abram to be among his own people. Alcuin had said that the Radhanites in Frankia clustered along the Rhone. 'Let's see how far Osric and Walo have already taken the animals along the Rhine before we change our plans,' I replied cautiously.

*

The sound alerted me three days later – a familiar yowling and yapping. The noise came from the direction of a low ridge that ran parallel to the highway, the width of a field away. We turned aside and when we topped the slope, found ourselves on the crest of an artificial earth embankment built to protect the neighbouring fields from flood. In front of us was the broad river, and we were looking down on a barge firmly stuck on a shoal a few yards out. The two ice bears were in their cage at one end of the vessel. The aurochs occupied a larger, heavier cage at the opposite end. The dogs were tethered between them, tied to a thick rope. They were jumping up and down, quarrelling and lunging at one another, tangling their leashes, and ignoring Osric's shouts of exasperation. Walo was nowhere to be seen. Closer at hand, standing on the muddy foreshore, was a huddle of what I took to be the barge men. They looked disgruntled and mutinous.

Osric glanced up and saw me. With a final angry yell at the dogs, he clambered over the side of the barge and squelched his way across the ooze to come to speak with me.

'Didn't expect you back so soon,' he said. His legs were slathered to the knees with grey sludge.

'Where's Walo?' I asked, dismounting.

Osric gestured upriver. 'He's gone ahead with a cart. Took the gyrfalcons with him.'

A sudden apprehension gripped me. 'You didn't let him go off on his own? Anything might happen.'

My friend was calm. 'He's training the birds. He does that every day. Says that they need exercise or they will lose condition. He's got them flying on a length of line, and coming back to a lure. Besides, one of the barge men went with him, to find some oxen.'

'They'll need at least twenty,' said Abram. He too had got down from his horse and was standing beside me.

Osric had begun scraping the mud off his legs with a twig. 'The barge men say that we can rely on the flood tide only for another fifty miles or so. After that, we'll have to haul and row the barge,' he said.

In a language I did not understand, Abram called back to his servants waiting at a discreet distance. One of them slid from the saddle, handed the reins of his horse to a companion, unlaced a bundle attached to a pack saddle, and hurried forward with a small folding table.

As the servant opened up the table and set it firmly on the ground, I caught Osric's eye. 'Abram has been appointed as dragoman to our embassy,' I explained.

Abram removed a leather tube from his own saddlebag, and extracted a scroll wound around two slim batons of polished wood. When the servant had withdrawn, he rolled the parchment from one baton to the next – it must have been thirty feet long at least – until he came to the section he wanted, then placed the scroll face up on the table. The parchment was sprinkled with tiny symbols carefully drawn and coloured. The most frequent symbol was a double-fronted house, its twin roofs coloured red. A number of oddly elongated dark brown shapes resembled thin loaves, and a few drawings looked like large stylized barns. Many symbols were linked, one to the next, by thin straight lines ruled in vermilion ink. Near these lines were written numerals in Roman script.

'We are here,' Abram said, placing a finger beside a double-fronted house. Next to it in small, neat lettering was written 'Dorestadum'.

It was an itinerarium, a road map, something I had heard of but never seen until this moment. An itinerarium was greatly prized, and I doubted if even the royal archive in Aachen possessed such a treasure.

'How far does your itinerarium extend?' I enquired. I noted that Abram had taken care to reveal only a small portion of the scroll.

The dragoman rewarded my knowledge of the map's name with a slight smile. 'My people would not thank me if I told you. They spent generations in assembling the information it contains.'

He turned his attention back to the map. 'Here we are, still close to Dorestad. This red line –' his finger slid across the surface of the map – 'is the route that the chancery in Aachen would have us take. Here we would leave the Rhine and continue along this next red line up through these mountain ranges marked in brown, and down into Italy, and finally to Rome.' His finger came to rest on a symbol, larger and grander than the others. It showed a crowned man seated on a throne holding a sceptre and an orb. Clearly the pope.

Osric was quick. 'Those numbers marked beside the road are the distances between the towns, I presume.'

'Or the number of days' travel required for each sector,' answered the dragoman. He shot me a mischievous grin. 'In Persia the distances are stated in parasangs, not miles.'

'What are you proposing?' I asked. From where I stood I could see that the short wavy blue-green lines represented the course of rivers. Areas painted a dark green were the sea. Every feature was distorted and out of shape, stretched in some places, compressed in others, so as to fit on the scroll. It was not so much a map as a stylized diagram that showed what mattered to a traveller – the important locations and the distances in between.

Abram looked down at the diagram. 'The further we proceed up the Rhine, the stronger the current will run against us. We cover less distance each day and risk reaching the Alpine passes when they are closed by snow.'

He traced a thin red line that went south-eastward. 'I recommend that we leave the Rhine at the tidal limit and go by waggon along this road to a different river, the Rhone. That river flows in our favour.'

I interrupted him. 'What about the difficulty of transferring the animals from one river to the other?'

'The road between the rivers is suitable for wheeled vehicles. It crosses low hills and rolling countryside, not mountains.'

His reasoning was sound, and yet I was reluctant to be persuaded. 'Every extra mile by land means additional costs – relays of oxen, fodder to feed them, wages for waggon drivers. Our resources may not be sufficient,' I told him.

His response was to point to a symbol on the parchment. It depicted a substantial building arranged around a hollow square. Even without the arches of what could only be a cloister, it was clearly the symbol for a monastery. I ran my eye along the new route Abram proposed. I counted five monasteries spaced at convenient intervals. I smiled to myself. I had told Abram about the skinflint in the royal treasury. The bookkeeper would regret giving me the written authority to requisition stores along my route. Every abbot in Frankia was obliged to obey that royal writ, and then reclaim the cost from the king. By the time I had finished providing for my waggon train that document would drain more money from the treasury than if the accountant had given me the silver I wanted.

Abram sensed that he had made his point. 'At the mouth of the Rhone we charter a ship to take us directly to Rome's port. The voyage lasts no more than four or five days,' he said.

Osric cleared his throat. 'The Rhone empties into the Mediterranean not so far from the territory of the emir of Cordoba.'

I recalled Alcuin's warning that the emir was a bitter rival of the caliph in Baghdad, and if the emir could interfere with our mission, he would do so.

Abram was unconcerned. 'When we reach the mouth of the Rhone, my contacts there will tell me if the emir's ships are too great a risk.'

Osric was still cautious. 'And if we cannot continue by sea?'

The dragoman fluttered a hand dismissively. 'Then we follow the example of the great Hannibal. He came out of Hispania with his elephants, crossed the Rhone and took his elephants to Italy through the mountains. The southern Alpine passes are easier than those that the chancery in Aachen wants us to use.'

Abram began putting away the itinerarium. 'When I was preparing to bring the caliph's elephant from Baghdad to Frankia, I studied Hannibal's route. I was thinking of using it, but in reverse. Unfortunately, I never got the chance.'

He slid the scroll back into its leather tube with a gesture of finality and turned to face me. 'Sigwulf, the route is your decision.'

Involuntarily, I glanced down at the aurochs, still standing in its enclosure on the barge. After months of captivity, the huge animal was still angry and dangerous. It bellowed and flung itself from side to side, trying to get free.

I made up my mind. 'I accept Abram's suggestion. We go along the Rhine only as far as the tide can help us. Then we head south overland and follow the Rhone to the sea.'

There was little point in having a dragoman, I told myself, if one ignored his advice.

*

Abram sent his men ahead to make the arrangements. By the time our barge reached the Rhine's tidal limit, they had paid carpenters to strengthen a massive four-wheeled farm waggon to carry the aurochs in its cage. Wheelwrights widened the axles so that the vehicle would not tip over when the beast thrashed about. A similar waggon for the ice bears was only slightly smaller. A team of four draught animals would pull each vehicle. A further three carts of a more normal size would carry stores and food. Nothing had been overlooked. There was even a lad hired to scurry up and down our line of waggons with a brush and a bucket of wool grease, daubing the grease on the axles so that they turned smoothly.

We lost no time in taking to the road. Our progress, after we had climbed from the river valley, was stately. We seldom covered more than a dozen miles each day, proceeding at a steady walk. The weather was glorious, with day after day of summer sunshine. As Abram had promised, the route was undemanding. Great tracts of rolling countryside presented little difficulty to the plodding oxen. July was the time for haymaking so their fodder was readily available. The meadows were full of workers scything the long grass, turning and stacking it when dry. The monasteries along our path owned extensive lands, and I had only to produce my letter from the royal treasury for the local steward to supply whatever we needed – loaves, ale and wine for the men, meat for the bears and dogs, pigeon breasts and day-old chicks to feed to the gyrfalcons. Each day we set out an hour after first light, rested at noon, then walked until the sun was halfway down to the horizon. One of Abram's servants rode ahead. He identified the open ground for us to stop and rest the animals for the noontime halt. He also made sure that water was available in a nearby stream or pond or drawn from a well by local people whom he paid in advance for their labour. When we reached our chosen camping place each evening, it was to find our tents had been erected and a cooked meal was waiting for us.

Men and animals thrived. Walo made wicker cages for the falcons. By day they were hung from a framework on one of the carts. At night he covered the cages with dark cloths. His training of them progressed so well that whenever we stopped, he could fly them off his hand and let them fly free for exercise before attracting them back with a morsel of fresh meat. He also fitted the five white dogs with collars and each animal was attached by its lead to a different vehicle so it, too, was properly exercised. In the evening after they had been fed, they were tied to stakes placed just far enough apart so they could not fight. The aurochs remained as truculent as ever, attempting to attack anyone who came close to its cage. It was extremely dangerous to feed and water the beast, and clear out its vast piles of dung. But the job had to be done.

Most of all, Walo concentrated on tending to his beloved bears. Try as I might, I still found it difficult to identify which was Madi and which was Modi. To me they looked alike and I saw no difference in their behaviour. Fortunately, they adapted to the summer heat. They kept their appetites and, with shade and water within their cage, they showed no sign of distress. Walo fed and brushed them, played them tunes on his wooden pipe until they laid their heads on their paws and slept for hour after hour.

I envied them. Despite the idyllic conditions I was plagued by disturbing dreams. In the four weeks it took us to make our ponderous way across country to the Rhone, there was scarcely a night when I did not wake up in the darkness, my heart pounding, covered in sweat. Occasionally, I was shouting in panic. My nightmares always concerned an elephant. Sometimes I was riding on its back, high above the ground, feeling the creature sway beneath me as we moved across a depressing, broken landscape of grey rocks and harsh mountains. The motion made me feel giddy and I would wake up nauseous. In other dreams I was on the ground and the elephant was deliberately trying to trample me. I would turn and run for my life, pursued by the monstrous, enraged beast.

My nightmares often woke Osric and Walo, who shared a tent with me. Neither of them said anything until one evening shortly before we reached the Rhone. We had completed our day's journey a little earlier than usual. Our road lay through an extensive forest of oak and beech and we had come upon a broad clearing where a spring of clean water had been chan-nelled into a pool lined with stone slabs. Charred marks of campfires showed that previous travellers had rested there before us. Very soon our waggons and carts were drawn up in a neat line, the draught oxen unyoked, and all our animals had been taken care of. There were several hours of daylight left, so we were relaxing in the last rays of sunshine before the shadows from the surrounding trees spread across the clearing. All traffic along the road had ceased, and the place was so quiet that I could hear the low mutter of the ox drivers talking among themselves as they prepared to spread their bedding rolls beneath the carts. Even the white dogs had fallen silent.

'I think I'll sleep under the stars tonight,' Osric commented, treating me to a meaningful glance. He, Walo and I were sitting by the embers of the campfire. We had finished our supper and Abram, who preferred to take his meals with his own men, had just rejoined us.

'I'm the one who should sleep outside,' I said. 'There's not much I can do about those dreams.'

'What dreams are those?' Abram asked.

I told him briefly about the elephant.

The dragoman smiled apologetically. 'That was my fault. I shouldn't have brought up the subject of Hannibal and his elephants.'

'What's an elephant?' interrupted Walo. He had been listening in.

'An elephant is a remarkable animal that the great ruler of the Saracens sent as a gift to Carolus,' I told him.

Walo's voice had been hesitant but his half-closed eyes were bright with interest.

'Some say that it is the largest animal that walks on land,' I added.

'Even larger than that one there?' Walo gestured towards the aurochs in its cage.

'Yes, much, much larger.'

'What does it look like?'

I started to explain what I knew about an elephant, its size and shape, but my words soon petered out. I had never seen the living animal and, for me, everything was hearsay. Abram was looking on with an amused expression.

'Our dragoman can explain better than me,' I was forced to admit.

Abraham chuckled. 'I doubt I could paint a word picture that would do justice to the strangeness of the elephant. For a start, its nose reaches to the ground and can be used as an extra hand.'

'You're making fun of me,' Walo said. He sounded hurt.

Abram's statement reminded me that there was a painted illustration of an elephant in the bestiary that Carolus had given me. Until now I had kept the volume carefully protected in my saddlebag. With a guilty pang I realized that I had never really explained to Vulfard's son what had led up to his father's gruesome death and why we were now halfway across Frankia. This was my chance to begin to do so. I went to our tent and brought back the book.

I had wrapped it for safety in a long length of heavily waxed linen. With great care I removed the layers. Walo came across and looked over my shoulder as I opened the cover of the book and turned the pages. The elephant was the sixth illustration. The copyist had drawn two elephants facing one another across a stream. They were coloured a sombre green. They had large, doleful eyes, white curving tusks, and their trunks were about to touch. I presumed they were male and female.

I heard Walo take an excited breath. 'Their noses look like trumpets, not hands,' he announced.

The artist had drawn the trunks so that they splayed at the tip like a musical instrument.

'Rightly so,' said Abram from the other side of the fire. 'If you've heard the voice of an angry elephant, you'll remember it for the rest of your life. It's like the hoarse blare of a giant trumpet, far louder and more fearsome than anything you have ever heard.'

Walo could not tear his eyes away from the drawing. 'If the

elephant is so big and dangerous, how did they manage to catch it so that it could be given to Carolus?'

I wondered if he was thinking of his father and the deadly pitfall in the forest. Below each picture in the bestiary a brief paragraph gave selected details about the animal:

'*The elephant has no joints in its legs,*' I read aloud, '*so it never lies down because it would be unable to get back on its feet. When it sleeps it leans against a tree for support. The hunters cut part way through the tree so that it topples over when the elephant rests against it, and the elephant falls. Then the hunters secure the helpless elephant.*'

I heard a barely stifled snort of disbelief from Abram on the other side of the fire. It occurred to me that the hunters would still need some way of getting the captive elephant back on its feet. Perhaps they dug out a sloping pit in much the same way we had handled the aurochs.

Walo reached out a hand to touch the picture with a grubby finger and hastily I moved the precious volume out of his reach. 'It is also written,' I told him, 'that an elephant lives for three hundred years, and is afraid of mice.'

'What else does the book claim?' asked Osric. I glanced across at him. He, too, wore a rather sceptical expression.

I read aloud further. '*The female elephant carries her unborn child within her for two years. When she is ready to give birth, she stands in a pool up to her belly. The male elephant remains on the bank and guards her against attack from the elephant's most deadly enemy, the dragon.*'

'Will I get to see a dragon on this journey?' asked Walo in an awed tone.

One of Abram's servants was approaching. He bent down to murmur in his master's ear. Abram rose to his feet. 'Please excuse me, there is something I must attend to.' Turning to

Walo, he said, 'I can't promise you will meet a dragon on this journey, but you will see something almost as extraordinary: men riding in small houses fastened to the back of the elephant.'

Walo waited until Abram was out of earshot before asking me, 'Is that really true, Sigwulf? Men living on top of elephants?'

I remembered Hannibal's story. 'They don't live there. They climb up before a battle, and wage war as if from a moving castle.'

Carefully I shut the bestiary, preparing to wrap it up again safely. The copyists in the royal chancery had been in a hurry. The stitches holding the pages together were uneven, and the book closed awkwardly, the covers slightly askew. Gently I opened the book once more, to straighten the pages.

'There's our beast from the forest!' exclaimed Walo.

He was pointing at a picture of a strange-looking creature. At first sight it did resemble the aurochs, for it had a bull's head and body, four cloven hooves, and a long whiplash of a tail ending in a tuft of hair. Like our aurochs, too, the animal had enormous horns and there was an angry glare in its eyes. The copyist had coloured it a rich chestnut brown.

'What does the book say?' asked Walo excitedly.

I consulted the description. 'It's called a bonnacon. It's not the same as our aurochs.'

'Are you sure?' Walo sounded disappointed.

'According to this book, the bonnacon's horns curl backwards so far that they are useless as weapons. The animal cannot defend itself with them.'

Walo giggled. He had noticed a comical human figure in the picture. A man dressed as a hunter was shown standing behind the rump of the bonnacon, his face was wrinkled in disgust. 'Why's he holding his nose?' he asked.

'According to the book, when the bonnacon is chased, it runs away at great speed deliberately shooting quantities of dung from its backside. The dung has a ferocious smell and burns anyone it touches.'

There was a furious outburst of barking from the tethered dogs. One of them had slipped its collar and was snapping and snarling at its neighbour. Walo jumped to his feet and ran off to deal with the situation.

Osric stretched and yawned. 'I've never seen Walo so animated. The pictures in the book draw him out. Perhaps you should show more of them to him when you have time . . .'

He waited until I had closed the bestiary and carefully wrapped it back inside the stiff linen cover, then added, 'Have you checked our pages from the Oneirokritikon for the meaning of those elephant dreams that have been troubling you?'

'There's nothing,' I answered, rather more abruptly than I intended.

Osric and I had agreed that our fragments from the Book of Dreams were too valuable to leave behind in an empty house in Aachen. They were hidden in the outer, double folds of the same heavy linen wrapper that protected the bestiary.

Osric frowned, searching his memory. 'Dreams of elephants were mentioned somewhere. Maybe in the complete version of the book. I remember translating them. What precisely have you been dreaming?'

'Mostly, that I was riding on the back of an elephant. But sometimes the animal is trying to stamp me into the ground,' I told him.

My friend thought for a moment. 'If I remember correctly, to dream of riding on an elephant means you will meet someone of great power and influence, a king or an emperor.'

'That sounds promising,' I said with more than a touch of

sarcasm. My vivid dreams were not only worrying. They meant that I had been losing sleep. 'Maybe we will get to meet the caliph in person. What about the dream of being attacked by an elephant?'

Osric ignored my ill humour. He was serious. 'If the elephant succeeds in crushing the dreamer, it foretells an early death. But if the dreamer evades the attack, it means the dreamer will face great danger yet escape with his life.'

'I wake up before the dream elephant squashes me to pulp,' I said. His words left me uneasy, and at that moment I felt the sudden sting of a biting fly on my neck. I reached up and slapped it. My hand came away with a tiny smear of blood and, despite my outward bravado, I wondered if it too was an omen.

My friend glanced across to where Walo had succeeded in calming the quarrelling dogs. 'Did anything come of your dream of Walo with those wolves and the bees?' he asked.

It was my chance to tell Osric that the bees foretold Walo's death. But I shied away from admitting that earlier I had kept the truth from my friend. Instead I described how the sight of Walo in Kaupang seated between the ice bears in Ohthere's bear pen was the fulfilment of my vision.

Osric heard me out in silence. 'And now? Does anyone else appear in your elephant dreams? Like Walo with those wolves?'

'Abram. I see him climbing onto the carcass of a long-dead elephant and delving through a slit in the grey skin. Then he pulls out great long white bones.'

A look of relief crossed my friend's face. 'Surely that dream is about the past, not the future. It's about the death of the elephant that Abram was bringing to Carolus.'

There was a sudden flicker in the air as a bat swooped over the dying fire in pursuit of a flying insect. The night was drawing in. Though the air was still warm, I shivered. 'I think

I'll stay in the tent after all. It'll save me from the midges,' I said as I got to my feet.

I made my way back to the tent, carrying the bestiary; something was nagging at the back of my mind. I crawled into our tent, slipped the book inside my saddlebag, and was fastening down the flap when, all of a sudden, I had a faint recollection that the Oneirokritikon did offer an explanation about elephant bones: someone seen extracting the bones from a dead elephant in a dream meant that the person would make a great profit from an endeavour. I racked my brains, wondering how the prediction might make sense. Then, in a flash of understanding, I knew: Abram was using our embassy as an opportunity to line his pockets. That explained the six laden pack ponies on the day he met me on the road outside Aachen, and the extra waggons hired for the overland journey to the Rhone. Our dragoman was carrying his own private trade goods, buying and selling as we travelled. As I tied the final knot in the leather lace, I wondered what items Abram was carrying that were so profitable. I decided I would not ask. If Abram wanted to keep his business dealings a secret from me, that was his affair. The dream of Abram and elephant bones was an omen. If he was to make a great deal of money from our journey then that, in turn, implied that our embassy would be a success.

That night, my mind at ease, I slept so deeply that Osric had to shake me awake when it was time to get up. He made some light-hearted remark that he and Walo had finally got a good night's rest, without my wild dreams to disturb them. None of us could have anticipated that what lay ahead was to be as bad as any nightmare.

Chapter Eight

IN THE LAST WEEK OF August a broken bridge halted us. The crumbling stone structure looked as if it dated back to Roman times. The central arch had collapsed into the river below, cutting the road. Several flatboats were drawn up on the gravel bank, ready to serve as ferries. Their narrow shapes reminded me of weavers' shuttles. Each had an ingenious arrangement so that the blunt bow and stern could be lowered to form a ramp and carts could be wheeled aboard. Worryingly, our oversize waggon for the aurochs appeared to be too wide to fit. Abram went forward to talk with the boatmen and when he came back after some time, I was surprised to see that he had a pleased look on his face and was carrying his itinerarium.

'Let me show you where we are,' he said to me, unrolling a section of the drawing and laying it out on the tailboard of the nearest cart. 'This dark wavy line is the river ahead of us. Our road meets it at a point close to where you see that symbol for a monastery.'

He unrolled the itinerarium another few inches. 'If you follow the line of the river you will note that it soon joins a larger one. That in turn flows into the Rhone.'

'You're suggesting that we travel by water once again?' I asked. 'The river here looks too small to be navigable.'

'I've checked with the ferrymen. They say that last spring

there was much rain, and there is still enough depth of water to take their craft downstream.'

I took a second look at the river. It ran sluggishly, its murky water an opaque green. 'Where do we find boats?'

He pointed with his chin towards the waiting ferries. 'With a little modification, those are suitable.'

I was still dubious and must have showed it in my expression because Abram quickly added, 'The local monastery owns the bridge and charges a toll to use it. But the monks have discovered that they can make more money by collecting fares for the ferry. The boatmen are obliged to work for the monastery a certain number of days each year, and they resent it. Several of them are willing to work for us.'

He gave me a sideways look. 'If the monks lose their boats, they'll be obliged to repair the bridge. You would be doing a service to other travellers.'

I had to smile at his deviousness. 'I'll go to see the abbot.'

As it turned out, the abbot was away on business. I met instead his deputy, the cellarer. A small, timid man, he was suffering from hay fever and used his gown's sleeve to wipe his streaming eyes as he read my letter from the palace treasurer. When I asked to be provided with the ferries, he let out a tremendous sneeze, then two more in quick succession, before recovering enough to tell me that first he had to consult with the abbot. I stressed that I was on royal business and short of time. I cautioned that, if necessary, I would simply commandeer the boats. He released another massive sneeze and used his sleeve again, this time to staunch his runny nose. It would be simpler, I suggested, if he agreed to my request and sent a claim for compensation to the king's treasury. In a gesture of goodwill I offered to leave our horses with the monastery since they were no longer required. His eyes filled with tears and his chest heaved as I waited patiently for his answer. He was helpless, sucking in air before the next volcanic sneeze. All he wanted was for me to leave him in peace. He waved one hand at me in desperation. I took it as his agreement and left.

As soon as I got back to the others, Abram set about organizing our transfer into the boats. Two were fastened side by side to make a surface wide enough to carry the aurochs' waggon. Supervised by Abram's attendants, a team of ox drivers backed the waggon down the riverbank and manoeuvred the vehicle aboard. The boatmen then removed the large solid wheels and, with a series of levers, carefully lowered the cage with the aurochs inside it to sit firmly on the platform. Next it was the turn of the ice bears in their waggon to be placed on a second boat – again the wheels were removed in what seemed to be a lengthy and needless operation but the ferrymen insisted it was done. By the time they were satisfied the light was fading, and we set up camp and held a farewell feast for the ox drivers.

The men built an enormous bonfire on the riverbank, and sat around it, guzzling their rations and swilling vast amounts of ale as if determined to bring home their carts completely bare. As the night closed in, sparks from the bonfire swirled up, carried high in the still air, their pinpricks of light reflected on the black surface of the river. Abram had paid them well, and there was a carnival atmosphere. The men shouted and guffawed, their local dialect impossible to understand. Someone produced a flute and began a tune to which the others sang drunkenly or banged on makeshift drums. Men stood up shakily and started to stamp and dance. The noise threatened to give me a headache so I left the circle around the bonfire and made my way down to the water's edge. The summer night was very warm and I was wearing a light shirt. Through the thin cloth I touched the thin scar on my side where the would-be killer in

Kaupang had missed with his knife. The wound was scarcely tender. Osric had cleaned it well. I wondered yet again whether the attack had been directed at me in person or was something to do with Carolus's embassy to the caliph. If King Offa had been behind the attempt to have me killed, every mile was taking me further from his reach. But if the Greeks in Constantinople had been responsible, then I should be increasingly wary as we travelled eastward.

Out of the corner of my eye I became aware of two figures weaving their way down the slope of the riverbank. Two ox drivers were stumbling towards the boats. They had the loose-kneed, lurching shamble of men who were very drunk, and occasionally they clutched one another to stop falling over. A snatch of drunken laughter reached me. My stomach gave a sudden lurch as it became clear that they were heading towards the boat with the ice bears' cage. They had to be intercepted. I scrambled up the bank, looking for Walo. I saw him at once. He was seated by the fire, playing his deerhorn pipe, his head wagging loosely from side to side to the rhythm of the music. It was clear that he too was completely drunk. There was no sign of Osric and I presumed he had gone off to our tent. There was no time to find him so I turned on my heel and set off at a run towards the boats. Ahead of me the two drunkards had already climbed aboard the boat and were standing next to the ice bears' cage. In the flickering light of the bonfire's flames they were capering stupidly, dancing and calling out to the bears, encouraging them to join in. I suppose they must have seen a travelling showman with a dancing bear and imagined that Modi and Madi would oblige them.

Desperately I hurled myself down the slope of the bank, shouting at them to stand clear of the cage. They did not hear me. One of the men stopped his capering and, egged on by his companion, he leaned up against the cage, thrust his arm between the bars and beckoned. Modi and Madi were already on their feet. The noise and music from the campfire had roused them. Behind me the flames flared up and in a sudden wash of brighter light I could see the two ice bears staring intently at the intruder. Their eyes were distinct black dots in their white faces. My shouts died in my throat as I recalled the foolish dog in Kaupang whose face had been slashed by the claws of an ice bear cub when he came too close. Modi and Madi were no longer cubs. Half-grown, each was bigger than a bull calf, and infinitely more dangerous.

I was too late.

With a deep-throated growl, one of the bears sprang forward. There was a glimpse of bared teeth and the jaws closed on the out-thrust arm. At the same moment the second bear rose on its hind legs and flung itself against the bars, seeking to attack the second reveller. The boat rocked with the force of the impact.

A terrible shriek cut through the blare of singing and drunken music. Behind me the noise of celebration faltered, then died away. Instead there was scream upon scream of pain, and a low-pitched growling, an awful sound, as the bear – I guessed it was Modi the angry – tugged and twisted at the human arm and tried to drag its owner into the cage. The other bear, Madi the strong, kept dropping back on all fours, then rising up again and hurling his weight against the bars, roaring as he batted with his front paws, trying to reach the other drunkard.

The bile rose in my throat. I was only a few yards away but felt helpless. The entire cage was shaking. Ripples spread as the boat rocked. The agonized screams made it impossible for me to think clearly. Several heartbeats later, someone ran past me –

Abram. He was holding a flaming branch that he must have snatched from the bonfire. He jumped onto the boat and thrust the brand between the bars, and straight into Madi's muzzle. By then the bear's victim was no longer standing, but slumped on his knees, his shoulder and arm pulled between the bars of the cage.

Abram was yelling at the top of his voice, jabbing at the bear with the flaming timber. On his right the second bear, Modi, continued to roar, swatting at the bars.

Reluctantly, Madi opened his jaws and released his grip on the mangled arm. Then the bear half-rose on its hind legs, spun round clumsily and retreated to the back of the cage. I stumbled forward, alongside Abram, and reached down to drag the bear's victim clear. Between us we carried the badly injured drunkard away and up the bank, his damaged arm hanging uselessly. Behind us Modi flung himself three or four more times against the bars, then he, too, dropped back on all fours, and began to pace up and down. Abram and I carried the moaning ox driver to the campsite and laid him on the bed of an empty cart. The arm was crushed; white bone gleamed through the mangled flesh. His comrades, suddenly sober, clustered round and clumsily tried to help. Osric arrived to wash the wounds as best he could and swathe the arm in tight bandages. An hour later a team of oxen was yoked and the cart had been driven away into the darkness, heading for the monastery infirmary.

*

Next morning the men were hung over and still in shock. They went about their work in silence, ashamed and morose. To add to the sombre mood the day was sultry and oppressive, heavy with the threat of a storm.

Walo also looked worse for wear, bleary eyed and pale. I did not have the heart to reprimand him for leaving the ice bears unattended. I suspected that the ox drivers had deliberately plied him with strong drink for their own amusement. Together we went to check on the ice bears in daylight. Both were asleep in their cage.

'Be careful with Madi,' I said. 'Abram poked him in the face with a firebrand to make him let go of his victim last night.' I could see a burn mark and a black streak of soot on the bear's muzzle.

'That's Modi,' Walo corrected me.

I looked again. 'But I thought that Madi was the angry one.'

'That's Modi,' Walo insisted. Ignoring me, he pulled out the peg that locked the heavy iron hasp that secured the door to the cage. I took a deep breath and told myself not to interfere. When it came to understanding and handling animals, I had to trust Walo's instincts.

I looked on as he swung open the door, climbed into the cage, shut the door behind him and went across to the bear and bent over to check the burn. Modi opened his eyes, raised his head and allowed Walo to rub away the soot.

I turned away, marvelling. On my way back to camp, it occurred to me that the events of the previous evening should be a warning to me that I was prone to making unfounded assumptions. Because Madi's name meant 'angry', I had presumed Madi had mauled the drunkard. But I had been wrong. Modi had been responsible for the attack. With Redwald I had made the same mistake, thinking that he was behind the attempt to kill me in Kaupang. In future, if anyone tried to do me harm or wreck the embassy to the caliph, I would be more deliberate. Instead of making a quick judgement as to who was responsible,

I would wait for the clues to make some sort of pattern. Of one thing I was certain: my difficulties were far from over.

By mid-morning we had shifted all our remaining stores and equipment, the gyrfalcons in their cages and the white dogs onto two more river craft. Then our newly recruited boatmen pushed our ungainly craft away from the bank, using long wooden oars, and we floated out on the slow-moving surface of the river. The ferrymen – two men in the bow and two in the stern – settled the oars into short Y-shaped crutches. Standing facing forward, they began to take slow, leisurely strokes. Our vessels drifted, barely moving. I was with Abram on the lead boat, carrying stores, and looked back towards our little convoy. A short distance behind us came Walo with the ice bears, then Osric on the vessel with the aurochs. The other stores boat brought up the rear. All three craft were low in the water and the double ferry, weighed down by the aurochs in its enclosure was scarcely visible. The huge animal appeared to be standing on the river's surface, the water level with its hooves.

An unseen eddy caught our boat and it began to rotate slowly. Our boatmen corrected the movement, holding us straight and in mid-river. The bank on both sides was steep, covered with thick brushwood. There was nowhere to land in an emergency. It was evident that it was now impossible to get off the river. We were committed to wherever it would carry us. Abram had left to me the final decision whether to continue by road or take to the river. If I had made the mistake, I had no one else but myself to blame for our situation.

A heron standing in the shallows watched us draw closer. We were moving so slowly that the bird did not consider us a threat. It turned its head, watching us along its spear of a beak, as we drifted past.

'This is even less than walking pace,' I complained to Abram.

'We'll move faster once we pick up the current,' he assured me.

Ahead of us the river curved to the left and out of sight. We drifted round the bend and passed a gulley where a stream emptied into the main river. Almost imperceptibly our speed increased for a few yards, then slackened again. Had I not been so dismayed by our dawdling pace, I would have enjoyed the tranquillity of the scene ahead of us. A large flock of wild ducks was feeding on the surface. They had blue beaks and wing tips, beautifully speckled brown breasts, and a noticeable streak of white just in front of the eye. They scattered in leisurely fashion, paddling just far enough apart to keep a safe distance from the dipping oars as we drifted among them, then came together again once we had passed. There was a small, rippling swirl almost within touching distance, and I had a momentary glimpse of the fin and green-bronze back of a fish as long as my arm before the creature sank from view. High overhead four swans flew, dazzling white against the grey, overcast sky. They were following the line of the river and overtook us in moments, the sound of their wing beats fading so swiftly that it made me feel as if our boats were anchored in one spot. From somewhere in the distance came a long rumble of thunder.

The hours dragged by. All that afternoon our little flotilla crept along at the same languid pace. Unlike a straight road-way, the river meandered and twisted in casual loops. Where trees overhung the bends, our boatmen were obliged to take a course to avoid branches that extended far out over the water. This increased the distance we had to travel. We never knew what we would encounter around the next corner or whether we would find ourselves heading north, instead of south. After four hours of travel I doubted we had progressed the same number of miles.

Just as I was thinking that our situation could not get any worse, there was a faint scraping sound. Our vessel had touched bottom. We were in mid-river and had been travelling so slowly that it took me a little while to appreciate that now we had come to a complete stop. The boat was caught fast on a shoal.

Our crew were waving at the boats behind us, signalling that they were to head for the bank, and not follow us onto the underwater obstacle.

The head boatman seemed unconcerned. A stocky, square man wearing a broad-brimmed straw hat, he rolled back his sleeves, revealing thick forearms covered with thick black hair. He probed the river bottom with a long pole. I thought he was searching for a deeper channel to get us over the shoal, but he was only trying to locate a firm spot where he could rest the tip of the pole, then push. He and his three comrades heaved and shoved until reluctantly our boat slid backwards into deeper water. Then, without a word to me or Abram, they began to punt our boat to join the others already nestled against the bank. There they rammed the bow of our boat deep into the reeds. One of them leaped ashore and fastened a heavy mooring line around the trunk of a sapling.

I was dismayed.

'Aren't you going to try to get past that shoal?' I demanded of the head boatman. He looked blank and Abram relayed my question in a language that I only partially understood.

'He only speaks Burgundian,' the dragoman explained after listening to the boatman's reply. 'He says that it is better we spend the night here. It is safer for us.'

I looked around. The river took its course through an

immense untouched forest. On both banks rose a solid wall of huge trees, heavy with summer foliage. There was no movement, no sign of life, no sound. Even the leaves were motionless in the muggy, still air. I wondered why the boatman sought safety when our surroundings were so peaceful.

'Please let him know that progress today was very disappointing. Ask him how far he thinks we will travel tomorrow. I'm worried we'll run out of food for the animals,' I said.

Another exchange of conversation, and Abram informed me that the boatman expected to make good progress the following day and to reach a town where we could purchase rations for the animals.

I accepted his response grudgingly and waited for our boatmen to go ashore and set up camp. However, they made no move to do so. Instead, they fastened extra ropes between our four vessels, drawing them even closer together until they were buried deep within the reed bed, their blunt bows almost touching the bank. It seemed that we were to spend the night on board.

Walo fed the animals from our stores, and Abram's camp cook dangled lines off the stern of our boat and caught several plump fish with silvery-gold scales. He alone was allowed by the boatmen to go ashore to light a fire and broil the fish. After the meal the head boatman insisted that he return aboard. As the evening shadows lengthened, I wondered yet again why we were not being allowed to spend the night on dry land, and what was so dangerous in the brooding forest.

Dusk came early beneath a lowering sky, the clouds massing together until their undersides took on the texture of curdled milk. From far away sheet lightning flickered over the leafy canopy. Rumbles of thunder reached us, but so faint that they only emphasized the deep silence of the great trees.

As the darkness settled over our little flotilla, a noise began, croaking and scratching. It rose gradually from the reeds as myriads of the frogs and insects began their chorus. The noise was muted at first. Then it grew louder and louder, reaching such a level that it seemed to vibrate the air with a constant humming, buzzing whine. Sleep was near impossible. The noise penetrated right inside one's skull. At intervals the din would die away. Then a few moments later it returned at full strength, interspersed with chirps and high-pitched whistles. I had never heard anything like it and it was a long time before I drifted off into an uneasy sleep.

I woke suddenly. There were neither stars nor moon and the night was so black that it was impossible to gauge the time. I could have been asleep for an hour or much longer. I lay still, wondering what had awakened me. The night chorus had eased to a low, background hum, as if the creatures in the reeds were exhausted. I felt the boat rock beneath me, a gentle swaying movement, as if it were encouraging me to return to sleep. I turned over and dozed. Moments later the boat rocked again, more violently this time. Close to my ear the water was rippling past the thin wooden hull, a sound that had not been there earlier. There came another shaking movement, and the boat bumped against its neighbour. I sat up and peered into the darkness. There was nothing to be seen. There was a rubbing and creaking from the ropes tethering the vessel to the bank, then a distinct crunch as the bow bumped on gravel. I could just make out the figure of one of our boatmen. He was crouching in the bow, attending to the mooring line.

Reassured, I lay back down and fell into a troubled sleep. When I opened my eyes in the grey light of another overcast dawn it was to sense immediately that something had changed dramatically. There was a heavy, rushing murmur everywhere.

I scrambled to my feet and looked upon a landscape transformed. The reeds among which we had slept were almost totally
submerged, only their tips showing. The lip of the riverbank
had been three or four feet above us when we arrived, now it
was level with the boat. I swung round and looked at the river.
The placid, flat surface I remembered was now a racing flood
the colour of oatmeal. Small waves rose and fell, apparently at
random, sweeping downstream on a broad torrent of dark, roiling
water. Pieces of flotsam, ranging in size from small twigs to
entire trees, rolled and twisted in the currents, now waving their
branches in the air, now showing their claw-like roots.

Our boatmen were conferring among themselves anxiously.
All of yesterday's lethargy was gone. They were tense and keyed
up. They must have been discussing what should be done and
had come to some sort of agreement, because they made signs
to Walo that he should feed the animals quickly. They helped
him throw fodder to the aurochs, and handed out cold food to
us. Then their leader shouted an order. One man from our boat
jumped ashore, leaping across the widened gap to the bank, and
went to the mooring rope that held the boat furthest downstream.
Its crew assembled, all four of them, with their poles against the
bank. The shoreman waited until they were ready, then, with a
cry of warning, he unfastened the knot and cast off. The crew
pushed in unison and their boat went sliding out from the reeds
and into the racing current. Within seconds the boat was whisked
away, rocking dramatically, gathering speed with every yard. In
frantic haste the crew switched to their oars to prevent the boat
from broaching sideways, and to bring her parallel to the current.
At the centre of the river, where the current flowed the strongest,
the vessel was picked up and thrust forward, bobbing wildly
through the patchwork of small, frothy waves heaping over the
shoal that had brought us to a halt the previous day.

Osric riding with the aurochs was next to be cast adrift. Then it was Walo and the ice bears. Finally it was our turn. The boatman on the bank untied our mooring line and flung himself across the widening gap as the current picked us up and sucked us out into the river. The boat spun crazily, a single wild revolution, before the oarsmen managed to bring it under control. Then we were racing along downriver in a wild ride that brought my heart into my mouth. The other boats had already disappeared around the next bend and I wondered if we would ever see them again.

'How did the boatmen know beforehand?' I called to Abram. I had to raise my voice, for the river was no longer silent. There was a sinister, constant growl as the flood water surged along, plucking at the riverbank, washing up against roots of trees, twisting itself into lines of small whirlpools.

'I already asked,' Abram shouted back. 'The thunder and lightning yesterday was where the river has its headwaters. They expected heavy rain to swell the river, but admit this was more than they expected.' He grabbed for a handhold as our boat struck a floating log and juddered.

'How long will the flood last?'

'They can't be sure – all today and maybe tomorrow.'

Now I understood why the boatmen had stopped us from camping on the riverbank. I had supposed that the risk had lain within the forest. In fact, the danger had come from the river.

The flood swept our boat as fast as a horse could canter. The boatmen stood poised, one man at each corner of our vessel. They watched for floating debris or sudden upwellings and rough water. Every so often one of them took several powerful strokes with his long oar and adjusted our headlong course. Despite their efforts we thumped up against large logs. A rogue tree, torn from its roots, slammed into the side of the vessel and nearly capsized us. The tops of the waves slopped aboard, and Abram and I bailed, using whatever was at hand to throw the water back into the river. Each time I looked up from the work it was to see that we were passing a new and different section of riverbank. I estimated that in the first half-hour we travelled further than the entire distance we had covered the previous day.

There was no sight of our comrades on the other boats until we entered a straight stretch of river, perhaps a quarter of a mile long, and saw them in the distance. Thankfully, all three vessels were still afloat with their live cargoes.

With each mile the river grew wider, though the turbulence of the flood water scarcely lessened. Our boat dipped and swooped as it passed over unseen shoals. Islands came and went, the boatmen choosing a channel past them. Their skill was reassuring, and our boat, being lighter and faster, gradually caught up with Walo and the ice bears. Ahead of them by another fifty yards, I could see Osric holding on to the aurochs' cage to steady himself. We eventually left the forest and the river took its course between low, fertile hills. On the river flatlands were fields of ripened wheat, orchards of plum and cherry, and coppiced woodland. We fled past several large farms, then a small riverside hamlet. There was no attempt to halt. The power of the flood was too strong. By mid-afternoon I calculated we had gone perhaps forty miles.

It was shortly afterwards that I heard the head boatman utter a grunt of alarm. Looking up from my bailing duties, I saw the river had narrowed again, and we were approaching the outskirts of a sizeable town. Modest timber-and-thatch houses extended along both banks. Each had a strip of vegetable garden that ran down to a small wooden landing stage on the water's edge. The boatman was staring straight ahead, frowning. I followed the direction of his gaze and my stomach dropped. Stretching across the river was the stone bridge that joined the two halves of the town. It was the twin of the broken bridge far behind us. Constructed of massive stone blocks, it had three semi-circular arches. The centre arch was slightly higher and wider than its neighbours, but all of them looked to be frighteningly low. The river surged through them, foaming where it struck the supporting pillars.

The boatmen on the lead boat were already plying their oars. They were aiming for the central arch, fighting to hold their boat straight so that the current would carry it safely into the opening.

I held my breath as I watched them being swept towards the arch and then – in one terrifying moment – they were plunged into the gap and swallowed up. I saw them no longer and I could only hope that they had safely made the transit.

Next in line was Osric's boat. Now I understood why the boatmen had gone to so much trouble to remove the wheels from the aurochs' cart and lash it down. It was to reduce the height of the cage for just such a hazard.

Beside me one of the boatmen muttered a prayer. Even with his expert eye he could not judge whether the aurochs' cage was low enough to pass underneath the span. If the cage was too high, the aurochs' cage would be ripped off or the boat would jam beneath the bridge. If the boat slewed and struck the pillars sideways it would be smashed to splinters. It was unlikely that any of the crew would survive. I knew that Osric could swim but I doubted that anyone could live in that raging flood.

We could only look on. The oarsmen struggled to bring their heavily laden boat onto the correct line as it hurtled towards the bridge. The aurochs, sensing the impending crisis, began repeating a long, wailing moan. At the instant before the boat plunged under the arch, the boatmen hauled in their blades.

One man in the stern was a fraction too slow. His protruding oar hit a pillar. The handle flew back as the shaft snapped and struck him in the chest. He was knocked overboard. He fell into the dark churning water just as the aurochs gave a final, echoing bellow of protest, and – from where we watched – the bulk of the vessel blocked out the daylight under the arch.

Abruptly the light returned as the river spat out the boat on the far side.

Now it was Walo's turn with the ice bears. This time I was close enough to hear the heart-stopping crunch of timber as an upper edge of their cage struck the underside of the bridge, followed by a tortured scraping noise as the current drove the boat onward and through the arch.

Moments later our own boat was thrust into the same gap. On each side the rushing river piled up against the bridge pillars in a sleek, lethal water slope. The bow of our boat dipped forward. Then we were careering through. I ducked. The underside of the stone arch flashed past, scored and chipped with centuries of collisions. The noise of the water reverberated with a great roar. Suddenly we shot out into open water, and I was blinking in the sunlight.

Fifty yards ahead of us men on Walo's boat were shouting to us and pointing urgently to our right. The noise of the river made it impossible to understand their cries, but a quick glance explained their agitation. A large up-rooted tree floated some twenty paces away, ahead of us and slightly off to our right. It was spinning and dipping in the raging flood water, carried along at almost the same pace as our boats. Our missing boatman was clinging to the wet, slippery trunk. Even as I watched, the tree rolled and twisted, and he was plunged underwater, only to reappear when the tree rolled again. It was a miracle that he had managed to retain his grip. It was impossible that he could hang on much longer.

Walo's boat was already past the castaway, and could not return. Only our boat had the slightest hope of rescuing him. Our head boatman yelled an order at his comrades and they began to row, angling our boat towards the stricken castaway. They threw their weight on the oar handles, panting with effort. It was obvious that we would have a single chance to save him before the river carried us past. The distance between us narrowed. The castaway raised his head, watching our approach. The tree rolled again, and he went under, coming back to the surface, spluttering, the water pouring off him.

Until that moment I had felt completely useless, a mere onlooker. Now I scrambled up to the bow and selected one of the ropes that had moored us to the bank overnight. I made a coil and stood ready to fling an end across the gap. If my aim was true, the castaway might be able to seize it and we could drag him aboard. With no warning, the free end of the rope was snatched from my hand and Abram was knotting it around his waist. 'Feed it out smoothly,' he ordered. Without waiting for a response, he plunged overboard, and began to swim. I helped as best I could, easing out the rope gently to reduce the drag, yet not so much that a loop pulled him downstream. Immediately it was clear that Abram was a very good swimmer. He was stroking forward powerfully, closing the gap. Yet it looked as if his courage was wasted. We would be level with the floating tree for less than a minute, and he would never reach the stranded boatman in time. Then a quirk of the current spun the tree sideways and it bobbed towards us. Abram reached out and seized one of the roots. He nodded to the boatman who let go his hold and slipped off the tree trunk. The current instantly

washed him into the curve of the rope. He grabbed hold, and
then all of us aboard the boat were hauling both men through
the dirty brown water until they were close enough to be hoisted
aboard. They flopped down into the bottom of boat, coughing
up water and wheezing for breath, utterly spent.

Chapter Nine

ALMOST AS QUICKLY AS it had arrived, the flood departed. Had I not seen it for myself I would never have believed that a river could switch so rapidly from untamed ferocity to placid calm.

'Rivers are like those serpents that swallow a deer or calf entire,' Abram explained to me. It was two days later and our little flotilla was gliding between banks thick with willow and poplar. In bright morning sunshine the swallows swooped and scythed over the silk-smooth, shimmering surface of the river, snatching up insects. Where the river divided around large islands it isolated patches of untouched wilderness, and the undergrowth along the bank teemed with wildlife. There were glimpses of otters, and startlingly bright blue streaks as king-fishers launched from low-hanging branches and sped away. All manner of small water creatures swam across our path, drawing out their telltale ripples.

'The prey becomes a bulge inside the serpent,' the dragoman explained. 'The bulge passes along the serpent's length as the beast digests. The crest of a flood is the same. It enters the head of the river and travels down its valley, swelling then subsiding.'

'It's difficult to imagine a creature so gross,' I said. The current was carrying us along at a rapid walking pace, and the boatmen only had to use their oars occasionally to keep us on course. The drama of the bridge seemed like a distant memory.

He laughed. 'When we get to Rome I'll show you a picture of Adam and Eve being expelled from Paradise. I think the artist had the same serpent in mind.'

'What else can I expect to see when we get to Rome?'

The banter left his voice. 'More important is what you don't see.'

'You sound like Alcuin.'

The dragoman was serious. 'In Rome the serpents don't swallow their victims. They strike with poisoned fangs. The city is a snake pit of intrigue, conspiracies and plots. Everyone is waiting for Pope Adrian to die and then . . .' He shrugged expressively.

I recalled Alcuin's warning that the pope was very old, and that no one knew who would replace him. 'And what sort of man is Pope Adrian?' I asked.

The dragoman shook a small purse out from his sleeve. The movement was so deft that I blinked in surprise. He noted my reaction and grinned. 'In my profession a discreet coin dropped quickly into a ready palm solves many a problem.'

He took a coin from the purse and passed it to me. 'Here's Pope Adrian for you.'

The portrait on the papal coin was very stylized: a man's head and shoulders, shown full face, the eyes staring boldly forward under some sort of cap or crown. Oddly, the upper lip of the face wore what looked like a short, trim moustache. Around the edge was written 'HADRIANUS P P' in raised letters.

'I presume that "P P" is short for "Pope",' I said.

Abram chuckled. 'In Rome the joke is that it means "in perpetuity". Pope Adrian is as hardy and tough as they come. He's already sat on Peter's throne for close on two decades, longer than anyone before him.'

I handed back the coin. 'If you remember, Alcuin gave me an introduction to the man who works for the pope as his Nomenculator. His name is Paul.'

'A very useful contact. By the time we arrive in Rome, we won't find any ship captain prepared to take us onward from Italy until next sailing season in spring. I strongly advise that we spend the winter in the city. The Nomenculator can help us find suitable accommodation. His office gives him considerable influence.'

I should have been disappointed by the thought of the long interruption to our journey. But the prospect of spending several months in Rome and seeing its fabled sights was something I looked forward to.

Abram's next words dampened my enthusiasm. 'Don't expect too much of the city itself. The place has been falling to pieces for centuries. It's a wreck.' He got to his feet. 'By contrast you'll find that travelling through Burgundy by water is a pleasure.'

*

The next ten days proved how right he was. We came to a region where mile after mile of vineyards extended up the flanks of the hills that overlooked the valley. It was the season for the grape harvest, and the farmworkers – men and women – toiled in the warm sunshine among the rich greens and browns of the vines, stooping to cut the fruit, then carrying it in wicker baskets to waiting carts. Most of the crop was then tipped into huge open-topped wooden casks set up close to the river landing places. Here barefoot men were trampling the grapes until the juice ran off into barrels that were then rolled onto waiting barges. More families were on ladders in the orchards, plucking plums and peaches, quince and mulberry, while their more agile children clambered into the branches to shake down the ripe fruit. Amid such bounty it was easy to obtain the supplies we needed for the animals. Every riverside town had its own market where Abram's servants purchased all we required, and we discovered that the ice bears were as happy to eat fresh rabbit as well as catfish and trout. Well fed, the animals settled down. The dogs were much calmer, and the ice bears spent much of each day asleep. By day, Walo took the thick cloths off the cages of the gyrfalcons so that the birds could preen and bask in the sunshine, and then covered them over for the night. By now he had them so well trained that, even from the moving boat, he could exercise them. One by one, he would let them fly free and, after a little while, bring them back to his hand holding out a titbit of fresh meat. Only the aurochs remained sulky and dangerous. It rolled its eyes if anyone came near, and thrust and battered with its great horns against the sides of the enclosure.

In the evenings, an hour or two before sunset, we would moor to the riverbank, as it was too perilous to use the river in the darkness and risk striking the occasional rocky shoal. We picked isolated locations to avoid attracting crowds of curious onlookers who might come to stare at creatures they had never seen before. Twice Abram asked us to stop within walking distance of a large town so that he could go ashore and spend the night with his fellow Rhadanites. From them, he told us, he could learn what we might find when finally we reached the sea.

Gradually the river grew in size. Large tributaries added not only their waters but also an increasing number and variety of river craft. We encountered ungainly rafts of timber floating down from the forests, barges loaded with great blocks of building stone, and scores of vessels bearing casks and barrels of wine. The river had become a great artery of commerce, and the bridges were high and wide enough to accommodate the traffic. We passed beneath their arches without incident now that the water level had dropped. On good days a breeze from the north allowed our boatmen to spread simple square sails and increase our speed. My spirits were lifted by the welcome sound of water chattering and lapping under the blunt bows of our ferries as we pressed onward. In such carefree conditions, Abram, Osric and I would exchange places on the different boats. Abram and Osric spent long hours talking together quietly, sometimes in the Saracen tongue. I joined Walo and his ice bears, keeping him company, for I wanted him to feel at ease in these strange, new surroundings.

It was always a challenge to find a way of engaging Walo's attention. He seldom spoke to others and kept to himself, passing the hours in his own special world, apparently in a half-daze. Yet he must have been taking note of what was going on around him because, like a shutter briefly being thrown open, he would come out with a sudden perceptive remark. He was at his happiest and most alert when dealing with our animals and that, in turn, provided me with a means to draw him out of his isolation: he loved to hear more about the exotic creatures depicted in the Book of Beasts. Whenever I joined him on the boat, I would sit beside him on the deck leafing through the pages until he pointed to an illustration that caught his interest. Then I would read out the information written underneath. In nearly every case the animal was as unknown to me, as it was to him.

'What's that lion with a man's face?' he asked one hot afternoon. Our boats were passing low gravel cliffs where the river had undercut its bank. Sand swallows had burrowed into the cliffs, and a cloud of the small brown and white birds whirled over our heads as they made their way to and from their nests.

'It's called a manticore,' I told him, reading the accompanying text.

'Those great teeth must mean it is a meat eater,' Walo commented.

The creature had the head of a man attached to the body of a lion. The artist had drawn a human face with a straggly beard and a wide open mouth armed with sharp fangs. The staring eyes were a cold blue but all the rest of the animal had been coloured blood red.

I quoted the text: '*The manticore has three rows of teeth and eats human flesh. It is very active and can leap great distances. No one can out run it. Its voice is like a whistled melody.*'

Walo was intrigued. 'I would love to see such a wondrous creature, even if it is dangerous.'

'But you would not want to come too close,' I said. 'Apparently the manticore can shoot poisoned spines from the tip of its tail.'

Walo detected the note of scepticism in my voice. 'Surely the book is telling the truth.'

'We'll never know. It says that the manticore lives in India, and we are only going as far as Baghdad.'

I could sense Walo's disappointment. His grasp of geography may have been non-existent, but he had a simple, direct shrewdness. 'We can test the truth of the book. Read out what it says about an animal we know, then we can judge whether it is right.'

I turned the pages until Walo pointed to an illustration of a flock of half a dozen tall birds standing in a group. They had long necks, pointed beaks like herons and stilt legs. The nearest bird was standing on one leg and gripping what looked like a round stone with the other foot, holding it up from the ground.

'Cranes!' exclaimed Walo. 'Flocks of them pass over my forest every spring, high in the sky, but they do not stop. They must be travelling to their summer home in a place I do not know. In autumn I see them as they return. Going back the way they came.'

'*Their Latin name is* Grus,' I said, reading. '*They travel large distances, flying very high so that the leader can see the lands to which they are going.*'

Walo nodded approvingly.

'*When the leader is tired, he changes places with another in the flock. As they fly, they post some of their number at the end of the line to shout orders and keep the group together.*'

'I've heard them calling to one another in the air. The voice is like a bugle,' said Walo triumphantly. 'You see the book tells the truth.'

'But what about the crane in the front of the picture,' I said, 'the one holding something in its claw? The book says that when a flock of cranes rests at night, one of their number stands guard. While the others sleep, he stays awake, holding up a stone in his claw. If he falls asleep, the stone drops and awakens him.'

Walo thought for a moment. 'I don't know about that. But why shouldn't it be true? Let's check on another creature that we both know. How about a wild boar?'

I found the relevant illustration. The picture was certainly accurate, a pig-like creature with a curly tail, cloven hooves, dangerous-looking tusks and a malevolent expression as it charged across the page. Even the colouring – a greyish black – was correct.

'*The Latin name is* Aper, *and it is named for its ferocity*,' I read. '*The boar is very rough when mating, and before they fight with one another, they rub their skin against the bark of trees to toughen it.*'

'I've seen boars doing just that,' Walo confirmed. 'In the forest you find places where the bark has been torn away. Boars also prepare for battle by whetting their tusks, sharpening them against trees.'

'That is what the book also says,' I admitted. 'The book claims, too, that a boar eats a plant called origanum to cleanse its gums and strengthen the tusks.'

'That I didn't know,' said Walo, looking over my shoulder as I turned the page to look for another familiar animal.

As luck would have it, the next page had an illustration of a large serpent. For a moment I wondered if this was the same sort of snake whose picture Abram would show me in Rome. But the man was not Adam, for he was fully dressed and there was no sign of Eve or an apple tree, and the serpent's home was a hole in a barren-looking hill that did not resemble the fertile Garden of Eden. The serpent body tapered to a pointed tail and, oddly, the creature had curved itself around and thrust the tip of its tail into its own ear. The artist had drawn a face on the snake, and the animal was grimacing, clearly in distress.

'That man is calming the serpent,' said Walo at once.

It took me a moment to see what he was talking about. A little distance from the snake a man was playing a stringed instrument. I recognized a viol from Carolus's banquets when musicians entertained the king.

'*The asp, or serpent*,' I read out, '*kills with a venomous bite. When an enchanter summons an asp out of its cave with incantations or music, and it does not want to go, it presses one ear to the ground and covers the other ear with its tail.*'

I paused and took a second look at the picture. 'Surely that's a fable,' I said. 'Serpents don't listen to music.'

Walo looked at me reprovingly. 'If ice bears do, why shouldn't serpents be the same?'

I returned to the book. 'It also says that there are many kinds of asp, and not all are harmful. The bite from one kind kills by causing a terrible thirst; another that is called the prester asp moves with an open mouth, and those it bites swell up and rot follows. Then they die. The bite from a third kind of asp brings on a deep sleep from which the victim never awakes. That one is called the hypnalis and it is the asp that killed Cleopatra the Queen of Egypt who was freed from her troubles.'

'We're going to Egypt, aren't we!' breathed Walo eagerly. 'Wouldn't it be magnificent if we found a hypnalis. I could play my pipe to lure it from its hole.'

The sun's glare was giving me a headache and I closed the bestiary and replaced it in its wrapping. If only I had paid closer attention to what Walo had just said, our journey might have turned out very differently.

*

By the tenth day of our journey along the Rhone it was evident that we were approaching the mouth of the great river. The current had become sluggish and the river had widened to nearly a half-mile from bank to bank. Far behind us were the prosperous farmlands; now we were passing through a flat, wild landscape of windswept marshes and lagoons. A few greyish-white humps, Abram told us, were piles of salt crystals scraped up by the inhabitants and awaiting collection. It was the only crop they could wrest from the waterlogged soil. Despite the lateness of the season, the weather continued fine and sunny with clear skies that produced spectacular sunsets. On just such an evening Walo and I stumbled on a discovery that obliged me to admit that the verderer's son had reason to believe in the strangeness and variety of the animals.

As was their custom, our boatmen selected an isolated spot to spend the night well away from the nearest settlement. They tied up our boats to the bank in an area thickly overgrown with tall bushes. Though it was difficult to get ashore, Walo and I managed to clamber onto the bank and found a faint path, leading inland. We followed it, Walo in the lead, until he stopped suddenly. He had seen something in the undergrowth. He veered off the path to investigate, then beckoned to me to join him. Lying on the ground in a small clearing was the body of a dead bird. From a little distance I thought it might be a swan. But as I drew closer, I saw that it was a bird unlike anything that I had remotely imagined. It was as if someone had joined the body of a large heron to the head and neck of a goose. The creature had once stood on very long stick-like legs and must have been nearly five feet tall.

'I wonder what food it eats?' wondered Walo aloud.

I looked at him sharply, then remembered how he had immediately deduced from the terrible teeth in the mouth of the manticore that it was a meat-eater. The dead bird lying on the ground before us had neither the flat shovelling beak of a duck nor the stabbing lance of the heron. Its beak was over-size, a misshapen excrescence like a large bean that curved downward at the tip. At the top of the beak were two long slits like nostrils.

'I don't remember seeing it in the Book of Beasts,' I said, 'though surely it should be in it.'

The most extraordinary thing about the animal was its remarkable colour. The body feathers were white shaded with a delicate pink that deepened in hue along the neck and towards the wing tips and tail until it became a bright, luxuriant red. The stilt-like legs were a shocking deep vermilion. The colours were so striking that even the most skilled painter would have had trouble in capturing its splendour.

'Perhaps Abram can tell us more about it,' I suggested. 'We had better be getting back to the boats.'

We were about to turn back when there came a confused, discordant clamour like the honking of many geese. It came from above us and I looked up. The tall bushes allowed a view of a small circle of sky. All of a sudden it was filled with the shapes of the strange birds, scores of them, gliding past on outstretched wings as they descended through the air, coming in to land nearby. They flew with necks stiffly outstretched and long legs trailing behind them. There was a glimpse of black underwings.

'Quick! We must go and see. Maybe they will appoint a guardian to watch over them while they are on the ground, just like the cranes,' Walo blurted, pulling at my arm.

'They're giant herons,' I guessed.

He shook his head. 'A heron flies with a curved neck. They flew with their necks straight, like cranes.'

He plunged off through the undergrowth, heading in the direction we had seen the birds descend. After some minutes we worked clear of the bushes and emerged on the rim of a broad lagoon. I caught my breath in astonishment. The lagoon was very shallow, no more than a few inches deep. Standing in the water on their weird stilt-legs were hundreds of the strange birds, clustered in a vast flock. They lifted their heads on their long, sinuous necks as Walo and I appeared, and turned to inspect us. A few had their heads buried underwater, and as they raised them, the water dripped from their glistening beaks.

At that same moment the setting sun eased from behind a cloud and flooded the scene with reddish light. The slanting rays gave the birds' plumage an unearthly glow, infusing them with every hue of red from pink to bright crimson. There was not a breath of wind and the still surface of the lagoon served as a mirror, doubling the illusion. It looked as if the entire spindly legged flock was about to catch fire.

*

As soon as we got back to the boats, Walo insisted that I search the bestiary to make sure there was no illustration of the wondrous creatures.

'Their picture must be there,' he pleaded.

'I'm afraid not,' I told him after I had checked every page. 'A bird called a phoenix glows red. But that's only at the end of its life just before it bursts into flames. Besides, it lives in Arabia.'

'Maybe the birds we saw flew here from Arabia, like those cranes that I see flying high over my forest each year.'

I was sorry to disappoint him. 'According to the book, only a single phoenix is alive at any time and it lives for five hundred years. When it is ready to die, it builds a nest in the top of a palm tree and bursts into flames. From the ashes arises another phoenix, a young one. It too will live for another five hundred years.'

Walo clung to his hopes. 'What about the phoenix's food?'

'The book states that the phoenix lives on the perfume of frankincense.'

'What's frankincense?'

'A sort of sweet-smelling gum.'

Walo's face lit up with a triumphant smile. 'Then those big slits in the beak are nostrils. That's how the bird takes its food.'

Abram, who had been listening, came to my rescue. 'They could have been huma birds,' he said with a smile.

Walo turned to him excitedly. 'What are they?'

'Huma birds are found in Persia. They glow like embers.'

Walo was agog with anticipation. 'Have you seen one?'

'I'm afraid not. A huma bird spends its entire life high in the air, never coming to land. Great kings wear its feathers in their crowns. Some people call it a bird of paradise. It is claimed that whoever sees the huma bird, even its shadow, is happy for the rest of his life.'

'I would be happy to see either a huma bird or a phoenix,' announced Walo firmly. 'If people speak of such creatures in Persia or Arabia, then they must exist.'

A surly grunt from the aurochs reminded him that the great beast had not been given its evening feed, and he headed off towards its cage.

Abram waited until I had put the bestiary away safely before he beckoned to one of his servants. The man clambered across from the adjacent boat, carrying the leather tube that contained the dragoman's precious itinerarium.

'It's time for another decision about our route,' Abram said to me, extracting the map from its container.

'Then I think Osric should also hear what you have to say,' I told him. I called out to my friend to join us. Osric, who had been trying his hand at fishing off the stern of one of the boats, laid down his rod and clambered across to where Abram had set up the little table.

As he had done the last time, Abram unrolled the itinerarium only enough to show the section he wanted. 'Note how the river we have been following divides before it reaches the sea. We are halfway along the eastern branch,' he said, pointing to the map.

'How much further to the sea itself?' I asked.

'Another two days, maybe less.' His finger traced the thick line shaded in green that represented the coast. 'We've come as far as is safe for our riverboats. On open water a sudden squall or large waves would quickly swamp them. So either we disembark and take the coast road towards Rome or we shift the animals onto a seagoing vessel and proceed to Rome by sea. The choice is yours.'

'I presume the sea route is faster,' I asked him.

'Without question. Given a favourable wind we can be in Rome in less than a week. By road it could take us almost two months.'

I thought back to the voyage from Kaupang with Redwald. The ice bears, dogs and gyrfalcons had all adapted well to shipboard life.

'I'm concerned about the aurochs,' I said.

The dragoman shrugged. 'I've seen live cattle shipped. If they are fed and watered, they survive well enough.'

Osric had been silent until now. 'And the risk from Hispania?' he murmured. 'If we take the sea route, we may encounter ships of the emir of Cordoba. He would not want an embassy between Carolus and the Baghdad caliph to succeed.'

'I've made enquiries along the river,' Abram told him. 'My contacts tell me that their trading voyages to Rome were trouble-free all summer. There's been no interference by pirates or hostile ships.'

I looked questioningly at Osric. He nodded. 'Then we go by sea,' I said.

Abram glanced up at the sky. The sun had dropped below the horizon, and the last few shreds of cloud had dissolved. In the west the evening star was already visible.

'When the air is still and clear like this in winter,' he

observed, 'it heralds a vicious gale that blows up suddenly from the north. It rages down the valley, lasting for days, and whips up these waters.'

'Then let's hope we are snug in Rome by then,' I said.

He flashed me a mischievous grin. 'The gale has been known to come at any other times of the year as well. Let's hope we come across a seagoing ship in the next few miles and can arrange a charter.'

*

The cargo ship moored against the salt jetty was nearly the same size as Redwald's stout ship that had carried us to Kaupang. But there the resemblance ended. This vessel's planking was grey and battered, the rigging sagged, and the mast had several splits and cracks bound up with rope. I supposed that she had been consigned to hauling humble cargoes of salt because of her advancing years. I doubted Redwald would have taken her onto the open sea, but Abram seemed relieved to see her.

'I feared that the jetty was no longer in use,' he admitted as our little flotilla tied up to the worn pilings of the dock. 'I'll go and find her captain and see if he'll accept a charter.'

Eager to stretch my legs, I decided to go ashore myself and explore. The dock was a mean, poor place. There was no sign of any cargo waiting to be loaded, though spilled crystals of salt crunched beneath my feet as I walked across open ground towards a collection of small shacks. Several mangy-looking dogs slept in the hot sunshine, slumped against their door posts, and there was no sign of human activity. Flat countryside stretched to the horizon in every direction, bare and bleached. When I peered into the darkness of one of the huts, I found that it was abandoned and empty and there was a musty smell.

I wondered where the occupants had gone and if they would ever return.

I jumped as a voice behind me said, 'Protis here is willing to take us to Rome.'

I swung round to find Abram with a slightly built young man whose dark skin and jet-black hair spoke of Mediterranean ancestry. The faint line of a carefully trimmed moustache emphasized that he was not yet old enough to have grown a full beard.

'Protis is the captain of the ship tied up at the dock,' Abram continued. 'He missed the last salt cargo of the season. Last-minute repairs to the hull delayed him.'

'It was just a minor leak, and it's now fixed,' the young man asserted. His self-confident manner more than made up for his youthfulness. 'Your dragoman tells me that you are looking to charter a vessel for the voyage to Rome.'

His Frankish had a heavy accent and he was visibly relieved when I answered in Latin: 'You've seen the cage containing the big ox on our boat, can you get it aboard your ship?'

Protis drew himself up to his full height of scarcely more than five feet. 'My ancestors taught the world how to use levers and pulleys. I can construct a machine to raise your beast in its cage and place it on my deck,' he declared.

With a quick, amused glance in my direction Abram intervened, soothing wounded pride. 'Protis's people are Greeks from Massalia. They settled there before Rome was even founded.'

'And,' added the young captain, 'the citizens of Rome would have starved time and again if my forebears' ships hadn't delivered the grain they needed.'

I refrained from asking how many centuries his own ancient vessel had been afloat. Instead I asked him to show me around.

Even to my inexperienced eye, the ship was barely sea-worthy. There were a great many patches where the timber had been clumsily replaced. The ropes were frayed and whiskery with age, and the canvas sails were threadbare. I peered into the open hatchway and saw the glint of deep bilge water in the bottom of the hold. Several times during our tour of inspection, sailors, of whom there must have been at least a dozen, hauled up buckets of evil-smelling, dirty water and tipped them over board.

Finally, I took Abram to one side. 'Are you sure the ship is safe? She seems to be ready to founder.'

'We could wait here and hope for another vessel to show up. But that's unlikely this late in the season,' he answered. 'And there's no guarantee that the next vessel will be any better.'

I scratched at an itch on the back of my neck, one of many welts that covered every square inch of my exposed skin. The biting insects of the lower river were ferocious, far worse than anything we had suffered previously. They feasted on us, both day and night. We smeared ourselves in rancid fat from the ice bears' food supplies, and our boatmen built smudge fires to discourage them, but it did little good. Our faces and hands were blotchy and swollen with insect bites. I flinched at the prospect of spending days being eaten alive while waiting at the dock for a vessel that might never come. As if in agreement, the aurochs let out an angry bellow. Bloody trickles ran down its flanks and neck, where it had been bitten by a local breed of voracious fly, the size of my thumbnail, which thrived on cattle.

'Very well,' I said to Abram, 'arrange the charter. Just make sure that we get on our way as quickly as possible.'

Protis made good his boast when it came to devising a way of lifting the aurochs and its cage. He and his sailors took a short, stubby mast from near the bow and repositioned it to project out over the side of the vessel. With a complicated web of ropes and pulleys they succeeded in hoisting the great animal, still in its cage, and placing it on deck just behind the main mast. The ice bears in their cage followed soon afterwards and were set down on the foredeck. In another of the young captain's inspirations he then had his men cut the smallest of our river ferries in half and one section brought aboard. His ship's carpenter built up the sides with extra planks, blanked off the open end, and re-caulked the seams. It transformed the vessel into a water tank for our menagerie. Meanwhile Abram's men had been scouring the countryside for supplies. Several cartloads of grass and fodder were delivered to the dock, along with crates of live chickens for the bears, gyrfalcons and dogs. When all was ready, Abram paid our river boatmen their final wages and the three remaining ferries towed Protis's venerable ship out into mid-river. There, her large, threadbare mainsail was let loose to catch the breeze. We began slowly to head towards the waiting sea, looking and smelling like a farmyard and leaving a trail of hay wisps on the murky surface of the river.

Chapter Ten

'I'VE MADE THIS VOYAGE a dozen times, and never a problem,' Protis boasted. We were standing on deck, side by side, and it was a splendid morning, the second of our sea voyage. The breeze was just enough to belly out the sail and the sun sparkled off a sea that showed a brighter, sharper blue than anything I had seen in northern waters. A flock of gulls wheeled and hovered alongside, attracted by the occasional splashes of water as our sailors dumped buckets of bilge overboard. Unsurprisingly, the hull of Protis's ramshackle vessel was far from watertight.

'I recall you saying that your family have been seafarers for generations,' I remarked, making conversation.

'As far back as any family in Massalia, and proud of it. My parents named me after the city's founder.' Our youthful captain liked to chat, and once he got into his stride he was almost unstoppable. 'The first Protis was from Greece, far back in the mists of time, a trader who dropped anchor in a sheltered bay along the coast. The daughter of a local chieftain fell in love with him, the two got married, and they and their people flourished. Massalia grew up around the same natural harbour. My family tradition is to name one of the sons after the city's founder.'

'So your father was also called Protis?'

He nodded. 'Though it brought him no luck. He went

down with his ship in a sudden, bad storm when I was just a toddler. My grandfather taught me my sea skills. He's now retired, of course. His eyesight's gone.'

That might explain the age of the vessel, I thought to myself. Protis had probably inherited it from his grandfather, a vessel put back into service after the family's other and newer ship had sunk.

'To lose one's eyesight is hard for anyone,' I sympathized.

The young captain smiled sadly. He was obviously fond of his grandfather. 'It's the worst thing that can happen to a mariner. He needs good eyes. We make most of our voyages following the coast or sailing from one island to the next one already visible on the horizon.'

He pointed away to our left. 'Right now we are staying well off shore for safety, yet close enough so that I can keep in sight those mountains.'

Judging by the number of other sails we had seen moving in both directions along the coast, it was how most captains navigated locally. Sailing from one port to the next in the Mediterranean did not appear to be as demanding as the conditions Redwald faced when finding his way from Dorestad to Kaupang.

'Do we follow the coast all the way to Rome?' I asked, trying to visualize what Abram's itinerarium had shown.

'There are one or two stretches where we lose sight of the mountains because the land is too low. At those places we will steer further off shore and take a more direct route to our destination.'

One of the sailors in the bailing team put down his bucket and came aft to speak with us. He said something to Protis in a language I did not understand and supposed was Greek.

'Excuse me a moment,' said Protis. 'There's something I need to attend to.'

He followed the man across the deck to the main hatchway leading down into the ship's hold and I watched as he climbed down a ladder. Several minutes passed and then he reappeared. He was looking perplexed.

'Anything wrong?' I asked.

'Nothing to worry about,' he answered airily. Turning to his helmsman, he gave an order. Our course altered slightly and the ship began to slant closer to the land.

'Just a precaution,' he explained to me. 'The bailing crew are having difficulty keeping pace with the water in the hold.'

Half an hour passed and I stood with him in companionable silence, enjoying the warmth of the sun soaking into my body, the easy rocking motion of the ship beneath my feet and the sensation of being carried effortlessly towards our destination. My reverie was interrupted by a shout from the bailing crew and this time there was no mistaking the alarm in the man's voice.

Protis strode forward to the hatchway once more, kicked off his shoes, and again disappeared, for longer this time.

I could see that something was seriously amiss. The deck crew had gathered around the hatchway and were casting worried glances at one another. The lookout stationed in the bows abandoned his post, and came back to join his companions.

I strolled forward and stood beside them. Peering down into the half-darkness of the hold I could make out several crew members up to their thighs in water. They were lifting up smooth round stones the size of a large loaf from under the surface and setting them aside. I recalled what Redwald had said about a ship needing to carry ballast stones low down to keep her upright. The men who had lifted the stones aside were also reaching down into the water, feeling around, then moving on to repeat the process nearby. Various odds and ends of loose lumber floated back and forth, nuzzling up against their thighs. There was no sign of Protis. Suddenly he surfaced with a splutter, took a deep breath, and immediately dived down again. There was a brief glimpse of his bare feet kicking at the surface, and then he was gone, swimming inside the belly of his own ship.

'What's happening?' I asked one of the crew, an older man with grizzled, close-cropped hair, and dressed in a torn dirty shirt and ragged trousers.

He understood my Latin well enough to answer. 'Trying to find exactly where so much water is getting in. The leak is bad, and gaining on us.'

One of the men down in the hold looked up, saw the circle of faces peering down, and gave an angry shout. Beside me two of the crew hurried off to fetch extra buckets and lowered them on ropes. They were filled with bilge water, then hauled up hand over hand, and their contents dumped over the side.

Abram had come up to join me and, after questioning the old man in Greek, he turned to me. 'The ship has a pump, but it is very old and it broke on the way to the salt jetty. That's why they're having to use buckets.'

'Can't the pump be repaired?' I enquired.

The dragoman shook his head. 'Apparently the pump is such an ancient design that the broken part is impossible to replace.'

Down in the hold Protis surfaced and waded across to the foot of the ladder. When he stepped out on deck, he was breathing heavily, his chest heaving. Water dripped from his sodden clothes and pooled on the sun-baked planks of the deck.

'A major leak,' he announced. 'But God only knows where it is.'

Osric had joined us from where he had been helping Walo set out bowls of drinking water for the dogs tethered along the ship's rail. They had to be kept well away from the aurochs' cage as their barking still enraged the great beast.

Now my friend asked mildly, 'Could the leak be something to do with the repair you mentioned earlier, the one that had delayed your arrival at the salt jetty?'

The young Greek treated Osric to a look that was both exasperated and condescending. 'Unfortunately there's no access to that section of the hull. There's too much ballast in the way.'

Osric remained composed. 'Maybe it would be worth stretching a canvas on the outside of the hull in that area, using ropes. That might slow the leak enough for us to reach harbour,' he suggested calmly.

I recalled that, earlier in his life, my friend had voyaged on trading ships from Hispania. He must have learned this technique at that time.

Protis gave my friend another look, more of surprise this time. 'I've heard of such a thing being done, but I've never tried it myself. I doubt if my men will agree. It's new to them and some can't swim.'

'I'm willing to go over the side and set the sail in place,' Osric volunteered.

Protis pursed his lips, uncertain what to do. It was the first time I had seen his self-confidence falter. 'It means stopping the ship while she's sinking and that uses up precious time. If it's a failure, the vessel will take on so much water that she will founder before we reach land.'

Unexpectedly, Abram spoke up. 'I will give Osric a hand if someone will tell me what to do.'

Protis seized his chance to reassert his captain's role. 'The principle's straightforward. The crew on deck lowers a spare sail overboard close to where we think there is a leak. The swimmers position the sail correctly and the inflow sucks the canvas over the hole. We then hold the sail in place with ropes around the ship and get her into harbour and mend her properly.'

'So there's no time to waste,' said Abram. He started to strip off his shirt.

Protis gave a quick grin of excitement. 'If this succeeds, it'll be the talk of Massalia!'

He shouted to the helmsman to bring the ship into the wind, and for the rest of the crew to lower the mainsail and bring aft the artemon.

The artemon proved to be a small square sail normally set on its own mast in the bow of the ship. While the men readied it as a patch for the hull, I reflected how strange it was to find ourselves in such serious danger when everything about us was so tranquil. The wind had fallen away to the slightest breeze and the sun still shone from a cloudless sky. Without the mainsail, the ship had come to a complete stop and lay rocking very gently on the calm sea. The gulls continued to circle and soar around us. A few settled on the glassy sea, stretching their wings for a moment before folding them in place, then paddling close around us and inspecting our activity with beady eyes, always hoping for scraps of food. Everything was placid, except that the land was uncomfortably far away and, if I listened carefully, I could catch the faintest sound of water lapping back and forth inside the hold.

Our ship was slowly sinking beneath us.

Osric and Abram got down into the small ship's boat. Normally towed astern, the skiff was drawn alongside and tied close to the suspected area of the leak. From there the two men directed the path of the little sail as it was lowered overboard and pulled under the hull. When it had disappeared underwater they took turns to dive down and guide it into place. From the rail above, Walo and I looked down as they worked. Protis ran back and forth, now encouraging his men as they hauled on the ropes, now rushing to the side of the ship to demand a progress report from the two men in the water.

Finally, Osric called up to say that the job was done. He and Abram climbed back aboard and an eager Protis ordered the mainsail to be re-hoisted, and the helmsman to set course directly for land.

'There's a small sheltered inlet a few miles along the coast,' he said brightly, his confidence returning. 'It's ideal, with a good hard beach where we can go aground. Then we'll lighten the ship and roll her over on her side so we can get at the leak. There are boat builders there who can help out.'

The ship slowly gathered way, though it was clear to all of us that she was very sluggish, barely moving with the weight of water in her hold. Anxiously we waited for the next report from the bailing team.

It was not long in coming. A cry of genuine panic had Protis sprinting to the hatchway and scrambling down the ladder again. When he reappeared, his face was ashen.

'It hasn't worked,' he groaned. 'The leak is worse than before – much, much worse.'

I stared towards the distant coast, trying to judge the distance. The heat haze made the brown mountains indistinct. At a guess we were still four or five miles offshore.

'Do you think we can make it to land?' I whispered to Osric beside me.

'Not a chance,' he murmured. 'With all that water already in her bilge, I'd say she'll founder before the day is out.'

I swung round to face Protis. 'We must save the animals! We've not brought them all the way from the Northlands to drown here on a sunny day.'

He ran his hands despairingly through his cap of black curls. Suddenly he looked very young and vulnerable. 'There's no room for them in the ship's boat.'

'What about seeking help,' I suggested, looking astern. Some distance away was the sail of a boat that had been within sight since dawn.

'We'll signal them, but I doubt they will respond,' Protis answered.

He gave the order for an old, threadbare sail to be ripped into rags, soaked in olive oil, and set alight. The sailors then fed the flames with short lengths of tarred rope until a thin wavering column of smoke rose from our stricken vessel.

For a full hour we watched the distant sail, willing it to change course and come towards us. It did change course, but away, growing smaller with each minute.

The elderly sailor to whom I had spoken earlier cursed savagely.

'They think we're pirates,' Protis said despondently, 'trying to lure them in closer.'

'Is there nothing else we can do?' I asked.

'We've no choice but to abandon ship.'

It was clear that our vessel was gradually settling deeper and deeper into the water. The hold was more than half full now, and the ship had a leaden, dead feeling. Without waiting for their captain's order the crew were already setting down their buckets and gathering together their few belongings. Two of them climbed down into the ship's skiff and the others began to pass down their bundles.

'At least let us take the gyrfalcons. They'll take up no space,' I pleaded.

Protis had the decency to look ashamed as he shook his head. 'I'm afraid not. The skiff will be overloaded as it is, and it will be a long row to reach land. We must leave all your animals behind.'

I felt a touch on my arm, and turned to find Walo; his face was working angrily. I had been distracted by all that was going on and had paid him no attention.

'Walo, we must leave the ship,' I explained. 'We cannot take the animals. They stay behind.'

Deep in his throat he made a distressed growling noise and, seizing me by the elbow, pulled me across the deck. 'For the falcons and the dogs,' he said, placing a hand on the water trough. It was the river ferry we had cut into two and converted. I ran back to where Protis was standing. He had a satchel slung over his shoulder, ready to abandon ship. 'We can use the cut-off ferryboat to carry the dogs and the gyrfalcons,' I cried.

'Impossible,' he answered flatly. 'It'll be swamped or capsize! My men aren't going to wait.' He cast a glance over his shoulder to where the last members of his crew were standing by the rail. The others were already in the ship's boat, setting the oars in place.

Osric limped over and announced that he was ready to try using the makeshift boat to get ashore with the smaller animals. I turned my attention to Abram. 'Are you willing to give it a try?'

The dragoman nodded immediately. 'I'll send my own men with the ship's crew. They can take our valuables with them.'

Protis threw up his hands. 'You're crazy, risking your lives for a couple of birds and some dogs!'

'It would help if you let us have some oars,' Osric told him pointedly.

Protis glared at him before stamping off to the rail and telling his men to hand up a couple of oars. There was a moment's hesitation and he had to shout angrily at them. Reluctantly, they obeyed. Protis brought the oars across to us and laid them down on the deck. 'This ship may still be afloat when I get ashore,' he told us. 'I'll try to organize a rescue boat to come out to fetch you and your precious animals.'

But from the way he avoided looking me in the eye, I knew he did not expect the ship, or us, to survive that long.

As the ship's boat pulled away, Osric, Walo, Abram and myself busied ourselves with the abandoned buckets. We emptied enough water from the trough to allow us to turn it on edge, and then tip out the rest. Abram found a couple of lengths of plank that he fitted for thwarts, and he knotted loops of rope to hold the oars when it came time for us to row. Osric and I used an axe and a crowbar to smash a gap in the ship's rail. By the time we had finished, the ship had sunk so far that there was less than three feet between the deck and the surface of the sea. We slid our makeshift vessel overboard with ease. It wallowed with barely five inches above the surface of the sea, but it floated.

Osric stepped carefully into it, and Abram handed across the gyrfalcons in their cages. The five white dogs were more awkward. They had to be restrained from leaping across the gap and upsetting the balance of the unstable craft. One by one, Walo picked them up and settled them in place to be watched over by Abram. I took a last look around. Walo had insisted on scrambling back aboard the sinking ship and had gone forward. He had already released the remaining chickens from their coop. Now he was unlatching the door to the ice bears' cage, leaving it wide open. He did the same with the aurochs' enclosure. Finally, he walked down the deck to join me and together we climbed into the boat.

We pushed off and, taking turns at the two oars, crept away from the sinking ship, looking on in silence as Modi and Madi pushed their way from their cage and padded up and down the deck. They sniffed curiously at the items that had been left behind. Only recently had I found a way of telling the difference between the two bears: Modi walked with a slightly different gait to his brother, his left front paw turned in at an angle. It was ironic, I thought, that I should have learned to tell them apart soon before I saw them for the last time. Quickly they came across the chickens that Walo had released, and there was a brief and dramatic chase. Terrified squawks ended abruptly in bursts of feathers, and the two ice bears settled down to gnaw happily on their catch. By then the aurochs had also emerged from its confinement. It went directly to the pile of dried grass that Walo had dumped at the base of the mast and began to eat.

Once or twice Walo tried to stand up to get a better view, and I had to tell him sharply to sit down or he would upset the boat. Strangely, he was showing no sign of distress as he looked back towards his beloved bears enjoying their meal. I wondered if it was Walo's intention that the animals would go to their deaths content, on full stomachs.

We rowed. Our progress was a crawl, and the sun beat down. Fortunately, the sea was a glassy calm, and there was nothing to do but sit very still and avoid disturbing the delicate balance of our unstable boat or take an oar when it was handed on. None of us spoke.

I was struggling to come to terms with the loss of the larger animals. Even if we succeeded in reaching the shore with the gyrfalcons and the dogs, they were not sufficient for what Carolus had had in mind when he had entrusted me with the embassy to the caliph. At best, the king might order me to return to Kaupang next year and start all over again with a new batch of white animals. More likely, he would abandon the whole scheme. In which case, my future – and Osric's – at the royal court would be hanging by a thread. Carolus did not tolerate a bungler.

Osric broke into my gloomy thoughts. 'That canvas patch should have kept the water out,' he observed.

'Protis's vessel was too badly neglected,' Abram told him. 'You saw for yourself the poor condition of the hull when you were underwater.'

'True, the seams were bad,' my friend replied. 'But if we had not delayed to fit the patch, as I suggested, maybe we could have got the vessel to land and beached her.'

I felt that Osric was blaming himself unnecessarily. 'That's all behind us now. I was the one who had made the decision to hire Protis and his ship. Let's concentrate on getting safely to shore in this tub.'

Osric shook his head ruefully. 'Even the most rotten hull shouldn't spring such a disastrous leak in a calm sea and with virtually no wind. Our luck has to change.'

His remark hung in the air between us. I found myself wondering if the sinking of the ship was just a freak accident, bad luck, or something more. I could not shake off the feeling that there was a link between the murderous attack on me in Kaupang and the recent calamity. It took the rest of the afternoon for us to reach the shore. By that time the sinking vessel was too far away and too low in the water for us to see any detail. Her mast was still visible so we guessed that she was settling into her grave still upright. Ahead of us, Protis and his men had already landed in a small cove. A group of a dozen men were gathered around their skiff where it was drawn up on the beach. I presumed they came from the community of boat builders that Protis had spoken of. Further up the beach were several half-built boats on the stocks, and there were untidy heaps of raw timber and long sheds that looked as if they contained the shipwrights' stores.

We were less than a stone's throw from the beach when, ignoring my warning growl, Walo suddenly stood up. The boat wobbled dangerously, and he let out a whoop.

I jerked around. He was pointing out to sea, his eyes shining. Directly between us and the sinking ship were two small dark shapes in the water, not half a mile away.

'Modi and Madi! They're swimming after us. That's why Walo let them free,' exclaimed Osric

'Quick!' I cried, after I had recovered from my initial shock. 'We have to be ready for them.'

We rowed the final yards. Protis and his men waded into the water and, helped by several shipwrights, dragged our makeshift vessel to land. Osric handed over the first of the gyrfalcon cages for it to be carried up the beach and set down safely on the ground. The dogs leaped out and bounded ashore.

'There are two large and dangerous bears on their way,' I announced loudly. The shipwrights stared at me. Then I remembered that they would not understand my language. A small crowd of onlookers had gathered at the back of the beach, women and children. I guessed they were the families of the shipbuilders, curious to see what the sea had brought. I yelled at the top of my voice to gain their attention, and pointed. The white heads of the two bears were now much closer. It was extraordinary how fast they were able to move through the water. In a few more minutes they would be on land.

I heard a murmur of astonishment from the crowd, a murmur that turned to a ripple of alarm as they realized what they were seeing.

'Abram, tell them that the bears are dangerous and we must have somewhere to contain them,' I told the dragoman.

One of the shipwrights was quick on the uptake. He ran to open the door of a boat shed.

Walo was already at the water's edge. He had his deerhorn pipe in hand. As the two bears came closer, he began to play. Behind me the crowd scattered. They scurried away, then turned at a safe distance to see what would happen next.

Madi and Modi came ashore side by side. They shook themselves, spraying water in all directions from their soaking coats, and looked around. They had grown into hulking brutes that could easily break a man's back with a single swipe from their great paws. Modi yawned, and the great pink gaping gullet caused several gasps of fear from the handful of the bolder spectators who had stayed for a closer look. In the distance there was the clink and rattle of pebbles as the more prudent on-lookers retreated even further up the beach.

Walo advanced towards the bears until he was no more than an arm's length away. Facing them, he continued to play his usual simple tune. The bears stood on the shoreline, their great pointed muzzles swinging from side to side. They were curious about what was happening. Carefully, Walo began pacing backwards, still facing the bears and playing his pipe.

The two bears padded after him. Walo backed away, step by slow step, towards the open door of the boat shed, and then inside. For a heart-stopping moment the bears halted at the dark entrance to the shed. They turned and faced outward, their small eyes inspecting the crowd of onlookers. I held my breath, knowing that if they chose to charge and attack, nothing could stop them.

Then the music worked its lure and they went inside. A shipwright darted forward, about to slam the door behind them. I grabbed him by the shirt and held him back. 'Don't startle the bears. Let them grow accustomed to their new home.'

The man could not have understood exactly what I said, but the message was clear. He waited beside me while we listened to the soothing sound of Walo's music for a few more minutes. Then together we went forward and softly half-closed the door, leaving a gap large enough for Walo to slip out when he judged the moment was right.

Osric let out a sigh of relief. 'We should have guessed that ice bears are good swimmers,' he said to me.

'A pity we can't say the same about the aurochs,' I replied.

The words were scarcely out of my mouth when there was another buzz of astonishment from the crowd. Everyone was gazing out to where the setting sun cast a long reddish-gold path across the mirror-calm of the sea. The head of the aurochs showed black against the red. The beast was swimming to land, more slowly than the bears, following them.

My heart leaped into my mouth. I had witnessed the creature's rage as it smashed Walo's father, Vulfard, to bloody pulp. Now I shuddered to think what carnage it might inflict on the crowd on the beach. To add to my alarm, the crowd was less fearful than when they had seen the bears approaching. To them, the aurochs looked little different from a common farm bull at that distance. They failed to note its great size and the menacing forward sweep of the deadly horns. There was a mutter of interest, but nothing like the general panic the bears had created.

I ran towards the crowd. 'Get back! Get back! I shouted, waving my arms frantically. I was met with stares of curiosity and incomprehension.

Osric joined me, gesturing at the crowd, trying to move them away. But the spectators dawdled, reluctant to leave.

The aurochs reached the shallows, and began to emerge from the water. There was a collective, appalled gasp. The creature was monstrous. It paused with half its huge body still under water and the great dark shoulders and neck gleaming wet. Then it lifted the great head, stretched its neck so that the muzzle pointed to the sky, and uttered a massive bellow that echoed around the cliffs.

At that moment Protis redeemed himself. The young man raced down the beach. He had a scrap of cloth in one hand as he dashed directly at the aurochs. I thought he had lost his mind. He sprinted into the shallows, tripping and almost falling as his feet hit the water. The aurochs immediately lowered its head and lunged at him with the deadly horns. Protis swerved and slipped past the attack. He flung himself against the creature's shoulder, and whipped the rag around its massive head, covering its eyes.

The aurochs tossed its head in amazement. Protis threw an arm over the creature's neck and managed to cling on. The beast shook its head angrily, and I was reminded sickeningly of the horror as Vulfard's spitted corpse had been thrashed from side to side. But Protis was behind the horns, and he hung on grimly until the shaking stopped and he had time to loop the rag in place. The great beast halted, confused and blind.

A vague memory stirred. I recalled my father's ploughmen coaxing reluctant oxen into their stalls.

'We need a heavy rope!' I called to Osric. He looked at me for an instant, and then understanding dawned. Together we ran to where the shipwrights had their gear, selected a length of heavy cable, and hurried down the beach, circling behind the aurochs. Abram and his two men joined us and together we stretched the rope and brought it against the aurochs' hindquarters. The sudden touch of the rope made the blindfolded beast start forward. It walked out of the water and, by keeping up the pressure on the rope, we guided it towards the line of boat sheds.

Two local men saw what we intended. They ran ahead and swung open the doors to the stoutest shed. All the time Protis stayed beside the beast's neck, matching it stride for stride, making sure the blindfold stayed in place. Together we somehow succeeded in steering the aurochs into its temporary home, then heaved shut the heavy door as Protis darted out to safety.

'The boat shed won't hold the beast for long. Ask the villagers to fetch fodder and water,' I said to Abram.

Protis was white-faced and trembling with relief. I thought he was about to faint.

'That was very courageous,' I congratulated him. 'I hope your grandfather gets to hear how you saved the day.'

He summoned up a shaky smile. 'The old man won't forgive me for losing the family's last and only ship.'

He looked past me to where his vessel was no longer to be seen. The sea was empty. The vessel must have slipped beneath the waves. The young Greek's eyes filled with tears. 'My family does not have the resources to build a new ship. And the moneylenders will think that somehow we are cursed with bad luck.'

'What will you do?' I asked softly.

'My men can find work on other ships, and I will have to hire myself out as a common sailor,' he answered.

He looked so downcast that I reached out and gave him a

reassuring squeeze on the shoulder. 'Your bravery saved the day. You'd be more than welcome to travel on to Rome with us.'

He lifted his chin as a trace of his former pride returned. 'I was hired to deliver you and your animals to Rome, and I will fulfil my side of the bargain.'

Chapter Eleven

ROME

*

ABRAM'S ITINERARIUM marked a road running parallel to the coast that would eventually bring us to Rome. The dragoman's attendants had brought the map ashore, along with my precious copy of the Book of Beasts and our other valuables, but all the travelling furniture – the folding tables and chairs, the tents and camping equipment – had been lost with the ship. As a replacement the ever-resourceful Protis, now once more bubbling with self-confidence, devised two houses on wheels for us – moving homes. He boasted these contraptions would save us from having to stay overnight in the hospitia, the flea-ridden hostels designed for pilgrims on the way to the Holy City. Equally practical and ingenious were the wheeled cages the shipwrights put together for the aurochs and the ice bears. The carpenters held a stock of curved timbers, normally used for the ribs of ships. They adapted them as bars for the cages so that our large animals travelled in elegant creations like skeletons of upturned boats. The effect was, as Osric remarked, to make our little procession along the road resemble a travelling circus.

It was late November by the time we finally reached the outskirts of the Holy City, and the weather had turned both rainy and cold. On Abram's suggestion I went ahead to find Alcuin's friend, Paul the Nomenculator, to ask if he could assist us in finding warm, dry accommodation where our embassy — including the animals — could spend the winter.

As Abram had predicted, my impression of Rome was that of a city falling apart. A steady drizzle made it a dull, cheerless morning as I passed through an archway, beneath what had once been an imposing bastion in the ancient city wall. Flaking plaster revealed rotting brickwork underneath, and there were no guards or sentries to be seen. I was on foot and carried Alcuin's letter of introduction, but no one asked me my business. I picked my way around a few farm carts loaded with produce on their way to market and dodged a small party of wealthy travellers on horseback, wrapped up against the weather in their fur-lined cloaks. But the majority of my fellows were families; men, women and children dressed in drab clothing, with hoods pulled up to keep off the rain. They trudged along under the unrelenting drizzle, many with backpacks. One man pushed a barrow with two of his children riding on top of their belongings. Eavesdropping on their assortment of languages, it was obvious that they were pilgrims from many countries and regions, all coming to visit the Holy City. But the miserable weather dampened the excitement of their arrival. The whining of children and the bickering of their parents prevailed over any expressions of wonder and anticipation.

As I walked deeper into the maze of streets, then across a bridge over a murky-looking river, I saw building after building that had once been grand and imposing. Now they were derelict and grimy. Most had been turned into squalid tenements occupied by the poor. Everything was so run-down and jumbled together that it was difficult to make out whether I was in a district that was residential or commercial. Respectable mansions gone to seed stood cheek-by-jowl with shops, warehouses, or smaller dwellings. From time to time I would turn a corner and find myself confronted by a crumbling structure dating back to the glory days of the Roman Empire: a triumphal arch, a long-abandoned theatre, a victory column, an ornate fountain long since run dry, public baths closed for centuries. One monument – a former theatre – was being actively looted for its material. A builder's gang was using crowbars to prise away the marble facing, then smashing the slabs with sledge hammers, before tossing the broken fragments into a smoky kiln to make lime for mortar. Luckily they understood my Latin well enough for them to tell me that I did not have to go as far as the office of the Nomenculator. The man himself had been seen with a party of papal officials inspecting a newly renovated basilica dedicated to Santa Maria not far away. Helpfully they despatched a boy to lead me there.

The church of Santa Maria in Cosmedin came as a pleasant contrast to the general urban decay. The building was conspicuously well maintained. Modest in size, it stood on the edge of an open space that I was already learning to call a forum. Seven round-headed arches that gave it a simple elegance pierced the plain red brick façade. A large group of servants lurked in a nearby alley, and in the portico of the basilica four or five men dressed in long dark tunics and cloaks sheltered from the drifting rain, conferring. My guide pointed to one of them – a short, heavy-set man wearing a broad-brimmed hat who was standing slightly apart from the others and rubbing his hands together to keep warm. He looked up as I approached, and – to my amazement – gave me a broad wink.

'I'm looking for the Nomenculator, Paul,' I said in my best Latin. A servant had detached himself from the waiting group of attendants and was hurrying towards me, doubtless to head me off before I bothered his master. My young guide promptly made himself scarce.

'My name is Paul,' said the man, waving the servant away, 'and judging by your accent you must be Sigwulf, the envoy from Aachen that my friend Alcuin wrote to me about. I've been expecting you for some weeks.'

He treated me to another broad wink with his left eye, screwing up that side of his face. I realized that it was an involuntary convulsion.

'I'm sorry to be late,' I said. 'We encountered difficulties on our journey that delayed us. I arrived only this morning, and my companions are waiting outside the city.'

'Then it is my pleasure as well as my duty to welcome you to Rome,' said Paul. His voice was husky, as if he was suffering from a cold, but his manner seemed genuinely well disposed. 'Alcuin asked me to be of assistance.'

'I don't want to disturb you. But we need to find lodgings urgently for ourselves and a place to keep the animals that King Carolus is sending to Baghdad,' I answered, rummaging in my satchel for Alcuin's letter of introduction.

'Ah yes. The animals!' said Paul, ignoring the proffered letter. 'Alcuin wrote to me about those. I'm longing to see them for myself. Don't worry about disturbing me. My business here at the basilica is finished.'

He turned to his companions and explained that he was being called away on an important matter. Settling his hat firmly on his head, he stepped out into the street and gestured at me to accompany him. I noted that half a dozen attendants followed us at a discreet distance. Clearly the Nomenculator was a person of importance.

'His Holiness insists on checks and double-checks, though they are not really my responsibility,' he told me as we walked along briskly. 'He's determined that the translations are success-ful. My fear is that they will only make the thefts worse.'

He saw my look of utter incomprehension and gave an apologetic chuckle. 'Forgive me. A lifetime of working at the papal court leads one to presume that everyone knows the obsession of the day. It creates a sort of tunnel vision.' He laughed again. 'A not inappropriate metaphor.'

'I'm sorry,' I said, confused. 'What translations must be successful?'

'Of holy bones. They must be moved into the city itself. To be better protected, and more accessible to the faithful.'

I gave him a sideways glance. I judged him to be in his late forties. His face was a blotchy coarse red. He had a bulbous nose and great bags under his eyes. He looked like a drunkard, and yet there was an underlying sharpness as well as genuine warmth. I found myself liking him.

'What bones are those?' I asked.

'Of saints and martyrs. In ancient times a municipal ordi-nance forbade burials within the city. So the bodies of the sainted dead were put underground in catacombs in the sub-urbs. Now we're trying to locate them, and bring them into the city where they can be properly preserved and venerated. As well as protected from grave robbers who would sell off the bits and pieces to whoever will buy them.'

He jerked his thumb over his shoulder. 'In Santa Maria's the workmen have excavated a new crypt. It has alcoves for the bones that will be brought in from the catacombs. I was there to check that everything was in order.'

'But I thought your office as Nomenculator makes you responsible for petitions to the pope, not overseeing translations, as you put it.'

'Quite so. Unfortunately, my passion is ancient history. I'm more familiar with the archives than the pope's librarian who, by the way, is a political appointment and an ignoramus. So I'm always being called upon to identify the catacombs where the martyrs were buried, and to authenticate their remains. Though, to be truthful, most bones look much like any others.'

'Santa Maria Basilica appears to be a very suitable place to keep holy relics,' I said, I hoped tactfully.

'When you have time, you should go inside and take a look around. It has some superb interior decoration, mosaics and painted plasterwork. All done by priests from Byzantium. Locally it's known as Santa Maria of the Greeks.'

The mention of Greeks was unsettling. I thought of the Byzantine gold solidus that one of the men who tried to kill me in Kaupang had asked Redwald to change for silver coin. 'Is there a large Greek congregation here?' I asked. 'I was told that the Holy Father and the Church authorities in Byzantium are at odds with one another.'

He sniffed, a sound that conveyed both amusement and disdain. 'Renegade Greek priests, refugee preachers, ambitious prelates. Rome is full of every sort of delinquent. Some genuine, some with a hidden agenda. I should know: many of them come to my office seeking favours.'

He paused for a moment. 'I'm a papal gatekeeper but the person I recommend for an audience with the pope doesn't necessarily get what he wants. There are other hurdles to clear before one benefits from the pope's patronage.'

It all sounded very much like Abram's warning to me that Rome was like a snake pit. I should be wary. I decided it was safer to turn the conversation to a more neutral subject, something closer to Paul's interest.

'I saw workmen ripping marble slabs from a fine-looking palace back there. Is that allowed?' I asked.

'That sort of thing has been going on for centuries,' he answered cheerfully. We had turned into a broad avenue dominated by a looming triumphal arch. Sixty feet high, its three archways were flanked with columns of yellow marble topped with over-size human figures draped in togas. Huge panels of carved marble depicted scenes of warfare and hunting, trophies, gods, Roman soldiers and defeated enemies. Sections of the frieze had fallen away and the surface was streaked with dirt. Wild plants had taken root in cracks in the stonework and grown into bushes high above the ground. It looked shaggy and forsaken.

Paul waved up at it. 'We're standing on the Triumphal Way. That arch was erected five centuries ago to celebrate an imperial victory. Yet already most of those marble panels were second hand. They were taken down from previous monuments and reused. We Romans have little loyalty to the past when it suits us.'

I should have been listening to him more closely, but my attention had wandered. An extraordinary structure dominated the skyline beyond the triumphal arch. The Nomenculator did not have to explain to me what it was. My teacher had told me about it when I was a boy and I had never expected to see it for myself. The Colosseum was everything that I had imagined – soaring up like a vast perforated drum, three layers of ornamented arcades perched each on top of the other and surmounted by a podium. There was a wide break on the side of the drum where a huge section of the edifice had collapsed, but the overall effect was still breathtaking.

Paul noted my amazement. 'The greatest structure of the Roman world. A feat of engineering and design that has never been equalled,' he said with more than a hint of pride.

'It is stunning,' I confessed.

He looked at me from under the wide brim of his hat, and a mischievous smile spread across the blotchy red face. 'That is where you and your embassy will be accommodated for the winter.'

I thought I had misheard, and stood rooted to the spot.

He had to repeat himself. 'That,' he said, pointing, 'is where you will be staying. It's your winter quarters and will house the beasts too.'

'But how . . . ?' I stammered.

His smile grew even broader. 'Alcuin listed the animals you were bringing. When I got his letter I wondered where on earth I could possibly put such creatures. It was like trying to find accommodation for a circus. Then, of course, it came to me: the very centre of Rome has a place designed precisely for circuses and their strange and curious beasts.'

'But the Colosseum was for gladiatorial contests.'

'It was, and sometimes the fights were between wild animals or between men and beasts. So the Colosseum has dozens of stalls to accommodate dangerous creatures.'

'And is it still possible to use them nowadays?'

His face twitched in the convulsive wink once more, and he laid a conspiratorial hand on my sleeve. 'Believe it or not, the Nomenculator can wield considerable influence when he wants to. Besides, the Colosseum is not as impressive on the inside as from where we stand. Those stalls and shacks should give you a clue.'

Around the base of the Colosseum squatters had thrown up a line of lean-to shops and poor dwellings. Like limpets, they rested against the outer wall of the amphitheatre. Here, as elsewhere, the citizens of Rome took indiscriminate advantage of their city's heritage.

Followed by his train of servants, the Nomenculator guided

me through one of the many entry archways in the Colosseum's lower wall. We walked down a dank tunnel smelling of rotting rubbish and excrement, and came out on the lowest of the spectator terraces. We were standing where the most important onlookers once must have sat, within yards of the gory action in the arena immediately below them. Now the spectacle was utterly different. On the far side of the amphitheatre a large part of the upper arcades had fallen inwards, causing an unsightly landslide of rubble. On the edge of the ancient arena was a small rustic-looking chapel made from salvaged stones. The floor of the arena close to the chapel was being used as a burial place. Crude stumps of broken marble served as grave markers. Much of the lowest arcade had been converted into makeshift dwellings. Smoke rose from their cooking fires. Higher up, the arcades had been abandoned, presumably as they were unsafe, but not before being robbed of building material, some of which still lay in untidy heaps in the arena. The only area that retained anything like its former function as a gladiatorial arena lay directly in front of us. A sturdy fence of wooden boards had been erected to make a semi-circular enclosure some thirty yards across. Inside the enclosure, the sand of the original arena had been cleaned of rubbish and swept. Several tiers of stone seats that looked down into the enclosure were intact.

'This place once held fifty thousand spectators,' Paul said, leading me down some broken steps and into the enclosure. 'Nowadays there's an occasional theatre show in this small part. For an audience of a few hundred.'

I said nothing. I was still coming to terms with how badly the Colosseum had deteriorated from what I had imagined.

'In the heyday of the Colosseum the wild beasts were kept underground,' Paul went on. 'A system of trap doors and pulleys hoisted them into the arena so they sprang up through the ground like magic. But all that mechanism is broken or rotted. Now you must be content with these stables at the back.'

We had arrived before heavy wooden double doors set into the high wall of the arena itself. The doors looked in good repair, and there was a sheen of oil on the metal hinges. The Nomenculator waited while one of his servants came forward, raised the heavy bar that kept them shut, and swung them open. We went inside, into a large antechamber with a high, vaulted ceiling, whitewashed walls and a stone-flagged floor.

'This is where the actors waited before going out to perform,' Paul told me. 'Gladiatorial contests were by no means the only public spectacles in the Colosseum. There were pageants and re-enactments, circus shows and dramas based on stories of their gods and goddesses. Many of them involved riders and horses.'

At the back of the antechamber was a broad passageway with several doors on either side. He led me to the first of them and opened it with a flourish. 'This is where they kept their nags,' he announced.

I looked into a large, well-appointed stable. A small window set up high in the rear wall gave light and air. There was a stone manger, a groove in the stone floor to carry away piss.

'This will be perfect for the aurochs,' I said, pleased.

'Alcuin claims that it is the only aurochs in captivity. I can't wait to see it,' Paul answered. 'There are adjacent stalls for your other animals. I'll have my people keep the open space in the arena cleared so they can be let out for exercise,' he let out a wheezy laugh, 'though not at the same time.'

'I'll write to Alcuin to let him know how kind you have been,' I said.

He acknowledged my thanks with a small shrug. 'For your

own accommodation I've arranged one of those houses on the lower arcade that we saw on the way in.'

We retraced our steps out into the arena where the Nomenculator's attendants were waiting. They had been joined by two men standing on either side of a large box with protruding handles. It reminded me of a deep bed with a canopy over it. I had never seen a litter before.

Pausing, the Nomenculator turned to me. 'One of my men will escort you back to rejoin your comrades. If there's anything you need, just let me know.'

He stepped inside the litter, half reclining on the seat. The two bearers lifted the vehicle and the Nomenculator's mottled face came back level with my own.

'Perhaps you and your colleagues could join me for a meal at my official residence? I'd like to hear about your journey so far,' he said.

'I'd be delighted,' I replied.

'If it's not too soon for you, I suggest supper tomorrow evening. I'll send someone to fetch you. A word of warning: avoid walking the streets of Rome on your own, especially after dark. I don't want to have to send a letter to Alcuin saying that something untoward had happened to you or your comrades.'

He gave an order and the two litter bearers began to move. I watched my new-found ally being carried away up the stairs, leaving me wondering why he showed quite such concern for our safety.

*

Next morning dawned with the same unrelenting grey sky though the drizzle had stopped, and we drove our boat-like waggons into the city and as far as the Colosseum. I worried about how to transfer the aurochs into its new home without endangering ourselves, until Osric drew my attention to an archway at street level wider than the other entrances. It was sealed with a massive gate that looked as if it had not been opened for a very long time. Behind it a passageway led to a second gate that opened directly into the arena. We forced open both the gates and backed the aurochs' wheeled cage into the entrance, then released the beast. Snorting angrily, it ran down the passageway and out into the arena. After making a couple of menacing circuits of the ring, tossing its head and looking for enemies, it came across the entrance into what had been the performers' anteroom. The brute trotted inside and eventually found its way into the stable prepared for it. Walo had been tracking the creature from a safe distance and he slammed the door shut behind it. He then undertook the easier task of bringing Madi and Modi to their new accommodation.

The house the Nomenculator provided for us was less than a stone's throw from where the animals were housed and we had transferred all our belongings by the time Paul's servant arrived to escort us to his master's residence for supper. Walo asked to stay behind to make sure that the animals were well settled, so Osric, Abram, Protis and I set out with our guide. He led us away from the centre of the city, up the slope of a gentle hill and into a very run-down area. Chickens scratched and foraged among the ruins of tumbledown houses. Overgrown gardens had been converted into small vineyards or turned into rough paddocks for goats and cows. Pig pens and cattle byres occupied the ground floors of dwellings whose roofs had long since fallen in. Amid all this decay the Nomenculator lived in a large square brick building with a colonnaded frontage that must once have belonged to a Roman grandee.

He greeted us in the entrance hall, his dark priest's gown in stark contrast to the bright patterns of the floor mosaics. 'There'll only be the five of us at table. So I've told my steward to serve the meal in one of the smaller side rooms.

I introduced my companions and asked why so many of the adjacent properties were unoccupied.

'The city's population is in rapid decline,' he replied, leading the way deeper into the building. 'Nowadays people prefer to live in the centre, close to the river, though I can't understand why. The low-lying areas are prone to bad flooding in winter, leaving the residents trapped in the upper floors of their tenements.'

We had passed into a second, even larger hall, and he pointed to the small pool in the centre of the marble floor. 'The city aqueducts are constantly breaking down so water for drinking and cooking has to be delivered by cart. Here we still collect the rain from the roof.'

The plastered walls around us were painted with scenes from ancient tales. Their colours were faded but the details in each of the pictures was still clear, and I sensed that Protis was having difficulty restraining himself from interrupting our host to tell us about them.

'This building is Church property and I am only a tenant,' Paul explained. 'Pope Adrian has decided it will become a monastery. I arranged the papal audience for the lucky abbot, and he agreed I could occupy it until he raised sufficient funds for the rebuilding programme.'

He gave me a sly glance as if to remind me that everyday life in Rome was underpinned by favouritism and intrigue.

Five chairs had been set around a small dining table in a side room where the wall paintings were of tranquil rural scenes. I had not eaten since breakfast and my stomach growled with hunger at the sight of green and black olives heaped in bowls, platters of cheese, dried meat and loaves of bread. As we took our places, the Nomenculator apologized for the simple food, saying that it was difficult for his cook to obtain fresh produce in the winter. But the first course was followed by a dish of coddled eggs, then a fish course with a pungent sauce, and finally small bowls of thick sweetened milk with a flavour that was new to me. All the while a servant came round behind our chairs and filled and refilled our glasses with wine. By the time the final course was cleared away, I was feeling light-headed. Finally, our host turned to me, screwed up the side of his face in one of his twitches, and announced, 'Now is the moment for you to tell me about your travels.'

Conscious that my comrades were listening, I asked for a cup of water and took a sip before launching into my account, beginning with my summons from Alcuin and the visit to King Carolus in his private chambers. The Nomenculator listened closely, his eyes flicking around the circle of his guests. Occasionally he signalled to a servant to refill a glass.

When I reached the point where I described my failure to locate a unicorn, Paul nodded sympathetically. 'You were look-ing in the wrong place. The unicorn is to be found in the Indies, not the northern lands.'

'What makes you say that?' I asked.

'In the archives there's mention of an ox-like beast with a single horn brought to Rome for a spectacle in the Colosseum. It was pitted against a bear. The bear won.'

'Was the animal white?' I asked. If the caliph in Baghdad already had a white unicorn in his menagerie, Carolus's gifts would look very meagre.

'Nothing is mentioned in that regard,' he replied. 'But please go on with your tale. What about the risks of travelling so far north?'

'The ice bears could have been difficult to transport. But it turned out that my assistant Walo has an uncanny ability to handle them.'

Osric coughed discreetly. 'You've omitted the knife attack in Kaupang,' he prompted.

Paul's eyes lit up with interest. 'Tell me about that.'

I described how two ruffians with knives had cornered me. When I finished, he looked thoughtful. 'If that had happened in Rome, I'd say the attack was more than an attempt at simple robbery.'

'It did seem to have been planned,' I answered, reaching to the purse on my belt. I took out Offa's gold coin which Redwald had given me and which I kept as a memento. I held it up for the Nomenculator to see. 'This man – King Offa of Mercia – would like to see me dead. One of my attackers had this coin in his possession. It could have been part of his pay.'

'May I see that?' Abram broke in. He was seated on my right and I held the coin out to him. 'Fascinating,' he said, taking the coin and turning it over. 'I've heard of King Offa, of course, but I've never seen his coinage before. It's a copy of an Arab dinar, but I would hesitate before trading it to a Saracen.' He smiled knowingly as he passed the coin on to Osric. 'I'm sure you can tell me why.'

Puzzled, I looked from one to the other as Osric also examined the coin. 'I see what you mean,' he said. 'Offa's name is in Saracen script. Whoever minted the coin couldn't read the writing for himself. It's upside down.'

He handed me back the coin, and I returned it to my purse.

Paul nodded to a servant to clear away the last of the little bowls of sweetened milk. Platters of dried fruits and nuts were placed on the table.

'You were very lucky to get away with your life,' he observed.

'It was Redwald who saved me, just as Protis here came to our rescue. Our mission has been lucky in its shipmasters.'

'Another adventure then?' said Paul expectantly. He selected a dried apricot and took a small, neat bite.

I described the slow sinking of Protis's ship and how we had been forced to row for shore. When I came to the moment when the aurochs emerged on the beach, Paul clicked his fingers delightedly. 'The bull from the sea no less!' he exclaimed and indicated the wall paintings that surrounded us. 'A picture in this house shows the tale. For his Seventh Labour Hercules had to capture the wild Cretan bull on its island. King Eurytheus set Hercules the task, but was too frightened to accept the bull when Hercules brought it back to his palace in Greece. So Hercules set the beast free and it ravaged the countryside until it was captured and killed by the hero Theseus.'

'I don't know that story,' I admitted. 'I was told that Theseus killed the Minotaur in the labyrinth.'

Paul took another careful bite from the apricot. 'The Minotaur and the Cretan bull may not be the same thing. Every story has its variations.'

Protis could restrain himself no longer. 'The Cretan bull was simply that – a very dangerous bull. The Minotaur was a wondrous creature half-bull, half-man.'

'Which half was which?' asked Abram, the ghost of a smile on his lips.

Protis took the question very seriously. 'Some artists depict the Minotaur with the head of a man set on the body of a bull; others prefer the body of a man with bull's head and tail.'

'Both sound highly unlikely,' Abram muttered under his breath.

Protis failed to hear him. 'The Minotaur,' he said, adopting a schoolmaster's tone, 'was the result of the queen of Crete mating with a bull. She hid herself inside the replica of a wooden cow and attracted the bull to her.'

Abram made a scoffing sound under his breath but Protis was still not put off. 'All sorts of strange-looking babies are born to humans. You've all heard of babies that have webbed hands and feet like frogs.'

I thought it was wise to intervene before Protis fell into an open dispute with our dragoman. 'We mustn't be too quick to dismiss the idea of a creature with the head of a bull and the body of a man,' I said. 'King Carolus's bestiary has several illustrations of creatures which could be the result of strange coupling. For example, the cameleopard is clothed in the spotted pelt of a leopard yet it has the shape of a camel. It could be the offspring of those two creatures.'

The Nomenculator was enjoying the discussion. He placed the stone from the dried apricot carefully on the table, took a cloth from an attendant and wiped his lips. 'There were cameleopards in those wild animal displays in the Colosseum I spoke about,' he said.

'What were they like?' I asked.

'Very timid, apparently. Two of them were brought from Africa, a long and difficult journey, and let loose in the arena. They galloped around the ring in a panic. Then hungry lions were sent in. It was very disappointing for the crowd. The lions pulled down and killed the cameleopards who put up no resistance.'

'If the crowds had seen ice bears, they would have been more impressed,' said Protis boldly. I suspected that the wine had gone to his head.

'But they did,' answered Paul mildly. 'I've come across a

description of how the arena of the Colosseum was flooded to make an artificial lake complete with small islands. Ice bears and seals were introduced so the crowds could watch how the bears hunted the seals. Remarkable.'

A thought occurred to me. 'Did your ancestors leave any clues as to how they managed to keep their captive ice bears alive?'

The Nomenculator was quick to follow my reasoning. 'Tomorrow I'll have a clerk start looking through the archives to see if anything is written about that.'

'I'd be grateful – the information would help Walo. He'll also have to keep them cool in the summer heat on the way to Baghdad.'

There was a lull in the conversation and Paul took the opportunity to whisper a quiet instruction to a servant and hand him a small set of keys. The man left the room and came back some moments later carrying a folded cloth which he laid on the table in front of the Nomenculator, and returned the keys to his master.

The rest of us watched, intrigued, as Paul unfolded the cloth and revealed a short twig, pale brown and a few inches long. He picked it up and handed it to me. 'What do you think this is?'

The twig felt very light, almost crumbly, as if it had been dried. On closer inspection it could have been a strip of bark, tightly rolled.

'Try smelling it,' suggested Paul.

I raised it to my nose and sniffed. There was a subtle, slightly oily, pleasant perfume. A moment later I recognized it as the flavour of the sweetened milk desserts we had just eaten.

'From my kitchen,' said Paul. 'It's very expensive, so my cook keeps it under lock and key.'

'What is it?' I asked, inhaling the intriguing scent once again.

'I presume that your Book of Beasts has a section on the more notable birds,' said Paul, twitching as he smiled.

I nodded. 'Gyrfalcons, among them. Ours are very special because they are white.'

'What other birds?'

'As I recall, cranes, eagles and a small black and white bird that can foretell the death of kings.'

'Anything about a bird and its nest?'

'The phoenix. Its nest catches fire in the rays of the sun and it deliberately burns itself to death. From the ashes emerges the next phoenix chick.'

The Nomenculator chuckled. 'You've overlooked a bird much more useful than the phoenix. Otherwise you wouldn't be holding the twig from its nest.'

Belatedly I remembered. 'Of course . . . the cinnamon bird!'

Paul smiled. 'Unlike the phoenix, the cinnamon birds are not unique, though where they live is uncertain. They gather the twigs from a certain fragrant plant to build their nests. The spice traders send their servants to throw stones to knock down the nests and gather up the twigs, later to be sold in the spice markets.'

He looked around the table, scanning our faces. 'We cannot deny the evidence of our own senses of taste and smell. Cinnamon exists and it flavours the food we enjoy. If you see living cinnamon birds on your travels – or any of the other rare creatures in Carolus's bestiary – I want you to tell me about them on your way back from Baghdad. That will be ample reward for any help I can give you during your stay.'

It was a gracious hint that our supper was at an end. We rose from the table and, as the others filed from the room, Paul drew me to one side. 'A word in your ear, Sigwulf,' he said in a low voice that held no hint of playfulness. 'From what you related about your journey, your embassy has met more than its fair share of setbacks and dangers. Are you familiar with the proverbs of Plautus?'

I shook my head.

'He's among Rome's finest ancient playwrights. It was Plautus who wrote: "frequently the greatest talents lie hidden".'

The Nomenculator gave one of his convulsive winks. 'It's not only the greatest talent that lies hidden, so too does a clever enemy.'

As I hurried to rejoin the others, I wondered if Paul's suspicion was justified, or whether he had lived too long in a city full of intrigue and conspiracy.

Chapter Twelve

THE NOMENCULATOR was efficient. Forty-eight hours later his messenger arrived at our lodgings in the Colosseum with a list of the different foods that the ice bears could be given safely. I had not expected it to include cabbages, lettuce, apples and even turnips and beans. Research in the archives had revealed that the Colosseum's animal keepers had kept their bears healthy by giving them vegetables and fruit with their fish and meat. Paul had added a note to say that if I would let him know what quantity of foodstuffs was required his staff would arrange a daily delivery. The messenger also brought me a document with a large crimson wax seal with the imprint of two crossed keys. It was from the papal secretariat: I was invited, with one companion, to attend the celebration of Mass in St Peter's Basilica. I read through the document, mystified, until I noticed the date. The invitation was for late December – on Christmas Day.

I would have preferred for Osric to have accompanied me but on Christmas morning he woke up feeling feverish and so it was with Abram beside me that I found myself cricking my neck to stare up at the gilded roof struts of the monumental church built over the spot where St Peter had been buried. The roof was at least a hundred feet above me, and the space inside the building was vast, by far the largest that I had known. Nevertheless, the chance to attend Christmas Mass with the pope was something ordinary people could only dream of so it was hardly surprising that the dragoman was crushed up against me by the throng of dignitaries, high officials and civic notables also invited to the event.

For the past two hours all of us had been waiting for the pope's formal entry, very little was happening and I was now bored.

My attention wandered and I gazed at the many marble columns; I twisted around to get a better view of the area immediately around the saint's shrine. Gold leaf had been applied lavishly to every free surface. On the wall of the apse was a vast mosaic. The figure of Christ was in the centre, handing a scroll to St Peter. On his left hand stood St Paul. Looming over the shrine itself was a silver arch. From its cross-beam hung a gigantic chandelier blazing with oil lamps, all of them lit despite the fact that it was daylight outside. The entire apse glittered and twinkled with thousands of points of light, reflecting gold and silver, enamel work and mosaic.

'The lamp is known as the Pharos,' murmured Abram, noting the direction of my glance. 'There are said to be more than one thousand lights on it. Both the lamp and the solid silver arch of triumph are the gift of Pope Adrian.'

I was about to comment that the pope must have amassed huge wealth to afford such an ostentatious gift when a flourish of trumpets announced the imminent arrival of the man himself.

The entire crowd turned to face towards the basilica's entrance and a hidden choir which had until now been keeping up a muted chanting in the background, suddenly burst into full-throated song.

All I could see over the heads of the throng was a three-foot-high silver-and-gold cross studded with jewels. Mounted on a gilded pole it was being held up in the air, swaying slightly as it advanced slowly up the nave and towards the saint's shrine. From time to time it disappeared from my view, hidden behind the purple and gold draperies hung between the marble columns on each side of the nave. I squeezed forward and stepped up onto one of the plinths at the base of a column in order to get a better view.

A choir dressed in long robes of white and gold headed the procession. They were singing away lustily in concert with the hidden choir. Behind them came the cross-bearer, and then another man holding up a similar pole topped with a smaller gold cross. Below it hung a large square of purple velvet, tasselled with gold and edged with a band of gems. Embroidered in pearls and gold thread on the velvet were two intertwined symbols that I recognized as chi and rho, the first two letters of 'Christ' in the alphabet of the Greeks that had been drummed into my head by the renegade priest who was my childhood teacher.

'The Laburum,' said Abram who had climbed up on the plinth behind me. 'Banner and symbol of the Holy Roman Empire.'

The church dignitaries solemnly pacing up the aisle behind the banner were gorgeously attired. Their flowing tunics of lustrous white silk had gold and purple borders. Long cloaks of richly embellished material were pinned at the shoulder with gem-studded brooches. A few were bare headed and had tonsures, but most wore square, four-cornered caps, black and crimson. They processed through the smoke curling up from the censers that some of them swung from gold chains. Others held velvet cushions on which were displayed various sacred items – a set of keys, holy books, chalices and vases.

'Adrian favours the veneration of images,' muttered Abram in a disapproving tone as one of the priests in the procession extended his arms and briefly raised up the picture of a saint he was carrying, turning it to left and right so that the crowd could see. More gold and enamel shimmered in the light of the oil lamps that hung the length of the nave.

Then came a short gap in the line, and I recognized Paul the Nomenculator. He was walking with a more soberly dressed group. These wore dark gowns, their hands clasped in front of them, faces fixed in solemn expressions. They had the appearance of notaries and scribes rather than bishops.

'The papal ministers,' explained Abram out of the side of his mouth.

The singing of the choirs rose to a crescendo, and at last I caught a brief glimpse of Pope Adrian. He was halfway up the aisle and looking straight ahead, his long aristocratic face composed and serene. His only concession to the winter chill was a short cloak of bright scarlet with a collar and trimmings of white fur. Under it, like the others, he was in a long tunic, though he was the only person in the procession to be wearing a long, gold-banded stole. Adrian might have been ninety years old but he walked with a firm step and it was clear that he had been a handsome man. On either side a senior official in dark ministerial dress was leading him by the hand in a gesture of formal support. The pope was half a head taller than they were, and the ridged cap accentuated a high forehead and strong features. He reminded me of an ageing and pitiless bird of prey.

A firm tug on the hem of my coat pulled me off the plinth, and I turned to find myself looking into the scowl of a burly spectator. I had been blocking his view. Abram had been treated similarly. I apologized profusely and slipped back through the throng to where I no longer had a view of proceedings. The singing had died away so the procession must have reached the saint's shrine. A hush spread across the crowd and then came the strong, clear voice of a priest summoning the faithful. The service had begun.

*

'The Nomenculator looked very drab compared to some others in the procession,' I commented to Abram some hours later as we made our way back towards our lodgings in the Colosseum. We were walking from the basilica downhill towards the river through an area of recently built wooden houses. Many of them were inns and hospices catering for the needs of pilgrims visiting the city.

'Appearances are deceptive,' he said. 'Those closest to the pope wield the most power. The two dignitaries you saw leading him by the hand are both his relatives. One is the Primicerius Notariorum, the other the Secundarius – the head of chancery and his deputy. Adrian wants one of them to succeed him, to keep it in the family.'

'You're very well informed,' I said.

He shrugged. 'I keep my ears open. All the gossip indicates that there's going to be trouble when Adrian finally passes on.'

'There are rivals?'

'Several.'

'Alcuin warned me about this sort of thing. Thankfully it doesn't concern us,' I said.

The dragoman wrapped his cloak tighter around himself. A chill wind had got up and there was a smell of rain in the air. Soon it would be dark. 'It might concern us,' he said carefully. 'Adrian and King Carolus are known to be close allies. Carolus even refers to Adrian as his "father".'

'How do you know that?' I asked, perhaps a little too sharply, but I was stung that the dragoman was more know-ledgeable about these matters than me.

Again he shrugged. 'It is common knowledge. Adrian may already have obtained an undertaking from Carolus to support a member of Adrian's family as the next pope.'

'That's pure supposition,' I objected.

'People in Rome have vivid imaginations, particularly when they are hatching plots.'

'But I still don't see how that affects our embassy,' I said.

Abram halted and turned towards me, his dark eyes searching my face. 'What if someone wants to send a warning to Carolus, to encourage him to stay clear of Roman politics? What would be a good way to do that?'

I felt a faint shiver of apprehension as I saw his meaning. 'Harm his embassy.'

'Exactly.'

'Abram, you're becoming as devious and mistrustful as those Roman conspirators you just spoke of,' I said, keeping my voice light though I remained uneasy. 'We can't look for enemies lurking down every alleyway.'

We continued our walk in silence as I thought over what the dragoman had told me. Despite myself, I looked around. It was dusk and the light was rapidly fading. What was it that Paul had said about not walking the streets unescorted after dark? I quickened my pace, glad to note that we were in a street lined with inns. A party of men was coming towards us, and they turned into the doorway just ahead of us. By their dress they appeared to be foreign pilgrims. They had been drinking and were talking loudly, laughing and joking with one another. With a sudden jolt I recognized their speech. They were talking together in my mother tongue: Anglo-Saxon.

I waited until we were well out of earshot before I said, 'Those men back there. They were from England.'

'That was a boarding house for English pilgrims. They pay

a very low rent to stay there, thanks to a donation from one of their kings some years ago.' There was enough light for me to see Abram's expression change as he realized what lay behind my comment. His eyes narrowed. 'Is this something to do with that coin you showed us the other evening? The one from King Offa?' he asked.

'I hadn't realized that some of his people would be here in Rome.'

It was Abram's turn to reassure me. 'Now you're the one who imagines plots and conspiracies round every corner! Dozens of your countrymen make the pilgrimage to Rome, especially to witness the Christmas celebrations.'

We walked on but I was unable to shake off the unwelcome idea that even in Rome I was within Offa's reach. The prospect of spending three more months in Rome had lost its appeal. The sooner we were on our way to Baghdad, the happier I would be.

*

The months dragged by. January and February were cold and dreary with slate-grey skies. A week of incessant rain caused the river to overflow and flood the low-lying parts of the city. The water rose above head height, obliging the residents to move to the upper floors as the Nomenculator had described. The Colosseum escaped the worst of the inundation, though there were days when several inches of standing water in the arena meant that the animals could not be exercised. They stayed in their stalls and were well looked after. Walo's feeding the ice bears with vegetables along with meat and fish, as Paul had researched, was a success. Modi and Madi thrived, and of course were very happy in the winter cold. The gyrfalcons also stayed in good condition and one morning Walo came to me, grinning with delight, to report that one of the dogs had given birth to a litter of four puppies. Two of them were pure white so we had more than we had started out with from Kaupang. The remaining pair had black and brown markings and, after they had been weaned, Walo made a present of them to the stable-hands who had the unpleasant job of cleaning out the aurochs' stable. That creature remained as bad tempered as ever.

Word had spread about our exotic animals and at exercise times there was usually an audience to watch them. The ice bears attracted by far the most attention. Entire families would sit in the Colosseum's former spectator seats as Modi and Madi padded lazily around the arena, and I was obliged to post attendants to stop children throwing stones to provoke them. Various members of the Roman nobility also came to inspect and admire the white gyrfalcons, watching Walo exercising them. The birds looked even more spectacular than usual as they circled high above the great bowl of the Colosseum. Our visitors' reaction to the sight of the surly aurochs, drooling, snorting and rolling its eyes angrily, was always the same: awe tinged with fear. Our benefactor Paul once paid an hour-long visit to see the animals, but after that we rarely saw him. His butler had found us a local cook and a house servant, so when Abram suggested that he and his three attendants move away to live with a Rhadanite family I agreed. It meant that the four Rhadanites could have their food cooked in their own style and observe their dietary laws. There were many days when Protis was away, visiting his friends in Rome, and Osric and I would tour the city's sights. We would either arrange to meet up with Abram as our guide or we would rely on a small book written for pilgrims that I had bought from a peddler in the porch of St Peter's Basilica. It listed the shrines of a bewildering number of saints. We dutifully joined the queues lining up to see their tombs or to inspect sacred relics. Invariably, when we emerged from a dark crypt into the daylight or stepped out from the doors of a church, it was to be pounced on by hawkers and street vendors offering to sell us medallions and pilgrim badges.

By early March I was beginning to believe that Abram's fears of an attack on our embassy were unfounded, so routine was our life in Rome. One evening after a fine sunny day that showed the first signs of spring, Osric and I returned to our lodgings footsore and weary, and rather later than usual. All the houses were shuttered and dark. Walo had gone to bed, and there was no sign of our servants, so I presumed that they had left and gone to their own homes. Osric and I headed to our separate rooms. I lay down in my underclothes for it promised to be a very cold night under the clear skies, and fell into a deep, dreamless sleep. Some time later, I awoke to the barking of dogs. I lay still in bed, listening. Several households within the Colosseum kept dogs as pets and as watchdogs. At night they often barked or howled at one another, and made sleep difficult. But the noise that awoke me was different. I recognized the distinctive high short yaps of the dogs we had brought from Kaupang. It was the sound they made when wildly excited. The noise was close at hand, which was odd. The dogs were always locked up for the night in their kennel deep within the stabling behind the arena, and any noise should have been muffled. My first thought was that Walo might have failed to confine them. I got up, pulled on some clothes and went out of my room and opened the front door of the house to see what all the noise was about.

The sight that greeted me was puzzling. The house we occupied was built on a former spectator terrace so I was looking down into the floor of the arena only fifty paces away. There was not a breath of wind. Above the jagged rim of the

Colosseum hung a bright three-quarter moon. It bathed the scene in a cold light, strong enough to cast deep black shadows across the tiers of terrace seats opposite me. The white dogs should have been in their kennel. Instead, they were out on the sand of the arena, barking frenziedly, running about in circles, dashing in, then retreating quickly as they harassed something invisible within the deep shadow under the high far wall of the arena. The dogs had cornered an intruder. From where I stood I noted that one leaf of the heavy double door into the rooms where the animals were kept was ajar. It occurred to me that a thief had come to steal the gyrfalcons. I hurried down the steps leading into the arena, about to call off the dogs. Then something in the far shadow moved. I came to an abrupt halt and the hair on the back of my neck rose. Out from the blackness stalked the aurochs. The spectral moonlight made the black shape of the beast more menacing than ever. The barking rose to a crescendo as one of the bolder dogs dashed in to nip at the aurochs' hocks. The aurochs swung its head downwards and sideways and hooked upward with its horns. A pointed tip must have grazed the dog's flank for I heard a high yelp of pain and the dog fled. The aurochs trotted forward into the centre of the arena and stopped there, swinging its head from side to side, looking for its next victim.

'How did the beast get loose?' said a voice. I glanced round to find Osric standing on the step behind me. He was looking grim.

'I've no idea. Have you seen Walo anywhere?' I asked my friend. He shook his head.

There was the slap-slap of sandals and Protis arrived, running down the steps towards us, almost knocking us over as he skidded to a halt beside us. He gazed at the aurochs with appalled fascination.

'Find Walo,' I said to him urgently. 'We have to work out how to get the aurochs back in its stable.'

Just then, I saw Walo coming down the steps towards us.

'Are you all right, Walo?' I called up to him. He appeared to be unsteady on his feet.

'I must have eaten something bad. I'll soon be better,' he answered.

'Walo, how did the aurochs escape?' Protis asked.

Walo stared down at aurochs, now pacing around the arena, ignoring the hysterical dogs. 'I don't know. I locked up all the animals as usual.'

I came to a decision. 'Walo, you head back to bed. The rest of us will take it in turns to stay here until daylight. We must make sure no one gets into the arena and is hurt. Then we'll devise a system to get the aurochs back inside.'

'What about the dogs?' Protis asked me. 'They could get injured.'

'If they've any sense, they'll learn to stay clear of those horns until morning,' I told him.

The words were hardly out of my mouth when Walo gave a strangled moan. He was staring towards the half-open door that led to where the animals should have been safely housed. The door had swung back and a pale shape had appeared in the opening. Someone had also let the ice bears loose. One of them was about to enter the ring.

In that instant the situation became a living nightmare. There was no doubt in my mind that we were about to see a fight to the death between the bears and the aurochs. It was to be a repeat of the blood bath of those ancient displays in the Colosseum when exotic wild beasts were pitted against one another. Whether the aurochs would kill the ice bears, or the other way around, I had no idea, though I found myself hoping that the ice bears would be the victors. Modi and Madi were our most valuable animals. If either one of them was injured or killed, it would be a crippling loss. Carolus's gifts of the remaining animals to the caliph would seem commonplace.

Walo slipped past me before I could stop him. He threw a leg over the low balustrade that topped the surrounding wall of the arena and dropped down onto the sand. His devotion to the well-being of the ice bears had overwhelmed his common sense. The head and shoulders of the bear had emerged from the doorway as the animal paused, gazing about to see what was in the arena. I saw the turned-in front paw and knew it was Modi. Behind him I saw movement and Madi's shape appeared. Walo was empty handed. Without his deerhorn pipe to soothe them, he would have to make them turn around and go back into their room. If they chose instead to maul him, he was a dead man.

But first he had to reach the open doorway. The aurochs saw the movement as Walo ran. The great beast spun on its haunches and lowered its head. Walo was alert to the danger and swerved away. But it was hopeless. There was no chance that he could get past the aurochs and reach the door. He stopped and turned to face the animal that had killed his father.

My mouth went dry.

With a yell of defiance Protis thrust me aside, hurdled the low balustrade and tumbled into the arena, falling on his knees. He scrambled back on his feet and shouted, waving his arms at the aurochs to get its attention. The brute whirled to face him. Protis shouted again, then pulled his shirt over his head and flapped it in front of the aurochs. He was taunting the beast, drawing it away from Walo, who stood for a couple of heartbeats and then sprinted towards the ice bears.

Time seemed to stand still. Protis kept up his clamour and

now he was joined by the dog pack. They were barking and dancing around him, leaping up with excitement. He was like a huntsman surrounded by his pack.

I stole a quick glance at Walo. He had reached the doorway and, hands extended, was pushing and shoving on Modi's head, trying to make the animal turn and go back inside.

Below me the aurochs pawed the ground, gouging the sand of the arena, still watching Protis. It rolled its great head from side to side, and then flicked up its horns as if rehearsing an attack. Then the great creature dropped its head and launched itself forward with a sudden thrust of the muscled hindquarters. I had witnessed the terrible speed of the creature when it rushed past me in the forest, running down Vulfard. Even so, I was appalled by how quickly it covered the distance to Protis. One moment it was ten yards away, the next it was almost on top of him. Protis must have planned to use his shirt to blindfold the brute. But what had been possible on a beach in daylight with an aurochs tired from a two-mile swim was no longer realistic. The enclosure of the arena was the brute's familiar territory, the animal was fit and in top condition and the flat moonlight made it difficult to judge distances. Worse, there was something truly evil about the hatred the aurochs displayed towards the human. It was as if all the months of being confined within a cage during the long journey were now concentrated in the ferocity of the onslaught.

Miraculously, Protis managed to dodge the attack. He leaped aside as the aurochs flashed past him, flinging its horns into the empty air. In the blink of an eye it had swung round on its haunches, lowered its head again, and was driving forward at its target. This time Protis did not even attempt to flap his shirt at the onrushing beast. He was only yards from the high wooden wall of the arena. He dropped his shirt, turned, took two strides and leaped upward, reaching for a handhold on the upper edge. He succeeded and hung on, drawing up his legs so that the horns of the charging aurochs smashed into the timber just below him with a splintering crash that I could feel from where I stood.

The aurochs drew back, shook its head as if slightly stunned, and turned aside. Then it trotted away a few yards, wheeled about to face Protis, and waited. The young Greek was dangling with both hands and at the full extent of both arms. He looked over his shoulder at the monstrous beast. It was clear that the vengeful aurochs was waiting for him to drop.

Osric and I bolted for the front row of the spectator seats. Protis was twenty yards away. If we could reach him in time, we could grab his wrists and haul him up to safety. As I ran I flicked a desperate glance towards the doorway where I had last seen Walo. The door was closed. Somehow he had managed to turn the bears around and push them back. What had happened inside, I could only guess.

We were so close to Protis that we would have reached him in a couple more paces, when he lost his grip. Perhaps he tried to pull himself upward onto the balustrade and miscalculated, or the palms of his hands had become too sweaty and he had slipped. He dropped away from us just as Osric and I arrived at the point where we could have saved him. We looked over the edge, aghast. Beneath us Protis was scrambling back onto his feet and turning to face the aurochs. Even then he might have escaped the beast's next attack if one of the dogs had not bumped into him. They had been circling hysterically, barking frenziedly the entire time. Now, as Protis stood up, one of them scurried behind him, brushing against the back of his knees, and threw him off balance. A heartbeat later the aurochs was coming forward and this time the vicious up-sweep of the horns caught Protis full in the stomach. He was flung high in the air. He cartwheeled and landed limp on the sand. The aurochs had already spun round and was on its victim in a flash. The horns hooked down.

Sick at heart, I watched the killing. It was like Vulfard's death all over again. The aurochs tossed the broken body repeatedly, picking it up on its horns after each time Protis's corpse flopped to the sand then flinging it up in the air. When the beast tired of that murderous treatment, it let the body lie where it fell, waited for a moment or two, then slowly and deliberately folded its fore legs and knelt and crushed the bloody remains of the young Greek into the sand. Finally the beast rose to its feet, looked around the arena as if satisfied and, ignoring the dogs, trotted away in the direction of its stall.

The door stood wide open. Walo must have succeeded in returning the bears to their enclosure and prepared a way for the aurochs to leave the arena. The hulking beast passed through the open doorway and headed for its stall of its own accord, for I saw it no more.

Numbed, I looked around the great empty bowl of the Colosseum looming over the gruesome death scene. The commotion had awoken people living in the other houses. A torch flame flickered in a window. My gaze travelled round the circle of the seats opposite me and my stomach gave a sudden lurch. In the dark shadow of a tier of seats slightly higher up, was a darker patch. It was difficult to be certain. Tucked in against one of the columns was what looked like the shape of a man. Someone was sitting there, watching. My spine crawled as I wondered if a spectator had been there the whole time, relishing the spectacle of Protis's death.

Osric and I went down into the arena. Protis's lifeless body was so badly mangled that Osric had to go back to our lodgings to fetch a blanket in which to wrap the corpse, so we could carry it away. As I waited for Osric to return, I looked up again at the spot where I thought I had seen a spectator. This time the place was empty.

*

A Greek priest from the church of Santa Maria in Cosmedin came for Protis's funeral. He conducted the service in the little chapel inside the Colosseum itself, and afterwards we buried Protis in the makeshift cemetery in the abandoned section of the arena. We placed a broken piece of marble to mark his grave. On the Nomenculator's advice we claimed that Protis had been killed in an accident while the aurochs was exercising. Paul said that it was the only way to avoid an official investigation by the city magistrates. If they got involved, we would not be allowed to leave the city for months. Osric and I had already agreed between ourselves that we would stay silent on the even more delicate question of how all the animals had been set free that fatal evening. Neither of us wanted Walo to be blamed.

The mystery of the watcher in the spectator seats preyed on my mind. I was unsure if my imagination had been playing tricks or not. So, on the morning after Protis's death, I climbed to the upper tier where I had seen the lurking shadow. The stone benches were worn and chipped, streaked with a winter's grime. It was hard to know if anyone had been there recently. I turned away, about to go back down to the arena, when I felt something crunch beneath my shoe. I had stepped and crushed the empty shell of what looked like a small nut. I went down on my hands and knees and saw three more half-shells, lying where they had fallen close beside the seat. They were greenish brown and wizened, more like the thin casings of large seeds. I picked one up and smelled it. There was a very faint whiff of some exotic flavour that I could not identify. Instantly, the unusual tastes of the meal with the Nomenculator came back to me. Paul loved exotic spices. He had also arranged for the animals to be housed in the Colosseum and had a vast knowledge of ancient Roman ways. I imagined him sitting on that seat, nibbling on dried seeds, and looking down into the arena when Protis died, enjoying the spectacle and indulging a perverted sense of history re-enacted. But that made no sense. It was Paul who had warned me that a clever enemy remains hidden. He would have been foolhardy or very arrogant to have taken the risk of coming to the Colosseum that night.

I sat back on my heels and thought about the Anglo-Saxons that Abram and I had met on our way back from St Peter's Basilica. It was possible that one or more of them were King Offa's hirelings, paid to get rid of me. But there, too, I saw a difficulty: releasing the aurochs and the two bears into the arena was not a sure way of getting me killed. Protis had died, not me.

Of course there was the simpler explanation: the spectator had been there by coincidence. Nevertheless, I was left with a disagreeable feeling that the shadowy watcher had known what would happen.

Carefully, I gathered up the half-shells and put them in my purse along with Offa's coin.

Chapter Thirteen

'THE ANNUAL NILE FLOOD — a great mystery,' Abram remarked. The two of us watched a fisherman throwing his net in the mud-laden current. The graceful flare and splash of his net was endlessly fascinating. Standing in a tiny, unstable boat hollowed from a tree trunk, he gathered up the fine mesh hand over hand, swung it inboard, and shook out a silver shower of fingerlings.

'Why a mystery?' I asked.

'The river rises when there is no rain in Egypt. So where does the water come from?' he answered.

'Doesn't your itinerarium provide a clue?' I asked.

'The itinerarium only extends so far,' he replied, pointing upriver with his chin. 'The source of the river is unknown.'

He had produced the map when we went to the Nomenculator to report what had happened with the aurochs. Paul had pressed us to leave Rome as soon as possible, saying it was for our own safety. He knew of a large party of pilgrims leaving for the Holy Land and he could arrange for us and the animals to accompany them to the port of Brundisium. From there the pilgrims would sail for Jaffa and Jerusalem and we could continue overland to Baghdad. Diffidently, Abram had proposed a quicker route by ship from Brundisium to Alexandria in Egypt, then onward. He unrolled the scroll to show the Nomenculator what he was suggesting.

'This is Alexandria on the Egyptian coast,' he had said, pointing to a symbol of a castle. 'Those lines, like a tangle of green worms, represent the delta of the Nile, each river finding its own way to the sea. And here' – he had slid his finger to a straight black line that met the most easterly of the rivers – 'is a canal that links the Nile to the Erythrean Sea. From there one can sail all the way to Baghdad itself.'

The Nomenculator had taken the opportunity to show off his erudition. 'Herodotus wrote about the canal, if I'm not mistaken. Built by the pharaohs. Emperor Trajan had it dug and cleared when it silted up.'

'Are you sure that the canal is still usable?' Paul had given Abram a worried glance. 'Shifting sand is difficult to keep at bay.'

'The map has been a reliable guide so far,' the dragoman had replied reasonably.

Paul had then turned to me. 'Sigwulf, I think your dragoman is offering good advice.'

'Then we go through Egypt and use the canal,' I answered. Months earlier in Aachen, Alcuin had suggested this same route, and indeed our voyage from Italy across the Mediterranean had been uneventful. In Alexandria we had been met by customs officials and taken to an interview with the city governor. His overlord was the caliph and when he heard of the purpose of our journey, he immediately gave his permission for us to proceed. Abram had slipped the port captain a generous bribe for his dockworkers to shift our animals without delay onto two large riverboats that regularly plied the river.

Now, less than six weeks after departing Rome, we were gliding along the braided waterways of the delta heading deeper into Egypt. Watching the fisherman cast his net again, I was confident that I had made the correct choice.

'That night in the Colosseum, did it involve those Saxons you were so worried about?' Abram asked.

The abruptness of his question caught me off guard as I kept my suspicions to myself, and I could only answer feebly, 'How do you reach that conclusion?

'The knife attack in Kaupang you described to the Nomenculator. Then Protis loses his life in the arena in the Colosseum. You could have been the victim just as easily.'

'Maybe someone wanted to harm the animals and damage Carolus's embassy to the caliph, as you had feared,' I said.

The dragoman tilted his head, squinting through half-closed eyes at the fisherman who was disentangling what looked like a twig from his net. 'We need to keep alert.'

I was taken aback. 'Even here? In Egypt?'

He turned to face me. I noticed how much browner he was now, tanned by the Mediterranean sun. He could have passed for an Egyptian himself. 'Make no mistake. Our arrival in Alexandria was noted.'

'But we are in the caliph's territory now. That is security enough.'

He treated me to a sceptical glance. 'Did you listen to the dock workers in Alexandria, or to the port captain when he spoke with his assistants?'

I failed to see the point of his question so he added, 'They were speaking Greek. Alexandria may be part of the caliph's possessions but in their hearts its citizens still think of themselves as Greeks. They were proud members of the Byzantine Empire for centuries and, if asked, they would still serve Byzantine interests.'

He did not have to explain any further. In Aachen, Alcuin had warned me of the hostility of the Greeks when they learned Carolus was sending gifts to their Saracen enemies. To them, the caliph was a foe. I also recalled the Khazar slave traders in Kaupang who would have passed through Byzantium on their way north. They had vanished a few days before I was attacked, and Osric had suspected them as being Greek agents. Unbidden, there sprang into my mind an image of the Greek priest in his dark robes officiating at Protis's funeral. The largest foreign community in Rome was Greek. They had their own churches, shops and guilds. For every Saxon pilgrim you might encounter in the streets of Rome, you were rubbing shoulders with fifty Greeks. They had the means and resources to organize the events that led to Protis's death.

'Protis was a Greek,' I said. 'If the Greeks have been trying to prevent our embassy reaching the caliph, we have to remember that Protis lost his life helping us.'

The dragoman was unimpressed. 'Protis was a Massalian. His Greece was the homeland of ancient heroes. Neither he nor his city had any ties to Byzantium.'

Both of us turned at the sound of a high-pitched cry of delight. It was Walo. He was in the bow of our boat, waving and shouting incoherently. I hurried forward to find out what was the matter.

'There! There!' he babbled.

His finger shook as he pointed at the reeds that fringed the river.

I looked in the direction in which he was pointing. The countryside of the delta was so utterly flat that my view was the empty washed-out sky and the thick wall of reeds, taller than a man, on both banks of the river. Wherever there was a small gap in the reeds, it offered only a glimpse of foreshore, a pattern of cracks and fissures where the water level had fallen and the sun had baked the mud into a pale brown crust. I saw nothing unusual.

'What is it?' I demanded irritably. I was still trying to come to terms with what Abram had just told me and Walo's simple-mindedness could at times be exasperating.

'There! Right down by the water!'

Osric had come forward along the wide deck and joined the two of us. 'What's Walo so excited about?' I asked him.

'A crocodile.'

Then I saw it. I had mistaken it for a dead tree submerged close to the reeds. A gentle ripple spread out. First a broad snout, the colour of wet bronze, and nostrils appeared, then two protruding eyes. The full size of the beast revealed itself as its armoured back and spine quietly broke the surface followed by the ridge of its long thick tail. I judged the beast to be fifteen feet in length. Beside me, Walo let out a gasp; part delight, part fear. Despite myself, I stepped back a pace, wondering if the animal could swim the short distance and lunge at our vessel. But our Egyptian boatmen appeared untroubled as we glided past the creature and it sank back down, reverting to being a drowned log.

Walo was breathless with excitement. 'Could you see tears in its eyes?'

'It was impossible to say,' I answered.

Walo had pleaded with me on the voyage from Italy to consult the bestiary and to make a list of the animals we could expect to encounter in Egypt and beyond. I had done so, though the book seldom made it clear which country each creature lived in. The crocodile was an exception. The bestiary stated that the crocodile was born in the Nile, and that its skin was so hard that it did not feel the blows of even the heaviest stones. It had fierce teeth and claws and laid its eggs on the land where male and female guarded them, taking turns. It was unique among all beasts in that it could move its upper jawbone.

'Walo, crocodiles can't weep,' observed Osric. Like me, he was not convinced that the information in the bestiary was always accurate. The book claimed that a crocodile shed tears just before and after eating a man, and from then onwards could not cease crying.

'You saw the creature for yourself,' said Walo obstinately. 'It was exactly like its picture.'

'But the book also says that the crocodile takes to the water only by night. It remains on land by day. So something is not right,' Osric pointed out.

'We should ask the boatmen what they know,' I suggested.

We squeezed our way around the aurochs' cage, which occupied most of the midships of the boat, and went to where the boat master squatted near the helm. An old man, he was wizened and scrawny, his white hair close cropped to stubble, and dressed in a grubby white gown. I questioned him about the crocodile and its habits, but he found my Saracen difficult to understand, and even when we asked for Abram to help out with interpreting, he still looked puzzled.

'Show him the picture in the book,' suggested Walo.

I fetched the bestiary from my luggage. The crocodile was illustrated twice. The first picture showed the beast on a riverbank. From its jaws protruded the naked legs of a man it was swallowing entire. The boat master looked at it with rheumy eyes, and nodded vigorously.

'You see,' said Walo triumphantly. 'The crocodile does eat men.'

My efforts at miming the beast crying tears were not understood so I showed the second illustration. Here the crocodile had an unpleasant-looking creature bursting out sideways from its stomach, through the skin. It was, according to the text, the crocodile's main enemy, a hydris. It was a water snake that hated the crocodile. If a crocodile lay on the riverbank with its jaws open, the hydris disguised itself as a ball of mud, rolled up to the open mouth and leaped in. From inside the crocodile's stomach the hydris then ate its way sideways, killing its enemy.

The old man frowned for several minutes at the picture of the hydris, and then shook his head.

'Why don't you show him that other Egyptian creature we doubted?' suggested Osric.

I turned the pages until I found the hyena. Neither Osric nor I believed the animal really existed. The humped shoulders, sloping backbone and ghoulish face were too grotesque. It was shown straddling an open coffin, and gnawing on a human corpse. To my surprise the elderly captain recognized the hyena immediately. He nodded energetically and made a sound like an odd coughing grunt, then smiled at us before spitting a gob of phlegm over the side. He pointed to the writing beneath the picture.

'He wants to know what's written there,' prompted Abram who had come aft to join us. 'If you read it aloud, I'll try again to translate what it says.'

With the dragoman interpreting my words, I read out: *'The hyena's jaws are so strong that they can break anything with their teeth, then they grind up the morsels in the belly. The hyena is male one year, female the next. It cannot bend its neck, so must turn the whole body to see behind.'*

I glanced at the old man to see his reaction. He squatted in the sunshine, arms against his bony knees, expressionless.

'The hyena can imitate the sound of a human voice,' I read on, *'it calls travellers by their names so that as they emerge from their tents, they leap upon them and tear them to pieces.'*

'How would a hyena know my name?' asked Walo with his usual unanswerable directness.

I ignored the interruption. *'If it wishes, the hyena's cry resembles someone being sick. This attracts dogs who are then attacked.'*

'That's what the old man was doing – imitating the hyena's cough,' said Osric. 'Mind you, if I heard that noise outside my tent at night, I think I'd prefer to stay where I was.'

*

Our travel plans were thrown into utter disarray three days later. Our boats had progressed through the delta, sailing and rowing against the sluggish current by day, tying up at night. The larger animals in our menagerie were bearing up remarkably well despite the increasingly ferocious daytime heat. The crew rigged awnings over their cages to keep off the Egyptian sun, and threw buckets of water over the aurochs and the two bears whenever they seemed to be uncomfortable. The Nile water was tepid, but helped them cool off, and the ice bears had the good sense to spend most of the daylight hours fast asleep in the shade, waking up at night. Walo had clipped the heavy coats of the dogs, and flew the gyrfalcons regularly for their exercise, watched by our boatmen who regarded him with something approaching awe. They took to acting as his lookouts – scanning the banks of the river and drawing his attention to the creatures that he might otherwise have missed. Crocodiles were commonplace. Often half a dozen of the ugly beasts were drawn up, side by side, on the dried mud of the bank, sunning themselves, mouths open. Walo triumphantly pointed out to me that the beasts did indeed move their upper jaws, just as the bestiary had claimed. But we never saw the hydris, the crocodile's deadly enemy, and it totally slipped my mind that Walo and I had also talked about the hypnalis, the asp that killed Cleopatra the Queen of Egypt.

Had I thought more carefully about the dried and cracked

mud of the riverbank I would have avoided the disappointment awaiting us. When we arrived at the junction where the canal met the river, it was to find a sizeable settlement of white-washed houses and reed-thatched storage sheds. Moored against the riverbank lay a score of boats, empty and idle. The canal itself was dry.

'If you had got here two months ago, it would have been different,' the canal superintendent told me, spreading his hands in a gesture of helplessness. 'The canal is only open when the water level in the Nile is high enough. When the Nile flood recedes, the canal empties out until just a few puddles remain.'

We were seated on cushions on the floor of his office where, at times of high water, the merchants came to pay the tolls that allowed them to use the canal. It was a large, comfortable room, furnished in the local style with low tables and carved chests that contained his ledgers. Slatted shutters over the window openings allowed any breeze to circulate, and the building's thick mud walls served as a barrier to the heat outside.

'Right now there are places in the canal where you couldn't float a child's toy,' he went on, shifting his weight on his cushion. He was very corpulent, his thighs bulging under his gown as he sat cross-legged. A thin gold chain almost disap-peared into the fleshy folds of his neck.

'Is there no way of retaining the flood water in the canal?' It was the sort of question that Protis would have posed. I felt a sudden wrench of sorrow that the young Greek was no longer with us. He would have loved to suggest an ingenious solution to a practical problem.

'There would be no point,' said the superintendent. 'If we sealed the mouth of the canal and trapped the water inside, the summer sun would suck it all up in a matter of weeks or it would seep away through bed of the canal. And there would have to be a system of lifting the cargoes from river level and loading them on canal boats.'

He paused and gave me a calculating look. 'You are not the first to have arrived here after the canal has shut.'

I waited for him to go on.

The superintendent swatted away a fly circling near his face. 'If the cargo is urgent, a caravan can be arranged.'

'A caravan?' I asked, feigning ignorance though I had been waiting for him to make the suggestion. Abram had learned that the superintendent supplemented his income by privately hiring out the labour force that should have been doing canal maintenance.

'A road runs alongside the canal almost as far as the eastern marshlands. There it branches off and goes directly to the port at al-Qulzum. The land journey only takes a few days more than if you had gone by water. Regrettably, it involves hiring waggons, draught animals, baggage handlers and guards . . . which, of course, incurs extra expense.' He paused to allow the last words to sink in.

I decided that, for appearance's sake, I should haggle. 'I don't understand the need for guards. Are the caliph's governors not charged with ensuring the security of travellers?'

'The guards are there to protect against wild animals,' the superintendent answered smoothly. 'Beyond the marshland the desert is infested with lions.'

'And hyenas?' I said, meaning to sound sarcastic.

Unexpectedly he agreed. 'Of course. Lions and hyenas. They go together and they prey on travellers.'

The superintendent was well aware that I had no choice but to hire a caravan. The canal would not reopen for many months and even if the ice bears survived the long delay, I did not fancy arriving in Baghdad late and with mangy, half-starved animals.

With heartfelt insincerity I told him that I would be most grateful if he would arrange a caravan to transport my menagerie across the desert. He struggled to his feet with an effort and assured me in the same spirit of fraudulent friendship that my well-being and the success of my mission were close to his heart. He would make sure that the caravan would be ready to depart within a week.

Walo was waiting for me outside, shifting from foot to foot with impatience. 'Can you come at once,' he blurted out.

Alarmed, I asked, 'There's nothing wrong with the animals, is there?'

'No, no,' he replied. 'There's something you must see.'

His face set in a worried frown, he led me down a side-street of modest whitewashed houses, their wooden doors warped and cracked by the sun. It was mid-morning and there was almost no one about. A few birds like starlings, dark brown with bright yellow bills and legs, flew down to peck at the piles of rubbish. We turned down an alleyway between high blank walls where the outer layer of mud was flaking off in scabby patches, and finally came to the rear of a long, low stable building. From the far side I could hear a medley of strange sounds. The background noise was a moaning and grumbling like a herd of cows in distress. Punctuating this clamour were sudden angry roars and enormous bubbling belches. I could not imagine what creatures would utter such constant complaints. Walo and I walked round the corner of the building and there in front of us was a row of bizarre creatures lined up beside a long water trough. On ungainly legs, they stood taller than a man and had serpent necks. Several of them swung their heads to look at us as we stepped into view, and greeted us with those loud, disagreeable groans.

Walo turned towards me, 'What are they?' he asked, obviously perplexed.

'Camels,' I told him. I had seen camels pictured in the church mosaics in Rome.

'But they don't look like the camel in the book,' he objected. That was true. The bestiary's camel had two distinct humps on its back. The creatures in front of us had a single hump covered with unsightly clumps of dark brown fur. They appeared to be moulting.

Walo and I approached closer. The burping and groaning and moaning grew louder and more insistent with each step.

'They could be the giant offspring of a deer and a cow,' said Walo. One of the creatures shifted on its great padded feet, lowering its head to inspect us more closely, peering past huge eyelashes. 'Look! The upper lip is split. It moves in two parts. Like a rabbit.'

He reached up to touch the creature's mouth.

The camel jerked up its head in alarm, and gave a gurgling grunt from deep within its gut. Its mouth gaped and I caught sight of long yellow teeth and feared it was about to bite. Instead it shook its head violently from side to side, the pendulous lips flapped, and out shot a thick gush of foul-smelling green soup. It splattered over Walo, drenching his head and shoulders. The smell was of rotten grass blended with dog excrement.

*

Twenty of the ungainly beasts laden with bales of fodder and baggage formed our caravan when we took to the road. Only the lead camel had a rider. The rest of us – guards, cooks, attendants, camel drivers, the men leading our dogs on leads, and assorted hangers-on – were on foot. The cages for the ice bears and the aurochs had been fixed onto ponderous wheeled platforms, each drawn by a pair of harnessed camels. A third cart followed with the gyrfalcons in their cages and a great barrel that contained a supply of water for our menagerie.

Our route along the canal bank led across an impoverished land dotted with poor villages where the peasants worked the thin grey soil with mattocks and hoes. Old men sat in the shade of dusty palm trees and veiled women held back their curious children as they peeked from the darkened doorways of mud-brick hovels. The only livestock were flocks of scraggy goats and a few donkeys. All life depended on the spindly wooden structures that, from a distance, I mistook for hangman's gallows. They were devices for raising water from the canal. A bucket dangled from the end of a long pole pivoted one-fifth along its length from a tall frame. A large stone fastened at the shorter end of the pole served as a counterweight so the bucket could be lifted and lowered with ease. The bucket scooped water, was swung over the bank, and the contents were tipped into a drinking trough for animals or into an irrigation ditch. I found myself wishing that Protis was still with us and could see for himself the ingenuity of this device. Where enough water remained in the bed of the canal, our camels were driven down to stand in the shallow puddles. Walo looked on from a safe distance as they noisily slaked their thirst. According to what I had read to him from the bestiary, a camel prefers muddy water, so it stirs up the silt with its feet before drinking. Our camels failed to do this and I could only presume from the look of mistrust on Walo's face that he doubted whether they were true camels. His faith in the Book of Beasts was unshakeable.

'If it gets any hotter, Madi and Modi may not survive,' I observed to Abram on the evening we camped on the fringe of the marshlands where the boggy ground was too soft even for pack animals. Here the road turned aside, striking into the wilderness.

'There should be enough water in the great barrel to sluice them down if they begin to show signs of distress, and one of my own men will stand guard over the water cart at night,' Abram said quietly.

The edge to his voice made me look at him sharply. 'You still think that someone might try to sabotage the embassy?' I asked. It had been on my mind too, but the dragoman's decision-making had been so astute thus far, I knew I should heed his advice.

'Draining the water tank would be a good way of doing it once we've entered the desert. It would be no harm to take precautions.'

Abram's concerns weighed on me and that first night I found it difficult to sleep. He had replaced all the camp equipment lost at sea when Protis's ship sank and Osric and I were sharing a small tent. While my friend slept soundly I tossed and turned, swatting away the humming insects, listening for suspicious noises, remembering the sounds that had awakened me on the night Protis had died. Shortly before midnight I got up and went to check on the water barrel, finding one of Abram's servants on guard and also wide awake. Relieved, I returned to my tent and when finally I did fall asleep, it was to drift off into a troubled dream: I was aboard a ship sailing, not on the sea, but across the land. I had to steer around rocks and trees, down the streets of towns and up the slopes of hills. It left me with a queasy feeling and when I opened my eyes I had a nagging headache and it was daybreak. Judging by the volume of camel grunting and bellowing, the beasts were already being loaded for the day's march.

Osric was already awake, kneeling to roll up his sleeping mat.

'Do you remember if the Oneirokritikon says anything about ships sailing on the land?' I asked him.

He sat back on his heels and waited for me to explain.

I described my dream to him. From outside came shouts and oaths, then the sounds of a stick being used vigorously. Someone was getting the cart-hauling camels under way.

'There's a straightforward explanation,' he said. 'You were expecting to cross Egypt along a canal by boat. Instead, we are obliged to go by land. That's a more difficult journey.'

He reached for the walking staff that lay on the ground beside him. It helped offset the limp from his crooked leg while we were on the march. 'But, since you ask, there was a mention in the Book of Dreams about a ship sailing across the land.'

'What does it say?'

'That to dream of sailing a ship across the land, while avoiding rocks and obstacles, foretells a journey beset with many difficulties and dangers.' He got to his feet and gently poked me in the ribs with the end of the staff. 'As far as I'm concerned, that's no prophecy. It's something we already know. You had better get up now or the caravan will move on without you.'

Later that morning, we found ourselves venturing out into a dun-coloured stony plain. There was no soil, just scoured rock and the occasional patch of sand or gravel. We walked deeper into the barren land, the wheels of the travelling cages crunching on the broken stones of the rough track. The sun was merciless, the bare rock throwing back the heat, and it felt as if we were walking into a gigantic oven. The only plants were weed, thickets of thorn bushes and a few stunted trees with twisted leafless limbs. Every couple of miles we paused to draw off buckets of water from the water cart so that our animals could drink. The water that remained in the buckets was thrown over them to try to cool them off. But it was no more than a gesture. Soon the ice bears were panting and their fur was a lifeless yellow.

'How many days will we be in the desert?' I asked Abram after the caravan halted for the night. The camels had been unloaded and hobbled in a tight group, their packs stacked to make an open square around them. Their drivers were lighting fires of thorn twigs. Under a clear sky it was going to be chilly.

'The guide says we should reach the sea at the port of al-Qulzum in four days' time,' the dragoman replied. He looked past me, over my shoulder. 'It looks as if Walo has found something.'

I turned to see Walo walking towards us, carefully holding something cupped between his hands. When he was no more than two yards away, he announced proudly, 'It's a baby.'

I looked to see what he was carrying so tenderly, then sprang back in fright. Cradled in Walo's hands was a small serpent. The length of my forearm, it had a thick body with dusty brown scales and dark markings. The head was broad and flat.

'It's a young one,' Walo repeated, holding up the snake so I could see it more closely. The hair rose on the back of my neck and I backed away.

'A young what?' I asked. I had broken into a cold sweat. I hate snakes.

'A young cerastes. The parents can't be far away.'

My mind raced as I tried to follow what Walo was talking about. I had an uncomfortable feeling that the serpent was venomous. Yet in Walo's hands it appeared completely at ease, not moving, though I could see its black tongue flicking in and out.

'Look at its head, above the eyes,' Walo urged, holding it up closer. It was as much as I could do to stifle a groan of fear as I swayed back out of range.

Now I understood what Walo was talking about. Above each eye of the little serpent projected a short spine like a tiny horn. There sprang into my mind the picture of the cerastes in the Book of Beasts. It was a serpent with a horn above each eye and, as I recollected, a body that had no spine so that it could tie itself in knots. As if to confirm my thoughts, the serpent slithered and twisted in Walo's cupped hands, rearranging its coils into tight loops.

'It was hiding in the sand, just as the book says,' stated Walo proudly. 'The horns were standing up, attracting the birds so it could ambush them.'

'I suggest you return it to where you found it,' I croaked, 'its parent might come looking for it, and that could be fatal.'

Casually, Walo lowered one hand and poured the snake from one cupped palm to the other, like a length of scaly rope.

One of the camel handlers was walking past. He took one look at the serpent and let out a yell of alarm, then took to his heels.

Abram came to my rescue. 'Walo, the cerastes' parents will be distressed if they find their baby missing.'

Reluctantly, Walo bent down and placed the serpent gently on the ground. There was a writhing motion and, before my eyes, the serpent began to move away sideways, propelling itself in a series of ripples. When it reached a patch of soft sand, it paused then, with a sinuous swimming motion, pushed up the sand around itself until it had disappeared. Only when I looked closely and very cautiously could I still see the sinister flat head just above the surface and the two protruding horns. I promised myself that whenever we camped, I would borrow Osric's walking staff and poke every suspicious mark in the ground.

That same night we heard our first lions. Their deep, hoarse roars sent shivers down my spine. They began at a distance, then came closer and closer and, finally, from several directions as the beasts prowled around our camp. The sounds were unmistakable, several long roars followed by shorter coughing grunts gradually fading away to nothing as though their lungs were empty. Creeping to the flap of our small tent I looked out and saw bright flames leaping higher from the campfires as the night watchmen threw on more dry twigs. The light cast flickering shadows on our animal cages. The aurochs was standing up, motionless, a hulking dark shadow behind the bars. I detected no movement from where Walo had chosen to sleep on the ground beneath the ice bears' cage, the dogs tied beside him. To my right and at the outer edge of the firelight, several pairs of animal eyes shone in the darkness. For a chilling moment I feared that our dogs had got free. I plucked up my courage and was about to crawl out of the tent and retrieve them when a branch on the fire flared up. The sudden strengthening of the light revealed the shapes of three or four wild animals. They had the shape of large dogs but oddly distorted. By the time I had recognized the coarse heads and over-size shoulders and the sloping loins, the creatures had wheeled about and darted away. Some time later I heard a new sound from the darkness, a chorus that was part howl, part laugh, and knew that I had seen hyenas.

The boldness of the lions was troubling. The following day, and the day after that, several of the tawny creatures kept pace with us, not far off. They were usually in twos and threes and made no attempt to conceal themselves. Our camel drivers took precautions. Men armed with spears and bows walked on each side of our column, and we stopped well before sunset so that there was time to cut thorn bushes and construct a barricade around the hollow square inside which they hobbled the camels. The bonfires they built were much larger than before, and they kept them burning brightly throughout the dark hours. On both nights, without fail, we heard the deep, coughing roars of the lions, followed by answering manic cries from the hyenas.

'They're laughing at us,' observed Osric. Our little group was sitting close to one of the bonfires as we began a third night in the desert. The calls of the wild beasts had started earlier than usual, even before it was fully dark. This night the hyena pack was leading the chorus.

'They're laughing at the lions, not at us,' corrected Walo. He showed no signs of alarm even though I had reminded him of the bestiary's warning about the creatures.

'Why would they want to mock the lions?' Osric enquired.

'Because they hope to shame the lions into action.'

Osric threw me a quick sideways glance. He was always careful not to make Walo feel as though he was being teased. 'I thought lions were meant to be courageous,' he said.

'The hyenas think the lions are foolish to be scared of the noise of our waggon wheels,' said Walo firmly. I realized he was reciting what I had read out to him months earlier from the bestiary: that lions fear the noise of waggon wheels and the sound of a white cock crowing.

Abram spoke up from the other side of the fire. 'And why aren't the hyenas fearful too?'

Walo was in no doubt. 'They are very hungry and must be fed. They want the lions to kill one of us so that after we bury the body, they can dig up the grave and eat his flesh.'

At that moment a great hoarse roar shook the air, louder than anything we had heard before. It came from somewhere in the darkness to our left, beyond the three waggons drawn up in a line as part of the barricade surrounding our camp.

'What do you think, Sigwulf? Are the hyenas encouraging the lions to attack us?' said Abram turning in my direction.

'It's possible,' I answered. 'Every night I've seen the eyes of three or four hyenas shining in the darkness, close to the camp. They've been watching us, and waiting.'

'Nasty-looking beasts,' agreed Osric. 'I'll be glad when we get to al-Qulzum.'

'The hyenas are patient because they know something will happen,' said Walo softly.

I heard Abram suck in his breath, a derisive sound, and was reminded how he had teased Protis for his belief in the Minotaur.

'Walo may be right,' I intervened. 'Maybe the hyenas do know what will happen. The Book of Beasts says that in the eye of a hyena there's a stone. If a man puts that stone beneath his tongue, he will be able to see into the future.'

'Can't be a pleasant taste, I'm sure,' said Abram with a yawn. 'I'm going to turn in.'

He got to his feet and went off to the tent he shared with his three Radhanite assistants. Walo, Osric and I stayed by the fire a little while longer, and when Walo left to make a final check on the ice bears, Osric and I retired to our small tent.

As Osric was taking off his heavy sandals, he suddenly turned to me. 'If the Oneirokritikon can help us interpret our dreams, maybe the stone from a hyena's eye really can help man look into the future.'

I was too tired to think of a sensible reply and, for the first time since we entered the desert, I found that I could shut out the noises of the wild beasts, and fell asleep almost at once.

*

'The aurochs has escaped!' The blunt announcement brought me sharply awake. I sat up, reaching for the cloak I had been using as a blanket. There was just enough light to make out Abram's head and shoulders thrust in through the tent flap. I guessed it was just before sunrise, that quiet, still hour when the world seems to be waiting silently for the dawn of the new day. In the background I could hear the bubbling and groaning of the camels. But there were no lion roars.

'When did it happen?' I croaked. My lips were cracked and dry.

Abram dropped his voice, now that he had roused me. 'Less than ten minutes ago. My man guarding the water tank heard the creature jump down from the cage. He came straight to me and raised the alarm.'

'Where's the aurochs now?' I asked, rolling off my sleeping mat and hurriedly pulling on my boots. I did not even pause to give them a shake in case some crawling creature had occupied them during the night.

'He says it ran off into the desert.'

'Thank God it didn't decide to go into the camp,' I said. I didn't want to imagine the havoc had the beast attacked the camels or gored the men.

I crawled out of the tent and together Abram and I headed at a fast walk towards the three waggons, dimly outlined against the sky where a sliver of moon hung close to the horizon. The bonfires were still alight, but had been allowed to die down. Firewood was scarce.

'My man guarding the water tank thinks he saw someone

near the cages, about an hour ago, but he couldn't be sure,' said the dragoman.

'What about the caravan watchmen?'

'I haven't asked them. I wanted to report to you first.'

We reached the aurochs' cage. The door was hanging half open. There was enough moonlight to cast faint shadows in the marks made in the sand by the animal's great hooves as it jumped down from the waggon. I clambered up and checked the hinges of the gate. They were undamaged. Normally the door was held shut by two heavy wooden bars, thicker than my wrist. They fitted into deep slots on either side of the frame. Both bars had been removed and placed to one side. I ducked inside the cage itself. There was a half-full fodder net, a bucket of water, and several piles of pungent aurochs dung. The aurochs had not broken out. It had been set free deliberately.

Abram's assistants were standing beside the waggon as I jumped back down to the ground. 'Are the ice bears safe in their cage?' I asked them.

'They were, just a moment ago,' answered one of the men. 'I woke Walo and he's gone to make sure that no one has interfered with the gyrfalcons.'

'The dogs?'

'All present and unharmed.'

So it seemed that only the aurochs had been targeted by the mysterious attacker. A figure loomed up. It was Walo.

'Everything all right with the gyrfalcons?' I asked him.

He nodded.

I became aware of an increase of noise from the hobbled camels, a hacking cough as someone cleared his throat, then spat, a stirring among the shapes of camel drivers sleeping on ground bundled in their cloaks. The camp was waking.

'We must track down the aurochs as soon as there's enough daylight. It should be easy enough to follow.'

'And when we find it, how do we recapture it?' asked Abram.

'I don't know,' I said, suddenly despondent. After my first, active response to the crisis I was beginning to succumb to an overpowering weariness as I grasped the extent of the setback. 'We'll think of something. Right now we must pack our gear as usual and be ready to move. The caravan can't linger or Modi and Madi will melt.'

It took another hour for the caravan to get under way. First came the morning prayer, then the camels were given their ration of fodder and the men sat down in small groups to breakfast on flat bread and a handful of dates washed down with a few gulps of water. By the time the camels had their packsaddles and loads securely in place or had been harnessed to the waggons, the tracks left by the aurochs were easy to see. It had walked straight into the desert.

Leaving Osric in charge of our remaining animals, Abram, Walo and I set off in pursuit. We had gone no more than a mile and were still within plain view of the caravan behind us when we topped a small rise in the ground and came to a sudden halt. We were looking down into a shallow depression in the desert's surface. The floor of the depression was a flat expanse of gravel dotted with small boulders. Stretched out on the gravel lay the body of the dead aurochs, the head and long horns twisted at an unnatural angle. Crouched on their bellies and feeding on the corpse were five lions. They were tearing and ripping at the flesh, their heads half buried in the entrails. One of the lions noticed our arrival. It raised its head and stared at us with its great, yellow eyes. We were close enough to see the jaws smeared with fresh blood.

For a long moment we froze, too shocked to move. Then, very slowly and cautiously we backed away, down the slope and out of sight of the great beasts.

My voice was unsteady as I whispered, 'There's nothing we can do. We must get back to the caravan.'

'What about the horns?' asked Walo.

I was so dumbfounded that I just stared at him.

'For the king,' said Walo. Only then did I remember the great silver-mounted aurochs' horn in Alcuin's room on the day when he had told me that I had an audience with Carolus. That time seemed impossibly far away.

'No, Walo. It's too dangerous,' I said. It would have been the duty of Vulfard, Walo's father, to present the horns of any large game animals to the king.

'If we wait until the lions have stopped feeding—' Walo began.

'No!' I hissed, angry now. I took a grip on his elbow in case he tried to get past me. 'We leave the aurochs where it is.'

We trudged our way back to the caravan, with frequent glances behind us to make sure no lion was following. In a strange way I was feeling relieved. From the moment I had first laid eyes on the aurochs in the forest I had disliked and feared the brute. It was a danger to anyone who approached it, even to give it food or water. Always angry and malevolent, it had killed both Vulfard and Protis. If the opportunity arose, it would kill again. Perhaps it was fanciful of me to think in such terms, but I detected something deeply wicked about it. Of course I regretted all the months of wasted effort it had taken to bring the beast so far, only for it to be torn to pieces in the desert. Yet I was thankful that it was the aurochs that had died, not the ice bears. I resolved that there was no point in brooding over the fate of the aurochs. What mattered now was bringing Madi and Modi and the other animals safely to Baghdad.

For that, I needed to find out who had set the aurochs free.

The answer was presented to me as soon as we caught up with the caravan. Osric had been making enquiries among the camel drivers.

'A man is missing. He disappeared from the camp during the night.'

I felt a surge of excitement. 'Does anyone know anything about him? Where he comes from?'

'Apparently he joined at the start of the caravan, offering to work as a general assistant for almost no pay. The other camel men were puzzled. He wasn't very good at his job. They say he behaved more like a town dweller than someone who had worked with the caravans. He got himself bitten by a camel.'

'Do they have any idea where he might be now?'

'The camel drivers think that he will have gone ahead. The road is easy enough to follow and we're little more than a day's journey from al-Qulzum. My guess is that he slipped away in the night before he was questioned.'

'As soon as we get to al-Qulzum we'll track him down and find out who he's working for,' I said grimly.

As it turned out, the interrogation was not possible. We resumed our march and not long after the halt for midday prayers there was a shout from the head of the column. A cloak had been spotted on the ground a few yards off to the side of the track. Someone ran to investigate and found the garment was bloodstained and torn. Another shout came from a man pointing towards a clump of thorn bushes some fifty paces away. Five or six hyenas could be seen trotting off into the desert, their loping strides unmistakable. The caravan halted and after a hasty conference between the camel drivers, a group of half a dozen men, armed with spears, headed cautiously towards the bushes.

Abram and I made our way to where the leader of the caravan was surrounded by several camel drivers. They were passing the torn cloak from hand to hand, talking among themselves in local dialect.

'They are fairly sure that it belongs to the man who ran away,' Abram translated for me.

Streaks of dry blood on the dusty ground were signs of a struggle. A line of scuffmarks led towards the distant thorn bushes.

'I'd say the lions got him as well, poor wretch,' said Abram. 'Then the aurochs came along and offered a better meal and they abandoned the corpse and went after larger prey.'

An empty water skin lay among the stones close to where the cloak had been found. A few paces farther on was a cheap cloth satchel with a shoulder strap.

I picked up the satchel and looked inside. It contained half a flat loaf of bread, a lump of mouldy cheese and a handful of dates. More than enough to sustain a man for a day's walk to al-Qulzum. I took out the food, set it aside on a flat rock, and checked the satchel again. There was nothing that might give a clue as to the identity of the owner; no money, no document. I put my hand inside and felt around. A cloth divide separated the interior, and my fingernail snagged on something lodged in a seam. I picked it out and held it up to show Abram. 'Do you know what this is?'

He glanced at it. 'The shell from a cardamom seed.'

'Cardamom?'

'A spice, from India. It's used for flavouring food.'

I flicked the shell away casually, held the bag upside down, and shook it. Nothing fell out.

There was a sudden buzz of excitement from the men examining the bloodstained cloak and we hurried over to see what was causing the fuss. One of the camel drivers was holding out his hand. On the grimy palm were four gold coins.

'He found them sewn into the hem of the cloak,' said Abram, listening to their excited chatter.

'Advance payment for setting loose our animals,' I said bitterly. 'Ask if we can take a closer look.'

Abram spoke to the caravan leader and one by one the coins were handed to him so that he could examine them, watched suspiciously by the camel men.

'Can you learn anything from them?' I asked the dragoman.

He shrugged. 'Not really. They're the caliph's coinage, local money – and more than a humble camel driver could earn in a year.'

He gave the coins back and we accompanied the group to the thorn bushes to see what they had found. It was a man's body, part eaten by wild animals. Flies were already gathering on the mangled flesh. There was little to glean about him except that he had been of slight build, with delicate hands and feet, and probably in his early thirties. Except for his sandals and a torn undershirt, nothing survived of his clothing. What he had looked like when alive was difficult to imagine. The hyenas had chewed off most of his face.

Chapter Fourteen

BAGHDAD

*

I HAD NEVER IMAGINED that Baghdad would be so vast, or so
hot. The breeze that filled the sails of the merchant ship that
brought us from al-Qulzum had kept us agreeably cool during
a trouble-free five-week voyage, so the scorching July heat of
the caliph's capital was all the more stunning.

'It must be the largest city in the world,' I remarked to
Osric holding up my hand to shield my eyes from the blinding
white glare of the sun. In Basra, now three weeks behind us,
Abram had arranged for our remaining animals to be transferred
to an upriver barge, and it was from the Tigris that I was
getting my first impression of the caliph's extraordinary capital.
It was huge. Docks, quays, residences, boatyards, gardens,
workshops, warehouses and steps for washing laundry lined the
banks. In the distance an enormous green dome seemed to float
above the low houses of the sprawling suburbs shimmering in
the haze.

'Baghdad is a thousand years younger than Constantinople
but already twice its size,' put in the dragoman, with more than
a hint of pride.

I gave him a sideways glance. Abram was no longer the

quiet and self-effacing guide I had known previously. He imparted his knowledge of the caliph's realm in a manner that was close to patronizing. I ascribed the change in him to a sense of relief that our long journey was almost at an end. I felt the same.

'Two generations ago this place was nothing more than a riverside village,' he continued. 'Haroun's grandfather, Caliph Mansour, picked the site, brought in the architects and city planners, and paid the wages of the masons, bricklayers, carpenters and other builders. A canal was dug to bring Tigris water to where the mud bricks were made.'

Abram nodded towards a riverside mansion. It appeared to have been abandoned. The boundary wall was crumbling, the garden overgrown, and the building itself was beginning to disintegrate. On either side of it the large houses were in perfect condition, trim and neat.

'Baghdad is built of mud brick, sun dried or oven baked. Quick to build, almost as quick to disintegrate. That palace probably belongs to a court high official, and he's found somewhere else he prefers to live. He's simply walked away.'

'And left it behind?'

The dragoman shrugged. 'Why not? Baghdad is constantly expanding. Thousands of people arrive here every month from the countryside. Land speculation is on a massive scale. A grove of palm trees given by the caliph to a court favourite ten years ago when it was on the edge of town is suddenly worth hundreds of thousands of dinars as the site for new housing.'

'And everything depends on the caliph's whim?'

'Nearly everything.' Abram turned to me, his tone sharper. 'Make no mistake. You are about to encounter the richest, most profligate, open-handed, and luxury-loving court on the face of the earth. A place where a singer whose sentimental song tugs at the caliph's heartstrings might receive a gift of enough pearls to fill his mouth. Or a poet writes a few successful lines and suddenly finds himself the owner of a house and servants so that he can spend the rest of his life at ease.'

'What happens to those who incur the caliph's anger?'

'If you get to meet Caliph Haroun in person, take a look at the grim-faced man always standing a few paces behind him. He's known as "the blade carrier of his vengeance" – the palace executioner. Last time I was in Baghdad it was a man named Masrur.'

The broad surface of the Tigris was swarming with water traffic. Barges, lighters, freighters and rafts rode the current loaded with their cargoes. With little or no wind, many were being moved with long sweeps or towed behind rowed boats. Passenger ferries shuttled from one side of the river to the other. Fishermen hung their lines from small skiffs and set and hauled nets. Pleasure craft had colourfully striped awnings under which their occupants sat on cushions, relaxing while hired boatmen or slaves worked the oars. Every few minutes yet another boat would emerge from the mouth of one of the small canals that joined the river and take its place in the throng.

'We'll be landing very soon,' warned Abram. 'We're nearly at the first of the three pontoon bridges that cross the river. I doubt that the bridge keepers will open up the bridge to let us pass.'

In Basra, Abram had met with customs officials and impressed on them that we were gift-bearers from the King of the Franks to the Commander of the Faithful. We had been promised every assistance, but opening a pontoon bridge and disrupting the city traffic was too much to expect.

'How far to where we can house the animals and find our own accommodation?' I asked.

'I expect we'll be allocated space inside the Round City itself. That's the caliph's personal precinct.'

One of the minor officials assigned to escort us from Basra was already coming along the deck towards us. Two assistants followed, carrying a large chest between them. They set down the chest and threw back the lid to reveal a store of neatly pressed garments made of fine white cotton. Walo and I had already taken our example from Abram and Osric and were wearing loose-fitting Saracen clothing suitable for such stifling weather. But our garments were travel-stained and crumpled, and it was a pleasure to put on the local costume – loose trousers and a wide-sleeved long shirt with pockets. Everything was crisp, clean and newly laundered. The official also insisted that we put on an additional over-gown of white cotton. This too was required of anyone who passed in through the gates of the Round City. Finally, we had to select our headgear because it would be considered uncouth to go about bare headed. Osric was comfortable with a dazzling white turban and from his own baggage Abram produced a white skullcap. Walo and I hesitated. Neither of us were expert in winding a turban around our head, or keeping it there. So the official issued us with small neat caps shaped like pots, around which he wound and then pinned in place a length of white cloth. The caps felt strange, but were sufficient to satisfy local custom.

By the time we were correctly dressed, our barge was slanting towards the western bank where a group of dock-workers was already waiting. Mooring ropes were thrown and made fast, the barge scraped against the quay and the labourers swarmed aboard.

'Please make sure that the ice bears are kept out of the sun,' I said to their overseer. After the months of practising the Saracen tongue with Osric, I could make myself understood.

Madi and Modi were in a very sad condition. Walo had done his utmost to keep them healthy. He had fed them their favourite foods, given them plenty to drink, doused them with water almost hourly during the heat of the day. But the sapping heat had taken its toll. Both animals were emaciated. There were great hollows in their flanks. Their fur was lacklustre, a dingy yellow, and they spent hour after hour, slumped on the floor of their cage, barely moving, taking shallow breaths.

They did not even raise their heads as the dockers lifted up their cage with levers, slid rollers into place, and began to shift it off the barge.

'Our reception committee seems very well prepared,' I said to Abram. On the quay a stout, low trolley was already in position.

'The barid, the caliph's intelligence service, will have told them what to expect,' he replied.

Walo, hovering beside the cage, was trying to explain something to the official in charge. Osric hurried off to help with translation.

'The barid has eyes and ears everywhere. That's how the caliph keeps his throne,' said Abram, lowering his voice. 'Be careful what you do and say.'

The shore gang was quickly on the move. At least twenty men hauled on ropes as they dragged the laden trolley away and down the nearest street. Behind them two men carried the gyrfalcons in their cages, and another group were leading the white dogs. Abram and I hurried after them.

Baghdad's houses were set close together, scarcely an arm's length apart, and they were a strange assortment. Some were modest in size, little more than cottages with small windows and sun-warped doors. The plaster on their walls was often patched and peeling. Other dwellings were far grander and larger, boasting intricately carved doors of oiled wood and outer walls decorated with patterns of coloured tiles in green, blue and yellow that glittered in the sunshine. All were single-storeyed and every house was built with a flat roof. Several times I saw people looking down at us, curious to see the little procession on its way past.

'This is a mixed district,' Abram explained. 'Merchants, traders, shopkeepers and manual workers, all living side by side.'

I asked why there were so few people in the street.

'It's still too hot,' he answered. 'People prefer to stay indoors until the worst of the day's heat is over. Even the homeless and the beggars try to find a spot of shade.'

'So there are beggars even in wealthy Baghdad.'

The corners of his mouth turned down. 'Beggars and vagrants by the thousand. While the caliph and his favourites live in unimaginable luxury, there are vast numbers of desperate poor. Often they are those who have flocked into the city, hoping to better their lives. That's another reason why the caliph needs the barid's eyes and ears. To be alert to any risk of mob riot.'

We walked for perhaps a quarter of a mile further, crossed a small bridge that spanned one of the canals that provided the citizens with water, and found ourselves confronted by a thirty-foot-high wall, topped with battlements. It needed no imagination to see why the caliph's residence was called the Round City. The great wall trended away on each side in a smooth curve, a circular design unlike anything I had seen before.

Abram noted my reaction with a knowing smile. 'Not like Rome with its conventional straight walls, is it?' he said. 'Caliph Mansour himself drew the initial outline of Baghdad in the ashes of his campfire. He sketched a circle, then jabbed his pointed stick in the centre. That spot, he told his architects, was where they were to put his palace so that he could be in the middle of all that was going on.'

I was finding the dragoman's air of superiority irritating but had to admit that the great wall was impressive. The base was a full fifteen feet thick, and we passed through the iron gates of an imposing brick archway into a hundred feet of open space – a killing ground. Beyond was an inner wall, even higher and thicker than the first, and a second iron gate. If the city mob did riot, they stood little chance of gaining access to the royal household.

Once through the second gate we turned to our left, still following the bear cage on its trolley, and continued along the line of the inner wall past a long arcade of shops and stalls that, I presumed, supplied the needs of the palace staff. Ahead was a high, square building that I took to be an immense warehouse. Gatekeepers held open broad double doors and we went inside. The smell made me catch my breath. It was like walking into a vast, stuffy stable. Behind the familiar mix of dung and hay there was something else – sour, pungent and fetid. Large windows set high up pierced the thick walls. Shafts of sunlight illuminated a long central passageway floored with wood blocks, and on either side a long line of heavy wooden doors. Instantly, I was reminded of the place where we had kept our animals inside the Colosseum.

An extraordinary sound made me jump: a shrill trumpeting blast, part squeal, part bellow. Just ahead of me one of the doors creaked open a few inches, pushed from the inside. A loose chain prevented the door from opening any further. Out from the crack slithered a thick grey serpent. It waved in the air, menacingly. I jumped back with a frightened yelp.

The grey snake heard me and turned in my direction,

reaching out towards me. I shrank away, shuddering. The head of the serpent was horrible. It had no eyes. Instead there were two slimy holes and above them a short fat finger that was moving up and down as if questing for me.

Abram guffawed. 'Don't be afraid. He's just curious,' he told me.

'What is it?' I blurted, still keeping well back from the serpent that now curled up and was withdrawing itself back through the gap in the door.

'You'll see in a moment,' he replied, grinning broadly.

A little further on, the upper half of one of the doors was open. When we came level, I looked inside, and caught my breath. I was looking at the animal that I had longed to see – a live elephant. My only mild disappointment was that it was not quite as large as I had expected. The animal swayed gently on thick grey legs and flapped huge ears with ragged edges and patches of mottled pink skin. Then it reached up with the long flexible nose that I had mistaken for a serpent and felt inside the hay net hanging on the wall. It tore off a wisp and, curling back its trunk, put the hay into its mouth. It stood there, chewing meditatively and watching me with tiny, bright eyes. The creature was as wonderfully strange as I had imagined. I looked on, delighted.

'Walo needs our help. We'd better hurry,' said Abram.

Ahead of us the team hauling the bear cage had stopped in front of an open door. Walo was waving his arms, arguing with the overseer of the slave gang. I looked around for Osric who had been acting as Walo's interpreter and saw that my friend had been distracted. He had found another half-open door and was peering over it at whatever creature was kept inside.

I hurried forward to help Walo. 'What is it?' I asked.

'They want to put my bears in there,' he said, casting an

unhappy glance into what looked like a perfectly ordinary stall. It had clean straw on the ground, and a large tub of water. The only drawback was that the stall was ill-lit and gloomy.

Walo was very distressed. 'Modi and Madi are very weak already. If they are put in there, they are likely to die. They must have fresh air.'

I translated what he had said to a small, grey-haired man who had appeared from further down the central aisle. I guessed he was the chief keeper of the menagerie.

He gave Walo a sympathetic glance. 'Tell your friend not to worry,' he said to me, 'we'll open shutters and allow fresh air to circulate as soon as the sun goes down. At this hour it is too hot outside for us to do that.'

I translated his words to Walo but failed to calm him. 'It would be better if the bears were taken outside, somewhere in the shade,' he insisted.

The head keeper saw that Walo was still troubled. Stepping past him and into the stall, he beckoned to Walo to follow him. Then the older man walked around the stall, patting the walls with the palm of his hand and repeating something in a soothing tone.

'What's he trying to say?' Walo pleaded with me.

I asked the head keeper to repeat himself, because what he had said was impossible.

But I had not misheard.

'He wants you to know that the walls are hollow, and they will be filled with ice.'

Walo gaped at me, his eyes wide with disbelief. 'With ice? How can that be?'

I relayed the question to the keeper and was told that great blocks of ice were brought down from the mountains every winter and stored underground in straw-lined pits within the

Round City. The purest ice was kept for cooling the drinks served to the caliph, his senior ministers and their guests. The lesser grade was used just as he had shown within the palace itself. Certain rooms in the palace had hollow walls that were filled with ice and, when that was not possible, trays of ice were placed where the breeze would carry the cold air into the rooms.

'This stall is constructed in the same way,' explained the keeper. 'We use it for sick animals who need to be kept cool in the summer. The caliph takes a keen interest in his menagerie and we are permitted to take from the ice stores when necessary.' He gestured towards Walo who was still looking dazed. 'If your friend wants, he can stay close by. There's a dormitory at the end of the building where the keepers sleep when they are on night duty. He can find a bed there and I will make arrangements for food to be brought to him.'

I was longing to see more of the elephant and other exotic animals, but our escort from the barge was growing impatient.

'What would Carolus think if he saw Baghdad for himself – how big it is?' I remarked to Osric as we went back out into the street, leaving Walo to watch over the ice bears.

'I'm more concerned about what the caliph will think of the animals we have brought him,' Osric replied in a low voice.

His tone caused a twinge of anxiety. 'What do you mean?'

'I had a look into some of the other stalls while you were helping Walo. There are animals in them that I have never seen before, animals so extraordinary that I wouldn't have believed they could exist.'

'What sort of animals?'

'One of them must be the animal our friend the Nomenculator thought was the unicorn.'

My heart sank. After all my searching for the elusive unicorn, it was already to be found in the caliph's menagerie.

Osric's next words were more reassuring. 'It does have a single horn. But that's the only resemblance. It's greyish black, like the elephant you saw, and not white, and no one would ever call it graceful. More like a stout ox or a very large boar with a wrinkled and armoured hide. The horn is a pointed stump growing on its nose. Not a unicorn's long spiral spike.'

My friend had also learned that the building we were visiting was not the only place where the caliph's exotic animals were housed. 'The keepers told me that there are at least two more similar buildings, as well as kennels, stables and mews for his hunting birds,' he told me.

'Did they say what other animals are kept?' I asked him.

'Wolves, several creatures whose names I didn't recognize, and thirty lions.'

I looked at him in utter disbelief. 'Thirty! That's impossible.'

Osric made a slight, helpless gesture. 'I know. It does make our gift of strange animals seem trivial. But I've no reason to doubt what the keepers told me.'

'I'd need to see those thirty lions with my own eyes before I'd believe them,' I said grudgingly.

'Maybe we will. I was told that when the Caliph wishes to impress an important visitor the lions are brought out and put on display. The keepers stand in a double line, each with a lion on a short chain. The visitor has to approach the caliph, walking in the aisle between them.'

'But where could so many lions have come from?' I said.

'From rulers in India,' Osric replied. 'Along with elephants. There are at least two dozen elephants in the royal collection. Only a handful are kept in the building we visited. Others are in an open-air park.'

'And next you're going to tell me the caliph already owns a dozen ice bears,' I said.

Osric smiled. 'He has bears of all sorts, large and small, brown and black. But there's not a single white bear in all of Baghdad.'

We had arrived at our destination, a substantial, high-walled building with an archway that opened into an interior courtyard. Our escort accompanied us inside and showed us to a set of rooms along one side of the courtyard. The rooms were spacious and airy, and our baggage had already been brought from the barge and placed inside. There was very little furniture apart from a couple of low tables, a scattering of large cushions embroidered with geometric patterns in red and green, and some expensive-looking carpets. The whitewashed plaster walls were bare but the doors and windows looked out directly on a fountain playing in the centre of the courtyard. The drifting spray made a rainbow in the rays of the afternoon sun and the sound of the water gave an impression of coolness.

Our escort informed us that a meal would shortly be provided and suggested that we might like to rest for a few hours. Later that evening, Osric and I would be taken to a private meeting at the palace of Nadim Jaffar, who had expressed a wish to meet us.

'Do you know anything about this Nadim Jaffar?' I asked Abram as the escort withdrew.

'Short of meeting with the caliph himself, you could not hope for a more promising introduction.' Abram went across to the doorway and checked that he could not be overheard. 'Jaffar is a member of Haroun's inner circle. "Nadim" is a title given only to the caliph's particular friends.'

'And this Jaffar is influential?'

'More than that. He is a senior vizier – a minister as well as being Haroun's chief advisor. His family, the Barmakids, wield extraordinary power, second only to the caliph's himself.'

'Why would he want to meet us so soon after our arrival?'

Abram frowned. 'Jaffar is the head of the barid. Perhaps he intends to check on the reports that he has been receiving about us.'

'And why weren't you included in the invitation?' I asked.

'As your dragoman, I have no formal role now that we have reached Baghdad. Besides, Jaffar will have been told that you speak good Arabic, so no interpreter is needed.'

'I would be easier in my mind if you accompanied Osric and me,' I said.

Abram treated me to one of his enigmatic smiles. 'I'm sure you don't need my help to make a good impression on Jaffar, and that way you could get to meet Caliph Haroun himself.' He paused for a moment. 'My only regret is that I won't have a chance to see Nadim Jaffar's palace. It is a byword for his opulent lifestyle.'

*

A decent interval after the call to evening prayer, our escort reappeared at our door. He walked with Osric and me to the bank of the Tigris. A private ferry was waiting at the quay, manned by a crew of a dozen oarsmen. All three of us settled ourselves on the benches and our vessel was rowed out on the river as the pink tinge of the sunset seeped from the sky. We steered directly for a row of blazing torches on the far bank, the reflection of their flames twisting and flickering on the water as we drew closer. The torches were fixed in brackets along a balustrade to show a flight of marble steps. Our guide led the way as we disembarked and followed him along a path through a garden half hidden in shadow. Dozens of torches and lanterns,

artfully placed, cast their light on beds of flowers in full bloom.
I marvelled at the effort and expense of growing such blossoms
in Baghdad's scorching dry summer. A hidden musician was
playing a stringed instrument so that the notes seemed to float
through the leaves of ornamental trees that lined the path.
When the music faded away, an unseen woman with a beautiful
voice began to sing a gentle, haunting song.

The pathway eventually brought us to an open space some
twenty paces across. Here the ground was spread with rich
carpets arranged around a shallow tiled pool. Pinpoints of light
slowly revolved and shifted on its surface. Tiny lamps of crystal,
set on lily pads, were drifting at random; the lily pads themselves were crafted from thin sheets of beaten gold. A low tree
leaned over the water at the nearest corner of the pool. On a
branch a kingfisher sat, peering down and poised to strike.
Everything was so lifelike, down to the outline of each feather
and leaf, that it took me a moment to understand that both tree
and bird were artifice. The tree was made of gold and silver,
and the brilliant colours of the kingfisher were close-set arrays
of gems, blue-green, burned orange and azure. As I looked on,
marvelling, the water beneath the bird's perch swirled as if to
tempt the kingfisher. A golden fish, a real one this time, broke
the surface briefly and the ripples spread. It was the movement
of the fish, I now realized, which made the lights on the lily
pads change position, for there was no breeze.

Seated on a low couch beside the pool was the man I
presumed to be our host. Some thirty years old, he was dressed
entirely in black, as was a lad of about nine or ten beside him.
Between them on the couch were ivory pieces on a chequered
board.

'Welcome to the City of Peace,' said the man, glancing
up. He rose to his feet and advanced round the edge of the

pool to greet us. My eyes had grown accustomed to the half-darkness, and I could see that he was remarkably handsome. Slim and graceful, he had a perfectly proportioned face. Dark, almost feminine eyes under long lashes gleamed with a bright intelligence. A thin belt studded with emeralds held in his black silk coat and accentuated his slender waist. A discreet spray of diamonds was pinned to the front of his black turban.

Our escort bowed and, without a word, left us, disappearing back down the path into the darkness.

'My name is Jaffar. It is my privilege to greet you on behalf of the Prince of Believers.' The man's speech was a match for his good looks, beautifully modulated and clear.

'We are honoured by your invitation and thankful to have reached our long-sought destination,' I replied respectfully.

Jaffar clicked his fingers so softly that I almost missed the sound. Instantly, a servant materialized out of the surrounding darkness. 'Cushions and refreshment for my guests, if you please,' he murmured. Turning towards the boy who still sat on the couch, he said, 'May I introduce my young friend Abdallah. He was about to beat me at chess, but checkmate must wait until you have told me what I can do to make your visit to our city agreeable.'

Before I could answer, a line of half a dozen servants came forward. Two of them carried an inlaid tray as large as a cartwheel, laden with small dishes Other servants brought large velvet cushions that they set down on the carpets beside the pool, arranging everything so that when Jaffar indicated to us that we should be seated, Osric and I were facing the nadim. He took his seat on the tiled surround to the pool. The lad Abdallah stayed where he was on the couch, watching and listening.

I opened my mouth to speak but Jaffar lifted a hand to stop me. 'First, please eat and drink. The evening is to be enjoyed.'

Two more servants silently appeared at my elbow. One held a basin, the other a ewer from which he poured scented water over my hands, before offering me a towel. The moment he withdrew, another servant brought forward a silver tray on which a small drinking bowl stood, eggshell thin and patterned blue and white. Yet another servant leaned forward with a matching jug and poured a pale gold liquid. I picked up the bowl and the cool surface on the palm of my hand told me that the drink had been chilled with ice from the mountains. I took a sip. It was a mix of exotic fruit juices slightly fizzy on my tongue.

Our host waited until we had sampled the food set before us – I tasted pickled fish, both sweet and sour, and chicken marinated in different sauces that, apart from orange and ginger, were impossible to identify. Among the sweeter dishes the flavour of cinnamon brought back a vivid memory of the meal we had shared in Rome with the Nomenculator.

'I'm on tenterhooks to hear about your journey, Sigwulf,' said Jaffar courteously, looking at me.

'Your Excellency, it would take far too long to recount everything that happened,' I answered, wondering just how much the nadim already knew. He had used my name though I had not formally introduced myself. It was a reminder, probably deliberate, that this man, so full of charm, was also head of the caliph's intelligence department.

'The evening is young, and tales of travel are never dull,' he replied. 'Tell me how your journey began.'

So I started with the day I had been summoned to Alcuin's study and seen an aurochs' horn, and how Carolus himself had instructed me to go into the Northlands and obtain the white animals that dwelt there. I said nothing about the unexplained attack on me in Kaupang, nor the strange events that followed in Rome and on the Mediterranean. As for the death of the aurochs, I explained that the creature had escaped and been eaten by lions, and made no mention that it had been set free deliberately. I wished to avoid distracting the nadim from the purpose of my mission – that the animals I had brought to Baghdad were a gesture of friendship from Carolus to the caliph.

Jaffar listened attentively, his head tilted slightly to one side. He interrupted only twice: firstly to ask me to describe Carolus's physical appearance and what he thought of the presents that he had received from Baghdad; then secondly to enquire about Alcuin and his role as an advisor.

'You and your companions are to be congratulated,' observed the nadim when I had finished my recital. 'It was a magnificent achievement to have transported those animals for such a great distance and kept them alive, except for that giant ox.'

Something in his voice made me wonder if there had been a hidden reason for wanting to hear my tale. His next words confirmed my unease.

'To return for a moment to the beginning of your story . . .' the nadim's manner was as soothing and courteous as ever. 'You say that King Carolus sent you to the Northlands to obtain white animals because these creatures would be rarities, previously unknown in Baghdad.'

'That is correct, Your Excellency,' I replied. 'King Carolus showed me a book, a bestiary, and pointed out the white animals I was to search for.'

'A book?'

'I have brought a copy with me, Your Excellency. It is another of Carolus's gifts to the Commander of the Faithful. Unfortunately, I did not think to bring it with me this evening.'

'There was no need,' said the nadim, with a graceful, dismissive wave of his hand. 'This evening is private and informal. I am sure that the Emir of the Believers will enjoy looking into this book. It will reassure him . . . and me.'

He must have noted my look of incomprehension for he added, 'The colour your King Carolus chose for the animals he sent us is surprising.'

'I'm sorry, Your Excellency, I do not understand,' I stammered. I was beginning to fear that something had gone very wrong.

For a brief moment Jaffar looked at me, judging my reaction. 'Some might say that the gift of white animals was provocative.'

It felt as though the pit of my stomach had fallen away. With a terrible certainty I knew that the nadim's jet-black clothes had special significance. 'But King Carolus was advised that white is the royal colour of the caliphate, that all must wear white when they enter the Round City . . .' I said shakily.

'The latter is correct,' Jaffar acknowledged. 'White is worn in the Round City so that no one can draw undue attention to themselves with costly garments or flamboyant colours. But anyone who enters the caliph's presence must dress entirely in black. It is the colour of the turban worn by Allah's Messenger – may Allah honour him and grant him peace – when he preached from the pulpit. Our caliph follows the true path. He wears the prophet's cloak and carries his staffs – may Allah honour him and grant him peace – and the colour of his house is black.'

'Your Excellency,' I blurted, 'King Carolus meant no disrespect.'

Jaffar leaned forward. 'It is equally evident that your king was unaware that white is the colour worn in the presence of the usurper in al Andalus, the false Emir of Cordoba.'

My throat was dry. I recalled vividly what Alcuin had told me of the feud between Haroun and the Emir in Andalus. Haroun's ancestors had slaughtered the Emir's family in the fight for power and laid claim to the true heritage of Islam.

Jaffar's eyes suddenly twinkled with mischief. 'Sigwulf, do not look so aghast. No one would be so crass as to deliberately insult the caliph in this manner and I shall tell him so.'

'Your Excellency, if King Carolus had known, I am sure he would have despatched me to find animals of the deepest black and bring them to Baghdad.'

The nadim flashed a brilliant smile. 'Sigwulf, your tale rings true, though I must confess that when I heard that Carolus was sending white animals I thought it was a less-than-subtle hint that he favoured an alliance with nearby Andalus and not with the Commander of the Faithful in far Baghdad.'

He rose to his feet. 'So now you will understand why the public presentation of white animals to the caliph is impolitic. I'm sorry.'

Clearly this announcement was the true purpose of our meeting. I felt utterly numb, stunned by the unexpected turn of events.

Jaffar saw my dismay and was swift to offer a consolation. 'Sigwulf, His Magnificence will wish to view the white animals, but discreetly. Also I'm going to recommend that he grants you a private audience so that he, too, can hear your remarkable tale.'

It was obvious that the evening was at an end. I stood up groggily, sensing that Osric beside me was equally confounded. Then I remembered something I had forgotten in my sudden confusion.

'Your Excellency, the elephant your master sent as a gift to Carolus was white. That added to our misunderstanding.'

Jaffar brushed my excuse aside. 'That is not a detail I am aware of.'

My knees were shaking and I felt my shirt sticking to my back. I was sweating; not from heat, for the evening had turned cool, but with a cold sweat from the realization that my mission was a total failure.

Jaffar was still speaking. 'The palace staff will send word when the date of your audience with the caliph has been settled. Meanwhile, you can oblige me by recounting the details of your remarkable trip to the scribes in the royal library. It will make a valuable addition to their collection of travel accounts.'

I gathered myself together sufficiently to thank the nadim for his hospitality and then a servant guided Osric and me back down the path to where our original escort was waiting at the wharf.

When we got back to the privacy of our rooms, we found that Abram had been waiting up, eager to hear our news.

'How did the meeting go?' he asked.

'A disaster,' I replied sourly. 'We should have brought black animals to Baghdad, not white ones. Black is the caliph's royal colour. White is associated with his rival in Hispania.'

Abram looked utterly taken aback. 'But everyone wears white in the Round City, that's a requirement.'

'Yes,' I said, trying not to sound aggrieved. 'But all who appear before the caliph on a formal occasion must be dressed in black. Why didn't you warn us?'

The dragoman spread his hands in a gesture of apology. 'As a Radhanite I've never been summoned to appear before the caliph in person. The inner workings of the court are shrouded in secrecy.'

'Both Jaffar and a young lad with him were dressed in black from head to toe.'

Abram's eyes lit up with curiosity. 'What young lad?'

I described Abdallah and when I had finished, Abram sucked in his breath. 'Do you know who that is?' he asked.

'I have no idea, except that he was listening to every word.'

'Abdallah's father is Haroun himself,' the dragoman said, clearly impressed. 'Not only Jaffar will report to the caliph what he thinks of you, so too will his favourite son.'

'Then I hope Abdallah liked what he saw and heard,' I answered peevishly.

The dragoman gave me an anxious look. 'Abdallah's mother is a Persian concubine. He has a half-brother, Mohammed, of the same age and born to one of Haroun's legitimate wives. Mohammed is the crown prince. There is much jealousy between the two youths.'

I shrugged. 'How would that affect us?'

'If Abdallah makes a favourable report to his father, then Mohammed will try to make your life in Baghdad as difficult as possible.'

'But Abdallah and Mohammed are both youngsters.'

'Sigwulf, you have no idea of the in-fighting that goes on beneath the glittering surface of the caliph's court. Each young man has his own supporters and they compete for power and influence, hoping their own candidate will one day ascend the throne.'

'You're sounding like the Nomenculator in Rome when he warned me about the hidden conflict for the selection of the next pope.'

'This is far more vicious than Rome,' said Abram grimly. 'The previous caliph, Mahdi, died before his time. Some say he was poisoned, others that he was smothered with cushions. He was Haroun's brother.'

'And Haroun arranged his death?'

The dragoman dropped his voice to a whisper. 'No, their mother did. She feared she was losing influence over her eldest son and preferred to see Haroun on the throne.'

Chapter Fifteen

'I STILL DON'T UNDERSTAND that mistake between black and white at the caliph's court,' Osric remarked to me the next morning. We had emerged from the menagerie building where we had gone to check on Walo. Despite not speaking Arabic, he had struck up a working friendship with the keepers and was comfortably installed in their dormitory. Madi and Modi were being given their proper food and the hollow walls of their pen were regularly replenished with ice. Walo was confident that they would soon be back to full health.

'I've been thinking back to my meeting with Alcuin and then the interview with Carolus,' I told my friend. 'Both believed that white was the royal colour in Baghdad.'

It was mid-morning and the glare of the sun was blinding. We were keeping to the shady side of the narrow street as we walked behind our escort, the same man who had accompanied us to the meeting with Jaffar. He was leading us to the palace library to meet the scribes who would record the details of our journey from Aachen.

'Did Alcuin or Carolus mention where they had got their information from?' asked Osric.

'No, and there was no reason for me to ask.'

'Yet it's unlike Alcuin to be so poorly informed.'

'I don't remember his exact words, but I think he only said

that anyone who enters the inner city must be dressed in white. And that's correct.'

Osric stopped for a moment to dislodge a pebble that had got trapped in his sandal. 'What about Abram? He should have known.'

'I didn't meet Abram until we got back from Kaupang. By then everything was settled, and we had the white animals. Besides, our dragoman tells me that he had never been admitted into the presence of the caliph. Only seen him from a distance.'

We were heading in the direction of the huge green dome I had noticed from the barge during our arrival in Baghdad. The dome loomed over the surrounding buildings and was evidently part of the main palace complex at the heart of the Round City. As we came closer, another defensive wall topped with guard towers became visible. The caliph's palace was a fortress within a fortress.

Before we reached the foot of the wall, our guide turned aside through an archway where two elderly porters sat half-asleep on a stone bench. We followed him into a large open courtyard. In the centre a fountain played, a feature that I was beginning to recognize as commonplace throughout the Round City. The courtyard itself had been designed as a perfect square, and contrasting lines of the grey and mottled-white paving slabs had been laid out in geometric patterns of triangles, circles and squares. Solid-looking buildings two storeys high surrounded all four sides of the court, each fronted by a portico with evenly spaced marble columns whose muted colours matched the courtyard paving. The overall effect was an atmosphere of austere calm, orderly and contemplative. It reminded me of a monastic cloister.

In the shade of the porticos groups of men were seated on the marble flooring. They were talking quietly among themselves or bent forward over low desks and busy writing. Many were greybeards, others barely out of their teens. I noticed that the usual pattern was for the scribes to work in pairs, an older man reading aloud from a book while a younger man sat at the desk and took down his dictation.

Our guide led us to the far side of the courtyard where a tall, painfully thin man stood waiting, his shoulders hunched and his hands tucked into his sleeves. Our escort introduced him as the caliph's librarian, Fadl ibn Naubakt.

'Nadim Jaffar sent word that you have recently arrived from Frankia. He instructs that we make a record of the details of your route,' the librarian said in a thin, scratchy voice. He blinked rapidly as he spoke and I wondered if it was due to the sun's glare or if he had spent so long over his books that his eyesight was damaged.

'My companion and I will be happy to provide what details we can remember,' I replied. The librarian sounded mildly aggrieved that his normal routine had been disrupted.

'Very good. I hope we will not take up too much of your time.' Fadl ushered us into the shadow of the nearest portico. 'I compliment you on your command of Arabic,' he said to me. 'I had assigned a Frankish speaker and one of our best notaries. But I can see that the former will not be needed. That will make the task go more quickly.'

We passed close enough to a pair of scribes for me to hear the older man reading aloud in a language I did not recognize. It had odd, bubbling sounds like water emptying into a drain.

'How many languages can your interpreters understand?' I asked the librarian.

'They're translators, not interpreters,' Fadl corrected me with a touch of pedantry. 'A good deal of our work here is the transcription of texts written in foreign languages and their scripts. We turn them into Arabic or Syriac. If the subject matter is judged to be very important, we make multiple copies for our library holdings.'

'What language is most in demand?'

'Greek,' he replied without hesitation. 'Last year we sent a deputation to Byzantium to buy classical medical texts. His Magnificence was most generous with the necessary funds, as was Nadim Jaffar, though his taste inclines more to philosophy.'

It was an unexpected insight into the interests of the head of the barid. 'Your deputation was well received in Byzantium?' I enquired.

The librarian blinked at me in mild reproof. 'There is no reason why not. Numerous Greeks live and work here in Baghdad and throughout the caliphate.'

I decided to let the matter drop. Alcuin had given me to understand that Baghdad and Byzantium were enemies, that their troops launched raids across the common border, and from time to time there was outright war. Perhaps this was another area where Alcuin was misinformed.

The librarian was speaking again. 'We produce a large number of original texts ourselves, in particular in the fields of astronomy and astrology. We consider those subjects to be the pinnacle of learning.' He nodded towards an old fellow who was sitting by himself in a shady corner of the portico. He had dozed off, his head slumped forward on his chest under the weight of an enormous turban that threatened to undo itself at any moment. 'Yakub is one of the leading authorities on planetary movements. He has been correlating observations at our own Baghdad observatory with the predictions in Indian texts.'

It crossed my mind that Yakub had been staying up late at night observing the planets, for he did not stir as we skirted around him and went through a door into a large, high-ceilinged room. Bookshelves lined the walls, and deep niches were piled up with scrolls. A row of small unshuttered windows allowed in light and air, but the place had a still, dead feel to it.

The only occupant of the room was a man who looked more like a heavyweight wrestler than a scholar. He heaved himself up from where he had been sitting in front of a low desk. Everything about him was oversize, from his barrel chest to his massive, entirely bald head. He did not wear a turban and there were beads of sweat on his shiny scalp.

'Musa will take down your story,' said the librarian. 'If you need to take a break during your narration, please do not hesitate to say so.' He stalked out of the room, closing the door behind him.

Musa waved us to cushions placed near his desk and when we had sat down, he took his place behind the desk, pen in hand. 'Perhaps you could begin with a description of King Carolus's palace,' he suggested.

It took the rest of the morning to repeat the tale I had recounted to Nadim Jaffar the previous evening. Osric helped me out. We took it in turns to describe all that had happened, each filling in details that the other had forgotten or overlooked. This time I also told of the attack on me in Kaupang, the sinking of Protis's ship and the young Greek's death in the Colosseum. Osric and I had agreed that a complete record of our journey should be written down and held somewhere safe, in case a further, possibly fatal, accident occurred, and the barid might wish to investigate.

Occasionally, Musa would interrupt, usually to ask us to repeat a place name or check that he had each episode of the journey in the correct sequence. When, finally, he had finished writing and had laid down his pen, he leaned back and stretched his meaty arms. 'You seem to have survived an unusual number of narrow escapes. Didn't Carolus consult with astrologers before sending you on such a hazardous venture?' he commented.

'As far as I am aware, there are no astrologers at King Carolus's court,' I replied.

'Really!' Musa's eyebrows arched in surprise on the great egg-shaped face. 'History tells us that every great ruler tries to look into the future. The Greeks consulted their seers, the Romans opened the entrails of chickens and goats.'

I paused before replying, not wanting to make Carolus seem too credulous. 'Carolus believes in his dreams.'

'Ah!' said Musa. His tone managed to be understanding and disapproving at the same time. 'And how does he know what the dreams mean?'

'He consults with family and his council, and . . .' here I hesitated – 'there was a time when he had access to a Book of Dreams.'

'I expect you mean the Oneirokritikon,' said Musa casually.

Osric and I exchanged glances. It was startling to come across Artimedorus's work in Baghdad, although our copy had been an Arabic translation from the original Greek.

'There's a rumour that you've brought a book from Carolus as a present to the Commander of the Faithful,' said Musa. 'I hope it is not the Oneirokritikon, because I'm fairly sure we already have a copy.' He levered his great bulk to his feet and walked to the book shelves, and within moments had pulled down a volume. 'Yes, here it is.' He looked up at us.

'No, no,' I hastened to assure him. 'We are carrying a book of beasts, a bestiary.'

'Our librarian will be pleased.' Musa's sardonic tone indi-

cated that he was not on good terms with the gaunt librarian.
'He already has a team working on a new volume of natural
history, a complete list of the animals and plants mentioned in
the various texts we own. A couple of artists are drawing new
illustrations. Nadim Jaffar ordered the book as a present for
the caliph on his birthday next year. Doubtless your bestiary,
as you call it, will be placed in this library once the caliph has
received it formally from you. It will be an additional resource
for us and much appreciated.' He half turned, about to replace
the Oneirokritikon on the shelves.

'I wonder if it would be possible to check something that
Artimedorus wrote?' I asked.

Musa swung round to face us. 'Of course. You read Greek?'

I shook my head, and thought it wiser not to say that Osric
and I had once had our own copy, and still kept a few pages.
'I had a couple of dreams on the journey here. They might
be significant. Perhaps the Oneirokritikon can offer an explanation.'

'What were they?' asked Musa.

'I dreamed of a man covered with bees and, in another
dream, someone was climbing inside the body of a dead
elephant.'

It took Musa some time to find the first reference, then he
read out: ' "To see a man covered in bees, who is not a farmer,
is to foretell his death." '

I was aware of the accusing glance that Osric flicked in my
direction.

Musa was leafing further through the book. Then he read,
' "If one dreams of a person breaking the skin and entering the
body of a dead elephant it means that person will one day derive
great riches." '

He closed the book. 'The problem with the Oneirokritikon is that far too many of the explanations deal with making or losing money. Very Greek . . .' He gave a throaty chuckle.

He replaced the Oneirokritikon on the shelf. 'And naturally the author covers himself against mistakes.' He thought for a moment and then quoted, ' "A dream that comes through a gate of horn is false; a dream that comes through a gate of ivory is true." '

His fleshy shoulders moved in a dismissive shrug. 'What on earth can that really mean?'

He reached down another volume from further along the same shelf. 'I don't suppose the librarian would approve, but we have an hour or so before he comes to collect you – why don't I illustrate how astrology is more reliable than dreams when indicating the future?'

He brought the large, heavy book across and opened it on the desk.

From where I sat I could see that the page was covered with columns of numbers, various symbols and drawings with lines and circles that vaguely recalled the geometric patterns in the courtyard.

'I'm no expert like old Yakub outside. I just dabble in these things. But if you tell me some of the key dates in your journey I may be able to put together a simple prediction of how it will end. For a start, I need to know the date when you started on your journey. Also the dates and places of your births.'

Osric and I provided the information as best we could, and Musa carefully wrote it down. He then spent a long time turning back and forth the pages of the great book and making calculations on a sheet of parchment. Finally, after a good twenty minutes, he sat back. 'Interesting,' he said. 'I've calcu-lated – very roughly, you understand – the star signs, the houses of the planets, mansions of the moon, both on your birth dates and when you began your journey, how the constellations varied along your path, and the timing of your arrival here.'

'What are your conclusions?' I asked. I was sceptical of the accuracy of such a method, but impressed by the amount of mathematical calculation. It seemed more arcane and intricate than merely dreaming.

'According to the astrology, your journey is not yet over. There will be more hardship, some disappointment and death, but — finally — great happiness. Life will change back to where it began.'

I was mildly disillusioned. Musa's predictions were hardly less ambiguous than the Oneirokritikon.

Behind us came the sound of the door opening, then the librarian's reedy voice announced that our escort had arrived and was waiting to bring us back to our lodgings. We got to our feet and thanked Musa for his help.

I avoided looking at Osric as we left the building. We had gone only a few yards before he asked in a low voice, 'Sigwulf, why didn't you tell me that your dream of two wolves and Walo covered with bees is an omen of his death?'

There was an uncomfortable pause as I struggled to find the right words. 'You forget that the Book of Dreams also states that madmen achieve what they set out to do, which is why I thought Walo should travel with us.'

When my friend did not reply, I added lamely, 'Walo has proved to be our lucky mascot, essential to our embassy. Thanks to him, the ice bears have reached Baghdad, not to speak of the gyrfalcons.'

Osric stopped abruptly and turned towards me, his eyes searching my face. 'And if this costs him his life?'

'My dream with the bees was nothing to do with his

impending death,' I said firmly. 'As I told you, a bear is called a "bee wolf" in the Northlands, and the dream was fulfilled the day Walo crawled into the cage and sat between the two bears without being harmed.'

Osric looked only half persuaded.

'Walo was rejected by his family, struggling to survive, teased and mocked by strangers,' I concluded. 'Whatever happens to him now must be better than if we had left him behind in Aachen.'

My friend managed a slight nod, as if to accept my reasoning but, as we walked on in silence, I felt that the foundations of our mutual trust had shifted slightly.

*

Nadim Jaffar kept his word. A servant called at our lodgings the following morning with a message that our private audience with the Commander of the Faithful would take place later that day. He also brought two sets of black clothes, so it seemed that Abram was not expected to attend. Indeed, we had seen little of our dragoman since he had obtained permission to find accommodation with his co-religionists outside the Round City. His role as a guide was largely redundant. Whenever Osric and I stepped outside, a guide was loitering in the street. Doubtless an employee of Jaffar's barid, sent to keep an eye on us, he insisted on accompanying us everywhere, showing us the sights. At the caliph's lion enclosures we had learned that Osric's information had been correct; we counted thirty of the beasts in captivity.

'No avenue of lions held on chains, I hope,' I joked nervously to Osric as we put on black silk shirts and long gowns, black trousers and belts, black slippers and tall, narrow hats made of straw and covered with black felt stitched with black brocade.

My hat was nearly the length of my arm, and threatening to topple sideways. Osric came across to straighten it. 'It would be tactful to wrap the bestiary in a length of black cloth before presenting it to the caliph,' he suggested.

I selected a spare black turban and wound it around the precious volume.

Soon after midday, the same man who had brought us to Nadim Jaffar's garden arrived to bring us to our meeting with the caliph. Instead of leading us towards the great dome of the central palace as I expected, he took us in the opposite direction, out of the city by the north-east gate and towards the river. We negotiated the narrow streets of a residential quarter and came to an imposing gatehouse flanked by brick walls too high to see what lay on the other side. Guards searched us, unwrapping the bestiary, and checking that it was not hollowed out to conceal a weapon. Beyond the gatehouse we emerged onto a broad, open terrace a hundred yards in length and built along the river front. It gave a spectacular view over the Tigris with its constant movement of boats across to the array of grand houses lining the far bank, and – a little downstream – the main city pontoon bridge. Overlooking this lively scene was a handsome palace in the Saracen style. Tiled domes gleamed turquoise in the late afternoon sun. Bands of polished marble – dark red, black and green – emphasized the symmetry of the rows of arched windows along the façade. The main entrance was framed by slender marble columns and high enough for a man to enter on horseback. This, our guide informed us, was the Khuld Palace, the Palace of Eternity, and here the caliph would receive us.

Veering off to one side, he took us to a side entrance half hidden by a screen of delicately carved stonework. Here he left us with a chamberlain waiting with two assistants, and they accompanied us down a long deserted corridor, past a line of closed doors. Tiled walls threw back the clack of our footsteps on the marble floor and, with our escort in such close attendance, we might as well have been prisoners on the way to their cells. The difference was the all-pervading scent of rosewater that perfumed the air. We were hurried up two flights of steps and then along a gallery that looked down on a large antechamber where small groups of black-clad men were standing and waiting, possibly for an audience with the caliph. There was no way of telling whether they were courtiers or officials. They did not look up, and it was clear, too, that our escort did not want us to be seen.

At the far end of the gallery, we were ushered into a room and the chamberlain and his assistants silently withdrew, closing the door behind us and leaving us alone.

Osric and I exchanged glances. We had stepped into a jewellery box. Panes of coloured glass in the ceiling illuminated gorgeous silk hangings covering the walls. Underfoot the thick carpets were richly detailed with intricate patterns of blossoms and fruit. Gold leaf had been applied to every exposed surface. Here the scent of rosewater was almost overpowering. Directly in front of us hung a curtain that divided the room in half. The fabric was gauze so fine that the slightest draught set it swaying. Daylight filtered through it, yet by a clever trick of the weave it was impossible to see what lay the other side.

I guessed we had been brought into one of the upper rooms of the palace with a window overlooking the Tigris. I strained my ears, trying to catch the sounds of the river when – bewilderingly – through the curtain came a succession of whistles and liquid trills. I recognized the song of a nightingale.

Osric and I stood facing the curtain, waiting politely for whatever might happen next. Several minutes passed. I wondered if someone was observing us secretly and I dared not turn my head and search too obviously for a spyhole. The birdsong stopped, then started again, then stopped. There was no other sound, no movement. Presently, the curtain in front of us swayed minutely, the barest tremor. I heard a faint rustling sound. Another pause followed. Finally, an unseen hand or some hidden mechanism drew back the curtain in a single, smooth movement.

The other half of the room was even more opulent. Matching mirrors extended from floor to ceiling on the side walls. They were positioned to angle the daylight pouring in through the window arch on the further wall and direct it onto hundreds of precious stones sewn into the fabric of the wall hangings. The gems caught the light and glowed in all their brilliance – amethyst, ruby and emerald. The cloth itself shimmered with gold and silver thread. Suspended from the ceiling by a silk cord in one corner was a golden birdcage. The drab brown of its occupant, the nightingale, made the surrounding colours appear all the more sumptuous.

Directly in front of us the floor level was raised to create a platform and oblige us to look upwards. There, reclining on two bolsters were two boys. I recognized one of them immediately. He was Abdallah, Caliph Haroun's son whom I had seen in Jaffar's garden. Something told me that the other boy was his half-brother, Mohammed the Crown Prince. Both were much the same age and identically dressed in long black surcoats and tightly fitting trousers, and both wore black turbans. While Mohammed's turban had a diamond brooch in the shape of a starburst, Abdallah's turban bore no decoration.

For a long moment we stared at one another without a word being said. Then, making me jump, one of the mirrors swung to one side and became a door. Through it stepped a tall, handsome and well set-up man about thirty years old, whose light complexion contrasted with a neatly barbered black beard some four or five inches long. He wore no jewellery but his long black silk gown was open at the front to show an under-robe of grey silk with discreet bands of embroidery at the collar and wrists. On his head he wore the same style of tall black felt hat as Osric and me, though his hat had a black turban wrapped around it, the free end hanging down his back. The two youngsters promptly sat up straighter on their cushions. Even without that hint I would have known that the man who had entered the room was their father, Haroun al Rashid, Prince of the Faithful, Caliph of Baghdad and Allah's Shadow on Earth.

Beside me, Osric immediately sank to his knees and pressed his forehead to the ground. A heartbeat later I followed his example, almost letting slip the bestiary I was clutching. We stayed kneeling until a quiet voice told us to rise. Getting to my feet, I found that the caliph had sat down between his two sons, only a few paces from me, and was scrutinizing us closely.

'You must be Sigwulf,' he said to me. 'Abdallah did not tell me about your eyes.'

I realized that the sunlight coming in through the window behind Haroun was falling full on my face.

'The great Iskander also had eyes of different colours,' Haroun continued. 'He, too, was a great traveller.'

My mind had gone blank. I knew he was talking of Alexander the Great and I tried desperately and unsuccessfully to recall what I knew about the extent of Alexander's journeys. I stood there tongue-tied and feeling foolish.

Abdallah came to my rescue. He leaned towards his father and whispered something.

'My son tells me that you have a book to give us.'

This was safer ground. My mind began to clear. 'Your

Magnificence, it is but one of the presents that my master Carolus, King of the Franks, sends you in return for your great generosity in the gifts you despatched to him, for which he thanks you.'

I realized that I was gabbling and forced myself to slow down. 'There are other items he hopes will please you – bears, birds of prey, specially selected –' I was still so flustered that I only just stopped myself from mentioning that the animals had been chosen because they were white.

Fortunately, the caliph cut across me. 'Nadim Jaffar has told me about these and Mohammed and Abdallah have been to see the bears. They are indeed remarkable.' He leaned forward slightly. 'The book . . . ?' he prompted.

It was clear that the caliph was in a hurry. I presumed that he was taking a short break from his official duties to hold this private audience, and was doing so to please Abdallah who had reported on the meeting in Jaffar's garden. Certainly Abdallah was listening closely to everything being said as if he owned the interview.

'Your Magnificence,' I blurted, hurriedly unwinding the black cloth from around the book, 'it cannot compare with the splendid volumes in your royal library, but King Carolus hopes that it will be of some interest.'

Abdallah scrambled to his feet. He came across the platform and I handed him up the book. He took it back to his father, and then sat down beside the caliph, who opened the cover. On Haroun's left, the other son, Mohammed, leaned in to look more closely.

There was silence as the caliph slowly turned the pages, pausing from time to time to study a particular illustration. At one point he stopped for several moments, then looked up at me, and turned the book around so that I could see the picture.

'What is this bird?' he asked. He looked down again, and slowly and carefully read out: ' "c-a-l-a-d-r-i-u-s." '

With a shock I realized that Haroun al Rashid had deliberately not looked at the Arabic translation that had been prepared long ago in Aachen. He was testing out his knowledge of Western script. I was dumbfounded. The contrast with Carolus could not have been greater. In Aachen, I had watched the King of the Franks looking through the pictures in the bestiary. He could write no more than a few words in his own language and struggled with reading the simplest phrases. In Baghdad, his counterpart, the Commander of the Faithful, could recognize a foreign script and, with close attention, even make out the letters.

On the page that Haroun then held out to me were two pictures. The upper one showed a man with a crown on his head. He was lying on a bed and looked very ill. At his feet a white bird vaguely like a magpie was perched on the bed frame, behind it an open window. It was clear that the bird had flown into the room and settled there. The bird was staring at the crowned man. The lower picture was identical except that the bird, instead of staring at the man, had turned its head and was looking away.

'A caladrius, Your Magnificence,' I explained, remembering the text written below, 'is a bird that can foretell whether a king who is sick will live or die. If the caladrius looks at the patient, the sickness is drawn into the bird. It then flies up into the sun and is burned away and, with it, the sickness. But if the caladrius looks away when he sees the ill king, then death is certain.'

Haroun's expression did not change. He turned the book around in his hands and continued to look through the pages. I wondered if I should have been more tactful in my explanation, then thought to myself that a translator in the royal library would eventually produce a full translation of the text written below the pictures, and that the caliph might see it. It was wiser to be honest.

The caliph reached the end of the book, and looked up at me again. 'Many of the animals shown here I recognize. Some are already in my collection. But others are not.'

On his right the young Abdallah looked pleased, doubtless glad that he had told his father that it might be worth looking through the book I said I was carrying.

'You are to be congratulated on delivering the bears alive – and the other animals – from such a great distance,' said the caliph.

I bowed in acknowledgement.

'It is pleasing that your King Carolus and I have a shared interest,' Haroun continued.

I cleared my throat and spoke as humbly as possible. 'My Lord Carolus has a menagerie, though not as varied as your own superb collection. He instructed me to say that if you could send him unusual animals he would be very grateful.'

'Did he mention any particular animal?' asked the caliph.

A clear memory sprang into my mind: Carolus showing me a picture in the book and saying that, if the opportunity arose, I was to ask the caliph if he could supply such a creature for the royal collection.

'Your Magnificence, King Carolus mentioned one creature of particular interest to him. It is shown, I believe, on the eighth page of the book.'

The caliph turned to the correct page, and studied the illustration for several moments. 'I find something familiar about this animal but can't place exactly what it is. Perhaps you can explain further. What is written underneath?'

He passed the book to Abdallah and listened approvingly as the lad read out: '"*The Griffin: It has the body of a lion but the wings and head of an eagle. Some say it lives in the Indian desert, others in Ethiopia. A griffin will tear a man to pieces or carry him to its nest to feed its young. Griffins are strong enough to carry away an entire live ox.*"'

The illustration showed a fierce, predatory creature with a cruel hooked beak and huge wings sprouting from the shoulders of a lion-like body. Its paws had long curved talons.

'That must be the same as our simurgh, that some call the rukh,' said the caliph gravely.

Mohammed, the crown prince, leaned in and spoke quietly in his ear. I did not like the sly expression on the youngster's face as he sat back straight and watched me.

'Naturally, I shall be happy to oblige your King Carolus,' announced the caliph. 'This animal is known to us, though only by hearsay. It is a great bird so fierce and powerful that it can even carry away elephants in its claws.'

He glanced approvingly at the crown prince. 'My son reminds me that the rukh is found in the lands south of the Zanj.'

The caliph turned his full attention back to me, and his tone of voice left no doubt that he was giving orders. 'I too would like to add a rukh to my animal collection. You and your companions have shown great skill in these matters and I will ask Nadim Jaffar to make arrangements for you to travel to the land of the Zanj and on to where the rukh lives. Bring back at least two of the creatures. One will be for my collection, the other to take back to King Carolus.'

I could only bow. The private audience had taken a totally unexpected and unwelcome direction and there was nothing for me to say. I had an uncomfortable recollection of Carolus telling me to find a unicorn.

The caliph spoke to Abdullah. 'I think our new emissary to Zanj should keep the book until he returns from his voyage. It may be useful.'

My hands shaking, I took the bestiary from Abdullah, and my consternation must have been obvious. The caliph looked down at me with the suspicion of a twinkle in his eye. 'You can place it with my royal library on your return, Sigwulf, and do not look so dismayed. Iskander travelled to the far ends of the earth, even to the Land of Darkness. In our Holy Book, it is said that he even reached the fountain of life. Take him as your example.'

With those words the caliph rose to his feet and the curtain that divided the room began to close. But before it drew completely shut I caught a brief glimpse of a grin of malicious triumph on the face of Abdallah's rival, the crown prince.

*

The moment Osric and I got back to our lodgings in the Round City, I sent for Abram. 'Where's the land of the Zanj?' I asked the dragoman when he arrived.

He gave me a surprised look. 'On the coast of Ethiopia. Far south.'

'Have you ever been there? Or any of your people?'

He shook his head. 'Not that I know of. Why do you want to know?'

'The caliph is sending us beyond the land of Zanj to bring back animals to add to his menagerie,' I said sourly.

Abram was visibly relieved. 'Then I'm afraid I won't be of any help to you. I have no knowledge of the languages of the people along that coast. You'll have to ask for a different interpreter to be provided.'

'But you know what the people are like?'

'Only that they are black.' He looked at me quizzically, 'And what sort of animals are you expected to bring back?'

Osric answered for me. 'The caliph called it a rukh, or simurgh. It's similar to the griffin pictured in the Book of Beasts.'

The dragoman regarded us with a mixture of incredulity and amusement. 'Do you think that such a creature really exists?'

'It's not for me to say,' I told him. 'The expedition was the crown prince's idea.'

The dragoman made a sharp intake of breath. 'What do you mean by that?'

'I'm sure that it was young Abdallah who persuaded his father to grant us a private audience. But it was his half-brother who suggested sending us to bring back a rukh from Zanj.'

Abram spoke slowly and carefully. 'Sigwulf, be careful. You're on dangerous ground.'

I waited for him to go on.

'I warned you earlier about the rivalries around the throne,' Abram said. 'Abdallah pleased his father by bringing you and Osric before him with the mysterious book. That would have made the crown prince jealous. Mohammed has devised a way of discrediting Abdallah by sending you off on a mission that he hopes will fail.'

I hesitated, trying to think how it might be possible to avoid going in search of the rukh when Osric spoke up. 'The rukh can't be any more dangerous to catch and handle than a pair of ice bears. Walo should be able to cope.'

Abram's response held more than a hint of condescension. 'I admire your confidence,' he said meaningfully. 'If a rukh does exist and is so easy to obtain, I'm surprised that there's not one already in the caliph's menagerie.'

Chapter Sixteen

MUSA WAS ABLE to provide a few more details about the rukh when Osric and I went to see him in the royal library. We found him in the same airless room as before, surrounded by books and scrolls.

'I never thought that there would be any use to the librarian's list of animals mentioned in our books,' he admitted, 'but I was wrong.'

'Our former dragoman doubts the rukh even exists,' Osric told him.

Musa mopped the sweat off his glistening scalp with a length of cloth. 'And until recently I would have agreed. But our archivists have turned up reports of similar animals.'

'Like the griffin in the Book of Beasts?' I asked.

'Nearly so. Our texts from India contain several references to a giant bird called a Garuda, large enough to seize an elephant in its talons. We also have a mention from China, of a huge bird known as a Peng. Interestingly, it is said to fly south each year to an unknown destination over the ocean.'

'To the land of Zanj?' I suggested.

'Let me show you on a map.' Musa lumbered over to a wall where hung a circular sheet of thin flat metal some two feet across. He unhooked it and laid it on the floor beside his low table.

'This,' he said, leaning over and prodding the centre of

the sheet with a thick finger, 'is where we are now, in Baghdad.'

The surface of the sheet was incised with interlocking and irregular shapes. It took me a moment to work out that each shape represented a country. I presumed that what was written inside each shape in Arab script was the country's name.

Musa's finger moved to a large empty space. 'This is the sea southward from Baghdad. And here,' he touched a curved line to one side of the space, 'is the coast of Ifriquia.'

The stark lines of the map brought to mind the geometrical patterns in the central courtyard of the library. It was an interesting way of seeing the world.

'Each year,' explained Musa, 'half a dozen of our shipmasters set out as a trading squadron. They sail south along that coast, stopping off at various beaches. They drop anchor and wait for the locals to come out to them to barter, buy and sell. There are no real ports.'

'Have any of the captains ever gone further than the land of Zanj?' I enquired.

'The shipmasters are fearful of being left stranded. It's a question of the winds. For four months a year the wind blows from the north, then there's a brief lull, and afterwards the wind blows from the south. If a ship goes too far, it may not be able to get back in the same season.'

The big man returned the wheel-shaped map to its hook on the wall, and came back to his desk. I concealed my disappointment. The map was so worthless for practical purposes and I remembered how useful Abram's itinerarium had been.

'Have the captains made any charts from their voyages to Zanj?' I asked.

'I'm afraid not. They rely on star books.' The big man gave a breathy chuckle. 'As I said when you told me about your dreams of the future, our preference is to look to the skies for guidance.'

*

Al-Ubullah, a roadstead and port adjacent to Basra, was where the trading ships were fitting out for the annual voyage to the land of Zanj. Jaffar's staff arranged for Osric, Walo and me to stay there in a merchant's house while we waited for the ship-masters to complete their preparations. It was a fine, substantial building made of whitewashed coral blocks, part storehouse, part residence, with large double doors that led from the street into a central courtyard where the owner stacked his trade goods. Al-Ubullah was not as bakingly hot as Baghdad, but the sea air was more humid and stifling, and we sweltered as the days dragged by. Sulaiman, the shipmaster whom Nadim Jaffar assigned to take us to Zanj, was a gnome-like figure, all skin and bone and with a rim of straggly white beard around his jaw. I put his age at approaching sixty but he had the bright eyes of a four-year-old and the sprightly energy to match. He invited Osric and me to inspect his vessel lying at anchor just off al-Ubullah's waterfront. The place echoed to the sounds of vessels being prepared for long-distance voyages: the work chants of dock gangs handling heavy cargo, the thump of mal-lets as rope workers spliced cables, the rasp of saws, and the long-drawn-out creak and squeal of wood on wood as spars were hoisted, checked and then lowered again, rubbing against their masts. There were smells of new-cut timber, foreshore rubbish, charcoal cooking fires and the fish oil smeared on hulls.

Sulaiman led us down into the dark gloom of the hold of his ship, clambering across a newly loaded cargo of sacks of dates.

'Not a single stitch broken after more than fifty years,' he said, pointing to the inside of the hull.

When my eyes adjusted to the dark, I saw that the planks were held together with thick cords, and similarly fastened to the ribs of the vessel. There were no nails.

I thought back to how Protis's ship had sprung a leak and foundered, and wondered what would happen if the cords burst. Sulaiman's vessel would disintegrate, the planks dropping away like the petals of a dying flower in autumn.

The shipmaster prodded a rope fastening. It was black with age. 'Soaked in coconut oil every season. It will see me out my lifetime,' he assured us. Tucking up his loincloth he scurried up the ladder and back on deck so nimbly that Osric and I lagged far behind him.

'When do we set sail?' I called after him, as we emerged into the bright sunlight. 'My companions and I are ready to leave whenever is convenient for you.'

'We leave on the *mawsim* for Zanj,' he said firmly, folding his legs under him as he sat down cross-legged on a tattered scrap of carpet on the stern deck. He gestured at us to join him.

'The *mawsim*?'

'The correct day of departure. I've sailed to Zanj more than a dozen times on the appointed day, and come back safely,' he answered.

'And when is this *mawsim*?'

'The end of the first week of October.'

'Can we not leave earlier?' I was eager to get the expedition over with as quickly as possible.

'We sail in company with others.' He gestured to the anchorage where three or four merchant ships, similar to our own, lay with their crews hard at work on mending sails and rigging.

'And how long before we reach Zanj?'

'A month or two, depending on the wind and the speed of our business. Nadim Jaffar agreed that I can stop at the usual places along the coast and trade.'

He gave me a sideways, conspiratorial look. 'If your interpreter could help out, it will reduce the time spent on these stopovers.'

I mumbled something about being prepared to assist in any way I could.

The shipmaster wanted a more definite undertaking from me. 'The further we travel along the coast, the more difficult it is to deal with the locals. We bargain in a mix of Arabic and the regional languages. Misunderstandings arise. They take time to untangle.'

'My interpreter will help out as best he can,' I promised.

Sulaiman burst out in a cackle of sheer delight. 'Not he . . . she!'

I blinked in surprise.

The shipmaster rocked back on his haunches, still chuckling, 'So you haven't heard the rumour. Your interpreter is to be a woman, and what a woman!' He rolled his eyes.

'I look forward to meeting her,' I said frostily. This was the first time I had heard that Jaffar was making such an unusual arrangement, and I felt put out.

Suddenly the old man became serious. 'I do not mean to sound ungrateful or frivolous. Nadim Jaffar has been most thoughtful in providing such an interpreter. Very few are fluent in the languages spoken along the coast –' he paused, 'and she cost him a very great deal of money.'

I decided it was time to turn the subject back to the practical arrangements for our voyage. 'How far beyond Zanj are you prepared to take us?'

'I have given my word to Nadim Jaffar that I will not turn back until my ship is as far south of Zanj as Basra is from Baghdad,' he said.

'And how will you know that?' I asked. 'I had understood that these are uncharted waters.'

The shipmaster reached into the pocket of his grubby gown and pulled a small, thin rectangle of wood, about an inch by two, with a cord through its centre. 'When this tells me so.'

He put the end of the cord between his lips, held out the tablet at arm's length to stretch the cord, and closed one eye. He held the position for a moment, then spat out the cord and grinned at me, showing worn brown teeth. 'Beyond Zanj I will have to find a different star, of course, probably Farqadan.'

I must have looked utterly mystified for he wound the cord around the little tablet and slipped it back into his pocket, then said, 'It will be easier to explain once we are at sea and under the great bowl of the heavens.'

*

On the morning before Sulaiman and his fellow captains were due to weigh anchor, Osric and I planned to walk to the harbour and make sure that there was to be no last-minute delay. But as we left our house, we came face to face with one of Jaffar's servants. I recognized the senior steward I had last seen in the lamplight of Jaffar's luxurious garden.

'Nadim Jaffar sends his sincere apologies for keeping you waiting,' said the steward after we had exchanged greetings. 'He asked me to say that he is entrusting to you the most precious of all his flowering plants.'

My glance travelled over the steward's shoulder to the small, veiled figure standing a few paces behind him. It took me a moment to grasp Jaffar's pun. Zaynab was the name of a fragrant flowering plant. It was also a popular name given to girls.

'Please come inside,' I said, stepping back into the house. The two visitors followed Osric and me into the courtyard. Only after I had shut the door to the street, did the steward gesture at his companion to draw aside her veil. Sulaiman had already hinted that our woman interpreter was special, but I was completely unprepared for Zaynab's good looks. She had dark lively eyes, a delicate mouth and a neat pointed chin. Her hair was still hidden beneath a shawl so I could only see her face, but it was her complexion that caught my attention. Her skin was the colour of the cinnamon that the Nomenculator had shown us all those months ago in Rome, and flawless.

I struggled to find something to say. Beside me Osric was equally speechless.

'Nadim Jaffar sent me to be of assistance to you on your journey,' she said, breaking the silence. Her voice was huskily melodious, and the way she phrased her remark confirmed that she was a slave.

I forced myself to stop staring. 'I understand that you speak the languages of Zanj.'

'Only some of them,' she murmured. She stood with her small, neat hands clasped in front of her, utterly composed.

'Our captain, Sulaiman, hopes you will also assist him in his trade negotiations.'

'If that is what you wish.'

Jaffar's steward caught my eye. 'If I may have a word in private.'

'Of course.' I walked with him across the courtyard to the side room our host used as a counting house. Behind me I heard Osric strike up a polite conversation with our new interpreter.

'Nadim Jaffar offers you Zaynab in obedience to the caliph's direct command,' the steward said to me once we were alone.

He hesitated for a moment as if unsure whether he was exceeding his instructions. 'One of the Zanj chieftains sent Zaynab as a gift to the Commander of the Faithful.'

His statement brought to mind the wretched slaves I had seen in Kaupang. It required a great leap of the imagination to equate them with the beautiful woman in the courtyard.

'My master was willing to pay almost any price to include Zaynab in his household. The caliph agreed to sell Zaynab for thirty thousand dirhem.'

I sensed that I was missing something. The steward's gaze searched my face, waiting for me to understand what he was hinting at.

Then it struck me: this was the crown prince's doing. Mohammed had suggested to his father that Jaffar despatch Zaynab to join the expedition. Jaffar was not only tutor but also the leading figure of his rival Abdallah's circle. By forcing Jaffar to send away a favourite slave worth a small fortune, the crown prince was twisting the knife.

'I shall make sure that Zaynab returns unharmed to Nadim Jaffar,' I promised with a confidence I did not feel. My recent experiences had shown how easily the lives of travellers were put in danger. During the days in al-Ubullah I had thought long and hard about the succession of delays and mishaps we had experienced on the way from Aachen to Baghdad. I had now come to the conclusion that some, if not all, of these events had been deliberate attempts to wreck the mission, and I had a suspicion of who had been responsible, though the underlying motive was still unclear.

Chapter Seventeen

AFRICA

*

SAILING TO ZANJ had a marvellous, dream-like quality. Each day seemed to repeat as if time was turning back on itself. Dawn brought a horizon, sharp and clear and infinitely distant, from which the sun rose into a sky where a scattering of puffy white clouds were all moving in the same direction as our ships. Far below, our little company of half a dozen trade vessels ran across a sparkling sea of the deepest blue. A favourable wind, fine and steady from the north-east, filled the huge cotton sails and our crew scarcely needed to touch the ropes. The breeze tempered the heat of the noonday sun so the deck was never too hot to the touch, and the air retained its pleasant warmth long after dusk. Sunsets were dramatic. A tremendous golden-orange glow suffused the entire sky, changing to the colour of pale parchment that diminished and retreated as darkness spread in from the east. Then the moon rose and laid a silver-white path across the black undulating surface of the sea. Wherever one looked upward, the heavens were alive with a multitude of bright stars.

In such idyllic conditions I fell in love with Zaynab.

On the third morning of the voyage, not long after sunrise, I was standing near the mainmast with Walo and waiting for the cook to hand us our breakfast of dates, bread and water. There was a sudden light slap as something struck the sail and fell close to where Zaynab was seated on the foredeck where the anchors were stowed. There was flapping and wriggling on the planks. Walo ran forward and I watched as he picked up what seemed to be some sort of small fish. He turned to Zaynab and must have asked her a question for she pulled back the shawl that covered her head and leaned forward to look at what he was holding. As Zaynab would be unable to understand Walo's Frankish, I walked across to interpret.

'Is it a fish or a bird?' Walo was asking her. I looked down at what he had in his grasp. The creature had a fish's body, six or seven inches long. There was a fish tail and a fish head, with round startled eyes.

Walo gently took the fin on the side of the fish between his finger and thumb, and pulled. Out swung a wing.

'Our name for it is "fish that flies",' said Zaynab.

Walo pulled open the second wing. The web between the bones was so fine and delicate that the light shone through it.

'Is it in the book?' he asked, turning to me.

'I can check,' I said uncertainly, my voice sounding odd in my ears. Zaynab's shawl had slipped down around her shoulders. Her dark hair was long and lustrous, piled above her head and fixed with an ivory comb. She wore tiny diamond studs in her small, shell-like ears, and the curve of her slender neck was so soft and perfect that it made me want to reach out and stroke it.

'What book is that?' she asked me, looking up. Her eyes held mine for a moment, and I felt a tingling shock. Never before had I met with an expression of such gentle kindness framed with beauty, yet tinged with melancholy.

'A Book of Beasts. It's a list of animals ... with their pictures,' I blurted. Suddenly I wanted to keep the full attention of this remarkable young woman with the cinnamon-coloured skin. 'I'll show you.'

Light-headed, I hurried aft to collect the bestiary and brought it to her. With Walo looking on, I opened the cover and leafed through the pages. I made a deliberate effort to keep both my hand and voice steady.

'Here's a fish with wings!' I announced, then read out, '"*The serra or saw fish. Also known as the flying fish. Named from the saw-tooth crest on its back. It swims under a ship and cuts the ship in half . . .*' My voice faltered. The insignificant little fish in Walo's hand was never likely to damage a ship's hull. I felt foolish.

Zaynab ignored my confusion. 'Is there a picture?' she asked.

I turned the book around and showed her. The artist had drawn a dragon-like animal emerging from the depths of the sea. It was very large, almost the same size as the ship it was menacing. The sailors aboard the vessel looked terrified.

'It does have two wings,' said Zaynab gently.

I was grateful that she had not laughed aloud. Her tactfulness only added to her attraction.

'Maybe the writer was muddled,' Zaynab murmured. 'In Zanj I remember being shown a big fish that had a long flat nose with a row of sharp teeth on each side, just like a saw. Maybe that is the fish that cuts up ships.'

I found myself gazing at her hands holding the book. Zaynab's fingers were slim and graceful, and she had drawn patterns on them in dark blue ink, whorls and curlicues that merged and flowed onto the palms of her hands and to her wrists. By comparison the artwork in the bestiary seemed clumsy and inept.

She noticed my rapt attention and gave me a demure smile, eyes cast down, as she handed the book back to me and tucked her hands out of sight beneath her shawl.

From behind me came a shout from the cook. He was summoning Walo and myself to collect our food. Hurriedly, I cast about for an excuse to speak with her again. I said, 'There are other animals in the book about which I know little, and which you may have encountered in Zanj. Perhaps I can consult with you again.'

'I would like that,' Zaynab replied. 'Maybe you can also tell me about the countries and peoples you have seen.'

*

That night Zaynab surprised all the crew in a way that none of us could forget.

At twilight it was Sulaiman's custom to find himself a spot on deck where he had a good view of the vault of heavens, as he called the sky. There he took measurements of the stars as they emerged.

'Try it for yourself,' he said to me, handing me the little wooden tablet on its cord that he had shown me in al-Ubullah. 'Place the end of the cord between your lips, stretch out the cord, and hold the lower edge of tablet on the horizon. Select a star, and see how high the star measures against the tablet's side.'

'What's the reason for the string?' I asked.

'So that the tablet is always the same distance from your eye. That makes the readings consistent,' he answered.

'Which star should I choose?'

'On the voyage to Zanj the best is Al-Jah. You Franks call it the North Star.' He gestured over the stern of his ship. 'Al-

Jah is fixed in the heavens. The further south we sail, the lower in the sky it is seen.'

'Even a child could use it,' I said after I experimented with the device.

'Now, yes. But when we reach the land of Zanj we will no longer see Al-Jah. It will have sunk below the horizon. Then I must use knowledge of other stars, where they are in heaven's vault at each season, to find my position.'

I gave him back the little wooden tablet and, choosing my moment, asked, 'How did you know that Zaynab was to be our interpreter?'

'I was the captain who brought her from Zanj when she was first sent to Caliph Haroun. I have followed her career ever since.'

'There must be other slaves in the royal household, just as beautiful.'

'None who can also sing with such sweetness.' His voice softened. 'I heard her sing just once on that first voyage, such a sad song. I'm told that is why Jaffar bought her from the caliph, for her singing.'

'Do you think she would sing for us?' I asked.

'Perhaps.'

Zaynab was the faintest of shadows where she sat away from the rest of us, on the small foredeck where the anchors were stowed. On an impulse I made my way over to her and asked if she would sing. When she made no answer I went to where the crew were clustered near the cook's charcoal box, talking among themselves. I asked them to be silent. For a long interval there was nothing but the creak of the rigging and the sound of the waves washing along the sides of the vessel as our ship shouldered south. Then Zaynab began to sing. She sang a dozen

songs, some plaintive, others filled with longing, one that spoke
of quiet joy, and we listened to her, enchanted. My spine
tingled when I recognized her voice. It was Zaynab who had
been singing among the trees when Osric and I had visited
Jaffar in his exotic garden.

When finally her voice faded away, no one spoke. We were
left with our own thoughts. The sky seemed infinitely far away,
a velvety blackness scattered with myriad bright points of
stars. Our vessel was suspended below it in a great dark void and
no longer part of the real world. Into that brief lull burst an
unnerving, eerie sound – a sudden heavy puffing and grunting
and splashing. It came from all directions and from the darkness
around the ship.

Walo cried out, 'Sea pigs! They came to listen!'

I recalled the picture in the bestiary where a shoal of fish
clustered around a ship on which a man was playing a lute. The
sound of music, according to the text, attracted the creatures of
the sea.

'They're not pigs,' muttered Sulaiman who was standing
beside me.

He sounded so disapproving that I felt I should defend
Walo though he could not have understood what the captain
had said. 'Walo has seen a picture of fish with snouts like pigs.
They root in the sand on the sea floor,' I told the shipmaster.

Sulaiman was scathing. 'Whoever made such a picture
knows nothing. Those animals are the children of al-hoot, the
largest creature that lives in the sea.'

I guessed he meant a whale. Turning to Walo, I translated
what the captain had said.

Walo was stubborn. 'They came to listen to Zaynab sing,'
he insisted.

I thought it wiser not to pass on his comment to Sulaiman.

Instead I asked the captain, 'If you don't believe in sea pigs, do you think we are wasting our time seeking the rukh?'

The shipmaster thought for a long time before replying. 'I don't know what to think. Ever since I first went to sea I've heard sailors speak about the rukh. They repeat stories about the rukh just as they have tales of how al-hoot grows so big it is mistaken for an island, with earth on his back and plants growing there.'

'But you don't believe such yarns.'

Sulaiman laid a hand on my arm as if imparting a confidence. 'When I come across a new island that I have never seen before, and it's small and low, with a few bushes growing, I approach very cautiously.'

'Then you are not so different from me or Walo,' I told him. 'Walo firmly expects to encounter the creatures whose pictures he has seen. I search for them because I believe there is a possibility that they exist. You hesitate to dismiss them as nothing but fantasy.'

The shipmaster chuckled. 'The only reality is my promise to Nadim Jaffar that, in searching for the rukh, I will take my ship further than any navigator before me.'

*

As Sulaiman predicted, Al-Jah had sunk to the night horizon by the time we arrived on our trading ground, the coast of Zanj. During the twenty days to get there I had done my very best to hide my growing yearning for Zaynab, and I believed that I had succeeded. It required painful self-discipline because I was longing to get to know her better, to tell her how I felt, and explore any feelings she might have for me. Not a day passed but that I ached to be alone in her company. Yet this was impossible and dangerous, and I knew it would place her in a difficult position. She was the only woman aboard the ship and she had to keep her distance, treat everyone equally and receive the same respect in return. So I forced myself to keep all my conversations with Zaynab to a minimum, and always in the company of Walo as together we looked through the pages of the bestiary. I took great care to appear casual and unconcerned whenever Zaynab appeared on deck, and I never spoke a word to anyone about the effect she was having on me. Not even Osric could have guessed how difficult it was for me to conceal my emotions whenever I laid eyes on her, or the fact that my thoughts lingered on the way she walked or sat and, above all, on her smile, so unhurried and enchanting.

The coast of Zanj brought me out of what was in danger of becoming a lover's trance. The land was lush and exotic. It extended from a fringe of white surf across the sandy beach, then into dense groves of palm trees that merged to make a broad expanse of vivid jungle green. Many miles away loomed highlands where towering thunderclouds built up every afternoon, dramatic and threatening, only to dissolve and drift away. The people of the coast were striking in appearance. Tall and well-built, with wide shoulders and big chests, they had fleshy swelling lips and shaved their tightly curled hair at the front, leaving it to hang down at the back in long strands soaked in butter. Their only garment was a tanned hide or a length of cloth tied around the waist, and their skin was a rich black with just a hint of brown. Their bare-breasted women dressed in similar fashion, carrying their babies across their backs in a cloth sling. They wore broad ruffs of copper wire, and strings of scarlet beans as anklets, necklaces and bracelets. They lived comfortably, growing vegetables in small gardens close to their thatched houses, raising goats and a few cattle, and, of course, they fished. As soon as we dropped anchor, they came out in small boats to trade or coax us ashore. They wanted our enamel goods, filigree and fancy metalwork, weapons, mirrors, spices, silk and embroidered cloth, as well as the more humdrum sacks of dates. In exchange they offered items they had been gathering for months from the inland tribes: packets of gold dust, coloured pebbles and nuggets of veined rock to be cut and polished into gems, the spotted skins of pards that were greatly prized in Baghdad, and – above all – quantities of elephant teeth.

Here we parted company with the other vessels from al-Ubullah. They lingered at the anchorages to trade at leisure, while Sulaiman kept his promise to Jaffar and barely broke our journey. We took on water and fresh food, traded for half a day at an occasional stopover, and then – sailing alone – pressed ever southward. We sailed past chains of islands, fringing reefs, isolated outlying rocks tufted with bushes, and shallow estuaries where the shore was lined with dense masses of a tree that grew on spidery roots, half in and half out of the water, and which Sulaiman called *gurm*. Within another week we had reached the limit of the lands that Sulaiman already knew and, quite by chance, our captain's purposefulness was rewarded.

To enquire about the rukh and griffin, we had made a cautious landing on a small strip of beach where a cluster of several dozen huts was half hidden among the ever-present palm trees. Two of Sulaiman's sailors paddled us ashore in the ship's boat. It was mid-morning on another hot, humid and sunny day, and there were just the three of us in the landing party – myself and Sulaiman with Zaynab as our interpreter. It was a struggle for me to keep my eyes looking ahead when I was so close to Zaynab, but I managed to keep my gaze on the beach, where a couple of small dug-out boats were drawn up at the water's edge and a number of nets hung on stakes. The people themselves were timid, watching our arrival from a distance and standing well back as we set foot in the shallows. Zaynab called out a greeting and, hesitantly, four of them came forward. All men, they were barefoot and wore only loincloths. Slits in their ear lobes held small silver plates or ivory plugs. Zaynab explained that we came in peace and were in search of a great flying bird, large enough to carry away an elephant. She had to repeat herself several times before she was understood, and I tried to help by sketching a rough outline of a griffin in the sand, though without much success. The lion's body could have been any four-footed beast with a tail, and the bird's head was more like a chicken than an eagle.

The villagers examined my feeble attempt of a drawing, muttered among themselves, and then all of them shook their heads.

'Ask if they've seen any trace of such an animal or even heard of it,' I suggested to Zaynab.

She relayed my questions and again there was some sort of a conference, more animated this time. Then one of the men hurried back to the village. He disappeared inside the stockade and re-emerged holding something in his hand. When he came close enough for me to see what it was, my hopes soared. It was half of a very large hooked beak. Jet black, it had a sharp, cruel point.

I took it from the man, and turned it over to inspect more closely. Fully five inches long, it was much the largest beak I had ever seen, and as tough and hard as black glass. I could easily picture the sharp tip driving into flesh, twisting and ripping, hacking into bone.

'Could this be a rukh's beak?' I asked Sulaiman, my excitement rising.

He did not answer me. He was staring at the object. 'Ask where they got it?' he said to Zaynab in a taut voice.

After a brief conversation, she replied, 'One of the fishermen picked it up on the shore about a week ago. It was in an odd-shaped ball of something he thought was a piece of rotten fish. But now he's not sure. Whatever it was, it had a bad smell and must have floated ashore when the wind was from the sea.'

I sensed that Sulaiman was hiding his eagerness, when he asked, 'That lump of rotten fish – does he still have it?'

Zaynab was told that it had been thrown away because it stank. It was probably still on the village rubbish heap.

'Can they find it for me?' asked Sulaiman.

One of the men turned and shouted out to the onlookers. A lad broke away from the group and raced away, running behind the huts and out of sight.

We waited patiently until the boy returned, gingerly carrying in both hands a lump of something partly wrapped in leaves. It was the size of a man's head and, judging by the lad's wrinkled nose, it still had its unpleasant smell.

Sulaiman was not put off. He took the object and peeled back the leaves. To my eye it resembled a misshapen lump of greyish-black wax, soft and streaky. I caught a waft of its foul odour. It smelled like cow dung.

Sulaiman was not put off. He poked the unpleasant mass with his finger, then turned it over gently so that he could inspect it on all sides.

'Tell our friends here that this is fish dung,' he said to Zaynab. 'I am willing to buy both the beak and the dung that surrounded it.'

The four men withdrew a short distance and stood talking. Finally the oldest of them came back to us, and through Zaynab told us that if we had fish hooks to sell, they would part with the beak for five hundred fish hooks and ten knife blades. Sulaiman could have the lump of fish dung for its weight in copper wire.

I was still holding the strange beak, and Sulaiman made me give it back to the villagers. 'I'll pay four hundred fish hooks for the beak and the dung, no more,' he said, wrapping the leaves around the foul-smelling mass and placing it on the sand.

It took at least an hour to conclude the haggling, and Sulaiman settled for 450 fish hooks for the beak and a length of embroidered cloth for the lump of fish dung.

'You paid a generous price for the beak,' I observed to Sulaiman as his men paddled us back out to his ship, the trade completed. 'Does that mean you're prepared to believe in the existence of the rukh?'

He nudged his foot against the rancid lump, again wrapped in leaves, in the bottom of the little boat. 'This is what I paid for.'

'What is it?'

'Phlegm!'

I thought I had misheard.

He cackled with glee. 'Al-hoot coughs it up, though others claim it emerges from the creature's backside.'

'When it's fresh and soft like that, it smells bad,' the shipmaster explained, 'but leave it in the sun for a week and it hardens and changes to a dark yellow, and the smell improves. Apothecaries in Basra pay a fortune for it to use as medicine and,' here he smiled, 'I will carry it in person to Baghdad and present it to Nadim Jaffar. He's one of the richest men in the caliphate and will reward me handsomely, then keep part for himself and sell on the remainder to his friends.'

He prodded the evil-smelling mass with his foot again. 'That's the largest piece of it I've ever seen. A double handful will pay the entire cost of this expedition and will still leave an excellent profit.'

I failed to see what use the fastidious nobleman would find for a stinking ball of fish phlegm. 'What does Jaffar need it for?' I asked.

'His perfume makers will melt it down, tiny morsel by tiny morsel, then add it to fragrant oils – rose, jasmine, all the flowers you can imagine. Just a few drops and their scents will be enhanced and last for many days.'

I thought back to my visit to Jaffar's garden, to Haroun's palace, and to a dozen other reception rooms in the Round City. Everywhere the air had been heavily perfumed. It was little wonder that the whale phlegm was so much in demand.

Sulaiman clutched the precious package to his chest as we clambered up the side of the ship, leaving me to show the strange beak to Osric and explain where it came from.

'If that's a rukh's beak, how did it finish up floating ashore encased in whale phlegm?' was his cautious reaction.

Walo, by contrast, was thrilled. He inspected the vicious pointed tip of the beak and assured me that it came from a large, flesh-eating creature that hunted other animals for meat. For him, there was now no doubt that we were closing in on a griffin or rukh.

*

The character of the coast changed as we sailed south. The vivid green of the woodland and jungle gave way to drier, more open countryside covered with sun-scorched grasslands, scrub and thorny trees. A brown, dusty haze frequently obscured what lay further inland. We noted that the people in these parts preferred to live in large settlements located on the bald hillcrests and they surrounded their villages with tall stockades. It gave an impression of a mistrustful, more dangerous place. Each night Sulaiman anchored as far offshore as possible for fear of being attacked. It was, of course, too risky to sail along an unknown coast in the hours of darkness. Our captain also showed the first signs of unease about the weather, frequently looking up at the sky or gazing out to the horizon. I asked what was troubling him and he told me that we were now close to the limit of the area where we could rely on favourable sailing conditions. To justify his fears, the winds were fitful, sometimes dying away entirely, and – more worryingly – once or twice they turned to the south, in the direction we were headed. Sulaiman warned that unless we came across the rukh very soon, we would have to turn back.

Our next landing was again to replenish our store of drinking water. All morning our helmsman steered as close as possible to the coast while the youngest and nimblest member of our crew perched on the great spar of the mainsail, high above the deck. Soon after midday, he called down that he could see a stream trickling down the face of a low cliff, leaving a stripe of green against the rock. The nearby beach appeared to be deserted. Sulaiman ordered the sails lowered, and we dropped anchor. Our sailors paddled cautiously ashore in the ship's boat. We watched as they scouted the beach and then one of them returned to say that it was safe for the watering to begin. Osric, Walo and I helped to lower the empty earthenware jars into the boat and then went ashore ourselves.

With more than forty jars to fill and transport back to the ship, the men would be busy for a while. There was still no sign of the local inhabitants, so I suggested to Osric and Walo that we explore a little distance inland. A narrow gulley offered a way up from the beach and we made a short climb that brought us out on an expanse of open, rough country covered with tall, coarse grasses, parched and yellow. Rocky outcrops rose like small islands in the sea of grass, and here and there were stands of flat-topped trees, their branches offering patches of shade in an otherwise empty landscape.

Walo was the first to see it. He was looking towards a grove of leafy trees when a movement caught his attention. He gulped with excitement and pointed, his whole arm shaking. I looked in that direction and could only see something small and dark, flicking back and forth beside a tree trunk. I mistook it for a bird. My gaze travelled upward and I caught my breath. High in the branches something else moved, a head. I stared transfixed, unable to credit what I was witnessing. Beside me, Walo and Osric kept stock-still, not daring to move and equally astonished. A bizarre-looking animal now moved from behind the tree and into full view. It stood on four very long slender legs that were totally ill matched. The front pair were so much taller than the back ones that the creature's body sloped downwards, ending in a cow-like tail with a tuft constantly flicking back and forth to ward off the flies. But it was the neck that made the creature so outlandish. Unnaturally thin and long, the neck alone was the height of two men and ended in a deer's head almost twenty feet above the ground.

'A cameleopard,' I breathed in wonder. It was everything that the Book of Beasts had promised, and more.

Swishing its cow-like tail, the cameleopard moved around the tree, grazing on its leaves.

'Why does it not have the pard's spots?' asked Walo. The bestiary had stated that the cameleopard got its name because it had the body of a camel and the spotted skin of the leopard. Yet the pelt of this extraordinary creature in front of us had a bold network of white lines on a yellowy-orange background. The colouring had blended with the dappled shadows under the tree. It was little wonder that we had failed to see the cameleopard sooner.

Walo was beside himself with elation. He tugged my arm as he crouched down. 'Come!' he begged. 'Let's get closer!'

Bending double we crept through the tall grass towards the feeding animal. Soon we were close enough to see the animal's long tongue licking out to twist off the leaves as it fed in the high branches. The creature swivelled its head towards us and the ears flicked out, listening. In place of large horns there were two short stumps on its head. 'It's a deer, not a camel,' announced Walo.

The cameleopard caught sight of us and took fright. Suddenly it wheeled about and fled, kicking out the long, ungainly legs and running with a rocking motion. Its panicked flight startled other cameleopards that we had not seen. They had been hidden in a fold in the ground, and now they appeared as if by magic. First their heads and then their long necks rising from the grass as they ran up the slope. All of a sudden we were watching an entire herd of them galloping away over the grassland.

The spectacle brought to mind the Nomenculator's story in Rome, of the timid animals that had been set loose in the Colosseum and hunted down by lions. Surely they had been cameleopards.

Walo was capering with delight. 'We must catch one and bring it home with us!' he cried. 'We can dig a pit like the one in the forest and put down leaves for bait!'

He was thinking back to the day he had seen the aurochs taken in the pitfall. Despite the day's heat I shuddered. I recalled seeing the aurochs gore his father to death.

For Walo the thrill of seeing a cameleopard wiped away the horror of that memory. He was beaming with anticipation. 'Catching a cameleopard will be easy!' he insisted.

'We should go back to the ship and speak with Sulaiman,' I

said, 'and ask him if it will be possible to transport a cameleo-pard aboard.'

We turned around and began to make our way back along the path in single file. Walo led, giving a little skip every few paces. At one point he turned to me, his face radiant, and said, 'This is the land where the beasts in the book have their homes . . . cameleopards, hyenas and crocodiles. We are sure to find the griffin!'

He carried on a few paces further and came to an abrupt halt. 'Look,' he called back over his shoulder, 'it is just as I said. All the beasts live here. There's an asp.'

He was pointing at an indistinct grey shape lying beside the path, half hidden beneath a fallen tree trunk.

The hair rose on the back of my neck, and I backed away so suddenly that Osric bumped into me from behind. 'Stay away, Walo!' I urged him.

But he ignored me entirely. He stepped off the track and approached the grey shape. It moved, shifting and twisting on itself. It was a serpent, scarcely a yard in length, but gross and fat, the head smaller than the bloated body, its skin a pattern of chevrons, grey on black.

It was coiling back, deeper into the overhang of the fallen tree trunk.

'You see! It retreats in fear just as the book says,' Walo exulted. He felt inside his shirt and pulled out his little deerhorn pipe, the same one with which he had tamed the ice bears. He put it to his lips, and played the same three notes.

The serpent coiled again, retreating even further.

Walo turned to me with a triumphant smile. 'The book was right. It fears the music.'

Despite my terror of the serpent, I half believed him. According to the Book of Beasts the asp dreads music. When an asp hears music it seeks to flee, and if that is impossible, it attempts to block out the sound, pressing one ear to the ground, and bringing the tip of its tail around and thrusting it into the other ear.

Walo blew a few more notes and – sure enough – the snake writhed and formed an extra loop, doubling back on itself, and its tail came near its squat, flat head.

I remembered how Walo had handled the little horned snake in the desert of Egypt and wondered if again he would show his uncanny skill with wild creatures.

He was moving closer, slowly and confidently, and playing the notes again. The serpent writhed as if in distress.

Walo took another step, bent forward and played the notes again. This time the asp reared up its head, and hissed loudly at him.

My blood ran cold.

Walo took another half-pace closer.

The asp was hissing constantly now, and its thick body was bloating and inflating, a grotesque sight. The flat head and upper part of its body began to rise from the ground. The mouth opened wide and pale, showing the throat. All of a sudden I knew that it was not about to thrust its tail into its own ear to try to block out the music. This was the warning of death.

'Walo! No nearer!' I begged him.

Walo ignored me and moved closer still. He was now within an arm's length of the asp, still bending forward and playing the pipe. His shadow fell across the serpent.

The asp struck. It happened almost too fast for the eye to see; a gaping pale mouth, a glimpse of fangs, and the asp had bitten Walo on his leg.

Walo did not flinch. He stayed where he was, still playing the whistle.

The serpent struck again, viciously and twice more, each blow as lightning-fast as the previous one. Only then did Walo stagger. The serpent turned, and its evil gross body slithered away beneath the log.

Walo seemed disappointed rather than distressed. He had been wearing loose sailor's trousers, and there were marks with patches of blood where the fangs had struck. 'I should have played a different tune,' he said meekly.

He was swaying, his face puzzled.

I ran forward as his leg began to crumple beneath him, and caught him as he fell. There was a ripping sound and I turned to see Osric tearing a strip of cloth from the hem of his gown.

'We have to bind the leg tight and get him back to the boat as quickly as we can,' said my friend. As a young man in Hispania Osric had been a student of medicine among the Saracens. In Hispania, too, there were serpents.

Together we helped Walo along the path, his arms around our necks. His injured leg was dragging on the dry earth.

On the beach we found that Sulaiman and his men had nearly completed watering.

'An asp has bitten Walo,' I told the shipmaster, near-panic in my voice, and he shouted to his boat crew to hurry to assist us.

We lifted Walo into the ship's boat and brought him out to the vessel. 'My leg is getting stiff. It hurts very much,' he groaned as we laid him on deck.

Zaynab placed a roll of cloth beneath his head to make him more comfortable but her face was troubled.

While the crew were rigging a length of canvas to shade Walo where he lay, she took me to one side and asked me to describe the serpent. It took only a few words, and when I finished she turned away, tears filling her eyes.

'Is there no cure?' I asked.

She shook her head.

*

Walo's death was painful and ugly. He was unable to move or bend the injured leg. A pale fluid mixed with blood oozed from the puncture holes where the serpent's fangs had pierced. Within hours he was feverish and flushed. From thigh to ankle the leg began to swell, puffing up as if in imitation of the asp that had bitten him. The skin turned a nasty purplish-grey. The next day it burst, splitting like an over-ripe plum. A long weeping wound revealed rotting flesh beneath. That evening Walo lay with his eyes closed, taking shallow breaths, losing the fight for life. Yet he still clung to his belief in the bestiary. 'That was a prester asp,' he told me, his voice so weak that I had to lean closer to him. 'If it had been the hypnalis, I would be asleep, like Cleopatra.'

He licked his lips and swallowed, struggling to speak. 'I remember you read to me that the asp called prester moves with an open mouth, and those it bites swell up and rot follows the bite.'

A spasm of pain racked him and he reached out and clutched my hand. 'The rare beasts are here! Take a young griffin from its nest and bring it home. Feed it meat, just like Madi and Modi.' Those were the last coherent words he spoke.

We dug his grave at the foot of the low cliff close to the spot where we had filled the water jars. The hole was deep enough so that the wild animals would not reach his body, and we put him in the ground within hours of his passing. Sulaiman was urging us to hurry.

As we left the beach, the shipmaster drew my attention to the heavy swell now rolling in from the sea.

'There's a storm somewhere out there,' he told me bluntly. 'If it catches us on this exposed coast, we'll be as dead as your friend back there.'

His words struck me as callous and I had to remind myself that on his voyages Sulaiman must have seen many deaths from accident, drowning and disease.

'We should head back to al-Ubullah,' I said. Until Walo died I had been prepared to give the bestiary the benefit of the doubt and was ready to accept its descriptions of outlandish creatures – after all, so many had come true. I blamed myself for not questioning the claim that music would tame the asp. Had I done so, Walo, whom I had brought on this venture, would still be alive.

'I will gladly set a course for home,' said the shipmaster. 'I've already taken us further beyond Zanj than I had promised to Jaffar, but first,' he nodded towards the south horizon where the sky was beginning to cloud over and show a peculiar colour, pearl grey with a hint of green, 'I think, we must put our trust in the All-Merciful.'

The storm that enveloped us later that evening lasted for a full three days. Had the gale come from the east when it howled in on us, our ship would have been driven ashore and dashed to pieces. Fortunately, the wind and waves came from the opposite direction and forced us out to sea instead. Faced with such a tempest our crew could only lower the spars and sails to the deck, lash them securely, then crouch in shelter, seeking to escape the blast of the wind and rain. To stand and work on deck was impossible. Sulaiman made no attempt to steer a course. He surrendered to the supremacy of the storm and let his vessel drift where the gale pushed her. The ship rolled and pitched wildly, shuddering to the repeated blows of the great waves that marched down on us. We thought only of survival, bailing water from the bilge, trying to keep the hatches covered so that the waves that often washed across the deck did not pour into the hold, and staying afloat. When the wind eventually eased, leaving a lumpy, grey sea, we were wet, hungry and utterly exhausted. The cooking fire had long since gone out, and we were eating handfuls of dates clawed from the last remaining sack of them in the hold. Yet throughout the ordeal Sulaiman had squatted near the helm, needing only short naps to keep himself alert. Whenever I glanced in his direction, he looked to be calm and unworried. I understood why the crew placed their confidence in his judgement and experience, trusting him to keep them safe. I knew that I had failed to do the same for Walo.

On the fourth day, as the height of the waves eased and they began to lose their white crests, Sulaiman climbed up on the lowered mainspar and stood there, one arm around the mast. With more than deliberate care he scanned the entire horizon before dropping back onto the deck, and coming over to speak with Osric and me.

'There's land to the south-east,' he said. 'We'll go there and find an anchorage.'

'Can't we set course for home?' I asked. Walo's death had affected me deeply. More than ever, I wanted to be finished with the voyage. My curiosity was at an end. No longer did I care if there was such a creature as a rukh or a griffin, and on the slim chance that it did exist, I did not have the stomach to go on with the quest when the lives of those precious to me were placed at risk: Osric and – of course – Zaynab. I would return to Baghdad and tell the caliph that Sulaiman had brought us further than any of us had imagined possible, and we had found nothing.

The old man shook his head. 'We must check the ship for storm damage. Then we head for al-Ubullah.'

'Where do you think we are?' I enquired.

'Tonight, if the sky clears so I can read the stars, I'll have a better idea. My guess is that we're off Komr or possibly WaqWaq.'

As far as I could recall, neither place had been mentioned when Musa had shown us the map in the royal library.

Sulaiman rubbed at the thin stubble of his beard. 'Captains from al-Ubullah picked up reports of those places while trading on the coast of Zanj. I've not heard of anyone landing there.'

He frowned at the distant dark line on the horizon. 'We need to find a gently shelving beach of clean, hard sand on which to beach the hull and check the stitching.'

I had forgotten that our vessel was held together with cords of coconut rope. 'What about the inhabitants? Will they be friendly?'

The old man shrugged. 'Maybe we'll find the place uninhabited.'

*

The unknown land, whatever its name, showed a flat coastal strip fringed with grey-green *gurm* trees. To seaward their tangle of roots presented an impenetrable wall, each root thrust deep into the sucking ooze, and it was midday when Sulaiman eventually found a small crescent of sandy beach protected by a tongue of land. By then the gale was no more than an evil memory, and we made the final approach on a gentle breeze, gliding across water so clear that Sulaiman could judge his moment and run the keel of his ship gently into the sand. It was a moment of utter relief.

'We wait here for two full tides,' said Sulaiman, 'to check and clean the hull, and we can stay longer if we decide on any repairs.' He looked across at me. 'That will give you and Osric enough time to explore inland if you wish.'

I declined without hesitation. 'Osric and I will remain with the ship. I want no more accidents.'

If Sulaiman had not sent two of his sailors to gather firewood I would have kept my word. But we needed to light a fire to cook and most of our firewood had been washed into the sea during the gale. What we still had on board was soaking wet. So the two men were despatched even before the tide had ebbed and we were waiting for the water to recede and the ship to settle on the sand.

They returned after a short while, bringing back an object that they had stumbled upon in the undergrowth.

They gave it to Sulaiman, who walked across to where I was standing with Osric.

'I think you should see this,' he said to us. It looked like a fragment from a broken bowl, no larger than the palm of my hand. Dirty cream in colour, the dished side was smooth and the outer surface was slightly rough.

I took it from Sulaiman and was surprised how light it was, much thinner than the heavy earthenware pots we had seen in Ifriquia.

'Whoever made this does fine workmanship. The people living here must be very skilled craftsmen,' I told him.

'My men found at least a dozen similar fragments, all lying close together,' said Sulaiman. 'They believe that they were not made by any human hands, and this frightens them.'

I looked again at the delicate pot fragment. 'I think we should go and judge for ourselves,' I said.

Guided by one of the sailors we walked up the beach and over a low ridge to find ourselves on ground overgrown with rough grass and straggly underbrush. The sailor stopped at the edge of a circular patch some four or five feet across. Here the grass had once been pressed down flat though now it was beginning to grow again.

Scattered on the ground were several more fragments of the bowls. Most were the same size as the sample I had been shown. Others were larger, seven or eight inches across.

'What do they remind you of?' asked Sulaiman softly.

It was Osric who answered. 'That looks to me like some sort of nest. Those fragments are bits of bird shell.'

I felt a fool for not seeing the truth sooner.

I stooped down, gathered up several larger fragments, and tried to fit them together into a single piece. The egg that they would have formed was enormous, more than a foot in length.

I looked up at Sulaiman. 'What do your sailors think?' I asked.

'They believe they are the eggs of a rukh,' he said. 'A small one, but nevertheless a rukh. That's why they're scared. They are frightened that the creature might suddenly swoop down on us and pluck us away.'

Oddly enough, I felt cheated. In my mind I had already abandoned the quest for griffin or rukh. To find signs of its possible existence was unsettling.

'Other creatures lay eggs,' I objected. 'Crawling creatures like the crocodiles we saw on the banks of the Nile . . . and serpents.' After seeing a snake kill Walo, the sight of the huge eggs had sent a shiver down my spine. 'If these are serpent eggs then the animal is huge and very dangerous. We should leave this place undisturbed.'

Osric disagreed. 'These are bird's eggs, Sigwulf. Serpents, crocodiles, turtles . . . their eggs don't have hard shells. If Walo was here, he would tell you the same.'

Mention of Walo jolted me. I knew what Walo would have done. He would have known immediately that they were eggshell fragments from a gigantic bird, just as he had known that the mysterious black beak found in the whale's phlegm came from a meat-eating creature. If he had been with us, he would have been thirsting to find the creature and learn more. The thought made me ashamed of my own timidity. If already I were responsible for bringing Walo to his death in Africa, soon I would find it even more difficult to live with the knowledge that I had chosen to throw aside the chance to carry out his last wish.

Standing there holding the pieces of a huge egg, I made my choice: I would locate a nest still in use by a griffin or rukh, take a couple of fledglings from it, and bring them to Baghdad and Aachen for all to wonder at. No one else need be involved.

'Why don't you and your men carry on attending to the ship,' I suggested to Sulaiman, 'I will see if I can find a rukh's nest that has got complete eggs in it, or even chicks, and be back by dark. Then we can decide what we should do next.'

'I'll come with you,' Osric insisted. 'Two people will cover more ground than one.'

The shipmaster did not argue. 'If you're not back by morning, my men will assume you have fallen victim to the rukh, and insist on leaving this place. I will not be able to prevent them.'

Without another word Sulaiman and his sailor headed back

to the beach, leaving Osric and myself standing by the abandoned nest.

I gazed inland where the heat haze obscured whatever lay beyond forest-clad hills. I was thinking back to my search for the white gyrfalcons.

'The griffin and the rukh are said to be like giant eagles. They build their nests among the mountain crags. Yet this creature lays its eggs on flat ground. That doesn't seem right.'

'Whether the creature flies or crawls or walks on legs, we would be wise to go cautiously,' said Osric. 'Let's start by looking around for tracks.'

Together we began to search the area. It was mostly scrubland with a few clumps of stunted trees among the tangle of thickets and rough grasses. We had been searching for perhaps an hour, circling the nest and checking the ground, when we found a second nest. This time it was in use. A clutch of half a dozen huge eggs lay on the ground. The undergrowth around the nest had been pressed down by a heavy weight, and the nest was less than an arrow's flight from a small lake. A well-marked trail led through the undergrowth towards the water. Several more tracks indicated that the creature patrolled around the margins of the lake, and that worried me. Thoughts of crocodiles and water serpents came into my head.

Osric went up to the nest and laid a hand on an egg. 'It is warm,' he said. 'The parent cannot be far off.'

He crouched down, listening, then touched the egg again. 'I think I detect something moving. I believe the eggs will hatch soon.'

A tight knot of fear gathered in my stomach. I was remembering the terror I had felt back in the forest when the aurochs had appeared behind Vulfard and me. 'We mustn't be caught between the beast and its nest. That could be dangerous,' I said.

'If it is a crawling beast that comes from the lake, then we would be safer if we were off the ground,' Osric answered. He pointed to a nearby grove of trees. 'If we can get ourselves up into one of those trees, facing the nest, we should be safe, and have a good view.'

We made our way to the grove and managed to find a tree into which we could climb ten or twelve feet off the ground. Branches and leaves partially blocked our view, but the path leading to the nest passed less than ten feet away.

For an hour or two we crouched among the branches, tormented by insects and growing increasingly uncomfortable as the branches dug into us. Lying in wait for the aurochs, beside Vulfard, had been damp and tedious but more comfortable. My shoulder wound began to ache again.

We heard the creature before we saw it. It was the sound of a large animal coming towards us through the underbrush, moving confidently, a little clumsily. Once or twice I thought I heard the sound of a heavy footfall.

We clung to the branches, peering down the track.

The creature stamped past, very close. Osric and I were nine feet off the ground, yet the creature's head was on a level with us. It was massive. I held my breath in case it turned its head and saw us. The eyes were bright and beady and the beak was a heavy, pointed spear and sharp enough to do serious damage. The body was covered with a heavy coat of dark brown feathery bristles. A glimpse of the massive claws at the end of its two scaly legs, thicker than my thigh, made me shiver. Each claw was nine or ten inches long.

The animal reached its nest, and stood there, peering about as if seeking an enemy. Then, squatting backwards, it lowered itself down to cover the clutch of huge eggs. Even when the beast was seated, the head on the snake-like neck was five feet above the ground.

Osric and I waited for the creature to settle before we cautiously climbed down and crept away, keeping the grove of trees between the beast and us.

After we had gone perhaps two hundred paces, Osric turned and looked at me. 'That was neither griffin nor rukh. It cannot fly,' he said. The wings had been little more than stumps.

'It's not in the Book of Beasts,' I said. 'There's a creature called an ostrich which it resembles. But it is nothing like as big and massive.'

'What do we do now?' Osric asked.

'Nothing,' I replied. I had already come to a decision as we were creeping away from the giant bird.

Osric gave me a look that was full of understanding. 'You're thinking of Walo, aren't you?'

I nodded. 'He was so certain that the Book of Beasts is correct and he died because of it. Today we've only learned that those huge eggs belong to a different beast, neither rukh nor griffin. That doesn't prove that such creatures don't exist some-where else.'

My friend knew me well enough to understand what I had in mind. 'So we report to Sulaiman that we failed to find the creature that laid the eggs.'

'Exactly. Then the search for the rukh and griffin will continue, and even be encouraged. The sailors already believe they've seen rukh's eggs.'

Osric considered before replying. 'If we bring back news of that extraordinary creature we've just seen, Musa's colleagues in the caliph's library can add it to the Book of Beasts and from there it will spread far and wide.' He treated me to a quick, conspiratorial grin. 'But I agree with you: it is better that we encourage the search for the griffin in the hope that Walo's trust will one day be justified. And I have a suggestion.'

I looked at him enquiringly. 'What's that?'

'We return to that empty nest, gather up as many fragments of the eggshells as we can find, and bring them back to Baghdad. Let others draw their own conclusions.'

Chapter Eighteen

THROUGHOUT THE LONG, dreary voyage back to al-Ubullah, everyone on board was exhausted and dispirited. Walo's grisly death continued to cast its shadow. Osric and I passed many hours in shared gloomy silence, and it was obvious that Zaynab had been deeply affected too. Quieter and more withdrawn than on the outward trip, her sadness revealed itself in the way she sat by herself in her customary place on the foredeck, staring out towards the horizon. Had the situation been different I would have gone over to talk with her and tried to ease the common sorrow. But Walo's death served to increase my previous reticence. I was very much in love with Zaynab and it made me fearful that I would mishandle the situation with a clumsy intrusion on her grief. Again and again I told myself to wait until we were back in Baghdad. There I would find the right moment to reveal my feelings. With a lover's stubborn blindness I pushed aside all thoughts that Zaynab was returning to her former life as Nadim Jaffar's costly slave-singer. Somehow the obstacle would be overcome. All that mattered to me was that somehow I would find a way into Zaynab's affections so that we shared the same feelings for one another, and together we would explore where it might lead. That heady prospect helped me endure the miserable ordeal of our homeward journey.

When we docked in al-Ubullah, the barid's agents whisked

Zaynab away to bring her more speedily to Jaffar's home while
Osric and I proceeded upstream to Baghdad by barge. There
Jaffar's steward was waiting on the quayside to bring us to meet
his master.

*

'I was losing hope of ever listening to my favourite singer
again,' said the nadim with a welcoming smile when we were
ushered into his presence. Attended by a secretary, Jaffar
received us in a small, open courtyard in his riverside palace
where the steward had taken us straight from the docks. The
nadim was evidently not due to meet the caliph, for Jaffar was
no longer wearing black, but dressed in loose trousers of white
silk, a long purple tunic, and a light cloak of the same colour
trimmed with gold. Bare-headed, he was standing in the shade
of a miniature pavilion of yellow-and-blue striped silk erected
among the immaculately tended flowerbeds. Even here in the
open air, I noted, the air was subtly scented with perfume and
I wondered how soon Sulaiman intended to deliver his precious
lump of whale phlegm to his patron.

Inside the carpeted pavilion were soft cushions and a tray
with a jug and cups for guests, but Jaffar did not invite us to
be seated. It was clear that he was in a hurry. 'My young friend
Abdallah will want to know how you got on with your search
for the rukh,' he said.

'Your Excellency,' I began, 'we found traces of the creature,
but not the rukh itself.' I unfolded the length of velvet I was
carrying and showed him the largest fragment of the eggshells
Osric and I had gathered. 'We came across what we believed
was a rukh's nest but it had been abandoned. Here is a piece
from one of the eggs.'

Jaffra took the eggshell from me and examined it. 'I shall

give this to Abdallah, though I doubt it will settle his argument with the crown prince about the existence of the rukh. I expect there will be a deadlock.'

He beckoned to a waiting attendant and handed him the eggshell. His voice took on a more formal tone. 'The Commander of the Faithful has instructed me to make the arrangements for your return to Frankia.'

Anxiously I waited for him to continue. A wild, irrational idea surfaced in my mind: maybe I could persuade Zaynab to come with me . . . that Jaffar would allow her to leave.

'You will be attached to a return mission to the court of the King of the Franks,' the nadim continued. 'The mission takes a further message of goodwill from the Commander of the Faithful.'

There was a brief interruption as someone appeared at the entrance to the courtyard. He looked like a member of the vizier's staff, anxious to call away his master. Jaffar flicked a dismissive finger and the man ducked back out of sight.

'May I ask when the mission is expected to leave?' I asked.

'In three weeks' time. There will also be gifts, among them another elephant. I am told that the previous animal he sent died before it had reached its destination.'

'I will do my best to ensure that the elephant survives the journey this time.' Abram, our former dragoman, must have reported to the caliph's secretariat what had happened to the first elephant. 'It is unfortunate that my assistant, the man best suited for caring for animals, lost his life in Zanj.'

'The health of the elephant need not concern you,' Jaffar assured me smoothly. 'The elephant will be given to the charge of experienced handlers. It is your experience of the route that will be valued. I would be grateful if you could give them the benefit of your advice during the journey.'

'I will do everything in my power, Your Excellency.'

Out of the corner of my eye I was aware of another movement in the archway. A different staff member was hovering, clearly anxious that the nadim should conclude the interview and attend to other business.

The vizier treated me to a quick smile. 'Prince Abdallah was telling me about that book you brought with you from Frankia, the one with animal descriptions. He found it fascinating.'

'King Carolus had it specially prepared for the Commander of the Faithful. It lists all the animals we know of, with notes in Arabic as well as Frankish.'

'Arabic and Frankish? Young Abdallah didn't mention that.'

'I took the book with me to Zanj and the caliph required that I place it in the royal library afterwards,' I volunteered.

'Then I'll have the librarian send it over to me in due course. It will be a good text for the prince to study. As his tutor I believe he should learn something of your Frankish script.'

Jaffar gathered his cloak around him, making ready to leave. 'I am sorry to hear about the death of your assistant,' he said graciously. 'A journey is often marred by mishaps, however carefully it is planned. With the help of God, your return to Frankia will be trouble free.'

Then he was on his way out of the courtyard, hurrying through an archway in a swirl of expensive silk, and leaving Osric and me standing in the exquisite garden. My friend cleared his throat with a small, strained cough.

'Sigwulf,' he said, sounding more serious than I could ever remember, 'I will not be accompanying you back to Aachen.'

I gaped at him. All my life I had known Osric, right from the earliest days when he had been a slave in my father's household. It had never occurred to me that he might choose to go his own way and no longer be my companion.

'You've decided to stay in Baghdad?' I blurted. 'Why?'

My friend looked me in the eye. 'I feel I have a future here.'

My head swam. 'A future? How is that? You know no one. How will you find employment? Somewhere to live?'

'I hope to be taken on as a member of Nadim Jaffar's household.'

'As what?' I demanded. I was so taken aback that I spoke more sharply than was justified.

Osric spread his hands in a gesture of apology. He knew he had shaken me. 'I have some medical knowledge, or I could join Jaffar's secretariat. As a senior vizier he needs a large staff. I could be useful to him.'

My thoughts were in turmoil. 'Have you approached Jaffar about this?' I demanded bitterly, my voice tailing away as I realized the truth.

The voyage back from Zanj had been long and sombre, overshadowed by the memory of Walo's death. On most days Osric and Zaynab had spent many hours together, sitting on the foredeck and talking quietly.

'Zaynab is asking Jaffar on your behalf, isn't she?' I said, trying not to sound accusing.

'Sigwulf, I'm hoping you will understand my decision,' Osric explained gently. 'I feel more at home here in Baghdad than I ever did in Aachen.' He gave a wan smile. 'Even with the summer heat, the weather suits me better. I have fewer aches and pains than in the damp northern climes.'

'And what happens if Jaffar will not add you to his staff?' I demanded.

My friend's answer was firm. 'Then I will offer my services

to the royal librarian. My knowledge of Hispania and the northern lands will help them in compiling maps and registers of foreign countries.'

'Are you sure about this?'

Osric shifted on his feet, but his steady gaze held mine. 'I've thought long and hard about the best thing to do. I would hate you to think that I am abandoning you, but I see my future here in the caliphate.'

'And Zaynab? Is she in your future too?' I knew I was sounding resentful.

Osric shook his head. 'She's less than half my age, more like a wise daughter that I never had. Remember that we share an experience of slavery and that makes one dream of a quiet settled life in charge of one's own daily existence.

'Yet Zaynab is still a slave,' I said.

Osric was patient with me. 'A slave for now, and a valued singer. Jaffar is generous, and he's more of a patron than a master. Last year he promised to give Zaynab her freedom as well as a present of money if she would continue to sing so beautifully. He says that the gift of freedom would remove the sadness from her voice.'

'And Zaynab agreed to his proposal?' A lump gathered in my throat as I asked the question. I already knew the answer.

My friend regarded me with such profound sympathy that I realized he had guessed my feelings for Zaynab. 'Yes, Zaynab has agreed. When she has her own house, she says, there will be room for me to live there if I wish.'

I felt as if I had been punched in the stomach with all the wind knocked out of me. In a single moment I had lost my friend and companion since childhood, and the woman I dreamed of had passed out of reach.

I could have wept with frustration and disappointment. I

knew Osric well enough to know that he would not change his mind. I had no right to expect him to fall in with my own plans. Long ago he had ceased to be my slave or servant. He was my friend and now I should wish him happiness.

What cut me to the quick was to be told that Zaynab saw her own future with no place in it for me or, perhaps, for anyone else. Given a choice, she preferred to be alone. For a bitter and savage moment, I felt betrayed. I loathed her for misleading me into a false dream. Then, with a great effort, I pulled myself together. I told myself that I should never have presumed on what Zaynab would wish. Her beauty and my delight in her company had been so overwhelming that I had projected onto her a desire for a loving partner that she did not share. Zaynab had not intended to deceive me. For whatever reason – her nature, her past experiences as a slave – she had built a wall around herself and was unattainable.

Nevertheless, I was crushed. I knew that if I saw Zaynab again, it would tear me to pieces. At that moment all I wanted to do was to leave Baghdad as soon as possible. From somewhere in the back of my mind rose an image of bald, sweating Musa seated in his room in the royal library consulting his star books for Osric and me. He had predicted from the star conjunctions that the future held death and great happiness and a return. Walo had died, and Osric was finding happiness. I, however, would return to Aachen on my own and this time I would ensure that fewer obstacles and dangers were put in my path.

*

There was a strained silence between Osric and me as we left Jaffar's palace. Neither trusted himself to speak without the risk of causing further disquiet. The steward brought us to the same lodging house in the Round City that we had occupied months earlier, and at the doorway I muttered something about needing to have some time to myself. I told Osric that I would join him later. Then I set out to walk the streets. My thoughts were crowding in on me – memories of Osric from my childhood, of when I was sent into exile, of campaigning with him in Hispania, and, most recently, the journey to the Northlands in search of white beasts. Osric had been with me either as guardian, companion or advisor – and always friend. He would no longer be a constant presence. I felt disoriented. The recollections of Osric mingled with painful visions of Zaynab. I struggled to stop myself from thinking of her but it was impossible. She was so easy to picture in all her loveliness. Zaynab was deeply entwined in my emotions and it would take months, maybe years, to disentangle her.

It was late afternoon, and I walked for an hour or more, with these notions tumbling back and forth in my head. Eventually my footsteps brought me by chance to the tall double doors of the massive building that housed the royal menagerie. There it occurred to me to check on how Madi and Modi were faring. It would divert me from my inner turmoil. I went inside. The interior was just as I had remembered it – vast, smelling of hay, piss and dung, while muffled snufflings and other unidentifiable animal noises came from behind lines of closed doors to the stalls. I walked down the central aisle to where I had last seen the ice bears. The door to their pen was open. Their enclosure was empty.

I turned away, intending to find a keeper to ask what had happened to the bears. But there was no one about.

As I walked back along the central walkway I heard a gentle clinking sound. I stopped and went to look over the open upper half of a door to one of the larger stalls. A great grey elephant was standing in the straw. The sound came from a slim chain, polished from much use, around the ankle of its back leg. The other end of the chain was fastened to a metal hoop set in the wall.

I was standing there, gazing in at the great animal and wondering why it had been tethered when I was conscious of someone standing at my shoulder. I half turned. It was Abram, the dragoman.

'There's a certain season of the year when a male elephant is dangerous,' he said quietly. 'They become difficult to handle, treacherous even. That dark matter oozing from near his eye and then down his cheek is a sign.'

He gazed over the door thoughtfully.

'Will you be accompanying the new mission to Aachen?' I asked him.

'No,' he said. 'Another of my people will act as dragoman. While you were away, I've been building up my commercial contacts in the caliph's empire. There's a fortune to be made here.'

I looked back at the elephant. It was standing swaying gently on its feet, the ears fanning slowly.

'Was the first elephant that Haroun sent really white?' I put the question casually and waited for an answer.

There was a long silence.

'Why do you ask?' Abram said.

'Because there was only your word that it was white. No one in Aachen ever saw it, and Nadim Jaffar didn't seem to be aware of the fact.'

Abram did not reply. He reached into the pocket of his gown and pulled out a dried seed. He prised the shell open with his fingernails and popped the kernel into his mouth, then held out the empty husk on his outstretched palm. The elephant shuffled its great feet in the straw and took a few paces until it reached the end of its chain. Then it reached out with the long snake-like trunk and, very delicately, picked up the tiny offering. The trunk curled back and the beast placed the shell into its mouth and the jaws moved.

'I was waiting for you to understand,' he said quietly. I caught a faint whiff of a familiar smell on his breath.

'On the voyage back from Zanj our captain Sulaiman had a great liking for those same seeds that you chew on,' I said. 'He told me they come from India.'

The dragoman was unflustered. 'That is correct. They sweeten the breath.'

'Those are the same shells that I found under the benches in the Colosseum on the morning after Protis died.'

Abram waited for me to go on.

'I had many hours on the voyage back from Zanj to think about that sequence of mishaps that so nearly destroyed the mission,' I said. 'As far back as Rome I realized that someone was deliberately trying to prevent it succeeding.'

'And what did you conclude?' the dragoman was gently mocking me.

'That, whoever it was, was remarkably well informed – wherever we were. It couldn't have been Osric or Walo, which left only you or your servants. Also, on the two occasions when the aurochs was set free – in Rome and in the desert – the dogs didn't bark. They knew the person or persons responsible.'

'And when was the start of this campaign against you and your mission, do you suppose?' Abram asked. He was supremely self-possessed.

'In Kaupang,' I told him. 'Though the attempt to kill me there didn't fit the pattern. I hadn't even met you at that time and I couldn't see how you might be responsible. Only later did

I recall a remark that a shrewd sea captain named Redwald made to me. He warned me that money has a long reach. On another occasion Osric said something similar.'

The dragoman allowed himself a knowing smile. The elephant was again reaching forward with its trunk, begging this time. Abram extended his arm and allowed the tip of the trunk to thrust up his loose sleeve, exploring. When the trunk withdrew, the elephant tasted in its mouth what it had found, rejected it, and then the trunk stretched out in my direction.

It seemed natural to accept what it was the creature was offering. I put out my hand. The end of the trunk turned up and I saw something shiny and held in place by the fingerlike tip of the animal's nose.

Something small and damp dropped into the palm of my hand, and I was looking down on a familiar coin – a gold dinar.

I admired the dragoman's sense of theatre. 'You didn't need that conjurer's trick,' I said.

I took out my purse and found the dinar from Kaupang that Redwald had given me as a memento. As I anticipated, it was the twin of the coin that Abram had produced. Both bore King Offa's name. 'You were the paymaster who arranged the attack on me in Kaupang.'

A brief flicker of regret appeared in Abram's eyes. 'For that I apologize. I had not yet met you by then. Had that been the case, I would have considered a different, less violent course of action.'

I made a point of sounding incredulous. 'You were behind all those other incidents, and yet you did not wish to harm me.'

'Neither you, nor your companions. After I met you, I had no wish to hurt you, certainly not to cause your deaths. I tried to thwart the mission without anyone being killed.'

I gave a snort of disbelief. 'I find that difficult to believe.'

'I managed to delay and divert the mission. I took it by a longer route, downriver to the Mediterranean and not over the mountains directly into Italy. I was hoping that something would go wrong, an accident that would make you abandon the mission.'

'Yet when an accident did happen and that raft hit the bridge, you risked your life to save the boatman who had been thrown into the water,' I said.

He gave a slight shrug. 'I repeat: I didn't want anyone to be killed because of me.'

My scepticism must have been very apparent because he added, 'Think back to when Protis's ship foundered. My plan was for the animals to drown, and your companions to get safely to shore. I overlooked the fact that ice bears can swim, and the aurochs too.'

I stopped him there. 'That was something else that puzzled me. I couldn't understand how you arranged for the ship to sink.'

He arched a mocking eyebrow. 'My people have excellent contacts along the river, and I sent ahead. Protis's ship was delayed for repairs and while it was in dock, the carpenters were paid to drill some holes in the hull and plug them with wax. An old technique, used by unscrupulous shipowners. They then claim the loss of a cargo that they never loaded, but had stolen.'

'And the wax comes loose and the ship sinks?' I said.

He grinned. 'But not fast enough. That was why I volunteered to swim overboard and put the canvas in place. It gave me a chance to knock out the last of the wax plugs.'

I found myself losing patience with his smug responses.

Clearly Abram had anticipated this conversation. 'You say that you didn't want to hurt us,' I snapped. 'Yet Protis died in the arena. I presume your servants let the aurochs go free – and then the lions killed that poor wretch in the desert.'

'I truly regret Protis's death,' said Abram, and he sounded as though he meant it. 'I never thought he would be so foolhardy, or that his head would be so filled with the heroics of the ancient Greeks.' He paused. 'As for that poor wretch in the desert, he had no reason to run off into it.'

I looked down at the two coins in my hand. 'These tell only part of your deceit.'

Abram grinned at me mischievously. 'Then explain to me the rest of it.'

'Offa might pay to have me killed, but he had no reason to wreck Carolus's embassy to Haroun.'

This time I had managed to throw him off balance. His eyes narrowed. 'Go on.'

'So you set up another suspect. Those men who attacked me in Kaupang were also paid in Byzantine gold. I was shown a gold solidus. On our journey here you reminded me repeatedly that the Greeks are at war with the caliphate, and would do anything to stop an alliance between Aachen and Baghdad.'

I closed my fist and shook the two gold coins together so they clicked softly. The elephant had remarkably acute hearing. He flapped his ears and the trunk came questing again towards my hand, then withdrew as I kept my hand clenched.

'Yet here in Baghdad I find that Greeks work for the caliph, and Arabs go to Constantinople to buy books. They are not at daggers drawn, as you had me believe,' I said quietly. 'Then I thought back to Christmas Day in Rome when I saw Pope Adrian with my own eyes as he went in procession in St Peter's

Basilica. He had a look of absolute self-belief, arrogant and implacable. I judged him to be someone who stopped at nothing to protect his Church.'

The dragoman was absolutely motionless. He did not contradict me.

'It occurred to me that Adrian, more than anyone, has reason to be alarmed by an alliance between Carolus and Haroun, between the Christian king and the Commander of the Faithful. That would be the worst of all possible worlds for the pope.' I chose my words with care. 'The Nomenculator said to me that everything in Rome has its price. That all is self-interest. I remember his exact words, "We Romans have little loyalty to the past when it suits us."'

I had Abram's full attention now. 'In Rome you knew about the inner workings of the papal office and Adrian and his ministers. That struck me as odd for someone who is a Radhanite. This is what I think is the truth – you passed through Rome on the way north with Haroun's gifts for Carolus. Pope Adrian offered you a large sum of money to make sure that the alliance between Carolus and Haroun never materialized. You became his creature.'

The dragoman cocked his head on one side. 'Truly, Sigwulf, you have a vivid imagination. Next you'll claim I killed the elephant in my care.'

I smiled mirthlessly. 'Perhaps so. The elephant died long before you reached Rome. If you remember, I did dream that you were extracting bones from a dead elephant. In the interpretation of dreams, this meant that you would make a great profit from an endeavour. Maybe it was an unfortunate coincidence, but it eventually made me question what you were really up to.'

The dragoman smirked. 'Sigwulf, I never thought you were

a dream believer. How do you explain Haroun's other gifts to Carolus – the mechanical clock and the other baubles? I delivered them safely.'

'That was when you made your really clever move. You claimed falsely that the dead elephant was white because white was the royal colour in Baghdad. You charmed Carolus's advisors with the idea that if there was to be a return mission to Baghdad it should take white gifts. You knew that would offend Haroun.'

Abram appeared to regain his poise, and that brought me a twinge of worry.

'Of course, Adrian has paid me well,' he admitted, giving me a pleasant, relaxed smile. Then to my astonishment he leaned forward and gave me a friendly pat on the shoulder.

'Sigwulf, if I were you, when you get back to Aachen, I wouldn't tell Carolus or Alcuin that the Holy Father tried to wreck their foreign policy.'

'Why not?' I retorted. 'Alcuin might be shocked, but Carolus is sufficiently worldly wise to accept that Pope Adrian's priority must be the Church itself.'

Abram gave me a look loaded with sympathy but a warning as well. 'Kings also don't like to be made to look stupid and ignorant.'

The dragoman was all too sure of himself. Again I sensed that he had planned ahead and out-witted me. 'What do you mean?' I asked cautiously.

'Think back to the day you met with Carolus and were given the mission to Baghdad. Do you recall that meeting?'

I could remember every detail. 'I had come back successfully from Kaupang, bringing the gyrfalcons, the white dogs and the ice bears,' I said slowly.

'And what did you give to him?' Abram prompted.

I thought back to the scene in the king's apartments and Carolus's reaction when I produced the horn of a unicorn. He had been like a child seeing a wonderful present.

'I showed him a unicorn's horn that Osric had bought in Kaupang for a princely sum,' I said.

'You told me that Carolus decided to keep it for himself, and not send it to the caliph,' Abram replied.

'That's true. He was delighted. He was going to show it to his sceptical counsellors who doubted the existence of the unicorn.'

Abram chuckled. 'And how would the king react if he knew he had been tricked?'

I stared at him. 'The king is known to have a notoriously short temper,' I said.

'It would be very unfortunate, then, if he learned his precious unicorn horn is nothing more than a tooth. What is more, it is a tooth from a large, fat sea creature that's more like a sea slug than a graceful deer.'

I stared at the dragoman. The triumph in his dark brown eyes told me that he was telling the truth. His threat was real. If I revealed the pope's plot to Carolus, Abram would make sure the king would learn that his precious unicorn's horn was a fake. My own future at court would be ruined.

I had to admire Abram's audacity. He had shown himself to be a past master at double-dealing. In my present disenchanted mood I was entirely ready to accept that my only sensible course of action was to let matters lie where they were: I would go back to Aachen, not mention Abram's treachery, and continue to pay lip service to the myth of the unicorn. It would be much the same as my clandestine arrangement with Osric to keep the secret of the so-called rukh's eggs.

'I agree to your terms,' I said reluctantly, holding out my

hand. 'I will say nothing to Carolus or to Alcuin about Pope Adrian's plot. In return, you will keep the secret of the unicorn's horn.'

Abram shook my hand. I turned on my heel and was nearly at the double doors on my way out of the menagerie when the elephant trumpeted angrily, either from bad temper or because he had been denied any further food. The hoarse sound echoed through the building and shattered my complacency like a physical blow. I heard again the aurochs in the pitfall bellowing in triumph over Vulfard's crushed body. My stomach heaved at the thought that while others were dying, Abram had taken his chance to serve two masters and line his pockets.

I hurried my steps, going first to the royal library for a private conversation with Musa, and then on to our lodgings where Osric was standing at a window, staring out at the fountain in the courtyard and deep in thought. He looked round, surprised at my sudden, urgent arrival.

'Osric, I need your help,' I told him. 'I've been talking with Abram.'

He listened as I described the extent of the dragoman's treachery. 'He can't be allowed to get away with it,' I concluded.

'What do you propose?' Osric asked.

'I'm relying on Jaffar's interest in our bestiary as a text book for Prince Abdallah. I've just spoken with Musa. He confirms that the book is in the royal library and has agreed to update the entry about elephants before it gets sent to the vizier.'

'What's Musa going to add?' Osric asked, puzzled.

I quoted the sentences I had so carefully composed to be written below the illustration of the two green-painted elephants, with their large, doleful eyes, white curving tusks, and their trunks about to touch. '*It is claimed that some elephants are white. The elephant sent by Caliph Haroun al Rashid as a gift for*

Carolus, King of the Franks, was reported by its escort to have been white.'

Slowly a smile began to spread across Osric's thin face. 'Prince Abdallah is sure to come across this claim in his lessons with Jaffar. He will demand to know much more about this white elephant, just as he did about the rukh.'

I returned his smile. 'And Jaffar will send for Abram, and then our former dragoman is in a fix. He may try to bluff it out. He can say that the elephant for Carolus really was white. And you and I both know what happens next . . .'

Osric finished for me: 'The Caliph launches another animal-catching expedition, this time to find and bring back a white elephant. Who better to be given the task than Abram?' He laughed.

I beamed at Osric, all awkwardness between us forgotten. 'More likely Abram's lie will be exposed. It's easy enough for Jaffar to check on the colour of the elephant that was sent. It will be found that Abram interfered with the Caliph's foreign policy. The "blade of his vengeance", the palace executioner, awaits.'

'You said you needed my help?'

'I think Abram was being truthful when he said he never wanted to bring about our deaths, only to wreck the embassy. So, if he does risk execution, can you ask Zaynab to plead for clemency? Try to get his punishment reduced to a ban on his ever carrying on any business within the caliphate.'

'Would that be enough?' Osric asked.

'It will put an end to his ambition to make a commercial fortune in the caliphate.'

Osric shook his head in admiration. 'Sigwulf, you really should stay on in Baghdad. You seem admirably adapted to the court politics.'

I stepped forward and embraced my friend. 'We lost an aurochs and never found a griffin nor a rukh, but we made sure that Carolus and Haroun will continue to exchange embassies. Whenever one leaves Baghdad, send me your news – and Zaynab's.'

Osric turned aside and picked up a thin sheaf of papers. 'You'd better keep these,' he said, placing our pages from the Oneirokritikon in my hand. 'I can always consult Artimedorus's writings in the royal library. But when you get back to Aachen, you may find yourself needing every signpost in an uncertain future.'

Historical and Zoological Note

In July of AD 802, the arrival of a live elephant created a sensation at Charlemagne's court. The elephant, named Abul Abbas, was a gift from Haroun al Rashid, the Caliph of Baghdad. The elephant's journey, except for the sea crossing between North Africa and Genoa, must largely have been on foot, an extraordinary achievement by the animal and its keepers. The exchange of rare and expensive presents – including exotic animals – was a feature of international diplomacy. Haroun despatched Abul Abbas after receiving from Charlemagne an embassy led by two Franks, Lanterfrid and Sigmund, and a Frankish Jew, Isaac. There is no record of what presents they might have carried with them but historians surmise that Charlemagne would have given horses, hounds and precious fabrics.

*

Why visitors entering the Round City were required to wear white clothes, when the household colour of Haroun's family was black remains a puzzle. Haroun was only twenty years old when he came to power and relied heavily on the advice of a Persian family, the Barmakids. His favourite was Jaffar, son of the Chief Vizier. Jaffar accumulated such influence and wealth that he issued his own coins. Archaeologists have found a gold dinar issued by Jaffar and dated AD 798 in treasure discovered on the coast of Zanzibar. Arab merchants traded to East Africa from the seventh century AD, perhaps earlier. They took advantage of the annual reversal of the monsoon winds to make the round trip from home ports in the Arabian Gulf and Oman, and developed a complex system of astro-navigation based on an encyclopaedic knowledge of the stars.

An even more unusual gold dinar came to light in Rome in the first half of the nineteenth century. The coin was minted in England by King Offa of Mercia and imitated gold dinars issued by Haroun's grandfather, Caliph al-Mansour, in AD 773–4. How it got to Rome is a mystery. The coin is unlikely to have been a gift from Offa to the pope because the inscription proclaims Allah as the only God. More probably the coin was intended for use as currency in Mediterranean trade. It seems that Offa's moneyer could not read Arab script because he inserted Offa's name upside down. The coin is now in the British Museum.

*

Many animals in the medieval bestiaries or books of beasts can be traced back to creatures listed in an anonymous second-century Greek compilation known as the *Physiologus*. The behaviour of the animal was considered to be as important as its size and appearance. Various classical authors, notably Pliny, also contributed descriptions of wonderfully weird beasts, as did garbled reports filtering back to Europe of unusual animals roaming foreign lands. The basilisk, for example, was said to be either a cross between a rooster, snake and a lion, whose gaze could turn a man to stone, or a small serpent with a breath so toxic that if a man on horseback struck it with a spear, the venom ran up the spear shaft and killed both rider and steed. In fact, several bestiary animals that might have been disbelieved by a sceptic as fantasies, were real. They included the ostrich, dromedary, chameleon and the remora. The latter, a suckerfish, attaches itself to a larger host fish or to a vessel's hull by sucker plates on its head. Additionally, the medieval mind credited it with being able to stop a vessel moving through the water, hence its name: in Latin *remora* means 'delay'.

Two of the imaginary bestiary creatures have had second lives. The little snake with a tiny horn above each eye that Walo picks up in the Egyptian desert is now known as a cerastes viper, a miniature version of the long-horned cerastes serpent shown in the Book of Beasts. In Central America the basilisk lizard (*basiliscus*) has crests or 'sails' on its spine, making it look exactly like the picture of its namesake in the bestiaries. The medieval observer would be amazed by the basilisk lizard's genuine ability to stand up on two hind legs and run for a short distance across the surface of water. The modern nickname is – Jesus Christ Lizard.

*

Ibn Khordadbeh, Director of Posts and Police for the caliphate, wrote the best surviving account of the Radhanites, the roving Jewish merchants, a hundred years after Sigwulf's imaginary journey. According to Ibn Khordadbeh, the Radhanites could speak Arabic, Persian, Latin, Frankish, Spanish and Slavic, and they ranged across an astonishing network of trade routes that extended from France in the West to China in the East, and included India. Khordadbeh describes the route that Sigwulf uses from Pelusium at the mouth of the Nile, by camel caravan across the desert, to Suez, where the Radhanites took ship 'on the Eastern Sea'.

*

The belief that the long, spiral tooth of the narwhal was an alicorn, a unicorn's horn, persisted until the sixteenth century. An alicorn was worth many times its weight in gold, as much for its presumed medicinal value as for its rarity. An alicorn was supposed to detect and react to poison. Dipped into a poisoned drink, it made the liquid bubble or darken. Ground into powder it was an antidote for poisoning, as well as a cure for epilepsy and a guard against plague and fever. Unsurprisingly, an alicorn was a popular gift for monarchs who feared for their lives. Queen Elizabeth I of England, Mary Queen of Scots, and Philip II of Spain all had alicorns in their treasuries.

That other royal gift, the elephant Abul Abbas, lived until AD 810 when he was in his forties. He died of pneumonia after swimming in the Rhine, so it is said. He will reappear in the third volume of SAXON.

extracts reading groups events
competitions books new
books discounts extracts extracts discounts
competitions new events
books reading groups discounts
events books extracts reading groups
extracts new reading groups extracts
new books discounts events
interviews new reading groups
reading groups events extracts extracts new books
discounts books extracts events interviews new books extracts
reading groups new books events events interviews new books extracts

www.panmacmillan.com

discounts extracts discounts books
extracts events reading groups
competitions books extracts new books